The Lost Mulattos

Front Cover Hanscome Candelabra Photograph

Antique ornate brass, marble and crystal prism girandole candelabra popular in France and Italy, 1750s-1850s. Brought by William Kissick Hanscome from Toronto to Minneapolis in 1880's. Author owned.

The Lost Mulattos

The Hanscome Trilogy

Dr. Joan Adsit Dickinson

Disclaimer:

This is a work of historical fiction based on the genealogy of the Hanscom(b)e family and is as accurate as genealogies can be. Sources include the author's research, wills, property deeds, court, birth, marriage, death records and Robert Hanscom's genealogical files given to the author. Other historical names, characters, places, events and incidents are either the products of the author's imagination or used in a fictitious manner and do not appear in the Hanscome diagrams or genealogy.

For my loving daughter Sarah

Contents

Acknowledgments

Thank you family and friends for reading *The UnPuritans* and your enthusiasm for the continuation of the Hanscome family story in *The Lost Mulattos*. Again, I appreciate your smiles and tolerance of my project. I must also say I wouldn't have completed the trilogy without three individuals' encouragement: Alex Rose, who likened my first effort to a history dissertation, and Jim Abrahams, who had faith in my ability to create a meaningful story from it, and Dianne Brown, who was my daily cheerleader.

I still am indebted to Bob Hanscom, my cousin from nine generations ago, for his prior research, Jordon's and Stringfellow's flavorful history of John's Island in *A Place Called St. John's*, the Charleston Library and the South Carolina Department of History and Archives for their gracious assistance as I gathered wills, deeds, marriage, birth and death records. I must also mention The Cathedral Church of St. James and Cemetery staff in Toronto for additional Hanscome records.

Many of these documents listed the actual names of slaves owned by the Hanscomes. Jenny and Ietrow were owned by Aaron Hanscome, 1685-1760, and willed to his grandchildren Thomas Hanscome, 1670-1831, and Ann Hanscome, 1757-1780s. Upon the death of Dr. James Hanscome, 1774-1812, one inventory of slave ownership listed fifty-five handwritten names, now etched painfully in my memory and my fingertips. I pause now in great sadness, as I did when I first read their names aloud.

Before writing *The Lost Mulattos*, I also read *Black Masters: A Free Family of Color in the Old South* by Michael P. Johnson and James L. Roark, *Black Slaveowners: Free Black Slave Masters in South Carolina, 1790-1860,* by Larry Koger, *A Gentleman of Color: The Life of James Forten* by Julie Wench and Rita Reynold's account of Nancy Randall, Rachael and Martha Inglis in her dissertation: "Wealthy free women of color in Charleston, South Carolina during slavery," (January 1, 2007). *Electronic Doctoral Dissertations for UMass Amherst.* Paper AAI3275800. My story is woven around these authors' scholarly contributions to slave, mulatto and Hanscome history. I am indebted to them for their tutelage.

The gift to me of all this joyous and painful research, jumping into my ancestor's skins in an earlier place and time and challenging my previous perceptions, while hopefully creating a plausible, historically accurate novel, is that when I meet eyes, dark like mine, I smile and wonder if we might be related. Of course, we all are.

John's Island 2014

Hanscombe's Creekside Plantation (Legare Farms)

Stono River

Creekside Old Oak Tree

Hanscom(b)e Genealogy

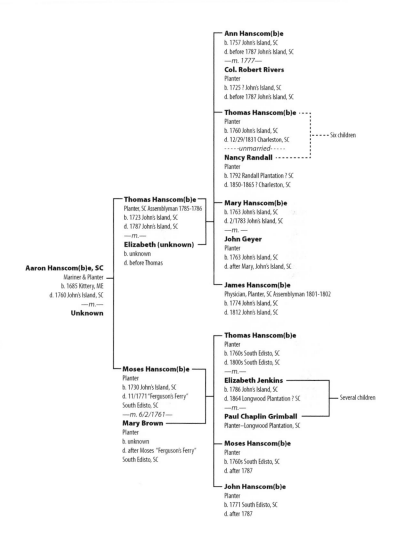

Ann Hanscom(b)e
b. 1757 John's Island, SC
d. before 1787 John's Island, SC
—m. 1777—
Col. Robert Rivers
Planter
b. 1725 ? John's Island, SC
d. before 1787 John's Island, SC

Thomas Hanscom(b)e
Planter
b. 1760 John's Island, SC
d. 12/29/1831 Charleston, SC
-----unmarried-----
Nancy Randall
Planter
b. 1792 Randall Plantation ? SC
d. 1850-1865 ? Charleston, SC

---- Six children

Mary Hanscom(b)e
b. 1763 John's Island, SC
d. 2/1783 John's Island, SC
—m. —
John Geyer
Planter
b. 1763 John's Island, SC
d. after Mary, John's Island, SC

James Hanscom(b)e
Physician, Planter, SC Assemblyman 1801-1802
b. 1774 John's Island, SC
d. 1812 John's Island, SC

Thomas Hanscom(b)e
Planter, SC Assemblyman 1785-1786
b. 1723 John's Island, SC
d. 1787 John's Island, SC
—m.—
Elizabeth (unknown)
b. unknown
d. before Thomas

Aaron Hanscom(b)e, SC
Mariner & Planter
b. 1685 Kittery, ME
d. 1760 John's Island, SC
—m.—
Unknown

Thomas Hanscom(b)e
Planter
b. 1760s South Edisto, SC
d. 1800s South Edisto, SC
—m.—
Elizabeth Jenkins
b. 1786 John's Island, SC
d. 1864 Longwood Plantation ? SC
—m. —
Paul Chaplin Grimball
Planter—Longwood Plantation, SC

---- Several children

Moses Hanscom(b)e
Planter
b. 1730 John's Island, SC
d. 11/1771 "Ferguson's Ferry"
South Edisto, SC
—m. 6/2/1761—
Mary Brown
Planter
b. unknown
d. after Moses "Ferguson's Ferry"
South Edisto, SC

Moses Hanscom(b)e
Planter
b. 1760s South Edisto, SC
d. after 1787

John Hanscom(b)e
Planter
b. 1771 South Edisto, SC
d. after 1787

Diagram B

xiii.

Hanscom(b)e Genealogy

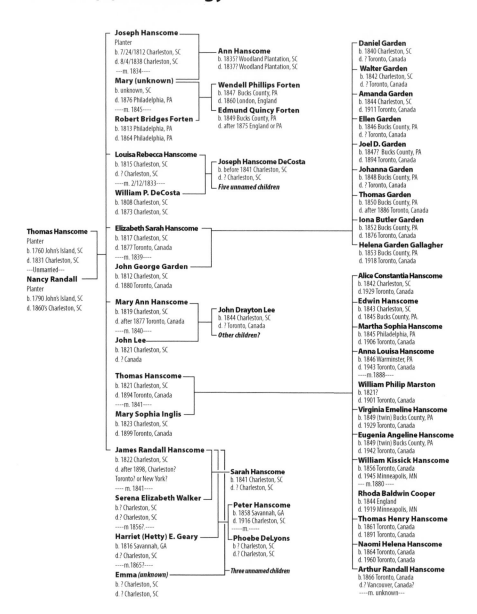

Joseph Hanscome
Planter
b. 7/24/1812 Charleston, SC
d. 8/4/1838 Charleston, SC
----m. 1834----
Mary (unknown)
b. unknown, SC
d. 1876 Philadelphia, PA
-----m. 1845----
Robert Bridges Forten
b. 1813 Philadelphia, PA
d. 1864 Philadelphia, PA

Ann Hanscome
b. 1835? Woodland Plantation, SC
d. 1837? Woodland Plantation, SC

Wendell Phillips Forten
b. 1847 Bucks County, PA
d. 1860 London, England
Edmund Quincy Forten
b. 1849 Bucks County, PA
d. after 1875 England or PA

Louisa Rebecca Hanscome
b. 1815 Charleston, SC
d. ? Charleston, SC
----m. 2/12/1833----
William P. DeCosta
b. 1808 Charleston, SC
d. 1873 Charleston, SC

Joseph Hanscome DeCosta
b. before 1841 Charleston, SC
d. ? Charleston, SC
Five unnamed children

Thomas Hanscome
Planter
b. 1760 John's Island, SC
d. 1831 Charleston, SC
---Unmarried---
Nancy Randall
Planter
b. 1790 John's Island, SC
d. 1860's Charleston, SC

Elizabeth Sarah Hanscome
b. 1817 Charleston, SC
d. 1877 Toronto, Canada
----m. 1839----
John George Garden
b. 1812 Charleston, SC
d. 1880 Toronto, Canada

Daniel Garden
b. 1840 Charleston, SC
d. ? Toronto, Canada
Walter Garden
b. 1842 Charleston, SC
d. ? Toronto, Canada
Amanda Garden
b. 1844 Charleston, SC
d. 1911 Toronto, Canada
Ellen Garden
b. 1846 Bucks County, PA
d. ? Toronto, Canada
Joel D. Garden
b. 1847? Bucks County, PA
d. 1894 Toronto, Canada
Johanna Garden
b. 1848 Bucks County, PA
d. ? Toronto, Canada
Thomas Garden
b. 1850 Bucks County, PA
d. after 1886 Toronto, Canada
Iona Butler Garden
b. 1852 Bucks County, PA
d. 1876 Toronto, Canada
Helena Garden Gallagher
b. 1853 Bucks County, PA
d. 1918 Toronto, Canada

Mary Ann Hanscome
b. 1819 Charleston, SC
d. after 1877 Toronto, Canada
----m. 1840----
John Lee
b. 1821 Charleston, SC
d. ? Canada

John Drayton Lee
b. 1844 Charleston, SC
d. ? Toronto, Canada
Other children?

Thomas Hanscome
b. 1821 Charleston, SC
d. 1894 Toronto, Canada
----m. 1841----
Mary Sophia Inglis
b. 1823 Charleston, SC
d. 1899 Toronto, Canada

Alice Constantia Hanscome
b. 1842 Charleston, SC
d.1929 Toronto, Canada
Edwin Hanscome
b. 1843 Charleston, SC
d. 1845 Bucks County, PA.
Martha Sophia Hanscome
b. 1845 Philadelphia, PA
d. 1906 Toronto, Canada
Anna Louisa Hanscome
b. 1846 Warminster, PA
d. 1943 Toronto, Canada
----m.1888----
William Philip Marston
b. 1821?
d. 1901 Toronto, Canada
Virginia Emeline Hanscome
b. 1849 (twin) Bucks County, PA
d. 1929 Toronto, Canada
Eugenia Angeline Hanscome
b. 1849 (twin) Bucks County, PA
d. 1942 Toronto, Canada
William Kissick Hanscome
b. 1856 Toronto, Canada
d. 1945 Minneapolis, MN
--- m.1880 ----
Rhoda Baldwin Cooper
b. 1844 England
d. 1919 Minneapolis, MN
Thomas Henry Hanscome
b. 1861 Toronto, Canada
d. 1891 Toronto, Canada
Naomi Helena Hanscome
b. 1864 Toronto, Canada
d. 1960 Toronto, Canada
Arthur Randall Hanscome
b.1866 Toronto, Canada
d.? Vancouver, Canada?
----m. unknown---

James Randall Hanscome
b. 1822 Charleston, SC
d. after 1898, Charleston?
Toronto? or New York?
---- m. 1841----
Serena Elizabeth Walker
b.? Charleston, SC
d.? Charleston, SC
----m 1856?----
Harriet (Hetty) E. Geary
b. 1816 Savannah, GA
d.? Charleston, SC
----m.1865?----
Emma (unknown)
b. ? Charleston, SC
d. ? Charleston, SC

Sarah Hanscome
b. 1841 Charleston, SC
d. ? Charleston, SC

Peter Hanscome
b. 1858 Savannah, GA
d. 1916 Charleston, SC
-----m.-----
Phoebe DeLyons
b ? Charleston, SC
d.? Charleston, SC

Three unnamed children

Diagram C

CH. 1. Eyes Glazed Over with Love

September 14, 1752

Charles Town

11:00 AM

"I do!" shouted Thomas to the rafters with so much bravado that the congregation's beaming smiles set the church aglow. Even his parents, Jane and Aaron Hanscome, had difficulty maintaining their proper decorum.

No, there was nothing meek or mild about this newly married heir to the Hanscome plantations. Creekside, the original 106 acre plantation on John's Island, boasted cattle and indigo, while their Craven's County 494 acre lowland plantation, acquired in 1737 to the north, grew the profitable Carolina gold rice. Their Charles Town mansion, 37 Meeting Street, laid middle ground between their two plantations. Although many a Carolinian planter family had tried to arrange a marriage with Thomas Hanscome to merge wealth with wealth, it was an outsider who finally turned Thomas' head and caught his heart.

Twenty-nine year old Thomas was quite the eligible bachelor - educated, charming and, don't forget, wealthy. He was uncommonly tall, over six feet, like his grandfather, Thomas Hanscome, who came to Salem in 1629 as an indentured servant at age twelve. Thomas was blessed with Aaron's gift of intense indigo blue eyes and auburn hair, streaked with a blaze of red, like his mother's fiery crown. Thomas was a most handsome Hanscome, indeed.

Privateer Aaron Hanscome, Thomas' father, had left Kittery, Maine, to defend England's honor against the French during Queen Anne's War in the early 1700s. It was only natural Aaron follow in the footsteps of his older brother, Captain John, who helped their disgraced sister Alice, who changed her name to Ann Downing, escape death at the Puritan's hands and flee to Charles Town with her two fair-complected, illegitimate children. Her mulatto son, William, was left in the care of Black Will, his soon to be freed slave father. After John became lost in the greed of the sea plunder, Aaron decided he would not cross the line to piracy. Yes, Captain John was never to be seen again in Kittery, Charles Town or the high seas. Instead, Aaron kept his honor, returned to John's Island and became ensconced in the noble wealth enabled by that *peculiar institution*, slavery.

What happened to Aaron's melancholy, his professed love for his mulatto nephew, Will, his guilt over slave-owning? He had long barred such feelings from his soul. Instead, he accepted the view from the pulpit that each has his anointed place in God's Carolina world. The slaves needed a ruling class, planters like him, to care for them. Aaron carefully controlled the thoughts he allowed entrance to his psyche. With one click, he tightly closed his mind and was magically free from sin. What a relief to be most honorable and to raise his two sons, Thomas and Moses, in the same lucrative planter tradition.

Young Thomas Hancome's wedding guests, of course, shared the same finely veneered planter ethos. The notable and fashionably attired guests could hardly wait to be introduced to Thomas Hanscome's bride. This wedding, yes, out of season, headlined the front page of the *South Carolinian Gazette*.

"Who is she?" whispered one guest to another.

"I can't tell - she is hidden beneath her veil," replied another.

"Who are her parents?" asked one curious about her lineage.

"The Smiths from Philadelphia," answered another, proud to be of service.

"Why the Anglican wedding when the Hanscomes always attend St. John's Presbyterian Church on the Island?" queried a third gossiper.

"The Smiths must be Anglican."

"More than likely they'd be Friends. Those stern and proper Quakers settled in Philadelphia."

"St. Michael's Anglican is a more suitable church than St. John's. It is Charles Town's newest and grandest."

"I had no idea it would be this cool inside. It must be all the imported elegant white marble from Greece, so cooling to the touch. I could be enticed to join."

"Your words would not endear you to your Congregationalist family. Your religious sentiments are, indeed, most shallow," teased her friend.

"Yes, I admit to being shallow," she laughed. "The social aspect of church keeps me praying. And, if I must pray, why not attend the best or at least the coolest church in Charles Town?"

"It will probably break 100 degrees this afternoon. I can see why they had a morning wedding."

"A morning wedding is hardly suitable. Heat aside, practical or not, this is an unseemly break from tradition. Yes, most uncomely. Why not wait until the proper winter season to marry?" huffed an erect matron with a flushed, prune face and plumped lips.

"Those Hanscomes like to test convention, true, but aren't we all enjoying a rare, fall social event? This wedding is definitely challenging the normal ennui of our fall season. It's a delight, if you ask me," responded her friend as she rose to excuse herself.

"Well, I don't like the stillness in the air – a big storm could be brewing."

"You worry too much, my dear. Forget the weather, forget the fears of the fever season, forget convention, we must make haste for the reception. I don't want to be the last to receive a libation."

Yes, most in Charles Town loved a wedding or any excuse for a party. Bitterness was rare. They were known for their graciousness and lightness of humor. Charles Town was in vogue.

The wedding reception

"May I introduce my bride, Elizabeth," said Thomas to the guests as they gracefully floated through the reception line at his parent's Meeting Street mansion.

"I am so pleased to meet you," replied Elizabeth with a warm smile and even warmer eyes that challenged none and embraced all. Yes, she was fair in face, framed by wavy, thick dark tresses and thin of waist. Thomas and Elizabeth made a most regal couple, most engaging conversation and welcoming in their bright eyes. Those wedding guests who missed marrying their daughters to Thomas soon relented. Elizabeth Hanscome was now one of them.

Champagne was delivered on sliver trays. The room was abuzz with gaiety. The servants silently glided through the room with huge, peacock plumes to cool the flushed faces and move the stilled, humid air. More than one guest questioned their sanity in attending a September wedding as they dabbed at their wet brows with their white, Belgium lace handkerchiefs.

A noon feast had been prepared by the slaves. With their smiling, dark faces, they stood at attention in immaculate white gloves behind the white linen covered tables, ready to please. Soon they would be serving tureens of soups, plates of meat, sea food, fruits and vegetables. The main serving table was lit with three tall brass candelabra, Jane's pride and joy, and displayed her Staffordshire salt-glazed white china and highly polished silver.

As a child, Thomas had been mesmerized by those candelabra and the rainbows cast from their dangling, crystal pendants. "Where do all the colors come from?" he asked his mother. "From God," Jane responded. "All beautiful things come from God."And Thomas smiled as he remembered his response. "Then God's love must be multi-colored." One day he hoped his children would also be fascinated with the prisms and their multi-colored light.

It was a lovely wedding, not too extravagant, Jane thought. Elegant. Some of their Charles Town friends had become competitive with their opulence. She knew there would be gossiping about the choice of a morning wedding, rather than the usual grand evening affair. She hadn't bothered telling her friends that Thomas and Elizabeth were sailing that very afternoon for England. Thomas wanted to return in time for the spring planting. It was, after all, their wedding, wasn't it? Let the guests think what they wanted.

"It will give the gossips something to critique. Why should I deprive them of their fun?" Jane commented to Aaron. Jane's eyes crinkled with glee when she entertained devious thoughts. She wondered how their wealthy planter friends had affected such aristocratic airs and forgotten their humble beginnings. Sometimes she wondered if she, too, had gone astray.

"I just love Elizabeth, Aaron. I am so glad Thomas chose her for his wife," whispered Jane, while appropriately smiling and nodding at their guests. "She is so warm and sincere."

"Yes, and she is charming, educated, beautiful, well-mannered and shiny-eyed. Thomas is entranced. Elizabeth is every young man's dream, true. However, her anti-slavery Philadelphia roots may turn her into Thomas' worst nightmare. I only hope she has a toughness I haven't seen."

"Oh? I am a planter's daughter of Kittery stock. Do you find me tough? Is that why you married me?" teased Jane.

"You are so tough you would only be good in a stew, most savory and tasty after a long simmer." Aaron loved to flirt with his wife of thirty-five years. "I meant to say that Elizabeth needs to accept slavery as a part of her life, truly embrace it. The labor of slaves is essential to the success of every planter, Thomas included."

"Don't worry, Aaron, I'm sure she will find slavery has advantages. She will be free to pursue the fine arts and philanthropies, rather than toil in the kitchen. I will ask her if she'd like to volunteer at the children's orphanage, truly a worthwhile endeavor."

"A fine idea. Let's lead this next dance," smiled Aaron, gallantly taking her arm. He was still inflamed by his Jane's bright, red hair and dazzling green eyes. They were in their sixties and still a most handsome couple.

Before the newlyweds left their celebration, Thomas took his wife to the kitchen to introduce Elizabeth to her new servants.

"Master Thomas, this is one of the happiest days of my life," cried Edna, giving him a warm hug. "If you don't take care of him, I will," Edna winked at Elizabeth. "Come here, honey." As Elizabeth became engulfed in Edna's warm arms, she was no longer apprehensive about owning slaves. She whole heartedly accepted whatever Thomas told her as the Gospel truth. Thomas had so kindly explained how Edna's songs had soothed him as a babe, that the slaves were part of his family and now they were her family, too. Did Elizabeth's Philadelphia family approve?

"We welcome you to our Smith family, Thomas!" warmly toasted Elizabeth's father. True her parents were Quakers, did not own slaves, but some of their tobacco growing relatives in Delaware and Maryland did. However, slavery was her parents' one hesitation in consenting to this union.

"Don't plan on changing his viewpoints, Elizabeth," warned her father. "This Thomas Hanscome comes with slaves. His wealth is built upon their backs. We like him, yes, but we have worked hard to abolish slavery. Talk with Thomas' cousin Joan seriously before you consent. She has become a Quaker, but she knows this Carolina life. It seems gay, but is it built on pretense."

Where was Joan, Thomas' deceased Aunt Ann's daughter and Aaron's niece? She and her husband John were dancing and guzzling champagne.

"You must admit, dear husband, Philadelphia is a bit staid," said Joan. "I think Elizabeth will embrace life here. I know I do miss Charles Town's extravagant parties and laughter. And weren't those horse races gay! Let's dance another dance, please?"

"Another dance, yes, but please, no more champagne. The lightness of your head is affecting your professed beliefs. I question how you can condone this decadence with your abolitionist views."

"This simply feels like home, John. I have no shame. I abhor it, forgive it and love it, strange as that may seem. Even my mother loved Charles Town. She was full of her admonitions, but underneath she loved the charm, the excitement, the merriment and all the black and brown faces. She wanted all free and educated, but her soul would have withered and died had she moved to Philadelphia."

"Listen to your contradictory words," Joan. "I do not understand how you can love your family, nor do I understand how they can own slaves when your very own brother, Will, who Aaron also professes to love, is a mulatto."

"It confuses me, too, but I love them all. I am not responsible for this hypocritical world I was born into. More champagne, please, dear husband."

"One more day until normalcy," John silently thought as he quickly waltzed his wife past the champagne. "Joan will see the falseness of this folly and justification of slavery once we return to Philadelphia. But will I ever understand her? Probably not. I only wish I could have met her mother, Ann Hanscome Downing, who was martyred, yes, lit on fire for her beliefs in equality, right here in Charles Town. Tonight Joan is simply seduced by this old familiar - the familiar warm, soft air, soft accents, graceful elegance, wealth and champagne. One gulp, taste or even sniff of her past life and her love of privilege surfaces. Was she ever her mother's daughter? Still, I love my charming, southern belle wife. I promised Joan not to challenge her relatives and tonight I also promise myself never to return. What were the Smiths thinking to allow their Elizabeth to marry into this planter society? She will never be their daughter again. Thomas will seduce her with opulence and she will greedily accept his sick belief in the necessity of slavery. Love me, love my family, love my society." John sighed. He understood the Hanscome logic ended with "Love my slaves."

Before the newlyweds embarked on their London voyage, Moses heartily bid farewell to Thomas.

"I intend to get married when you return. You had best give me a good report."

Thomas embraced Moses, his best man, his best friend and his younger brother. Then he embraced John Randall, his groomsman and life-long companion. John's parents, now deceased, had owned the plantation next to Creekside and generously offered Aaron and Jane quarters, truly a slave hut, when they were first married and building their home. Yes, the very same John Randall, who's mother Amy, Jane's best friend, had died of fever in child birth when the boys were a mere six years old. Jane and Amy had used Indian medicine to conceive and shared their excitement of having yet other children, who might also be best friends. Moses Hanscome lived, but Amy Randall's babe died with her. Yes, the very same John Randall, who attended Ann Downing's school with Thomas and was raised by his Mammy Pearl and his father. He was like another brother to Thomas.

"God bless!" yelled well wishers as Elizabeth and Thomas boarded the ship.

"Good luck!" cheered other friends, showering them with rice. Wasn't it true that rice was the basis for prosperity? It was called Carolina Gold for a reason.

The voyage

Thomas and Elizabeth stood on the ship's deck and waved farewell to their friends.

"It will take me years to get all this rice out of my hair," smiled Elizabeth.

"Truly years, dear?" teased Thomas.

"At least until we reach England. My trousseau is covered. I think your slaves had fun filling our luggage and supplying all our guests with rice."

"Indeed, they might have. That's one of the benefits of owning a rice plantation."

Thomas' levity was quieted by the thunder and lightning he heard in the distance.

"Elizabeth, look at this dark sky that looms on the horizon. We could be in for quite a storm. I do hope we will not be spending our honeymoon in Charles Town."

"Our wedding day has been perfect, thus far. I would hate to return and spend the whole evening entertaining your parents' friends. I am tired of fielding question after question."

"Then full sails around this storm, anything to please the new Mrs. Hanscome!" shouted Thomas into the gusting wind. Soon enough the ship sailed smoother waters and their honeymoon excitement returned.

"I want you to meet my Cousin Thomas and hear his stories about India."

"I must say, there are so many Thomas' in your family, it confuses me. Why didn't your father name you Aaron, after him, and start a new tradition?"

"My parents had two sons before I was born. Both died right after birth. It is a subject that still brings tears to my mother's eyes. They had named both sons Aaron. Thus, my father painfully declared, 'We will name no more sons Aaron. I need not leave an Aaron legacy. I just want a living son. I will continue the Thomas tradition for my father.' So here I am, a Thomas. Of course, my Cousin Thomas is also named for our mutual grandfather."

"And will you name our first born son Thomas?" Elizabeth flirted.

"First, we need the honeymoon," Thomas lustily replied.

"Oh we will have children, of that I'm sure. And for girl's names? Have you a preference?" she asked.

"Ann," Thomas said without hesitation. "Next to my mother, Aunt Ann was the woman I have admired most, that is, until you. Unless you'd prefer Elizabeth for a daughter's name? You can name the girls, as in the Indian tradition."

"Your name choice surprises me. Wasn't your Aunt Ann an abolitionist?"

"Abolitionist is a new Philadelphia term, but today the meaning would fit her. She wanted freedom and equal education for all – girls, boys, free, slave. Education was her life's purpose. Unfortunately, she could never entice my father to read or heed her warnings about the ills of slavery. She almost moved to Philadelphia to be with Joan and promote her ideas. But my Aunt Ann was no coward. She was forced from Kittery and very determined not to be forced from her precious Charles Town, too. Run away from slavery? She looked it straight in the face. Now here's a secret no one but our family knows – and for good reason. Ann's first born was a bastard, mulatto son. Did I tell you that?"

"No, what a surprise revelation, indeed. She must have been raped. Is her son in Charles Town? Do you know him?"

"No, I haven't met him, but her other children, my cousins Joan and Thomas, knew their brother Will. My father grew up with Little Will, as he affectionately calls him, took him under his wing as he is only six years older. They say Will's as English and as educated as we are, except for his complexion. He lives north of Kittery on an island he owns and has an English wife and children. My father took them all to Will's Island on his ship for a family reunion. My parents fell in love on the return voyage.

"Do you have a great imagination or did I just marry a charming liar? I can hardly believe this tale. Do tell me more about your most uncommon family."

"My Aunt Ann and Will's slave father, Black Will, each received forty lashes in the Kittery town square for their sins. Father's whole family was ordered to witness her shameful beating. My father still remembers his beloved sister Alice, that was Aunt Ann's name before, lying in a bloody heap, near death. Alice and Black Will almost died, yes, for love. Finally, the family helped her escape from the Kittery jail and her witch's fate of being burned at the stake for yet another bastard babe, the very Thomas we are visiting in London. Then John, my privateer uncle, sailed her away to Charles Town to begin anew. My father credits Aunt Ann, who was like his second mother, for turning him from privateering and choosing his wife, my very mother. Aunt Ann was a pillar of strength, highly spirited and well-respected. She promoted the early Charles Town credo of tolerance and accepted, even relished, Charles Town's different cultures," said Thomas.

"I can tell you loved her," said Elizabeth, unbelievably puzzled by the incongruity of beliefs in her new Hanscome family.

"She was beyond love, my dear Elizabeth. I didn't want to share her laughter with my friends. I wanted her selfishly all to myself. She was that magical." Then Thomas grew somber. "There was not a person who attended her school who did not morn her death. Her funeral was well attended. But others say the fire that killed her and Uncle James was deliberate, because of her anti-slavery views. Do you know that before the Negro Act of 1740 was enacted slaves could be educated and had freedom of movement?"

"No, I thought those restrictions were always there."

"No, they weren't. When my father first bought his land, he and my mother lived together in the same small huts as the indentured servants. That was before we owned slaves and became wealthy."

"What an unbelievable story. My parents would have been mesmerized by your tale, too. I want to hear more about your Aunt Ann. What other secret family scandals did you forget to tell me about before we married?" teased his new wife.

"It's good we have a long voyage ahead," laughed Thomas. "When we reach England I hope you'll still be grateful to my cousin Joan for our introduction."

"I will always be eternally grateful to Joan for your visit to Philadelphia," replied Elizabeth gazing into Thomas' big blue eyes, forgetting about the ominous, dark sky.

The captain sailed due east, rather than hug the Carolina coast northward. It was important that they race to England ahead of the storm fed by the warm seas to the south. Did they make it? Yes, they did.

Did they wonder about the storm's impact on Charles Town? No, they did not. Thomas and Elizabeth eyes were glazed over with love. When they came up for a breath of fresh air and finally left their stateroom, they spoke only of their grand tour of Europe. Why look homeward? They would be gone for seven long months. What an extravagant honeymoon. Did Elizabeth entertain second thoughts about the wisdom of her marriage? Heavens no. Elizabeth could hardly believe her good fortune.

CH. 2. Eyes Glazed Over with Fear and Grief

September 15, 1752

Charles Town

"How fortunate Thomas' and Elizabeth's ship was able to sail before this gale arrived," said Jane as she and the servants readied the Meeting Street house for the hurricane. Fierce September storms came every year and this one promised the usual flooding, broken windows and damaged ships in the harbor. All knew the safety drill, nonetheless, their eyes glazed over with fear with the arrival of every hurricane. The fear was always the same. Would this be the storm to wipe away their existence?

"Make sure we have fresh water in every basin and tub, Edna," ordered Jane.

They could handle the wind and the rain, but they'd die without clean water. After the fierce winds and slashing rain subsided, the most damage could come from the storm surge on a clear, sunny day. The water pushed into the harbor would calmly rise, like a tea cup overflowing its brim, unstoppable. Oh, how they prayed for low tides.

"I have already given those orders," huffed Edna, who was in charge of the help. "Jess and Charles are latching the Bahama shutters. Sarah is bringing all the priceless silver and china upstairs for safekeeping. We are madly cooking cornpone and smoking meats. We will have our larder filled for a week's time. Luckily, we have all the left over wedding food."

"What would I do without you?" smiled Jane.

Jane realized how fortunate she was to have Edna by her side. Her father had given Edna to her as a gift when Moses was born. They were almost the same age. "Do not treat her as a slave, but as your confidante and friend," was her mother's advice. And Edna was quite the gift. She anticipated Jane's needs before she even knew she had them.

"Edna, I wish Aaron had not gone to the Craven's plantation, but he was so worried about the high tide and the rice ready for harvest. An inflow of salt water will ruin the whole crop."

"I told him that those sand bags would only break his back and not stop the steady sea," chided Edna. She had always given her opinion quite freely to both her mistress and master. And they valued her for her candor. They trusted her, even above their planter friends.

Jane smiled, "These storms are like having a baby. Boil that water! We prepare, but it is futile. No storm is the same. It's probably better Aaron is out of our hair."

"Oh, Miss Jane, truly you miss him. The Master would be comforting to you, particularly when the lightning and booming start." Jane smiled at Edna's words. Edna saw through her pretense of bravery. Jane had always been afraid of the hurricanes.

"What about Creekside?" asked Edna.

"I think Alfred can close up the house and organize the slaves to keep the livestock from stampeding," replied Jane.

"Well, if you ask me, and I know you didn't, he is not a good overseer. I don't trust him. I don't like his smile. I don't like how he looks at the young girls. I told Master Aaron that, but it truly is not my business. I wish Master Aaron had gone to Creekside and let the rice go."

"This talk is doing us no good. Let's sing, Edna. And when we have done everything we can think of to be ready, let's have another wedding feast, china and silver and all. Yes, and we will all toast to Thomas and Elizabeth on their new life together. And we will have another toast to the glory, power and beauty of this storm."

"I will remind you of your party idea when we are washing yet another set of dishes," laughed Edna. But she knew the laughter would chase away the fear.

"I hear the thunder and lightning. The shutters are rattling. It is all starting. Call the servants to the table. Let's eat," invited Jane.

And did the servants continue to laugh? Yes, they made light of the storm as they enjoyed the wedding feast. But the laugher stopped when the water crept under the doors and seeped through the window casings. The water rose and all evacuated to the safety of the second story.

"Edna, keep me company. Bring your candle to my room. I am frightened," implored Jane. "The whole downstairs is flooded! This has never happened before."

"I have sent Charles to fetch Master Aaron. I gave him one of those safe passage notes, so he won't be apprehended as a runaway. But Lord, who would be out looking for runaways in this storm? He took the gray horse. He would do anything for the Master. Pray they both come back alive."

"Pray with me," said Jane. "Let's hold hands." They knelt by Jane's bed in the eerie light of the lightning flashes. Their prayers were drowned out by the crashing, banging and roars of thunder.

Creekside

The slaves at Creekside were making their own storm preparations.

"This is the time to leave," whispered Samuel to Caroline. "If we are to be free, we must flee - now. I have all the preparations in the sloop. Alfred is too busy with the animals to notice us."

"We could be killed by the lightning and dashed to pieces upon the shore in this small craft. I'm frightened!" cried Caroline.

"Do you want to stay here and keep fending off Alfred's assaults? I am your husband in God's eyes and I will crush his bones if I witness him touch you one more time. We won't know whose babe you carry in your belly until it's born."

"And if it's white? What then? Will you discard me, like an old shoe?"

"I don't care if it's purple. I will love it, but we must be free to have any family."

"Master Aaron would never separate us. He keeps families together."

"He is old now and I hear nothing about his manumitting us upon his death. We will just be passed to young Thomas and Moses. They could separate us or sell us."

"Sell us?" Caroline stared at Samuel. It was every slave's worst fear to be separated from family.

"Don't cry, please. We need to leave, now, Caroline. This storm will get worse before it passes. We need to hide the sloop in the islands to the south. Then we can wait out the rest of the storm. No one will be slave catching today."

"Are you sure we will be freed in Florida?" she asked, needing reassurance.

"I don't know, Caroline. We do know what lies here for us if we remain. How can Florida be worse?"

Charles Town

"I must go downstairs, Edna. I hear a banging on the door. It must be Aaron returning with Charles from our Craven's County Plantation."

"You stay abed, Miss Jane, I will go," Edna replied. But Jane could not wait. They each had a candle and peered down the circular stairway. Again, they heard banging from beyond the front door.

"How can anyone be on the other side? The noise must be a loose barrel. The water inside is halfway up the stairs," Edna cried. "I have never seen the water so high."

"High water or no, I must see if it is Aaron. The door must be locked." Jane clung to the banister as she descended the stairs into the water. In an instant the banister cracked and as she fell, the water engulfed her. Edna's screams were answered by Charles' and Aaron's battering through the door. Aaron was able to pull Jane out by her flowing nightgown. She was limp in his arms, but as he threw her over his shoulder and pounded her back, she sputtered back to life.

"Oh thank you, Master!" cried Edna from the top of the stairs. Gingerly, Aaron found his footing on the slippery stairs and carried Jane up to safety.

"Find some dry clothes while I make her purge her stomach of the filthy water. The whole town is a sewer," commanded Aaron. After Jane regurgitated her wedding feast, Edna helped Aaron put her to bed. In the middle of the night, Jane turned hot with fever and lost control of her bowels. Was it dysentery, yellow fever or both?

"No!" cried Aaron. "Jane must fight this fever. Pray with us, Edna."

And they prayed, fervently. In one day's time the winds subsided and the sun broke through. Edna opened the shutters.

"What a beautiful sunrise!" Jane smiled at Aaron as he held her hand. But when the next predictable bands of straight-line winds and pelting rain hit, she became delirious again. Would Jane survive this fever? Was this the last sunrise she would see?

Jane passed quietly in the roar of the renewed thunderbolts. Edna and Aaron cried together.

John's Island

The funeral service was held at St. John's Island Presbyterian Church. Edna and Charles sat in the balcony with all the other slaves. Noticeably absent were Samuel and Caroline. Isaac and Elizabeth Remick, Jane's parents, sat with Aaron and Moses in the Hanscome family pew. Jane the daughter, Jane the wife, Jane the mother and Jane the mistress was soundly mourned. Aaron wondered how he could go on without her. At the closing of the service, the pastor thanked God for sparing all present from the worst hurricane in their history. Over one hundred perished, but the accompanying fever took uncounted others. Aaron's Craven's County plantation rice crop was lost, but he thanked God for the safety of his precious sons, Thomas and Moses. Plantations can be replanted. More slaves can be bought.

After the service, the family buried Jane in their new family cemetery, a plot of land called The Point adjacent to Creekside. Aaron assumed he would be next.

Moses sent a copy of their mother's obituary to Thomas's address in Italy. Perhaps it was futile, but he must try to reach Thomas. Moses also sent copies to his cousins - Joan in Philadelphia, Thomas in London and the Remicks in Kittery, Maine. After a silent reflection, he also prepared a copy for a William Black on Casco Bay, Maine. Shouldn't William know his cherished Uncle Aaron's wife had died?

"We were as inseparable as Thomas and you were, Moses," said his father about his relationship with his mulatto nephew, Little Will. "Of course, Little Will was so bright; he had never been a slave."

In the same newspaper as Jane Remick Hanscome's obituary was the following ad:

South Carolina Gazette September 18, 1752

Reward for return of two runaway slaves, dead or alive: Five pounds for Samuel, a good grassier and mild mannered. Four pounds for Caroline, excellent house domestic and cook. Both are young, backs clean of stripes and strong. Both speak good English and are Carolina born. They stole guns, a sloop, blankets, food, clothes, knives, cooking pots, utensils and plates. They escaped the first night of the hurricane. If found dead, please return bodies for a decent Christian burial. The sloop, supplies and slaves are property of Aaron Hanscome, Creekside Plantation, John's Island.

Moses winced as he read the ad and cut it out. "On second thought, I best send nothing to William Black," sighed Moses. "I see our hypocrisy most clearly and I must jump off the fence. I am tired of my father's guilt and I will never give up my slaves."

In the same *Gazette* issue appeared a dialog of discontent with the Crown's governance. Why was the Governor hedging on the promised restoration of Charles Town and the plantations from the hurricane? First, the Carolinians chafed at the Lords Proprietors' rule and sought the Crown's rule. Now, they were disenchanted with being a Crown Colony. Was freedom from England fomenting? Yes, the planters and merchants all wanted their freedom. Of course, so did the slaves. But none of the Hanscomes could see that truth.

What happened to Caroline and Samuel during the storm? Did they make it to freedom in Florida? Did they thank God for giving them a dark-complexioned, Negro baby? All we know is that no one collected the reward for the return, dead or alive, of Aaron Hanscome's runaways.

And Thomas and Elizabeth? They missed the notification of his mother's death. Their European honeymoon was a romantic success. They looked forward to the beginning of their family. Thomas surprised Elizabeth with a wedding gift of more land, an additional 165 acres on John's Island, a £1000 pound purchase. When he told her, she was most pleased, just as she had been when he allowed her to buy expensive house furnishings, paintings, fabrics, rugs, whatever she desired, in every capital of Europe. The seven months passed quickly.

Charles Town

"I'll build you a mansion to house all our treasures," promised Thomas as they sailed into the Charles Town Harbor.

"You spoil me, indeed, dear husband," she happily replied.

"We Hanscomes always do our best to please the fairer sex."

"And for that you deserve a place in heaven."

Their joy quickly faded when they disembarked to the news of Jane's Hanscome's passing. Yes, his mother was a shocking loss, but Thomas was doubly undone when he glimpsed his father. Aaron, a mere shadow of his former robust self, was frail.

The honeymoon was over. Thomas' eyes glazed over with grief.

CH. 3. Building Prosperity

1757

Creekside Plantation

Cries of "It is a girl! It's a girl!" rang out up and down the halls and in and out of the kitchen and out into the fields where even the slaves smiled. Elizabeth beamed as she placed her first-born babe in Thomas' arms. "Are you pleased?"

"It is a good omen to have a baby girl. If only boys are born the prophecies predict a future of wars. I have seen too much death to welcome more. It is high time for a baby girl in the Hanscome lineage. I couldn't be more pleased, dear Elizabeth. As a sign of our gratitude, I will be handing out cigars." Elizabeth smiled. She had grown to appreciate Thomas' love of words, even if his exuberance was at times over the top and she wondered if he'd ever stop digressing and get to his point.

"I thought those precious cigars, worth their weight in gold, were only awarded for boys," teased Elizabeth.

"True, it is more customary for boys, since they build the family prosperity, but in our case, no one need toil. She will be a princess, waited on hand and foot – I will see to that!"

"And what will we name this priceless princess?" asked Elizabeth. "Ann?"

"I would be honored if we named her Ann – for my Aunt Ann and my Kittery grandmother Ann."

"And what if our Ann holds those same anti-slavery viewpoints?"

"She is going to enjoy being a planter's daughter too much to adopt an attitude that would make her a pauper. Times are different now. Our slaves are content."

Charles Town

On the same day in a mansion on Tradd Street, another happy man was giving out cigars.

"It is a boy!"

The smiling parents of baby Henry were none other than John and Samantha Randall. Thomas was most relieved at the news. He hoped John's son would help sustain his marriage. Thomas winced as he recalled an ominous conversation with his best friend, just prior to John's wedding six years ago.

"It is so like you, John, to abide by the best wedding protocol – a proper night time wedding and ball," toasted Thomas at the race track where their planter friends feted John's upcoming nuptials.

"Unlike you, I won't run away with my bride from the worst hurricane in Charles Town's history after the hottest wedding we ever attended," retorted John.

"Touché, John. You are in fine form today. I see we're off to as good a start as these races. I'll drink to the finest wedding Charles Town will ever see," said Thomas holding his glass high in another toast. "Hear, hear!" was echoed jovially round the old group of fast friends. Indeed, what a clever start to a great bachelor party.

"Look at those thoroughbreds win - race after race," applauded Grimball. "There is no miscegenation there!"

"Actually those thoroughbreds are not as pure in their lineage as you think. Their strength and endurance come from the mixing with Arabian studs," responded an already inebriated John.

"Like you with your Charles Town concubine?" jested another friend. All laughed except for Thomas who saw a fight brewing, by the look on John's face. It was his responsibility as best man to protect the groom.

"So do we all get a turn with your special Grace – as a sign you have changed your preference for Miss Samantha, your bride to be?" joked another.

"Be generous, share your slave whore and we'll keep your secret," taunted another.

"Grace is no slave and no whore," retorted John, barely able to contain his wrath. "And I'll kill you if you touch her or harm her in any way!"

John was too drunk to see the fist, but the blow enraged him more. At this moment he loathed his friends and lashed back.

As Thomas had predicted, the fight began in earnest. Fists flew, heads cracked, knuckles bled and eyes puffed and closed until all lay in a tangled heap. It was soon over but no one was left unscathed. Thomas had stood by John's side and absorbed blows intended for his best friend. After everyone dispersed and he put bloodied John to bed, Thomas stealthily crept into his room, hoping to escape Elizabeth's scrutinizing eye.

"What happened at John's party?" asked Elizabeth, quite awake and most aghast. "Your face is bloody and swollen!" Thomas simply sighed and managed a feeble smile through cracked lips as Elizabeth continued. "You need not defend yourself, Thomas. I believe I have a vivid picture of events from just looking at you. These bachelor parties are a hideous custom. Now put some cool water on those bruises and hope you don't look like a drunken sop for the wedding."

"My face will be better tomorrow. Hopefully, none of the wedding guests will take notice of me. They will be too busy noticing the pulverized faces and black eyes of the groom and all his groomsmen. No punches were spared in the drunken brawl tonight," said Thomas, wincing as he wet his face with cool water.

"Do you want to discuss it?" asked Elizabeth, not angry, but curious.

"No. I just want to go to sleep. I am too old for all this carousing. But tomorrow I will be busy salving wounds worse than mine. Indeed, I hope this wedding happens. There are as many bruised feelings as bones."

Early the next morning Thomas visited John Randall.

"I am relieved to see you," said John. "If my memory is right, I could have sparred all night."

"Yes, unfortunately you are correct. However, I am concerned we sparred over the honor of the wrong woman, Grace, and not Samantha, your wife to be."

"I had never planned on marriage, Thomas. I wanted to be true to my Grace. However, my father convinced me otherwise, or his inheritance did. He wants our planter lineage to continue into perpetuity."

"And that is what Samantha is to you? A mere breeding mare - a liaison between planter families?" asked Thomas, disgusted.

"Yes, sadly that is true. It will not be easy, but I do intend to maintain both Grace and Samantha. I will not give up my Grace, my true reason for living."

"You mean your dalliance with a slave, Grace?"

"She is not a slave. Grace is a freed mustee – and an accomplished seamstress and a most loving woman," answered an affronted John. "Aside from you, she is my best friend and companion."

"I know you have always had an affinity for women of color, none of my business really, but this bodes ill for your marriage. Why can't you just let Grace be?"

"I love her!" shouted John.

"Lust or love?" asked Thomas, expecting this conversation.

"I would marry Grace in true bliss, if the laws allowed it. We don't like England's meddling in our business affairs - collecting taxes or creating tariffs. I don't like the state meddling in my heart's affairs. Why do you think marriage between the races is illegal?" asked John.

"Surely you know the answer to that question. Don't play the fool, John," scolded Thomas.

"And don't patronize me. I ask you sincerely - Why? Why can't I form a legal union with my heart's choice?"

"They are an inferior race! Mestizo or no, freed or not, Grace is not your equal. She is part Negro and not fit to be the mother of your children."

Thomas shocked himself by the intensity of his words. This was the first time he had admitted to holding the prevailing planters' beliefs. What would his Aunt Ann think of his words? Thomas thought he was a champion of the Negros. Hadn't he argued for Negro education? Hadn't he called for fair treatment of slaves? He thought he was beyond the venom he just spewed. But he apparently wasn't.

"Ah, you have spoken just like my father," said John sarcastically. "We did not learn such tripe at your Aunt Ann's school. I for one do not believe such a silly rationale of superiority. We just keep the Negros uneducated and childlike because we might be over-run by their sheer numbers, or perhaps out-witted. We are afraid! We have created a nightmare with this slave class. Look at how the mulattos are thriving in Charles Town. And love, not simply lust or rape, created many. Why aren't we planters honest about it? We are the ogres here. We are all people, regardless of color."

"And you would rather our white planter class disappeared into this sea of color? The laws against miscegenation protect us, protect our way of life."

"The sheer numbers of freed mulattos indicates the law is not very successful. We love those we live with. It's that simple, Thomas. I do not remember my mother, Amy. Mammy Pearl was my true mother. I loved her. So did my father. Our Randall slaves are brown, not black. Miscegenation is the rule, not an aberration. No one except a fresh slave from Africa is black. Not one. Think about it. Our Carolina laws are a sham."

"Lust or love is not the point. Grace's children don't carry your name, your planter lineage. If we had no laws our way of life would disappear. I don't see you giving up your slaves. I see you flaunting your wealth, just like the rest of us. You are the worst kind of hypocrite."

"And I feel guilty about it. I drink myself into oblivion every night I am not with Grace."

"Feeling as you do, please do not get married today. This is too unkind to Miss Samantha. Or promise to give up Grace."

"I know the nasty Carolina rules by which we play our game of life. I know it would be the better course for me to marry Samantha and deny my Grace. Perhaps I shall," answered John with a sigh.

"There is no dishonor in calling off this wedding," said Thomas with a softer tone. He was sickened to think he had just spoken so harshly to his best friend. Yes, and sickened at John's honesty and the true chord it struck deep inside. Thomas knew John was right and he was wrong.

"Perhaps you and Grace can go to the Barbados or even Africa where tolerance still reigns for mixed marriages. I'd rather lose you, than see you waste your life in a sea of booze, miserable. And Samantha with her dowry of thousands will have no difficulty finding a better match. She deserves an honorable man. And you deserve to live your truth."

"I will consider your suggestions. If I am not at the Church, you will understand."

Did John deny his heart?

No. John married Samantha, but did not relinquish his Grace.

What was John's truth, the truth that Thomas had observed for years? Why was he so attracted to Grace? Was it because he was raised by his father's slave, Pearl, after his mother died? Was it because Pearl's hands fed him, her open arms comforted him and her songs lulled him to sleep? Was it that he suspected that Pearl also comforted his father? Did big brown eyes in a kind, dark face mean love? Although nothing was ever said to him, some of his father's slaves were too light-skinned not to be his younger brothers and sisters. They were his playmates, true, but weren't they also his family? Yes! In his heart John knew they were his family, but his father did not claim them, so how could he? And with that knowledge John's guilt imploded, releasing a toxic self-hatred.

Yes, John mirrored the love he found in the eyes and the smiles on the darkest faces, but no one discussed it. Not even his father. And definitely not his best friend, Thomas. But they all knew the truth.

1760

John's Island

"It's a boy!" exclaimed Thomas as he handed out the cigars to his friends after the Sunday church service. "His name is Thomas."

"Congratulations, Thomas!" said their good friends - the Randalls, Legares, and Grimballs.

"We thought the baby had arrived when we noticed Elizabeth's absence from your pew today," said Samantha Randall, proudly carrying her newly born son. Her two older boys ran for the safety of their Mammy, just arrived from the balcony, where the slaves listened to God's word every Sunday.

"Yes, we are truly blessed this spring. Little Ann is already mothering her new baby brother and Elizabeth is doing well." Thomas' eyes were never brighter. "I thank the Lord for all our abundance and I thank you my dear friends for your support and friendship all these years. I regard you as my family, too. Have another cigar."

"We would like you all to join us for games at our plantation this afternoon," invited Sarah Legare. "I look forward to an afternoon of whist and music on the south veranda. The children will have a grand time playing together. The boys can fly their kites, test their archery skills or trade their marbles. It is a shame to waste the breezes of this perfect spring day. I intend to open up the whole house. And the girls can play hopscotch, jump rope or chase the boys in a jolly good game of tag. My servants were making the best smelling cakes before we left for church. I'm sure they will be quite sumptuous with our afternoon tea. We can celebrate all our new little planters' births."

"Yes, a tea sounds lovely," said one friend.

"We are long overdue for a spring fling," chimed another.

"Regretfully, I must bow out as I want to share this day with my family. I just don't think Elizabeth is up to a buggy ride," said Thomas.

"And I must bow out, too," said John. "Had I known earlier I could have made other plans, but I have an obligation in Charles Town."

Thomas noted Samantha's strange smile at John's departure. He sighed. Samantha was no fool. All their planter friends knew John had another family with Grace in Charles Town. Why wouldn't Samantha also know? But no one spoke of it. Many planters also had such duplicitous arrangements.

Charles Town

In Charles Town, where most planters had second homes, the ratio of Negros to English was five to one. Many of the lighter complexioned were freed and gainfully employed in the trades – as blacksmiths, barbers, seamstresses, carpenters, hoteliers and cooks. Of course they all knew their proper place on the lively streets, but behind closed doors the mulatto class was born and thrived. Their white planter fathers manumitted them, sometimes recognized their parentage, gave them their surnames and set them up in businesses. Yes, Charles Town was the center of culture and permissiveness.

Were they hypocrites, supporting two families? Perhaps, but John Randall had done his duty. And duty was more important than love. Wealth flew to all the planters, including the Hanscomes.

Creekside boasted 250 head of cattle and fields of sweet potatoes, corn, peas, onions and beans. The markets in Barbados bought as much as they could supply. The Hanscome's biggest cash crop was indigo. But soon the luscious, long, soft Sea Island cotton would surpass indigo's profits. Moses had convinced Aaron that rotating the cotton with the indigo would be the most advantageous. And it was. The blue indigo cakes were in high demand in England and the cotton market was just beginning to flourish. The Sea Island cotton was unique in that the seeds were easily extracted, not true of the shorter cotton varieties. But the biggest boon to cotton, the cotton gin would bring unheard of profits after 1794.

And the Carolina Gold? The Craven's County rice plantation recovered from the hurricane of 1752, thanks to Thomas' keen oversight. He listened to his West African slaves, who rivaled the Chinese in their rice cultivation knowledge. The most challenging dilemma was harnessing the tidal flows, while not saturating the tender roots with salt water.

And the need for slaves? It was as one would suspect - the more labor intensive crops of rice and cotton demanded more slaves. The plantations became seas of black arms working in rhythm. Few white faces were spotted in the heat of the summer.

"Why are our slave expenses so high this year?" asked Aaron of his two sons as they examined their ledgers in his Meeting Street study.

"Slaves are becoming more expensive to purchase," replied Moses. "And the death rate of slaves, particularly on the rice plantation, is quite high. Have you ever asked yourself what causes the great disparity between the cotton and rice workers life spans?"

"It is the swamp fever," answered Aaron. "Yes, it is true that more of us, English and slaves alike, all die in the fall."

"Yes, but what causes the swamp fever? I think Aunt Ann was right. The mosquito carries the dreaded disease," added Thomas. "They multiply in the moist swamps all summer and we succumb in the fall. If this is true, we need to do what we can to keep our slaves free from the deadly pests. One of my slaves says that in Africa they inoculated all against the swamp fever."

"Can we do that?" asked Moses. "That would save many lives."

"Dr. Smith says it is a ridiculous notion, that only a good bleeding will purge the deadly fevers, but I no longer believe him. Bleeding hasn't cured anyone," said Thomas. "I am going to heed my good slave Earl's wisdom. Earl will inoculate everyone at the rice plantation, including me."

"I'd like you to reconsider being inoculated by Earl," cautioned Aaron. "I'd hate to see my son poisoned by his slave. You know that has happened recently at other plantations."

"Don't be ridiculous, Father. I treat my slaves well, but if it would make you feel more comfortable, I'll wait a year – see if the inoculations save slaves' lives."

"Please do, I don't want to outlive you," laughed Aaron.

"How can you jest about your death, Father?" queried Moses. "I don't find that very amusing."

"I accept that my time will soon come. I want you to also accept death as an inevitable condition of life. It is my final gift to you. When I am gone, you will truly be emancipated - free to be your own person." Aaron paused and then smiled, "Free, unless you allow my voice to haunt you. But while I live, let's get back to the business at hand. We were talking about the new slave expenses and how they would easily be offset by more years of service. Please continue, Thomas."

"I also want us to protect all our slaves from mosquitoes, not just the Craven's County slaves. I suggest we spend more on decent, fine, white cotton fabric for the slaves' clothes – two changes per person. Earl said long pants, shirts and hats would protect them better – from the sun as well as the pests. If they have one change, the dirty shirts can be cleaned and drying. Earl says the mosquitoes are attracted by sweat and dirt. I am also going to spend more on netting for their beds. Too many young women and children have died. The more their increase live, the less our future expenses."

"Now I see why your anticipated expenses are so high," sighed Moses. "However, I am for the inoculations if it means we can increase our labor numbers and not have to buy new ones from the slave market."

"Yes, Moses," grinned Thomas. "The more we can keep from dying in the fields or the cradle, the fewer slaves we will need to purchase. No one wants to lose loved ones, not even slaves. They will be much happier and productive with healthy families."

"I think the added expenses will save us money in the long run," agreed Aaron. "I like your ideas, Thomas. You could also, by your good example, rejuvenate interest in slave welfare among the less kind planters. Some just don't seem to understand that slaves are people. They need to understand that the happier the slave, the better they toil and the bigger our profits will be."

"If this inoculation saves lives, I've promised Earl that he can hire himself out to other planters and keep part of his wages. You should have seen his eyes light up!" Thomas was pleased with his plans and astute financial acumen.

"Does Earl want to buy his freedom?" asked Moses.

"Yes, his entire family's freedom. Do you have a problem with that?"

"Only that he is so bright; it would be nice to keep him as long as we can," ventured Moses.

"It will take him years before he has saved enough money. Once he is freed I will offer him the job of overseer. First, we need to see how this experiment works. I suggest we start the inoculations right away before the mosquitoes hatch. We should know the results before winter."

"And that brings me to the topic of my will," said Aaron.

"I do hope you don't plan to leave this world soon," said Thomas, gently placing his hand on his father's.

"There is no need for pretense my sons. I am aware that I lost much of my stamina after your mother's death. I had hoped to recover, but as you can see even my thin skin sags. Yes, I am failing, but I am not sad. I am pleased with my life. I have sailed the seas, seen the world, fought for the Queen, vanquished the Indians, honored my parents, loved my wife and been blessed with two fine sons. I have tried to be a godly, decent man, good for his word and a stalwart steward of our land. In return, providence has given me unforeseen prosperity. I am content."

"I do hope you plan on surviving until my wedding next year. Mary's parents are insistent upon a long engagement," said Moses.

"Oh, who can tell when God will claim me, but I am pleased with your choice. Mary will be a good planter's wife. She has the singing voice of an angel and is very kind to her sisters. Kindness is more important than gaiety, education or wisdom. Not that she is lacking in those qualities, but kindness makes the affection true. Treat her with the utmost respect and you will be rewarded, Moses."

"If I can do as well as Thomas, I will be pleased. He and Elizabeth have a special rapport, unique among our friends. Prey, what do you advise me, brother?"

"Well, thank you for the compliment. Here's my secret, Moses. Listen. Listen carefully and include Mary in your decisions. Heed her counsel. Women are truly not the weaker sex, but they will feign weakness if that is what you expect – quite boring I think."

"You will make of your marriage what the two of you desire, of that I am sure," added Aaron. "If you give it nothing, you will have nothing. But I have greater things on my mind today – my will.

"My solicitor has given copies to Solomon Freer, Thomas Arnold and Daniel Holmes. Here are your copies. As you can see it is short, very straight-forward. You two will share the executorship and equally divide all my properties and assets, after subtracting my debts and funeral expenses. If you cannot agree, as sometimes brothers are wont to do, I suggest selling everything. If you want to keep the land, then I suggest you receive appraisals, accept them as fairly accurate and move forward. I wish to be buried in our family cemetery plot on the Point, next to your mother.

"In addition, Thomas, I bequeath one child slave to each of your children. Little Jenny, with her increase will be left to little Ann and her heirs forever. My mulatto boy, Ietrow, will be left to baby Thomas and his heirs forever. I know I have left your future issue nothing Moses, but I cannot foretell the future. I only know that if you and Mary are blessed with children there is ample in my estate to care for their welfare for their lifetimes."

Did Aaron live to see Moses' wedding to Mary Brown? No, he did not. He died peacefully in the spring at his beloved Creekside, attended by his family. He was content to have built a legacy of prosperity for his sons. Moses married the following June. With his inheritance, Moses bought a plantation on the South Edisto, just in time to prosper in the Cotton is King era.

1763

Creekside

"It's a girl!" heartily announced Mary Hanscome, Moses' wife, who served as mid-wife for Elizabeth.

"What should we name this girl?" asked Thomas as he tenderly kissed his tired, but smiling wife. "We could call her Elizabeth after you."

"I owe her life to Mary's help, thus I'd like to name her Mary, after her Aunt. You have two boys and no girls, Mary. How does that suit you?"

"To have a namesake is always an honor," said Mary. "I always wanted a little girl."

"It is unfortunate that my father isn't here to hold her. I just can't get used to his passing," said Thomas. "It seems like yesterday, but now I know what he meant about how time slides by faster and faster the older one gets. I can't believe that Ann is six and Thomas is talking up a storm at three. He and Ietrow are the best playmates."

"Yes, and so are Ann and Jenny. Your father was so thoughtful to bequeath those slaves to our children."

"Do you think we should buy a slave for wee Mary?" asked Thomas.

"What a thoughtful way to celebrate her birth. But let's buy a girl older than Mary, so she can take care of her personal needs. Jenny was initially more work for Mammy than help. Only now is she able to be of service."

1770

Charles Town

"Open the letter, Mother, please! It's from England!" begged fourteen year old Ann. She had snatched the letter from the mail courier. The Hanscomes, like most of the planters, were in Charles Town for the high season.

"The letter is most exciting, Ann, but since it's from your father's cousin, Thomas, I think he should have the pleasure of opening it. We will give it to him before the ball tonight. Are you prepared for your debut?" asked Elizabeth.

"Yes, I am ready, Mother. Jenny and I perfected my curtsies and dance steps all morning."

"Yes, I heard your giggles – I didn't know that curtsies were all that humorous," smiled Elizabeth.

"Well, Jenny does the best imitations of all possible suitors. She thought I should be ready with quick retorts for each type. It is never wise to be too ingratiating or unprepared."

"I agree this courting ritual is a bit silly on the surface, but the consequences of not mastering the fine nuances could cause you to lose the best suitors," counseled her wise mother. "Then you'd be stuck choosing between a man who would give you ugly, dull children or only desire your father's wealth. Would you like that, Miss Ann?"

"I'm not sure I want any suitors at all, Mother," quipped Ann.

"You are young - consider tonight's debut practice for your future. Who knows who might strike your fancy? Remember, the ball etiquette calls for elegant grace, not giggles. Ann, mirror me in the proper deportment, please," smiled Elizabeth. Ann slowly followed her mother's lead and gracefully curtsied with barely a hint of a smile. She batted her eyelids several times, not too many or too fast, then, demurely lowered them.

"Lovely, Ann! You are most beguiling. Now repeat the whole sequence as slowly and artfully as possible. A proper gentleman is required to watch your whole performance."

"A performance, Mother?" asked Ann.

"Yes, this is exactly like a play – each player exquisitely acts his or her part. It is the same with the dance postures. The ensnarement depends on your first captivating curtsy after the formal introduction."

"Pretend you are setting a trap for a wild animal," offered Jenny.

"Let's hope he's more like a gentle hare," responded Elizabeth. And they all laughed.

"But Mother, what about truth and honesty?" asked Ann. "Father and you do not seem as actors in a play – full of pretense."

"The pretense of the play allows you to carefully glimpse the true character beneath – without prematurely disclosing your heart. It is meant to be a gay charade, to sample the suitors without inflicting hurt. That is why you are to dance with all who sign your dance card. Remember, the rule is no more than four dances with any one partner."

And so Ann and Jenny practiced. After Ann's dance skills were flawless, she practiced her vocal trills - accompanied on the grand piano by Jenny. Ann knew musical talents were as important to a proper education as reading fine literature. Yes, she wanted to be an accomplished lady.

The true test was Ann's performance with her father when he arrived home.

"I would sign your dance card for every dance, if I were a suitor," affirmed her father as he whirled her around the room until they were breathless.

"Would you, please? It would make me most happy to only dance with you, Father," replied Ann, as she gracefully curtsied. "And now, Mother, can we please open Cousin Thomas' letter?"

Elizabeth handed Thomas the letter from London.

"Please don't keep us waiting, Thomas," said Elizabeth. "This letter is as exciting as the ball."

However, Thomas was not to be rushed as he eagerly and privately digested his cousin's news. First, his cousin expounded on London's political news, particularly, would England wage war against the colonies that sought their freedom from taxation and tariffs. "There will be no need for a rebellion in the colonies. Why would England kill their cash cow?" were his cousins exact words. Thomas felt a bit reassured, then read the rest of the letter aloud to Elizabeth and Ann.

"I am quite fit and jolly at seventy-six, but I cannot portend the future. I entreat you to visit me, before I am history. London has never been more fashionable. I would love to fill your children's psyches with all things English and see your lovely countenance, my dear Elizabeth. And if you could turn the plantation oversight over to a trusted servant and accompany them, dear Thomas, my prayers would truly be answered. Whatever your decision, please consider sending Ann and Thomas for at least a year. Many a prosperous planter has found an English education creates success for their children. Before I close, I assure you my health is solid, but my sister Joan's passing in Philadelphia last year did remind me of my own mortality."

"He seems as witty as ever and his penmanship is steady, both signs that he is quite well," commented Thomas.

"What do you think of a trip to England?" asked Elizabeth. "We have put it off for one reason or another. I think what Thomas is saying is that his open invitation may not be open for long."

"In truth, I cannot take even six months away from the plantations," sighed Thomas. "I remember our magical honeymoon only too well. I also agree with Cousin Thomas that even my superficial knowledge of England and Europe has helped me keep a balanced perspective on our Carolina politics. Some of these hotheads, blood thirsty from their war games against the Indians, call me a fence-sitter."

"The planters have been threatening for years. I doubt that in six months we will rebel against the Crown. I think you inflate your need to be here. Why can't you trust the overseers to manage our plantations? We have so much abundance that even if they faltered in their duty, we would not notice the difference," said Elizabeth.

"It's not profit that chains me here. It is the increasing intolerance abroad of the institution of slavery that makes me uncomfortable. When my grandfather arrived in Salem, as a bondsman, slavery was common practice world-wide. It mattered not what you called the laborers - slaves, indentures or serfs. In practice there was little difference among them. Now we are outliers in the practice of slavery and a thorn in the conscience of the civilized world. We could have an uprising, any day. We could have a war with England, any day. We could also have an overreaction by some of the hotheaded planters, any day."

"Do you really believe your presence will change the course of any of those tides?" confronted Elizabeth. "Planter paranoia is nothing new."

"I hope your optimism is warranted, Elizabeth. Nevertheless, I have made my decision to stay."

"And the children?"

"I think both Ann and Thomas are prime for an English education. Ann could benefit from the music and artistic lessons and Thomas from intellectual stimulation - of any sort. He is only interested in shooting, hunting, horse racing, sailing and gaming with his friends. Only games of chance make his eyes light up like candles."

"Weren't you just like him when you were young?" teased Elizabeth.

"I was, but I did learn to dance and speak French," defended Thomas. "He barely passes his subjects."

"Does Gullah count as a language? He can communicate better with the slaves than any planter, other than old Legare," laughed Elizabeth.

"That indeed is an asset for a planter. I've seen him plant rice in fine Negro rhythm. He's as fast with his heels and toes as any good field hand. If I couldn't see his white face, he could pass for a slave. But he'll never learn the dances for the balls. He just needs *taming*, as Aunt Ann said my Kittery grandfather needed."

"That is precisely why some time in England would benefit Thomas. He spends way too much time with the slaves. His skin may be white but his soul is too colored. Proper elocution lessons would help him appear more genteel and educated. And by the way, I've asked you before to keep him from those rice fields in the summer heat. He could get the fever!"

"Young Thomas has a mind of his own in regard to the plantations. I agree he should be gone this summer. And next fall he'll be back in school in Charles Town. He needs more polish as a gentleman. I'll arrange passage so you'll be back by then. I will miss you dearly, Elizabeth," he said as he tenderly embraced and kissed his wife.

"And I, you. We have not been separated since our wedding day. I will send mail on every ship Carolina bound."

"And I will write as frequently as I can," responded Thomas. "We had best begin right now, making up for the loss of our time together," said Thomas whisking his wife to their bed.

"Do you have any idea how long it took me get laced, coifed and powdered for this ball, dear man?" protested Elizabeth in her flirtatious, encouraging way that endeared her so much to Thomas.

"Yes, I do, but we have plenty of time to repair the damage and, as you recall, I can be as speedy in lacing as unlacing that nasty corset. I actually prefer the shade of your natural rouge and will remind you during every dance of how you deliberately tempted me with your abundant bosoms. All at the ball will think you the debutante with your rosy glow."

"Just remember those bosoms are due to your children I have nursed."

"I find it difficult to believe that you are the mother of my children and not a vamp of the night in Charles Town. Perhaps we should make another, unless our three are *plenty* enough for you," teased Thomas using the old Hanscome family *plenty* joke.

"Oh, I'm sure I could manage one more," confessed Elizabeth as Thomas had his way with her, artfully and slowly.

Finally, they surfaced in their massive four-poster mahogany bed, hearing the girls' giggles in the hall.

"I do believe it's time to take our princess to the ball." Thomas laughed as Elizabeth groaned, yes groaned as he unmercifully cinched her waist while she clung tight to the mahogany bedpost.

"I am not your prize heifer you are roping," she scolded.

"But am I not your best bull?" he quipped.

"Now I've let out my breath, please stop making me laugh or you will have to lace me again. Not so tight, please."

"My pleasure," he replied as he kissed her neck and gently laced her corset. They barely had time to scurry downstairs before the girls appeared. Yes, Elizabeth was rosy. And Thomas' eyes reflected her love.

As the young girls floated down the circular stairs, in that genteel southern way that made them appear footless, Jenny looked as regal as her mistress Ann. Her bronze skin was glowing, her figure erect and elegant. Was she going to the ball? Of course she was. She was wearing a lovely old golden gown of Elizabeth's. Would she dance? Absolutely not. Would she eat or drink? Yes, she would. Jenny would eat in the ladies' dressing room after Ann was flawlessly prepared. She would then retire to the balcony with the other slaves to watch the festivities. Why then did Jenny look so happy? She imagined she was already dancing with the most handsome gentleman in the room. Imagination had always been Jenny's best friend. Well, why not?

"Look how lovely our Ann is," whispered Elizabeth to Thomas. "She is positively flushed with excitement."

"Hopefully, our Ann is flushed with the heat of this room and not the reason for your blush," whispered Thomas in return. "Let's not be so anxious to find her a suitor tonight. I like the idea of her going to London first."

And what a ball it was. The gala was held at the very grand and very private St. Cecelia's Concert Hall.

"I might faint, Father," admitted Ann on his arm. Her name was the next to be announced. Her debut was seconds away. Ann Hanscome was coming out.

"Ann, pretend you have blinders on, gaze straight ahead and your smile will captivate all," counseled her father as he patted her dainty, milky-white hand. "One deep breath, one low, graceful bow and society will embrace you."

"Ann Hanscome, escorted by her father, Thomas Hanscome," the guardian announced.

"I feel like a purebred filly on parade," murmured Ann as she stepped forward.

"And you are," whispered Thomas as he proudly released his daughter to society.

Elizabeth controlled her tears of joy at the ceremony that stamped her daughter as eligible for courtship. Thanks to her arduous practice with Jenny, Ann's performance was flawless. What a curtsey. What fluttering, glittering eyes. What a tiny waist and rounded bosoms. What a radiant glow of complexion. What young man could resist such a temptress?

Champagne flowed. Hundreds of candles in crystal chandeliers set the ballroom aglow. Slaves in white gloves fanned the guests and served. The opulent grandeur created the perfect ambience for Charles Town's princesses. The stage was set for the feast by the heady aromas of flowers, food and wine. Pheasants, turkeys and hams were on display, carved and warmed. Crabs, fish and oysters were properly cooled. Cheeses, fruits, puddings and cakes that tantalized the pallet on the dessert tables reminded the laced and cinched debutantes to eat sparingly.

The dances were ready to begin. Ann played her role of princess to perfection and, as expected, her ornate silver embossed dance card was quickly filled with the names of sons from the most prominent planter families. She coyly twittered and tittered as she gracefully accepted compliments from her dance partners.

What was on the mind of many of those planter princes, besides Ann Hanscome's beauty? They wondered how much the wealthy Thomas Hanscome would offer as a dowry. Ah, such were the economic realities of marriage and the partnerships of the planter class. Some of the lesser planters courted the wealthier ones with the finest cigars in the gentlemen's lounge.

And Jenny? She was dancing on the dance floor in her mind's eye with every handsome suitor. She glided in her chair in rhythm to Ann's dance moves. From her balcony bird's eye view, Jenny rated the desirability of each young man on her empty dance card. Yes, she enjoyed the ball. She had lived vicariously through her mistress. Jenny's special treat on the carriage ride home was Ann's gift of her rose scented nosegay.

"I couldn't have done this without your tutelage," whispered Ann to her lifelong companion. "Thank you, dear Jenny."

Later, Ann and Jenny spent the night together laughing as they compared their ratings. That night, as Jenny slept, as usual, at the foot of Ann's bed, she dreamt of her own debut. Did Jenny realize she was a slave? Oh yes, Jenny had no illusion as to her proper place in society. Still, Jenny thanked her lucky star in her evening prayers. "If I have to be a slave, Ann is the best mistress."

The next day plans were made for their voyage. London would provide another debut for Ann and a proper gentleman's training for the incorrigible, untamed Thomas. Even young Mary would study languages, literature, the arts and music. Lessons, lessons, lessons! Artful conversations, delivered with finesse and knowledge were important to every planter's liaisons, and liaisons ensured prosperity.

"I don't know how I could possibly function without my Jenny," fussed Ann. "We must take her, Mother."

"We will have other servants in London," replied her mother, firmly.

"I won't go then. I won't go to London without my Jenny!" Ann crossed her arms in defiance and pouted.

Ann had definitely become her father's version of a perfect princess. He had indulged her at every turn and she in turn indulged her Jenny. Thomas laughed - sometimes it was difficult to tell who was slave and who was mistress. Thomas was certain that Jenny would claim she was the luckiest slave alive.

Thomas and Elizabeth discussed Jenny's future at great length. Why? Slavery in England was illegal, albeit not strictly enforced. In 1706 the courts determined that as soon as a slave stepped on English soil he was freed. Would Jenny return? Would she be loyal to her Mistress Ann? Legally, she was Thomas' property until Ann reached eighteen, but then Jenny would become Ann's, as was Aaron's intention. Elizabeth and Thomas decided Ann could take Jenny, but would risk no other slave losses. Jenny alone could be sold for £1000 pounds. Why was she valued so highly? Jenny's English diction, elocution and domestic training were hard to match, true, but the value of her increase, assuming she was fertile, made her truly valuable. As long as she was a slave, her issue would be slaves. The fact that she was mulatto was of little significance.

Elizabeth promised new clothes for all in London, thus instructed her children only to bring proper ship attire. Did they heed her instructions? No, they did not.

Mary at eight years old ordered her slave Dora to pack all her dolls, picture books and puzzles. What else would she play with on that dreary, foul smelling ship? Once Mary learned that Dora was not going to London, she threw herself on the floor, kicked her feet in protest and screamed, "I do not want to share a slave with Ann. It is not fair!" Mary didn't like sharing – oh no, not at all.

And young Thomas' reaction? If it hadn't been for his trusted Ietrow's supervision, Thomas wouldn't have packed anything. He didn't care about clothes. He didn't care about London, but he did care about spending months aboard this dream of a ship. He intended to befriend every mate and spend his days climbing the masts and manning the helm. He wanted to pretend he was a privateer like his Grandfather Aaron or perhaps the famed pirate Blackbeard. His father had regaled him with Aunt Ann's stories about the Carolina pirates, their booty, bounty and romantic escapades. They were so fantastic; surely his tales were not true. But if those tales were true, why hadn't he been born then, before all the rules? Did Blackbeard truly marry so many women, all at the same time? His Great Aunt was a respectable school directress, or so he had been told. Had Blackbeard truly courted her? And did his privateering Grandfather Aaron truly purchase his first land with gold coin from plundering? Yes, he longed to live in that era, before the rules of how to daintily raise the proper silver fork or choose the proper spoon for the proper dish. Yes, before it was unseemly to work beside your slave or allow your skin to reach its deeper tones. Yes, before the carefully choosing of words and clever affectations. Thomas longed just to be free and race his marsh tacky through the brush and swamps. To be free! Being wealthy carried too many obligations. He had more fun with his slaves who seemed to know and appreciate him better than his own family.

"Son," laughed his father, reading his mind. "You will like plantation life much better than being a dirty, thieving pirate or a common toiler in the field. But first, you must allow Cousin Thomas to teach you to be a proper gentleman. It is an honor and a duty that belong to few. We privileged planters have the obligation to set an example of fine living."

Early 1771

On the day they departed, Thomas' brother Moses, his wife Mary and their two sons - Thomas (yes, another Thomas!) age four and Moses age six, accompanied them to the wharf. They had traveled from their plantation at Ferguson's Ferry on the South Edisto just for this special occasion. Mary had also wanted to spend time with her dear friend Elizabeth for a few days before their departure. She had a reason.

"I am pregnant!" Mary confided. "It won't come until you return, that is if I can carry it. I know you have lost babies, Elizabeth, but I have lost so many, the thought of losing another just breaks my heart."

"I will hold you in my prayers in England. All we can do is thank the Lord for the babes that are meant to be born. I had thought you might be pregnant and prepared this herbal potion for you. It is an Indian medicine that should prevent an early birth. Please dear Mary, do not dwell on a possible loss. Think of how healthy little Moses and little Thomas are. These are good times in our lives. All that are living are thriving. We must be grateful. And I will find some special English gift for this newest Hanscome."

"Bon Voyage!" yelled Thomas to his family. He had a lump in his throat watching Elizabeth and his children wave to him from the passenger deck. Soon the ship was just a dot on the horizon. His heart sank as they disappeared. Had Thomas been a fool to stay behind or to let them go? Unfortunately, it was too late for him to change his mind. Thomas had to shrug off a new feeling for him, loneliness.

Was Elizabeth's assessment of Thomas' planter paranoia correct? Yes, it was increasing. Freedom from the overbearing English was the only talk he heard. "No more taxes!" was the cry. For years the Carolinians felt ignored, wanted English protection from the Spanish and the Indians. They actually sought the status of being a Royal Crown Colony. Why not? They were English and wanted the same protection and privileges as Londoners. But now that they had England's full attention, they wanted to be emancipated. How ironic, thought Thomas with a deep sigh. The thought that his slaves might similarly want their freedom simply escaped him, but then, they were property. Slaves were valued in pounds and had lost their humanness.

It was on this backdrop of political uncertainty that Thomas sent his family to sea. His fears began to get the better of him and caused sleepless nights. Would his family receive a warm welcome in London or would they be snubbed? Would they return before war was declared or would they be captured indefinitely in London? This last fear was the unthinkable.

CH. 4. Blinders On

The voyage

1771

Did Thomas' family at sea share his worry? Heavens no. They were having the times of their lives. Young Thomas could have dedicated his life to the sea, right then sworn an oath to the captain to sign on for life. What had happened to young Thomas' deep love for the land? He now dreamed of being a pirate, saving an adoring damsel in distress and feeling the hefty weight of gold in his hand. During the day he climbed the masts to serve as a lookout and at night he wagered with the mariners. The captain affectionately renamed him *Tommy Boy* and the name stuck. He ignored his family, which made Elizabeth smile. Just in the nick of time, she thought. London will surely tame him.

"I claim this life!" shouted Tommy to the wind from the top of the mast. "I want gold, but please dear Lord, spare me from wigs, silver spoons, high mannered teas and polite conversations. I despise pretense and seek honor. A mariner's life rings true and a planter's life false. I will conquer the waves and vanquish the foes."

London

Eyes wide open and mouths agape, Elizabeth led her crew from their ship into the fairy land of the bustling, hustling London harbor. Their blinders from their provincial Charles Town were quickly tossed aside. Never had they seen so many tall ships loading and unloading precious cargo, mariners grunting, crates smashing and captains commanding. Never had they seen so many beggars thieving, hawkers selling and couriers urgently scurrying. And never had they seen such a fine looking, sophisticated, yet jovial, gentlemen as the silver haired, bespectacled Thomas Downing.

"Welcome to London, the center of the world!" greeted their father's cousin with warm embraces for all, including Jenny. His servant made short work of loading their few belongings into the carriage.

"I expected to hire another carriage for all your baggage," laughed Cousin Thomas at seeing their meager belongings.

"I told the children to pack lightly because they may never wear their Charles Town attire again after they see London's high fashion. We may need several wagons for the return trip as I intend to buy new furniture," responded Elizabeth. "Thomas is planning to surprise me with an actual mansion at Creekside and an expanded Meeting Street mansion."

From the carriage windows on their ride to his residence, Thomas schooled his charges with the names of sculptured gardens, statues, fountains and palatial homes with domed roofs, broad arches, tall Grecian marble columns and massive churches with Gothic spires and towers. They were suddenly amazed and proud of their English heritage. Why would they want independence from all this magnificence? As they crossed the London Bridge over the Thames they spontaneously broke out in song, "London Bridge is falling down, falling down, falling down... my fair Lady!"

Thomas' elegant two story town home in the city boasted a lovely portico and front door of intricately carved black ebony from Africa that swung wide to introduce an interior of wonder. Inside warm rosewoods from India lined Thomas' study. To Tommy's delight, over the fireplace mantle hung an elephant's head with long white tusks. To Elizabeth's delight, books with new titles lined his bookshelves, just waiting for her to open. To Ann's and Jenny's delight, the chamber organ waited for their deft fingers to produce booming melodies that shamed their piano. And young Miss Mary? To her delight, she eyed a cabinet filled with fine wood dolls in elaborate dress and a garden to host pretend tea parties. She was in heaven. London was, indeed, a miracle place.

"I have to fit years of education into six short months, so we have no time to waste," declared their father's cousin. "Where should we begin? The theatre, the orchestra, the art salons, the grand balls, the fine tailors have all been waiting for your arrival." Ann, Elizabeth and even Jenny swooned with the cultural choices, but Tommy remained a bit skeptical until his cousin added, "I see your mother and sisters are enthralled, but perhaps you might like to visit the horse track with me? I believe we might acquire some proper fox hunt training for you, Tommy. This is not the land of the marsh tackies and you must sit a horse properly."

Yes, oh yes, Cousin Thomas soon became a pied piper to all. What happened to the six months? Like the old English expression, the time simply flew out the window.

August, 1771

The hunting lodge

"How will we ever return to Charles Town after the London theaters and concerts?" asked Elizabeth, wistfully. "I don't know how to thank you enough, Thomas. Young Thomas has even learned to dance the most fashionable waltz and his French is quite passable."

"You have Jenny to thank for his tutelage in both," smiled Thomas.

"And your fox hunt bribes for good deportment and elocution helped even more. Look, here gallops Tommy, even as we speak. I hope he will not be too despondent when he realizes this is his last hunt."

"Watch me, Cousin!" yelled Tommy as he swiftly jumped the pond with his roan. He was practicing for the fox hunt tomorrow.

"Your jumping has improved, but your style is as abandoned as if you were still racing your marsh tacky through the swamps," laughed the elder Thomas. "Mind your posture! Sit in style! Put your blinders on and only look ahead!" coached his cousin.

"And weren't you a racer when you lived on the Island?" inquired Tommy as he came to a dashing halt in front of the hunting lodge where his cousin was sitting with the ladies, drinking afternoon tea.

"I never was a wild, lowland country youth – like you. I lived in Charles Town and assumed the serious demeanor of the head of the family, not that my resourceful mother needed me to play that role."

"That surprises me, Cousin. My father always said you lived life with merry abandon."

"I traded in my seriousness when I learned my dear departed mother, Ann Downing, was not as prim and proper as she appeared. What a breath of fresh air that discovery was. I felt free to live my own life. That and she also married, but I'm sure he was the one to follow her lead. My Emma and I traveled to the far reaches of China, India and Africa. Oh yes, I was a trader of exquisite goods, but we always followed our hearts' desires. I didn't know it then, but I do believe I was fortunate to have found a wife as entertaining, and yes, as talented as my very own mother."

In the morning, all the lodge guests gathered for the hunters' breakfast. It was held in the open air in a clearing in the woods. The servants had spread a sumptuous feast of roast pork, mutton, pheasants, fruits, jams, custards and breads on tables covered with white linens, china, silver and candelabra. The sun was welcoming the day, a rare gift. The dull, gray English landscape magically turned a dazzling, emerald green when awakened with the sunshine.

"What a beautiful day! How can I leave this cool, refreshing English air?" asked Elizabeth. "I believe I will hilltop with Cousin Thomas. Chasing a fox through the thickets is not my cup of tea. Ann, dearest, are you hunting or watching?"

"I am hunting. I find the chase as exhilarating as Tommy," she replied.

"I believe she is referring to the chase of Robert Rivers, not the poor red fox," teased Tommy.

It had been a surprise to see a fellow sea island planter staying at the same hunting lodge. He had come to England as an envoy to encourage England to lessen their tariffs and loosen their reign on the Carolinas.

"Colonel Rivers is too old to receive Ann's innocent attention. I would speak with him, but he is leaving tomorrow for London," Elizabeth whispered to Thomas.

"That is not an uncommon arrangement, my dear Elizabeth," commented Thomas, looking at Elizabeth's worried face. "One day you must let her go. You and I both married our peers. However, today there are few rules about marriage and even fewer about attractions. I would have thought my Emma would have survived me, but that was not the case. I still miss her."

"We were sorry to hear of her passing. If you ever feel you would like to return to the Carolinas, we have room for you," offered Elizabeth.

"I thank you for your concern and offer, but if I were to relocate, I would choose India. Emma and I loved the culture so. But that is highly unlikely. I am quite content here. Emma's family has embraced me as one of them, which helps since we had no children."

"Jenny, please watch Mary until we return," ordered Elizabeth. What a wise choice to have brought Jenny to London. Living with only one servant was new for all. Elizabeth tried not to overload her with requests. And Jenny seemed content to be included in all the outings, just like one of the family. Jenny tried her hand at painting when Ann and Mary had their art lessons. The three girls sang, practiced their music lessons and read together. Yes, Jenny could read and write. Ann had taught Jenny everything she learned since she was a young child. It was against the slave code, true, but the Hanscomes did not discourage their slaves from reading. Now, Mary had her own private tutor in Jenny. How fortuitous.

The bugle sounded and the hunt master in his red coat signaled all riders to their mounts. The red fox was swiftly released and wisely ran for his life. The hounds instantly howled, barked and strained to be free of their leather restraints. Soon they were released. The race was on! What a pageant to behold. It took Elizabeth's breath away to watch her two children jump their horses. Soon the hunters were out of sight and the hounds' barks barely audible as the chase went deep into the woods. Elizabeth pulled out her sketch pad and her skilled fingers made the scene come to life. "I must catch all this on my canvass before it escapes my memory."

Who, pray tell, killed the fox? Why Colonel Rivers, of course. And Tommy was right on hand for the thrill of the kill. Elizabeth and Thomas watched from the lodge porch as the gay but tired riders returned. Alongside Colonel Rivers rode Ann. And Tommy, broadly smiling, was covered head to toe with mud.

They stayed two more days at the lodge before returning to London. Tommy was in heaven shooting birds and boar alike. However, Tommy also studied his French. He knew his father would expect some progress, even slow progress with his studies and his manners. All three children also improved their English diction and grammar with their elocution lessons. Even Jenny was dropping her Gullah inflections and words. Elizabeth planned to adorn the walls of their Charles Town mansion with English pastoral scenes. Her best painting was simply called *The Hunt*.

London

Thomas' carriage and servants were kept busy taking Elizabeth and Ann to the best shops. What did they buy? Everything fashionable. Everything expensive. Elizabeth was in her best glory, pointing her jeweled fingers at paintings, statues, beveled mirrors and gilded wallpapers. And books. Ann's library needed the latest editions. Her new drawing room demanded exquisite paintings and the music conservatory must include a grand piano and organ. Her appetite grew insatiable; she needed more. Thomas would be so proud of her refined tastes. And not so refined, but indeed necessary, were her twenty additional hand-painted porcelain chamber pots depicting London Bridge, fox hunts and the pastoral scenes she had tried to capture on her canvas. One cannot ignore one's natural functioning, now can one? All her purchases sent the servants scurrying while the shopkeepers served them tea and they rested their weary feet on finely brocaded ottomans. Shopping was indeed exhausting.

"I want to create unparalleled beauty in each of our residences. Yes, heaven must be portrayed in each room, like the ceilings in the Sistine Chapel. I want to entertain exquisitely with flair, with the most graceful and tasteful of furnishings. They must be ornate, but not gaudy. What do you think of my selections thus far, Ann?"

"I do believe your tastes are impeccable, Mother. And to think I wanted to go to the park with Mary and Jenny? How silly of me to miss this most important lesson in being a fine lady. I must say I am enjoying your command performance," said Ann with a new appreciation for her mother.

"It is important for us to take advantage of this trip to England. All of our purchases will be one of a kind and stand out among our friends. I believe in spending money to acquire the best. These nice things will also be a part of your dowry and legacy. Our things outlive us and reflect who we are, even after death, dear Ann. I do intend to be remembered well." Elizabeth laughed, realizing her own absurdity. Had she really outgrown her modest Quaker beginnings? Did she really believe the necessity of such ostentation? Apparently so.

"And now it is your turn, dear Ann. It is time to buy you a hope chest. Let's see what a good time you can have filling it."

Ann's first selection was a gilded, delicately carved mahogany chest with cedar lining. She soon equaled her mother in her shopping ardor. Her favorite selection was a pink ivory African statue that would grace her parlor.

"What do you think, Mother?"

"Here are a few questions to ask with each purchase. Would you like to look at this for the rest of your life? Does it speak of refined beauty to you? Do you enjoy rubbing your finger across its smooth finish?" tutored Elizabeth.

"Yes. I love it, but what if my husband doesn't?"

"If you love it, he will love it. As a wife it is your position to educate him on the beauty of things. He may see the functionality of an object, but not its beauty. And now to fill your hope chest with fabrics that enhance your beauty."

Ann's confidence grew with each selection. She lifted each fabric to her face to see how her color was enhanced, as a shop girl followed her with a mirror and words of praise for her fine tastes. Ann felt and smelled the heavy brocades, lush velvets and light, filmy silks. Next she selected the mandatory three sets of china - breakfast, lunch and dinner dishes, with silver, crystal, and linens for each set.

"Think of how your favorite flowers will look with all you purchase," coached her mother. Now you must select the proper vases, pitchers, trays - all the details even to the smallest saltcellars. And don't forget a magnificent silver tea service. Picture how all will grace your tables."

What was the grand finale? It was Ann's very own grand piano. Harpsichords were passé. Pianos were in demand.

"Oh thank you, Mother! What a trousseau I will have. What a dowry!"

"This is only the beginning. It has been my pleasure to share this fine London day with you. My next desire is to help you find a deserving, young man."

CH. 5. Blinders Off

August, 1771

London

"I must speak to you, Elizabeth," said Thomas, more serious than usual, on the eve of their departure. Elizabeth, puzzled, accompanied him to his library as he somberly closed the door.

"Why the seriousness, dear cousin? Are you ill?" inquired Elizabeth. She knew something was dreadfully wrong, but what could it be? They had all had such a lovely time with Cousin Thomas. And he had lamented they could not stay longer. Surely he was not irritated at them for overstaying their welcome."

"I won't mince words with you, Elizabeth. Your sharing your children with me has been a great source of joy. Now, however, I must inform you of a serious decision I have made. I want you to have this valise - keep it safe as it contains a good deal of money that I wish you to give to Thomas. Go, ahead, open it and read the legal papers that explain the purpose of the money."

As Elizabeth opened the bag her eyes grew wide at the amount of money. She was even more astounded as she read the papers.

"Oh Thomas! How could you do this? I don't know whether to be angry or cry. I am flabbergasted!"

"Yes, I thought you would be. Please catch your breath, Elizabeth. I didn't know any nice way to broach the subject of my buying Jenny from you. These documents are legal, but truly unnecessary as you know Jenny was free the day she stepped on English soil. However, I was raised a Carolinian and I want to honor my family ties with you in this fashion. Thus, I am asking you to sign the bill of sale in Thomas' place." He paused. "Elizabeth, I know this is a shock. Would you like a refreshment while you review the documents?" Elizabeth nodded. Thomas served her a drink and sat patiently as she studied the papers.

"I wish we had days to reflect on this decision, Thomas, but since we are leaving tomorrow, that is not possible. Why did you wait until now to make your wishes known? Did Jenny request this? Have you been plotting this since our arrival?" asked Elizabeth, barely able to contain her fury.

"No, Jenny did not and does not know of my intentions. And to answer your other questions, I would never plot against you, my family. I want this to be an honorable exchange. I selfishly did not want to mar the lovely time we have had together by bringing this up earlier."

"But Jenny is part of our family! She is not for sale - not at any price. She and Ann have been constant companions, as was your Uncle Aaron's intention. They are like one person! He bequeathed Jenny to Ann!"

"It seems you have totally forsaken your Philadelphia roots, my dear Elizabeth. You cannot have it both ways. Is Jenny your family? Or is she your slave? I thought we could discuss this with Jenny, but out of my deep respect and love for you, I wanted to inform you first. There are several options, but I'd like Jenny to choose."

"Your words confuse me. What do you mean - is Jenny family or a slave?"

"I have wondered since you arrived if Jenny might not be my Uncle Aaron's child. That would make us cousins. Why did he specifically name her in his will? Why did he not just say she could be auctioned off, like any slave he owned? Why, Elizabeth, did he will her to Ann and not your husband? Did he not want that bond to be close - so that Jenny would be treated decently for life? She is mulatto. Take your blinders off! My Aunt Jane had died, bless her soul. All planters, sorry, many planters take slave women for comfort and companions and not all by force. They are caring and loving women. Why not?"

"Oh!" was all Elizabeth could muster, again wide-eyed. "I can see you are your mother's son, Thomas. I have never seen so much fire in your eyes."

"And do you remember that Jenny is not the first mulatto in our family? I have a brother, William Black, whom I have visited several times in Maine. My wife Emma found both Will and his wife, also an Elizabeth, quite charming. I have invited them to England to visit me – our last hurrah, so to speak. They should arrive within the month."

"I fail to see what they have to do with Jenny. William Black was never a servant or a slave."

"True, he was not. Will has made his way in the world. He and his wife may be able to help Jenny make her way as a freed woman. I simply want to help my possible cousin."

"Are you intending for Will to take her back to Maine?" asked Elizabeth, bitterly.

"I have no plans for Jenny, Elizabeth. She must make her own choices. I am only supposing. Truly, I do not know that she is Uncle Aaron's daughter. But my Uncle's will makes me think she could be. It could be that Jenny is the product of one of his indentured bondsmen, perhaps an Irish, who many feel are lower than the slaves, and an unknown slave. Many planters breed their servants, Negro and white, just so they don't have to resort to buying fresh slaves from the market, just like produce. Today slaves cost more than the land. Homegrown slaves are more docile, never tasted freedom, thus accept their fate and the crumbs from our prosperity. Crumbs, stripes and rape. Those are our gifts to them!" Thomas could hardly believe the feverish intensity of his very words, so foreign to the logical, calm self he knew. He took a deep breath, before continuing.

"Actually, none of my suppositions are important. I need to settle my emotions, Elizabeth, for that I apologize. I have grown fond of Jenny over the last few months. She is so quick witted, talented and yes, even elegant, for which she has you to thank. Simply, I want her not to be chattel. She no longer needs to sleep at the foot of Ann's bed. I want to help her. William Black could help her. She deserves to be freed. She has served you for twenty years. I have just bought my first slave, my cousin."

"If I take your words correctly, you have closed out reason and discussion. I see I have no choice. But I am more than surprised, that with no proof you suppose her to be Aaron's child."

"You are correct; I give you no say in this matter. Oh Elizabeth, I mean you no disrespect. If I don't buy Jenny, I will just advise her to walk away from you. Or she can choose to go back to Charles Town with you as a slave. I will then take my money back. But a bill of sale and a manumission paper would be in Jenny's best interest."

"And her other choices?"

"She can be freed and return to Charles Town with you. Or she can stay in England with me. Or she can hire herself out and live on her own. Or, as I told you, Will and his wife may take her back to Maine." He paused. "But what I find unconscionable is for Jenny to spend the rest of her life in the balconies of the churches or the ball halls, or at the foot of Ann's bed, treated as an inferior."

"She loves her life with us. We treat her well!" cried Elizabeth.

"I do not doubt you do. But do you love her like a mother, Elizabeth?"

"Yes, I do."

"Then let her go."

Silence.

"There is also Ietrow's freedom to consider. Is he also mulatto? He was awarded to Tommy by Uncle Aaron, named specifically in his will. I have not met him, but I am willing to purchase him in similar fashion. It could be that he and Jenny could help each other if she decides to return. I could set him up as a merchant in that society of successful free mulattos in Charles Town. She wouldn't be alone."

"Why is this necessary? Why free Ietrow? Isn't Jenny enough?"

"No! Jenny is not enough," raged Thomas. "And my reasons? There are many, but reason aside, slavery is morally wrong. Because I don't want to die knowing I might have slave relatives owned by my very family! I believe Uncle Aaron's melancholia was due to his guilt. Yes, his guilt over building his wealth, only one generation removed from his indentured father's mistreatment, on the backs of slaves. His guilt over his abandoning his sister Ann, who raised him like a mother, yes, fed her to the flames of Charles Town's paranoia over slave rebellions. His fear and inaction set fire to my very mother! And not least, his guilt over turning his back on my brother and his beloved nephew, William. And most important, his guilt over not freeing his two mulatto children, a very accepted practice in wills. Why didn't he claim his progeny and set them free? And his worst guilt was that he knew what he was doing when he found comfort in the arms of his slave."

"Thomas, did you lure us to London with your kind invitation for your own pleasure of releasing your rage against your Uncle Aaron? Against us? Against my husband who held you in such high regard? Slavery is a reality."

"Reality refers only to the unchangeable in life and slavery is changeable. Oh, I must settle myself, Elizabeth. I am not angry with you. Had I been raised as Thomas I might hold his same viewpoints. But I wasn't, fortunately. You, your Thomas and all good planters have your blinders on. Your vision is as distorted as the thoroughbreds you race. At my older age I've learned we can't see the follies of our own time, until it's too late. Your Thomas was raised different from his father, Aaron, who knew that slavery was inhumane. I did not know the depth of my rage at Uncle Aaron until your visit. And the truth be known, Uncle Aaron was like my very own father, since I never had one. I worshipped him. I respected his determination to not to own slaves. Then I married Emma and left. Uncle Aaron's image crumbled in my heart and soul as he became the very greedy man he taught me to loathe. It is very possible my rage today matches my grief over his recent death and my own guilt over never returning to a Charles Town I learned to hate. I loved him, yet I abandoned him. As he let others down, so I let him down. Where was I when my mother needed me? I abandoned her, too. Yes, we are all guilty."

Silence.

"I hear your grief, your guilt, your pain, your abolitionist views that mimic your mother's and now England's, who denies our labor needs in the Carolinas. I must say the depth of your misplaced anger surprises me. Our 'planter paranoia' is real. The civilized world wants to punish us for the institution of slavery they once foisted upon us for their greed. We are England's chattel. Now slavery is necessary to our life, but it no longer serves England's purpose. We are the abandoned!"

Silence.

"Again, I ask you - is Ietrow mulatto?"

"Yes, he is."

"Then I will double the money in the valise and include documents for you to sign for his manumission."

"And if Thomas chooses not to honor Ietrow's sale to you and manumission?"

"There is nothing I can do from this distance. However, it's an honorable price for the sale of Thomas' property. And, in lieu of his signature, I will have you sign copies for me."

Silence.

"I will not sign any documents for Ietrow. He need not ever know of his possible heritage and your offer," said Elizabeth. "You have created a nightmare and dishonored your newly deceased Uncle Aaron. How will I ever tell Thomas? You have betrayed my husband, your true cousin, for a bastard of perhaps Aaron's seed!"

Silence.

"Have you forgotten that I, too, am a bastard? That Joan and William are bastards as well? I hear your insults, but I will continue my course of action. I intend to keep no secrets from Jenny or your children. They will know of my offer to purchase Ietrow."

"You dare use blackmail against me?" accused Elizabeth with fire in her eyes.

"You dare keep family as slaves?" Thomas retorted. "The whole system of slavery is archaic and inhumane. Slavery will end. When is the only question that remains."

"We are at an impasse," sighed Elizabeth. "Please do not lecture me on our Carolina life or the future. Not even you are clairvoyant."

"I will have Ietrow's papers for you in the morning. I see an impasse here. Are you ready to summon Jenny?"

Silence.

Thomas rang the bell for his servant who, in turn, summoned Jenny.

"Jenny, please sit down," said Elizabeth, smoothing her skirt and sitting most erect. Jenny was alert – and cautious. Rarely had she been invited to sit in the presence of her mistress. "I am asking you to read these documents, slowly digest their meaning and then we will discuss your future."

Silence.

"I understand I am to be freed," said Jenny with a shaky voice. "Mr. Thomas has bought my freedom. I also understand that his payment is not necessary - that I am freed just being on English soil." Jenny seemed as frightened as she was amazed. Why had no one told her that just being on English soil meant freedom?

"That is correct," answered Elizabeth as calmly as she could. "Now you need to decide whether or not you want to return to Charles Town with us or to stay with Thomas. He has offered to help you begin a new life."

"I am a slave. Miss Ann's slave. I have never made choices. I don't know what to do!" cried Jenny.

"Do you want to remain with us?" asked Elizabeth. "We can rip up these papers, return to Charles Town and you can serve Ann as before. Or you can be freed."

"Yes! Oh yes! I want to be free – every slave dreams of freedom!"

"This may all be quite overwhelming, Jenny," said Thomas. "It may be too early for you to make a final decision. I invite you to stay in London with me while you give freedom its due. If you later decide to return to Charles Town, I will then arrange passage for you.

"First allow me to ask you a few questions. Do you know who your father is, Jenny? Do you know who your mother is? My Uncle, Aaron Hanscome, your old master, willed you to Miss Ann. Do you remember anything at all of your earlier life before his death? You could have been from three to five years of age when Uncle Aaron died, but you could have been older – perhaps eight." Then Thomas addressed Elizabeth. "Do you know how old Jenny is?"

"No, I really don't. We don't know the ages of most of our slaves."

Thomas was aghast at Elizabeth's answer. How could Elizabeth purport to treat Jenny like a daughter when she didn't even know her age?

"I only remember my life with the Hanscomes – with you Mistress Elizabeth. I can't remember any other life. But freedom? Yes, I want you to buy me, Mr. Thomas. I want the papers saying I am freed. I have prayed for this day."

"Then I will help you," said Thomas. "This is a shock to all. And Jenny, I want you to also know I have offered to buy Ietrow's freedom. He may actually be your brother. You may both share the same father - Aaron Hanscome."

"I have a brother? I had a father - Master Hanscome? I am again in shock, but I should not be surprised. I know slaves who are the children of planters who forced themselves on their mothers. They are not freed. Some are treated poorly, flogged for no reason. I blessed my mulatto features that kept me from the fate of the field slave, but I never expected my dream of freedom to come true. I felt privileged to be owned by Miss Ann and serve her. I find it unbelievable she could actually be my niece!"

"Jenny, I am merely surmising your parentage, but the truth of it may never be known. Regardless of your parentage, I want you to be free."

Silence.

"Elizabeth, why don't you call Tommy, Mary and Ann? You have much to discuss. I will excuse myself and prepare Ietrow's papers. I'll see you in the morning." After Thomas left, Elizabeth and Jenny simply stared at each other. What was there to say?

In the morning, a haggard looking group gathered for breakfast. Was it that no one wanted to return to Charles Town or was it that they had stayed up all night discussing Jenny's freedom? As Jenny passed the breakfast room on her way to the kitchen, Thomas called to her.

"Please sit with us, Jenny. You are no longer a slave." And with that he rang the bell for the servants. Was it ironic that Thomas never questioned his own need for servants? His servants, paid a mere pittance, were indeed free, but they had little spare time as they worked from sunrise to sundown.

Breakfast was served.

Silence.

"The porters will be here later this morning to take the luggage to the ship," announced Thomas. "It doesn't sail until the outgoing tide this afternoon."

Silence. Finally Elizabeth cleared her throat.

"I will speak for my children. Jenny's loss to us was unexpected and unwelcomed," said Elizabeth, mustering her best civility and acceptance. Then she turned to Jenny. "We have cried all night with you, for you, about you and for us. We will all begin anew, ready or not."

"What have you decided, Miss Jenny?" asked Thomas. His use of a respectful address was not lost on anyone in the room.

"I have decided to accept your kind invitation to stay. I may want to also accept your offer of passage back to Charles Town after I have adjusted to my new freedom. I would like some time to decide."

Jenny sat more erect this morning, Thomas thought. Her gaze evenly met their eyes. Ann's finishing education, tutoring, the elocution lessons, trip to Paris, had not been lost on Jenny. She was quite the young English lady.

"You will always be welcomed home," said Elizabeth with sincerity. "If you decide to return to Charles Town as a freedman, we will sponsor you, vouch for your fine character and sign your guardianship papers."

Elizabeth still harbored feelings of betrayal toward Thomas, but she was too exhausted to be hurt or angry. She simply wanted to go home. She did recall her conversation with her husband before they left. They both knew Jenny's freedom was at risk if she went to London. They chanced it anyway. Elizabeth did expect to rise one morning and find Jenny gone, but not by the hand of Cousin Thomas.

"I feel like I have lost an arm or a leg. You are my sister!" cried tearful Ann, as she excused herself from breakfast. "How could you do this to me, Jenny? Or you, Uncle Thomas? I feel betrayed. This is a nightmare! I wish father were here."

"Your father can do nothing. I have bought Jenny, but only because I want you, Ann, to receive the money your grandfather wanted you to inherit. I want you to think well of me. Please understand Jenny was free the day you arrived." Tenderly Thomas took Ann's hand. "I know you love Jenny, but her remaining in London could be a gift – to you both. Jenny was never your equal. And you will learn to be more resourceful. Your mother never had slaves as a girl. It makes her more capable. And your mother is quite capable."

Silence.

"Isn't anyone asking me?" cried Tommy. "I don't want to live without your smile, Jenny! And my slave Ietrow, freed too! How will we manage?" And with that he stomped out of the room. Mary pouted, said nothing, but followed her brother in a huff.

Silence.

"I know my role seems strange to you, Elizabeth. I don't want to further insult you by saying I care deeply for you and your family. But I do. I don't want you to feel betrayed. Your visit has been one of the highlights of my life. Thank you for signing Ietrow's documents. I know you and Thomas will help him begin a new life."

Silence.

The voyage home

There were no goodbyes at the wharf. There was no gaiety. Jenny and Ann had become overcome with grief earlier. And did their grief last? No, it did not. Life went on.

Jenny? She grew accustomed to her new freedom. She continued her music and art lessons, improved her French, visited the museums and attended concerts with her Cousin Thomas. He was talking about taking her to India. Jenny called him Cousin Downing, which made Thomas' old eyes smile.

And Ann? She was delighted to find that Robert Rivers was aboard ship. Her days were spent primping and scheming how she could "accidentally" greet him.

And Elizabeth? She was too busy keeping her children in sight and doing Jenny's role of tending. Did she mind her added responsibilities? Not really. She was enjoying her children and looking forward to seeing her husband.

And Mary? What a surprise to see her become an agreeable child, but then she had more of her mother's attention.

And Tommy? He was again climbing the masts, catching fish and even swabbing the decks. However, he remembered his polite manners and elocution lessons, at least around his mother.

And Robert Rivers? He promised Elizabeth he would stand his distance, but Elizabeth had no control over Ann's flirtatious looks at the Colonel.

It was smooth sailing back to Charles Town. Yes, London had been exciting, but home was best.

November, 1771

Charles Town

As soon as Elizabeth greeted Thomas on the wharf, she knew he had bad news.

"What's wrong, Thomas?" she asked as she embraced her husband.

"Moses is dead, Elizabeth. My brother is dead!"

"What happened? This is a shock, indeed! I am so sorry, Thomas. When did Moses die?"

"Just a few days ago – Mary is beside herself with grief. They tried to treat his fever with sassafras tea and cinchona bark, but poor Moses only became weaker. The burial is this afternoon. Do you think you and the children are up to it? If you need to rest, I will go myself."

"Has Mary's baby been born?"

"No, but she is distraught."

"That is to be expected. Of course, we will all go to the funeral. I will stay to help her with the birth, if she wants my company. And the children can help with their cousins. How are the children handling their father's death?"

"Our nephew Thomas has some understanding about death but poor little Moses just keeps asking for his father. I told Mary not to worry, that I will help her execute Moses affairs and will. She may decide to sell their plantation and move to their Charles Town home, but this is all too new."

"And you, Thomas? How are you doing? Moses was your baby brother," asked Elizabeth tenderly. She could see the strain in his face.

"I hate it! Moses was only forty-one and healthy. Earl's inoculations reduced some deaths from mosquitoes, but did not protect Moses. These fevers show no favor – men, women, old, young, Negro, planters. It's as though our land is poisoning us or perhaps punishing us for our prosperity."

"Do you really feel that way, Thomas?" asked Elizabeth. "Moses' death is no one's fault. It is no evil omen."

"Yes, you are correct, dear. I'm being ridiculous. I'm just tired and angry at the fevers. I do want someone or something to be held accountable. I don't like being powerless. We need to learn more. One day we will have that knowledge. I think Moses might have lived if he'd taken that cinchona bark earlier. It has helped many. I want us to lay in a supply at all of our plantations. It is all we can do, Elizabeth."

"We can do more," said Elizabeth emphatically. "We can leave. I want you to think about selling our plantations and moving before next summer arrives. Will you please entertain that notion? We have enough. I want our children to live. I want us to live, Thomas."

"This is our home! How can I leave what I have built?"

"The price of our prosperity is too exacting. It is killing us," said Elizabeth, softly.

Silence.

"Elizabeth, where is Jenny?" Thomas had just noticed her absence.

"She is in England. As we feared, she chose to remain free on English soil. What we did not consider is that Cousin Thomas would purchase her. I have the money for both Jenny's and Ietrow's freedom, to be held for Ann and Tommy until they come of age."

"Why Ietrow?"

"Thomas thinks Ietrow and Jenny have Hanscome blood, are actually Aaron's children by a comforting slave after your mother died. He said we have our blinders on."

"That thought never entered my mind!" Thomas laughed at the thought. "My father was a repentant Christian near his end. Perhaps he had more to repent than I imagined. On the other hand, those two mulattos could have sprung from the Scottish bondsman's loins."

"It's nice to see you smile, even if it is the idea of your father's indiscretions that fosters such mirth."

"I should have gone to England with you. I hope Thomas' guilt is assuaged by the price he paid for Jenny and Ietrow. It seems that I missed some entertaining conversations with my cousin. I think he's the one with the blinders on. Every day it seems more likely we will have a war with England over the tariffs."

"Thomas said we would be fools to think we could win such a war against the mighty English empire. Thomas, I am afraid. What do you think?"

"I don't know, Elizabeth. I wish I could tell you the talk of war is only talk, but the patriots are crazed."

"What will we do, Thomas? Stay and fight or leave?"

"I don't know, Elizabeth."

Silence.

"And how are you and the children doing without your number one slave?" asked Thomas, changing the subject.

"I miss Jenny. I feel a good soul has abandoned us to fend for ourselves. She had such a fresh spirit, worked hard and made us all laugh. I never thought Ann would get over losing her lifelong companion, but the minute she saw an interesting southern gentleman on board the ship, her countenance brightened. Our Tommy and Mary were upset, but the call of the sea for Thomas and the extra attention Mary received from me seemed to help. And you? I expected you to be angry."

"No, I am not angry. I enjoyed Jenny, but no slave is indispensible. They are simply property. Thomas is my abolitionist Aunt Ann's son. How could I expect a different attitude from him? Hopefully, his purchasing two slaves will satisfy his conscience. May he glide into heaven with all the other abolitionists. Jenny will do well as a freed mulatto in London, particularly with Thomas' guardianship. She served us well."

"And Ietrow? Will you honor the agreement I made with Thomas to free him?" asked Elizabeth.

"Yes, I will honor that sale, but when is the question. When will be the best time for Thomas to lose his childhood companion? And when will he be mature enough to manage his money from the sale? We can discuss it later."

"Tommy is expecting Ietrow to be freed soon, but certainly this subject can wait until after Moses' funeral."

"What I am dismayed about is this new odious name - *Tommy*? Who gave him such a name? His name is Thomas." And it was Elizabeth's turn to smile.

"The ship's captain named him Tommy Boy. And Thomas loves it! You did miss out on such levity. One other thing - guess who accompanied us on the ship home and turned your daughter's head?"

"Who?"

"Colonel Rivers."

"I will put an end to that dalliance. Our Ann is way too young for Robert Rivers - or for any man." Thomas' wheels were turning in yet another direction. "We will need to discuss who we wish to encourage for her future husband."

"It is good to be home. I missed you so." Elizabeth laughed, giving Thomas another affectionate embrace. "We have much yet to discuss and you have much to see. I bought out the finest London shops."

And they talked and laughed and smiled all the way to Ferguson's Ferry on the South Edisto. Sadness was an accepted part of their life and for now the sadness of Moses' death could wait. The talk of war could wait. Elizabeth and Thomas always made the most of their time together.

CH. 6. I'll Be No Slave

1774

Charles Town

The *peculiar institution* of slavery lived on and on, even as the fervor of freedom from the English grabbed hold of many planters. How ironic! Didn't Carolinians see their own desire for freedom mirrored in the very eyes of their slaves? As the privileged Hanscomes continued their justification of slavery, other parallel tales began. Charles Town was a true sea of diversity and yes, opportunity, but not for all, of course, hardly for all.

"She's too light-complected for the fields," declared a planter strolling through the Charles Town slave market to the trader who was displaying a young girl's naked assets – hoping to turn a good profit. "I'd buy her for a lower price for domestic work, but she'd die in a few months in my rice fields. I long for the days when we could get those black Angolan or Senegalese slaves. Today, no planter wants to sell their darkest Negro issue, at any price."

"I am in the market for a young domestic. Where is she from?" asked a well-dressed, haughty lady, tilting her fancy parasol to get a better look at the young, slave girl. "She's not Negro."

"She was captured by the English from a pirate ship near Morocco," answered the trader. "The English corsairs snatched her from the Moroccan pirates, who snatched her from the Ottomans, who were transporting her whole family to her wedding day in Algiers. Weren't the English smart to turn the tables, exact booty from those pirates for a change? This little Lucy and the whole human cargo were headed for England, but the captain turned the ship to Charles Town to make a pretty penny – sell them as slaves instead of indentures. What a shrewd captain he was, if I do say so. Take this little Lucy. Her value is increased ten-fold as a slave. The profit of indentures diminishes to nothing once their bond has been paid in full. If she was a virgin when she left Morocco, she surely has been seasoned by now. Ripe for the picking, she is!" laughed the trader, impressed with his cleverness.

"Turn her for me. Does she speak English?" asked the lady, not interested in the history of her capture or the trials of the poor girl.

The trader prodded and poked the young girl, like a cow, until she turned in a full circle. Then she spat on him with great contempt.

"I do speak English," replied the fiery-eyed, surly girl. "But I'll be no slave. I am the loyal subject of the Sultan of Morocco. It is against our laws to enslave Muslims."

"We are tolerant of all slaves' religions here at the slave market, except those papist Catholics," retorted the slave trader. "Unless you want to be flogged, you insolent wench, I suggest you hold your tongue."

The trader held a gleam in his eye as he readied his whip, but he was no fool to stripe her back. English speaking, clean slaves were at a premium, even those of the lighter skin shades.

"Stay your whip. I'll buy no damaged goods. How do you price her?" asked the lady.

"£1000 - a great bargain for you Mistress. What did you say your name was?"

"That price is far too high, a fair price for a strong, dark-complected man, but not this puny wench. And my name is Miss Sarah Smith."

"She'll be gone before noon with her fine English and her potential for increase," scoffed the trader. "She could bring you five more slaves in five years, easy. That's a good return on your property investment."

"I am not looking for a broodmare who has no time for work. I will offer you £500. You will not get a better price for such an insolent one. These new slaves show no humility or fear, but what can we do? We must take what we can get."

"You are a thief, my lady," replied the trader with a mocking bow.

"If you want to sell her, have your apprentice deliver her to my home on Church Street, cleaned and clothed before tea time. Don't forget the properly signed and stamped bill of sale." Sarah Smith interrupted her grand exit with an afterthought. "What is her name?"

"Lucy. We call this one Lucy Moor."

Lucy was left standing naked. Did the trader think he would get a better price for her? Perhaps, but an offer for one so light of skin might not come at all. He thought of having his way with her this evening, teach her some true humility, but 500 pounds in his pocket would be more satisfying. The trader sighed. The day was still young; perhaps an even better offer would present itself.

In the meantime, the girl hung an imaginary veil over her nakedness to protect her from the gawkers. She was raised that modesty was a virtue. She stood tall and straight, as if to challenge the onlookers. Charles Town, at least the slave market, reminded her of the bazaars in her home of Tangiers. She prayed the rest of the town was more humane and civilized.

How had this happened to her? She thought her capture was an evil dream, even now. She had prayed for freedom. She had recited her tale of woe to herself over the past month's sea voyage. No one else would listen. And why would they?

"My name is Houda," she grumbled to herself. "Why do they name me Lucy? But perhaps Houda died with the rest of my family and this tough shell, this new Lucy is all I am."

Houda remembered the vivid nightmare of her family's voyage from Tangiers to Algiers:

I was so proud to be given in marriage by my father to a man of great import in Algiers. My mother was equally pleased. My future children and I would have an honored, abundant life. Allah had blessed us all.

I was overseeing the proper stowing of my gifts to my future family when I heard the yells of my father. My mother and I ran from our cabin just in time to see a pirate run my father through with his sword. "Father!" I screamed as I ran to him, but I was too late. Pirates had overcome our ship and bloodied bodies were strewn everywhere.

Soon order was returned and the pirate captain bellowed, "Be still, lest you meet the same fate as those who protested. If you want to live, be still. This ship and all its cargo, including you, are mine!"

My mother and I huddled together with the other passengers while we witnessed the remaining live mariners being bound with ropes and chained together. Slaves? I asked my mother, but she quickly shushed me. That was the last utterance to pass her lips. We were then brusquely separated and I was tied with two other girls my age, before we were hauled away to the captain's quarters and thrown on his bed. We waited, silently, too afraid to speak behind the locked door. I watched the shadows of the sun grow longer on the floor and pondered my fate. Suddenly, another ruckus began. More screams. More commands. More scuttling on deck. What did it mean? Then the cabin door was splintered open.

English! I wept for joy. I was saved. The pirates had been over taken by a British ship. But my joy faded as I smelled smoke and viewed another massacre. The pirates were being thrown into the sea and the vessel was afire! Was I to be burned alive? No, I was yanked from the bed and loaded with the other passengers onto the British ship. In vain my eyes searched for my mother, but I never saw her again. I was for the first time in my life alone.

"Dues!" the English captain yelled. "I will play the tribute and obligation game with you pirates, you vermin! We've paid tribute for years, now you are obliged to repay us," laughed the captain, shaking his fist at the drowning pirates. He was crazed, worse than the pirates, that English captain.

I watched the pirate vessel burn as we sailed away in haste. How could this be happening to me? I am a good Muslim girl. My fate became clear when the first mate came to me that night. Yes, he was the one who ripped my garments, took me, soiled me and spoiled me for any honorable man. I try to block from my memory the tears I cried from the bruises I suffered. Yes, just like a baby, I cried. No Muslim man will marry me now, but I no longer care. I bite my thumb at them all. I am not beautiful or sweet anymore, but I am no man's fool!

"You'll find good company in Charles Town," said the first mate to me after his last use of my body. "Moroccans, both Muslims and Sephardic Jews, have made it their home since its beginning over a hundred years ago. Some came as slaves, but most as indentured servants. Many of their children are free now, that is if they're still alive. Look for The Turks, that is what your people are wrongly named. And count your blessings if you're sold as a domestic. With your light skin you will die in a few months in the fields."

Did this riff raff, dirty mate truly think I would forget his animal acts? Has my life come to this? Me or him? I will kill him if I can.

Killing went against every tenet of Houda's faith. Every truth she held dear had vanished. She felt despicable, vengeful and ruined. She kept her mouth shut on the voyage, but carefully tucked away every piece of information she heard and hid her rage. She learned Charles Town was one of the few ports that still traded slaves. It was the clearinghouse for all slaves coming to the New World.

"Mistress Sarah Smith does not look like a blessing," Houda thought as she returned to the present. "I have been abandoned. Where is my Sultan's protection? Is this Allah's will? If so, Lucy Moor I shall be. But I'll be no slave!"

Later that afternoon she was delivered, clean and clothed to Mistress Sarah Smith. Indeed, Lucy Moor was a slave.

CH.7. The More Things Change, the More They Stay the Same

1774

Charles Town

"It's a boy!" announced Thomas Hanscome as he handed out cigars to his friends at St. John's Island Presbyterian Church.

"And what is his name?" asked Sarah Legare.

"James," replied proud father Thomas. "We thought the Lord had finished his gifts of children to us, but we were blessed again. Our Ann has just celebrated her seventeenth birthday."

"And when do you expect to marry her off, Thomas?" asked Grimball.

"We have been trying to find a suitable young man for her, but she turns up her nose at every advance."

"Rumor has it she is taken with Colonel Robert Rivers, but he is old enough to be her father," joked another friend.

"He is most involved in the war preparations against England. Too busy I hope to seriously court our Ann," said Thomas. "Eventually she will find an eligible man, a much younger man."

"If you listen to Colonel Rivers, the war with the British is only days away. You truly must admire his record for killing the last of those Indians, Thomas. And our tea party in the Charles Town harbor certainly sent the message that we will pay no more tariffs on tea from India, or any other British goods. Are you still a fence sitter, Thomas?" asked yet another friend, yes, a Patriot.

"Indeed, I remain on the fence. The British are just whetting their appetite on my long fibered cotton. Can you imagine what will happen to our new cash crop, if we go to war? I think we are being foolish to seek independence from the Crown. We will lose all our prosperity. I think you are swayed by the northern colonists who have little prosperity to lose."

"Do you truly believe cotton is that important, that it will replace rice and indigo, our golden cash crops?"

"I am making less indigo cakes and planting more sea island cotton at Creekside. It doesn't have those nasty seeds. And I don't want my cotton dumped in the London Harbor as retaliation by the Brits."

April, 1777

Charleston

"I, Ann Hanscome, take you, Robert Rivers, to be my wedded husband. I promise to love, honor and obey…"

The ceremony was flawless. The ambience was perfect. The sun's last rays were playing with the crystal prisms on the candlelit chandeliers, giving a handsome glow to the elegant St. Cecelia's ballroom. The bride's Belgium lace white gown, long veil and even longer train were stunning. However, Ann's untouched alabaster skin and adoring eyes far surpassed her finery. Was she real or just every planter's dream? The Colonel, quite handsome in his military dress uniform, thought her regal and pure.

Yes, Thomas Hanscome had reluctantly given his consent to this marriage. How could he refuse a hero of the battles with the Cherokees and the English? The dashing Colonel and wealthy planter had captivated Ann's heart.

The best man, young Thomas, looked a man at seventeen. Would he be the next Hanscome married or would it be his younger sister? Mary, the blushing maid of honor at fourteen, had already mastered the fine art of coquetry and turned many heads of Charles Town's finest bachelors, particularly that of one John Geyer. Mary and John had secretly set a rendezvous for later that very same evening. After all, who would notice their disappearance amid all the wedding festivities?

And little James? At three he was thought too young to be a ring bearer, but he aptly fulfilled his responsibility with due pomp and circumstance. If applause were permissible at weddings, he would have received an ovation from the amused guests.

Moses Hanscome's sons, Thomas, Moses and little John, sporting gardenias on their lapels, were also caught up in the wedding magic. Their mother, Mary was present - alone. After Moses' death, she had proven to be quite adept at running their plantation and denied the customary suitors. Even if she were to reconsider a second husband, few suitors were to be had. The back country skirmishes among the Cherokees, English and Patriots had taken so many men, sadly too many men. Unescorted ladies were quite noticeable when the wedding guests were announced by the guardian at the door. Behind their ostentation and the pretense of superiority, these women still possessed that settler survival spirit and toughness. Like all planters, they lived in the present. They knew their lives could be cut short by disease every fall. Tonight they were elegant and gay; tomorrow they'd manage the overseers of their fields, slaves and most important, profits.

"This wedding truly exemplifies St. Cecelia Society's motto - *To seek the beautiful and the true.* It's exactly what the architects desired - this unparalleled tribute to refined culture," commented a matron glowing with great pride.

"Thomas looks surprisingly pleased at his daughter's choice of husbands, although rumor has it that he had discouraged Robert Rivers for years. I wonder what made him change his mind?" asked another guest.

"When that old *Swamp Fox*, Francis Marion, came courting Ann, poor old Thomas immediately warmed to Colonel Rivers. The thought of Francis' hands on his precious daughter was repugnant to him," gossiped another guest.

"What was wrong with Francis?"

"He may be our hero in war, but his conquests of the Cherokee women are reputed to be most savage," laughed another.

"You may laugh at his poor conduct, truly unfitting a planter, but what if he desired your daughter?" asked another, quieting the first gossip's smile.

"I do not understand Thomas' ever discouraging the fine Colonel Rivers. What wealth and charm! How many plantations does he own now, four?"

"I don't believe most men want their daughters marrying someone their age, regardless of wealth. You know we planters have means, but we don't have longevity."

"Or perhaps it is because Ann fell in love with Robert Rivers. I believe Ann's stubborn affections for the Colonel outlasted her father's reluctance."

"Well, if you ask me, I think the match is ideal. Only the best - for the best!"

"Don't you just adore weddings?"

"It is a welcome relief not to discuss our current war and economy," said another.

"I don't like the change from Charles Town to Charleston. Our city is still named for King Charles II. We should have chosen a new name."

"At least we aren't named Georgetown after George III. He's a crazy King, that one."

"If you ask me, the French are correct in their astute observation of political changes: the more things change, the more they stay the same."

The heady aroma from the spring blooms floated through the open French doors. The verandas were filled with Carolina notables waiting to greet the wedding party. The ballroom was being prepared.

Who would have guessed that these same guests had been fighting battles just yesterday? The English and their cohort loyalists would not easily concede. Independent states? United States? Only last year the Declaration of Independence had been signed. Only two years ago the English Royal Governor had left hastily in the dead of night from Charles Town harbor. And now? The optimistic celebrations of Independence had faded. The economy had faltered. The new State Troopers were all but defunct due to desertions. The South Carolina state assemblymen had conscripted the riff raff for troopers, even promised them land for service. However, those actions hadn't brought enough recruits. They were now discussing paying the Troopers wages. How absurd.

And the planters? They were not unified in their sentiments – a third were patriots, a third were hidden loyalists and the rest, like Thomas Hanscome, were fence-sitters. He found no consolation in his dire predictions coming true. Thomas wondered how these new United States planned to protect their property, meaning the institution of slavery. He was concerned as a majority of the states outlawed slavery following the Declaration of Independence. How would South Carolina benefit from tariffs that, while pleasing to the newly prospering northern merchants, only served to increase southern merchandise costs? The Loyalists thought that continued governance by the Crown would have been the best choice. And Thomas? For a time he had supported complete independence, from both the Crown and the union of states. After all, Charles Town was the most prosperous city in the colonies. But since that option was not widely supported, Thomas privately went back to his position on the fence.

"Governor Rutledge, I believe you have met my daughter and her husband," said Thomas in his most jovial manner.

"Yes, I have Thomas, and for the rest of the evening please dispense with the formality. It is a pleasure to see you again. I am, as you know, quite happy that you have rallied to our patriot cause."

"How could I not? My new son-in-law would not tolerate any more fence-sitting from me."

"Let us drink a toast then to our new state of South Carolina, our new city of Charleston and our newly married couple, the Rivers!" said Governor Rutledge, holding his glass high.

Privately, Thomas whispered to Elizabeth. "I think John Rutledge is interested in having our Thomas join the State Troopers, but I have emphatically told Thomas, no. Absolutely not. He is only seventeen and the dust on this independence has hardly settled. The tide could turn at any minute."

"I agree, Thomas, but Ann's husband is certainly a persuading patriot. Young Thomas' decisions may be out of our hands," said Elizabeth.

"Thomas is still not of age. What do you think of sending both Mary and Thomas to France, to boarding school for a year or two? They could sail with Ann and Robert in a few days. I'm sure they would see them safely enrolled in Paris before continuing their honeymoon travels. Certainly our politics will have settled within the year."

"How would you have liked to have your brother Moses accompany us on our honeymoon?" teased Elizabeth. She smiled sweetly as she confronted her husband. She knew that more than anything Thomas wanted to protect his children from the strife. Many of the loyalist planters had recently abandoned their plantations and sailed for England. They simply left.

"I wouldn't have allowed anyone on our honeymoon," agreed Thomas with his mischievous grin, "but we were not at war then."

"Do you want to forsake our lives here and return to England? Or sail for France? We could sell all to our good patriot friends, the Legares. Their optimism for our new union keeps them sending their young men to the cause," replied Elizabeth. "London is wonderful, if we want to be English."

"I am not fleeing anywhere. Tonight we celebrate Ann's and John's new beginning. Would you like to dance, my dear Elizabeth?"

Later, Thomas brought up the idea of studying abroad to his son.

"I do not want to go to France, Father, nor return to England with the cowardly loyalists. Your ploy to keep me out of the revolution only alienates me. But worry not, I will not join the State Troopers. I do not want to be a soldier. They are all thugs and beggars." Yes, young Thomas was learning to stand up to his father.

"What do you want to do then? We cannot keep our heads buried in the sand. John Rutledge is calling for all South Carolinians to swear loyalty oaths to the State and give up all allegiances to the Crown. Of the paths open to us, I will support our new government. I will not give up our land. But you need to carefully consider your choices. If you want to be a doctor or a barrister, no one would fault you for leaving and furthering your education. If you stay and do not join the military, you may be held suspect and could even be imprisoned as a traitor."

Above all else, Thomas was concerned for his son's safety.

"I want to work with you, help you protect our property and keep the loyalists and Brits from stealing our crops and our slaves. Need I remind you of the plantations that have already been looted, burned and slaves carted off to waiting English ships? Like you, this land is my spirit, my soul. You will need my help. I will tell my friends I am fighting - I am fighting for our land. And we will support their Patriot cause with food."

"I accept your plan, son. I also want you to consider manumitting Ietrow as per my deceased Cousin Thomas' wishes. If we give him a decent wage, I believe he will help us oversee our plantations. But he is your slave and the money Thomas paid for his purchase is rightfully yours. What do you think?"

Was Thomas actually seeking his son's counsel? Yes, he was. Young Thomas finally felt like a man.

"Yes, I think the time is right. I don't need a nursemaid or a valet anymore. Ietrow is a good organizer. Let's see what he can do with the slaves. I will use some of the money for a larger cabin for him close to the big house. If he starts a family with a slave, the value of his issue will make up for our expenditures on his behalf."

And so it was. Ann and Robert Rivers took their honeymoon trip by themselves. They left their laughter in every European city, except for London, which Robert refused to visit. They returned in the fall to Charleston.

Legare Point

Once their ship docked, the honeymoon couple immediately boarded a small sloop for the Sea Islands and their new home on Legare Point.

"Oh Robert, how can we live here?" Ann was crestfallen as she looked at the devastation, not caused by the Brits but by the fierce tropical storms. The house was a shambles.

"Do you still want to live by the sea?" asked Robert, as he surveyed the storm damage.

"If I only look at the beach, yes I do. I saw nothing in Europe that rivals the beauty of this place. But this house needs to be razed. It is uninhabitable."

"Then, raze it I will do. I will build you another house, on ground higher than these storm surge marks, with sturdy cypress shutters that will protect it from the hurricanes. It will be a mansion fit for Charleston, with verandas and French windows all around to catch the sea breeze. The front door will open to the sea, where we can watch our children play in the surf." Robert was most expansive.

"And if a hurricane finds it again?" asked Ann.

"Then we will rebuild again and again. We are wealthy, my dear. My military service is finished. Our plantations on James Island, Long Island, and in Cravens County are flourishing. As opportunities occur I might even purchase more!" Robert started shedding his clothes. "Come Ann dear, let's refresh ourselves with a swim."

"I have no proper swim attire," laughed Ann.

"Let's not be proper. This is our first night home."

And were they proper? No, they were not, but only the moon and the sea witnessed their spirited frolic. For such an older man, Robert's stamina equaled his desire.

And did Robert buy more property? Oh yes. The remaining loyalist planters, and there were many, fled for England. Opportunities for cheap land abounded.

May 12, 1780

Creekside

"Governor Rutledge has fled to North Carolina! Our government is in exile! Charleston has been taken by the British! The remaining Patriots have been imprisoned or sent to St. Augustine!" The courier's horse was lathered as he found the Hanscomes in the field. Yes, laboring in the field with their slaves.

"Thank God the English did not wait until June to attack," said the older Thomas to his son. "They would have caught every planter and officer in Charleston for the swamp fever season."

"What will you do, Father? Have you changed your mind? Will you join the Patriots?" Was young Thomas afraid? Not outwardly, but his eyes sought reassurance from his father.

"I have done my service as State Tax Collector. Unfortunately, our state coffers will be drained once again by this war effort. Who knows how long this siege will continue? I must now focus on retaining our personal financial solvency.

"This is what I propose we do: We will keep our plantations in order. We will keep the news of the English siege of Charleston from the slaves, for as long as we can. We will improve our slave cabins. We will help our neighbors and friends. We will plant more crops at Creekside. Our exports to England have ceased, and they were our biggest indigo market. The war effort needs food. We will keep our rice production. We will train our overseers to be ready for battle. We don't want the British finding us weak prey and we don't want them enticing our slaves with promises of freedom." Thomas fiercely emphasized the *we* in his plans for the near future. He and his son were a team.

"Won't all these changes decrease our profits?" asked young Thomas, a bit puzzled.

"Our profits have already dwindled. England is buying nothing from us, but the northern states may starve without our food next winter. Today, survival is our only goal. We must focus our energy on living. But do not worry son, like the tidal flow, our prosperity will come again."

The determined Hanscomes hunkered down. They held onto all their property, slaves included.

December, 1782

Others were not as fortunate as the Hanscomes. Francis Marion, the old "swamp fox," had been appointed Brigadier General of the militia by Governor Rutledge, while he was still exiled in North Carolina. After two long years, the siege of Charleston was finally over. When the English were routed in December of 1782, Francis Marion's plantations had been burned and his slaves freed. He had to take loans from other planters to start over. Finally, he married his cousin, to the great relief of Thomas and other planters who felt indebted to him for his service. No one wanted such a fox to marry a daughter of theirs.

Mary Hanscome also breathed a sigh of relief. She wanted no marriage of obligation. She was now able to marry her choice, John's Island planter, John Geyer. What had begun in innocence at Ann's wedding years ago had blossomed, indeed. They had already sworn their love to each other in secret passionate exchanges by the sea. Had they not been able to marry, Mary had decided they still would be lovers.

What happened to propriety? Oh, as usual, propriety went underground, as it had during most wars since the beginning of time. Indeed, does even war change a culture? It seemed to be the case that the more things changed, the more they stayed the same. Love seemed timeless: ardent young love, fatherly love and so it seemed the love of slavery.

"Must we spend all our profits on Mary's wedding?" complained young Thomas.

"Yes, we must. In addition, we will celebrate the end of the siege and the return of our prosperity. For the first time in three years our exports are up. Wool, indigo, even fruits and vegetables are in high demand in the northern states. Who could have foreseen that? Perhaps this union will work to everyone's advantage. The New England soil is too rocky for profitable farming. They are focusing more on ship building, sail making, textile and timber mills. Harnessing those fast rivers was a superb idea. And now that our rice and indigo have stronger European markets, our dependency on England is less. Yes, our profits return." Thomas clicked his heels and jumped for joy while his son laughed. "It is time we turned our fields back to the overseers. I am too old to toil in the fields anymore."

"I doubt that, Father. From what I observe by your mid-air click of your heels trick and the glint in your eyes, I think field work agrees with you. I know you have earned the respect of many of our slaves."

"And I am glad I built those new cabins for them. They work very hard. I am so glad they appreciate our kindness."

Pray tell, what was Thomas missing? Was he blind? Did he ever gaze long enough in his slaves' eyes to know? No, he didn't. He mistook downturned eyes as humble gratitude, homage, ignorance and not contempt.

And young Thomas? Oh yes, he knew. Yes, he met his slave's eyes with his own. He always had, before he knew slaves were slaves and not family. He saw their rage, no longer hidden from him. He knew their love. He felt their pleas in his heart of hearts. But more important, above all, he yearned for his father's approval. And here it was. Finally. He would no longer be ripped apart by dual allegiances. He chose. He was a planter. He was a Hanscome. Superior. Entitled, at last. Why had he ever questioned his proper fate? How ridiculous!

"But back to this extravagant wedding for Mary? What if I want to marry? Will there be money for me? Or must I still keep the yoke to my back?" he teased.

"When you select a wife, I suggest you choose a wealthy planter's daughter with a large dowry. How about a Middleton? Or an Inglis? Our dear Robert could match you with one of his suitable Rivers' cousins. Or a Legare? A Hext or a Freer? It is the bride's responsibility to pay for a fine wedding – not ours." Then he hesitated. "Or do you already have a charming heiress in mind?" They were both enjoying the lively banter. The war was finally over. Young Thomas had chosen his side. The Hanscomes were on to next, father and son together.

"No Father, I do not have an heiress in mind. After the last several years in the fields, I am ill suited to the old Charleston life. I find many of those spoiled debutantes, who fled to France during the war, vacuous and too carefully practiced in their conversations and manners. They are like the French marionettes. Dead," complained young Thomas.

"Be understanding of their attempts at being fashionable, Thomas. They are young and playing their version of perfection – to catch their perfect husband. But I implore you - don't return to your race track cronies. They are not good substitutes for a wife."

"What if I want to breed thoroughbreds? I can think of nothing more lovely than a fine race horse."

"Why not breed Hanscomes!" replied his father. "I suggest you look at Mary's wedding for a suitable spouse – not a horse. You might find a wealthy young widow who manages her own plantation, like your Aunt Mary, who is as adept in the fields as in the ballroom. There must be many refined beauties without the European affectations. The tally of our war widows has reached the one thousand mark. Yes, one thousand! If gentlemen had dance cards, I'm sure yours would be filled. But you'd better brush up on your dance etiquette and fine manners. Your sister will tutor you, if you ask politely. You've been spending far too many nights with our slaves."

"I hear you, father. I love all women, equally."

"Thank God for that. Now find a white planter to marry."

And they laughed. This Hanscome father-son duo had developed a great repartee over the last several years of hard manual labor. They knew each other's secrets. Thomas wanted his son to live the life of the gentleman planter, not a rough overseer who found his pleasure in the dark of the slave cabins. Yes, Thomas worried. He did not want his son following the path of his old friend John Randall who would love no one else but his Grace. Thomas found comfort in the fact that his son had been raised by his white mother, Elizabeth, not a mammy. Well, not unless he counted the lovely Jenny, Ann's mulatto slave, but she was in England, thank God. Thomas knew that it was human nature for people to love the familiar, those they lived, worked, laughed and even fished with. Thomas remembered his Aunt Ann's great love for a slave, Black Will. He wanted no scandal for his son. And he knew he was most happy with his mate, his Elizabeth. Surely his son would follow his suit.

Thomas dismissed his fears. Like the Hanscomes before him, his greatest love, his only love, was his family. Yes, his brother had died, but they were fortunate compared to other planter families where all the lineages were wiped out from disease or wars. Instantly, those families were finished, extinct.

Thomas also had great hopes for little James, now eight. Elizabeth had sequestered James safely inside during the war. Unlike his older brother, James had developed a voracious appetite for the written word. Would he become the scholar? Thomas hoped so.

And the marriage between the Geyers and the Hanscomes? Neither family minded the secret trysts between Mary and John. Oh yes, there were no secrets on John's Island. Never. Thomas always had Mary's horse readied for her "secret, spur of the moment" rides. What a gold mine, the joining of these planter families. Thomas thanked God every Sunday at St. John's Island Presbyterian Church for his blessings, as his father Aaron had taught him.

"I thank you Lord that my Mary has found a wealthy planter to love. And Ann loves her wealthy but old husband, Robert. I hate to be callous, but grant them children soon, before he dies. Oh, I know I ask too much, dear Lord, but please take care of my heir Thomas. He is unbridled, untamed and a loving man. He needs a wife soon, a loving white wife, a planter wife. Amen."

January, 1783

Charleston

"I, Mary, take you John, to be my lawfully wedded husband - for better, for worse, for richer, for poorer, in sickness and in health, until death us do part."

Mary had chosen to honor her older sister, Ann, by wearing her wedding dress, altered for Mary's diminutive frame. With her wispy blonde hair, fair skin and palest of blue eyes she looked like a fairy princess as she floated down the aisle at St. Cecelia's on her father's arm. Her brother Thomas was again best man, but his boyhood frame had become well-muscled in the last few years. He had become another handsome Hanscome with his auburn hair and blue eyes. He caught his father's eye and smiled. His father was right. The guest list had a high preponderance of attractive, young widows.

Were the wedding guests despondent? Oh no. They were prospering. Cotton was the new king of crops. Even England wouldn't close their harbors to profit. How smart were the Hanscomes.

Did any belle catch Thomas' eye? Yes, a cousin of Robert Rivers. Actually they had met many times over the years at the Rivers' plantation that adjoined theirs. In fact, Thomas wasted no time as he asked to sign her dance card even before the wedding ceremony. And was she widowed? Yes, she was. And did she have an inheritance? Yes, she did - a six hundred acre rice plantation, complete with slaves. How fortunate. After the war of independence from England the slave population was decreased by thirty thousand. What happened? Many had runaway, fought for the British and either died or sailed away with them when they admitted defeat. Now slave labor truly cost more than the land.

"Father, Mother, I'd like to introduce you to Vanessa Jones, a cousin of Robert Rivers. Perhaps you remember Vanessa from Ann's and my childhood?"

And so the courtship started. Elizabeth and Thomas relaxed, hoping that their son would rejoin Charleston society. He just needed some polishing and *taming*. Thank you, Vanessa Jones.

CH. 8. Extinction

February, 1783

Charleston

Elizabeth fervently and angrily prayed to God while Thomas held her and their sons watched. Helpless. They felt so helpless.

"Take me, Lord, not my children! It is not fair for the young to die. First you took my newborn babies, now our precious Mary. Where is your mercy? We are not meant to bury our children!" Elizabeth keened and wailed in Thomas' arms and lamented, "I curse this fever laden country, Thomas!" Thomas glanced at his sons as he gently led their hysterical mother to her room, leaving them to cope with their own grief.

"I wish you back to life!" howled James as he hurled himself on his sister's small frame as she lay too silently in her bed. "Don't leave me! Please, Mary, don't leave me! Help me, brother Thomas. Help me bring her back to life! "

"We must let Mary go," Thomas said softly as he pried James from his sister Mary's still warm body. Thomas' heart was torn, first by Mary's death and now by watching his younger brother's torment. How could he help him understand death when it still made no sense to him? "She is with God now," was all Thomas could think of to say. Did he believe it? Thomas didn't know, but he'd heard it often enough in church. Mary was a beautiful bride one day and a wasted skeleton the next. What other lame comfort could he give James?

"But it isn't fair! Mary was so kind and good!" James yelled. "How can God be so mean? Why did this happen to us?"

"I have no answers for you, James. It seems to me death is just nature's way. Some are chosen while others are passed by. Death doesn't discriminate between good and evil. I make no sense of it. I wish I had better words." Hollow. Thomas felt inadequate and hollow. "And, you are right, it isn't fair."

How had this happened? Less than a month married, Mary had a terrible upset stomach. She could hold nothing within her, not even water. Whatever had poisoned her, she was too thin to fight it. She had been bled with leeches, but to no avail. Her skin held a tinge of blue color as she died. Her weeping slaves unpacked the trousseau they had just readied for the young Geyers' honeymoon trip. Now they would wash and dress her for the vigil.

James had asked a good question in his grief. Why did this happen? Had Charleston become tainted during the British occupation? Was death by disease their parting gift? True, the British had left a dirty city, but these recent deaths had nothing to do with fevers. Mary was not yellow in color. The doctor called it influenza, the grippe, and it was reaching epidemic proportions since the Brits had left. Not knowing the exact cause the doctor ordered, "Burn everything Mary touched. Wash and cook all your food. Boil your water."

Was it a cholera epidemic? Yes, it was. The good doctor guessed well. It was the polluted water.

The young bridegroom, John Geyer, was inconsolable. He and Mary had patiently waited years to legally marry, but they had always been married in their souls. There were few matches so special. Undoubtedly, he would marry again, but not in his heart. The planters needed to reproduce or they would become extinct, like the Indians. John must put his grief behind him, but not so soon. Please, not too soon.

And neither could the Hanscomes afford to be undone. Elizabeth still had a young son, James, to rear with hope for the future. She needed to be resilient. They must all be resilient.

1784

In the new Charleston, Christmas strollers brightened the waterfront promenade and laughter reigned once again in the holiday balls. Life was promising. The war was won and finally done. Prosperity was returning.

Even the Hanscomes moved past their grief. What a relief. Ann was expecting a baby, due in February. She had lost several babies before birth, but the Rivers were most hopeful. Vanessa and young Thomas were engaged, with a wedding planned in March, after the baby's birth. Thomas had been asked to run for the State Assembly and he consented. The harvest of last spring's cash crops surpassed their profit expectations. Creekside was ideal for the long fibered, Sea Island cotton plants, sought for the finest linens and lace of Belgium. It was far superior to the traditional cotton boll, whose stubborn seeds were time-consuming to extract.

1785

Creekside

Fire! No! Not all of them? Yes! The Rivers' mansion at Legare Point had burned, sparing no one - slaves and masters alike. What a surprise to see that sturdy cypress landmark ignite like a tinderbox. Fire was every planter's fear. Someone must be blamed! Who? Who could have done the unspeakable? Not the Indians. Those who survived the wars had migrated west or south, if they hadn't become extinct. Not the British. Although fire was a favorite weapon of war, they had left several years before. Could it have been the loyal slaves, who from time to time murdered their masters while they slept? Or the wild winds and lightning strikes? Or just simple carelessness? No one would ever know. It was sickening.

Who was dead? Robert and Ann Rivers and their unborn child. And all the house servants. Who heard their final screams? Only the howling winds. That's what made Thomas vomit when the rider barreled into Creekside with the news. They died alone.

And Elizabeth? How did she handle the deaths? She heard their screams for help every night in her dreams until the day she died.

And young Thomas? He said nothing. He refused to cry. He withdrew. He rode his marsh tacky as fast as the wind. He drank by himself. He stopped seeing his friends. Vanessa tried not to worry and gave him time. Surely he would heal. They no longer discussed their wedding, as though by mutual decision. He worked until exhaustion in the fields. Was there no relief? No, there wasn't.

And James? "I want it to stop. I want death to stop choosing our family!" he shrieked. This time he understood the nature of death better. He knew death could not be undone. This time he refused to be sad. He was angry.

"Your life is ahead of you. Do not lose grasp of it, dear James. Life is too precious to waste in mourning or anger," consoled his father. "I am going back to the Assembly and I want you to return to school. Your mother has not left her bed and needs our help to rejoin the living. We are all leaving for Charleston tomorrow. If your classmates pity you, realize that not one of them will be spared a great suffering at some point in his or her life."

Charleston

And so James dedicated himself to his lessons and his mother.

"How can I help you?" asked James, sweetly holding his mother's hand. "It has been a month and you refuse to leave your bed. I want you to join us for dinner tonight, please. Thomas will be coming from Creekside and Father from Goose Creek. And it would brighten my life if you would just rise. No one was meant to be disconsolate in Charleston. Let's take a carriage ride and catch the merriment in the streets. This is a fine morning!"

"You are right, dear James, it is time I rise. Dinner would be lovely. Summon my servant and I will dress for that carriage ride with you. I want to hear all about your studies. And send a currier to see if Vanessa will honor us with her presence. It has been far too long."

Elizabeth even smiled in response to James' big grin. She did not want James to feel responsible for her health. She was the parent and he was the child. "I must see beyond myself. I have two living children," she reminded herself. That night Elizabeth seemed her old spirited self at dinner. And young Thomas' eyes shone when he saw Vanessa. "Good," thought Elizabeth.

"Let's drink a toast to being together, again," smiled the elder Thomas. Yes, he was most pleased with the lively dinner conversation. "We have not discussed your wedding date, Vanessa and Thomas. Is this a good time?" And it was.

1786

Charleston

"I, Thomas, take you, Vanessa, to be my wife… for richer for poorer, for better or for worse, in sickness and in health, until death do us part."

James at twelve was a bit young to be best man, but Thomas would have no one else. The wedding at St. Cecelia's Society Hall was small and informal. It was considered to be in poor taste for a widowed woman to wear white on a second marriage. Nonetheless, the guests invited for the reception, dinner and ball expected nothing but elegance. Were they disappointed? No, they weren't.

"I cannot believe my good fortune at finding you, Vanessa," said Thomas gazing into Vanessa's green eyes as they danced the first dance. Her flaming, red hair matched the passion she had for life, her plantation and yes, Thomas Hanscome. "I never thought I would find a wife who cared more for a good ride on a swift, marsh tacky than attend a ball."

"Actually, I love them equally," laughed Vanessa. "I love to dance. I love to ride unencumbered through the swamps. I like to move - and be moved."

"And do I move you?" Thomas teased.

"Yes, you do. Just wait until our honeymoon."

"Oh, I will wait, but not too patiently."

Did it bother Thomas that Vanessa had been married before? No, it did not. However, friends at his bachelor party had no mercy. Most of them had married years before and were ready for a feting.

"Vanessa will be no blushing virgin. Are you sure you are up to it, old man?" said Legare.

"Oh, I enjoy riding a well-trained horse," responded a jovial Thomas. "The breaking of a horse is too much work!"

"Well, some horses never are a good ride," roasted another.

"And perhaps she's out of practice!" toasted another.

Was Vanessa up to it? Of course. She laughed heartily as they waltzed at their wedding.

"I've been a widow far too long," she seductively whispered in his ear.

If the other guests on the dance floor saw the groom blush, they didn't mention it. What an evening of fun. Even the senior Hanscomes needed some merriment.

"Did I ever compliment you on your fine dancing?" Elizabeth asked her husband Thomas.

"No, you never have, thank you. I hope you enjoy all our activities, particularly our private afternoon pleasures," answered her husband with his endearing, mischievous grin.

They were enjoying their usual banter, but Thomas noticed how slight Elizabeth felt in his arms. It was probably nothing. The next day as they waved farewell to the young couple, Elizabeth was her cheery self.

"The bride and groom seem blissfully happy, don't you agree, Thomas?"

"Yes, they must have had quite a night because they also look most tired," grinned Thomas.

"And you, Thomas? Are you as tired as I am?"

"Weddings are a great deal of work for you, Elizabeth. I am looking forward to having your company all to myself."

Thomas and Vanessa decided not to take the time for an extended trip to Europe. Instead, they booked the honeymoon suite on the new American passenger ship. They would visit Philadelphia, New York and Boston, among other ports of call. Forget Europe. They were excited to learn more about their new wonderful country, the United States of America.

In the following weeks, Thomas couldn't help but notice that Elizabeth barely ate. She grew thinner and the light in her eyes grew dull, faded. She was failing. She was growing frail, right in front of his eyes.

"I don't know what is wrong with her, but you are right to be concerned," said the doctor to Thomas as he shook his head. "Elizabeth is dying. Her heart is not working properly."

Thomas buried his head in his hands and cried. The doctor didn't think she would last until Vanessa and Thomas returned from their honeymoon. How could he tell James?

But Elizabeth spared her husband the pain of that discussion. One day after school, Elizabeth took James' hand, smiled and looked him squarely in his eyes.

"Look at me, my dear son, and listen without interruption. I am dying. I think you know that. I also want you to know I am at peace. The Lord will soon be taking me to his kingdom where I will be reunited with Mary and Ann. I only wish I had been younger when you were born so I could see you marry and raise your own family. As it is, you have given your father and me great joy. I also wanted to discuss what you want to do when I am gone. You can stay with your father, who would like your company, or you could live with Thomas and Vanessa. I want you to have some choice about your future."

Silence. Finally, James spoke through his tears.

"I knew, Mother. I just knew you would not recover. It makes me more than sad. I cannot imagine my life without you, but be assured I am almost a man. I will go on, live on. And I will honor you the rest of my days."

"James, it relieves me to hear you speak so. I want you to live a happy life and not mourn me forever. Life is for the living and meant to lived to the fullest. That is how you can honor me."

"I will do my best. I also know what I want, Mother. I will stay with Father, but I don't want to be a planter. I want to be a doctor. I want to help people live. When I am sixteen I would like to study medicine in England. Do you think Father will mind?"

"I think he will like that. I know your choice makes me happy. Your brother has the planter blood running through his veins. You never did. You have had too much death in your young life. Helping people live better is a good mission. Truly, we don't need help dying."

One morning Thomas woke next to Elizabeth's cold wasted frame. She died well. Peaceful. She simply passed in her sleep, without fever, without pain. As Thomas held her, he cried and prayed:

"Give me strength, dear Lord, to face life without my dear Elizabeth. Give me strength to help my sons. Please forgive me, Lord, for selfishly putting the love of this land over my family's welfare. Elizabeth begged me to move and I refused. I am guilty! Punish me, take me, but please do not punish us with extinction."

As the months passed, Thomas became resigned to his own death. He was not sad or angry. He put his affairs in order, finalized his will and quit the South Carolina State Assembly.

1787

Creekside

Thomas Hanscome died at age sixty-three. His friends said grief killed him. James sadly moved in with Thomas and Vanessa. Thomas was the executor of the estate. Provisions had been made for James' medical education. When James turned twenty-one he would receive half of all property: land, sheep, mares, horses, slaves and their future issue. Each man, woman and child was individually named in the will and none of his father's loyal slaves were manumitted. None. James received the Charleston house on 43 Meeting Street and the 600 acre plantation his father bought from Thomas Ladson that abutted the deceased Robert River's plantation. And Thomas received 650 acres, Creekside Plantation, the animals and slaves, also individually named.

Surely Thomas' passing heralded the end of the Hanscome death knell. But it didn't. Vanessa died of swamp fever the following fall and took their unborn child with her. Thomas wanted to run away from the demise of his family. Other planters' families had become extinct. Would that also happen to the Hanscomes? For the first time in his life, he saw no purpose in tending the land. He hated it. He could not escape from the voices of his father, mother, sisters and his dear Vanessa. However, he did promise himself to stay alive. Thomas' sole mission was to help young James become a man.

Thomas booked passage on the first ship to England after Vanessa's burial. Thomas' friends agreed to oversee the overseers and plantations. John Randall, their father's friend since childhood, took them to the wharf. Was he still living between his wife Samantha and his true mulatto love, Grace? On no, both his wife and his mistress had died, but Thomas heard rumors that John Randall was not alone. It was a subject his father had refused to discuss with him. Thomas told John they might not return for some time. James, age thirteen, would be attending school in London.

Who could blame them for leaving? Perhaps they'd never return.

CH. 9. The Light, London Air

1788

London

The black fog of death lost its grip on the Hanscomes when the ship lost sight of the Carolina shore. And the rest of death's memories relaxed into bearable images by the time they glimpsed London. Was hope on the horizon? Yes, it was. And for Thomas Hanscome her name was Jenny.

"This is the London I remembered best," Thomas said to James and Jenny as they strolled through the blossoming gardens along the River Thames. "I can finally breathe this light, summer air. Winter was much too gray, drizzly and dreary."

It was one of those rare and glorious sunny days, when the green English landscape challenges the beauty of the finest emerald. All it ever needed was the sunshine. Yes, summer in London.

"I so prefer this Richmond area to the foul smelling quays in London. This crisp air is just what the doctor ordered. Right, James?"

"I'm not a doctor yet - that will take years of study, dear brother, but I do appreciate your encouragement," smiled James. "However, if fresh air is your true desire, the Oxford air is much more invigorating and enlivening than even this George III country air of Richmond. But I suspect it is the air of the stables and your gambling pastimes that truly stimulate you. Cricket, steeple chases, anything that claims your money excites your senses."

"You besmirch your brother's fine character. He is no shallow, gentleman dandy," laughed Jenny. "I think it better that he bets on the races and games than participates in them. You should have seen your brother at the hunting lodges when he was not much younger than you, James. It was a contest to see who would be killed first, the fox or Thomas!"

"I still intend to kill a fox, my dear Jenny," responded Thomas with false braggadocio. "And James, do not worry. I am not squandering your tuition money at the track, nor wasting my time. I am doing research on blood lines. I might even take a champion thoroughbred back to Charleston when we leave. There is money to be made in horse breeding. Americans are just whetting their racing appetites, now that their prosperity has returned. It is a veritable gold market."

"I know you love your horses, but Oxford is not a far journey from Ascot. Why not live with me, rather than London? It's not too late to take up the pleasure of the arts," said James, knowing that was not among his brother's passions.

"Don't you like boarding at Oxford? Making friends? Immersing your mind in intellectual pursuits, unencumbered by your guardian?" teased Thomas.

"Yes, I admit I am in my element at Oxford. I should just content myself with seeing you on the weekends. But I must say I am enjoying your company, now that you are so light-hearted and gay."

If either had asked, and neither did, both brothers would say leaving South Carolina was their smartest decision. Their departure wasn't just for James' education. Grief had consumed them, but they couldn't even identify their fog until it magically lifted. In England their losses were in the past and their present was exhilarating. The brothers' best discovery had been each other. And yes, Jenny, who had been Ann Hanscome's slave and possibly Aaron Hanscome's child.

"If I moved to Oxford, I would find little of interest, James. You would feel smothered and I would be bored. In London I can attend to the commodity markets. The planters are thanking me for ferreting out the best merchants and the best prices for our goods. Our cotton is in prime demand. I will be converting more of our land to its cultivation."

The three finished their walk and rented horses at the stables. The deer park had hundreds of acres for them to explore. While Thomas touted London life and all that was in vogue, he felt most at home in the wide-open spaces. He spent more of his days hunting and shooting with merchants than on the wharves. He had always found that friends made the best business partners and hunting solidified friendships. Did Thomas socialize with nobility? Oh no. The loss of the colonies was a bitter pill for the nobles to swallow. Many nobles not so secretly blamed King George III's tyrannical ways for the loss, but befriending a Carolinian was still considered extremely bad form. However, in the merchants' eyes, money reigned supreme. Why should they pledge allegiance to an insane King when their profits were at stake? Thomas was invited to all the finest men's clubs, but he devoted his weekends to his brother and Jenny. Riding horses was an interest that all three held in common.

"I knew you chose to ride in Deer Park today for another reason. You are a scoundrel with an ulterior motive," exclaimed James as his brother escorted them into the cricket match at Lord's Ground. In truth, James delighted in his brother's weekend surprises.

"Yes, today is a double treat," confessed Thomas. "First the ride and now the match. It is time to put your money down," smiled Thomas. He was in his glory.

All three studied the win records of the various jockeys and horses, then confidently placed their bets. Who won? Jenny, of course.

How did Jenny become part of this Hanscome camaraderie? In a moment of nostalgia, Thomas rode by his deceased Cousin Thomas Downing's London home. Life seemed so beckoning and innocent at age eleven. His mother and sisters had been enthralled with London. He was the apple of his Cousin Thomas' eye. That had been seventeen years ago. Now Thomas was twenty-eight. Indeed, he had been shocked when Jenny was manumitted and chose to remain in London. Their sad departure day was etched in his memory. She was like his older sister, albeit a slave sister. After Cousin Thomas died, Jenny's name was never mentioned at Creekside again.

Thomas hesitantly rang the bell at the old Downing home. Imagine his surprise to see Jenny open the door.

"Hello!" was all Thomas said, trying to hide his amazement. He had expected to greet a stranger, not a vision of beauty. Did Jenny recognize this handsome man who stood before her?

"Hello, Thomas," she smiled in return. "What a surprise this is. Please, do come in. I am finished with my music pupils for the day and was about to have tea. Would you care to join me?" Without waiting for his reply, Jenny simply rang for her servant.

Once he sat down in the familiar parlor, Jenny served him tea, with the same graceful composure his mother had. Jenny was fashionably dressed, lovely. Why was that surprising? Jenny was taught, right along with his sister Ann, all the fine nuances of perfect grooming and etiquette. Thomas tried hard not to stare at her. Jenny's mannerisms were so similar to his sister's. It was the way Jenny arched her little finger as she lifted her teacup to her plumped lips. It was the way she smiled as she remembered Thomas took one lump of sugar and no milk in his tea. Jenny's small habits and patterns of speech brought tears to his eyes. This tea he had lived before. His sister was reincarnated before his very eyes. Jenny's golden glow and deep brown eyes only enhanced her allure.

Their conversation flowed easily, as if there was no time lapse, as if that last fateful night of her manumission had never occurred. Soon they were laughing as they recalled amusing Creekside incidents, like nearly escaping the alligators' jaws when their canoe flipped. And they both cried when Thomas told her how all the Hanscome's had died in such a short time span. Yes, Mary, Ann, his parents and his wife, Vanessa.

"James was like an orphan with the saddest, blue eyes. And after my Vanessa died, I, too, was a lost soul. But the voyage brought us together. We hardly knew each other before."

"I'd like to meet young James," said Jenny.

"And you shall!" said Thomas as he stood to leave. "What a pleasant afternoon. I enjoyed recalling some happy memories of my family."

"Did you know that Thomas and I married?" she asked, waiting for a reaction.

"No, I did not. Jenny Downing, it is then. Yes, that is a bit of a shock, even now," admitted Thomas.

Was Thomas horrified? No, but that a Negro, even a freedman, could marry a white was outside his realm of experience. His psyche had to let that information settle.

"Mother wondered how it came to be that you had the Downing name, when you wrote that he had died. She thought it strange, since you weren't his slave, for you to take his name. She thought Cousin Thomas had adopted you. She didn't stop to consider the English marital laws were different."

"There is no law in England prohibiting marriages between races," Jenny clarified, "but it is still frowned upon. Thomas had to pay a pretty penny to have a justice perform the ceremony."

"But Cousin Thomas was so old!" blurted out Thomas. He had meant to be more tactful, but he was still a bit stunned.

"Yes, he was old. However, I'll never forget our honeymoon trip to India. I truly cared for him and he adored me. At times I forgot I ever was a slave and that he was old. At last I had a true family, a real family, not one fabricated in my mind. I even had my own servants. Imagine that! Sadly, Thomas only lived five more years. Since then I have taken total charge of my life. He willed me everything. I am truly free, carefree and financially free." Jenny's eyes twinkled, apparently quite pleased with her accomplishments. "I have my music students because I love to teach, not because I need the tuition. And I have many friends among the East Indian wives of the British merchants. They have been intermarrying for years. I am content with my life."

"I can see that London suits you well," smiled Thomas as he took his leave. Then Jenny ever so lightly touched his arm.

"Please accept my invitation to dinner this Saturday eve. I will prepare a notable Hanscome feast for you. And please bring James."

"What a kind invitation. I accept, for the both of us."

Thomas could hardly wait to tell James his discovery of Jenny and her invitation to a real Carolina dinner.

And how did James react?

"Jenny's a slave," said James with a horrified face. "Do you really think it's a good idea to socialize with her?"

"She's not a slave and we are not in Charleston, James. Why not let her entertain us? She intends to prepare a Charleston feast, just for us."

"She's a Negro, was our slave."

"She's a freed mulatto and a probable blood relative of ours."

"How preposterous! I've never heard that story. Do tell me more." Oh yes, Thomas had James' full attention.

"I thought this might pique your curiosity. Cousin Thomas thought Jenny was his Uncle Aaron's, our grandfather's, child. That's why he freed her. She could be our Aunt, James. And she is our cousin for sure, as Cousin Thomas married her."

"That's even more bizarre news."

"I can see I need to tell you all the secret Hanscome tales," laughed Thomas. "Did you know that Ann Downing, our great Aunt from Kittery and Thomas Downing's mother had a mulatto son? Did you know that Cousin Thomas and his sister Joan, were also bastards?"

"No, I did not!" James was shocked again. His mother had always said he came from a good family, the best of families. "You continue to amaze me brother. Bastards? Mulattos? Next you'll be claiming pirates as our kin."

"Oh, we had some of those, too, like our Grandfather Aaron."

"I thought he was an honorable privateer before he settled on John's Island."

"Privateer or pirate, our father said they were the same, plunderers. And Aaron's older brother John even cavorted with Blackbeard."

"In truth?" James' eyeballs were truly bulging from their sockets.

"And what's more, Ann Downing's love knew no conventional boundaries. In addition to her romance in Maine with the slave Black Will, she had a tryst with Blackbeard."

"Thomas, I do believe I don't believe a word you've told me. I may be gullible, but I'm no fool."

"It's all true. You see Jenny is only a mild part of our colorful, family history. Anyway, do not worry. No one in London will pay much attention to the company we keep. She was a part of my childhood, a good part, and I intend to see her. Do you want to come to dinner with me, or do you pass?"

"Of course I will come. I just have to get over my amazement. I wouldn't miss this enlightenment for the world. And yes, the food, too. I do believe I am a bit homesick for those Carolina flavors."

And so the friendships began. Was it that Jenny's fine meals fed their souls as well as their bodies? Or was Jenny simply family? All the Hanscome brothers knew or cared about was that they laughed heartily, once again.

Or was there something else in the sweet, light London air? Yes, there was. James was young, but no fool. He knew love when he saw it.

CH. 10. Nancy Randall

1790

John's Island

"I am in my last days, Louisa. I am dying," confessed John Randall to his colored mistress of twenty years as she plumped up his pillow.

John was the son of the first Robert Randall whose plantation abutted Aaron Hanscome's plantation on the Stono. He was also the lifelong friend of the elder Thomas Hanscome who recently passed. When John's mother Amy died, he was lovingly raised by his mother's slave, Pearl. Then John met the love of his life, Grace, a freed mustee, who bore him children in Charles Town. However, he succumbed to his father's wishes for heirs and married Samantha, who bore him three sons. After Samantha and Grace both died, John took Pearl's granddaughter, Louisa, as his mistress. She was also John's slave. It just seemed natural for them to be together. While they could not be married and she could not sit in his pew at church, the planter society knew Louisa was his consort. The planters had given up on finding John a respectable wife.

"You just have a touch of the flu. Don't be talking death with me," Louisa gently reprimanded him.

"I am sixty-seven. I thought I would live to be one hundred, with your fine care, but it is not to be. It seems this Carolina country is too hard on us white planters. What if I had your dark skin, my dear Louisa?" he said somewhat in jest.

"If you had my dark skin, you never would have been a planter. You would be a slave, like me," laughed Louisa.

"Yes, I do believe you are right on that account. I don't believe I know a colored planter – many freed merchants, but no Negro planters. But mark my word, Louisa, before you die there will be Negro plantation owners. There are already Negro slave owners."

"Colored plantation owners! I don't see it," said Louisa. "As I've told you before, this whole institution is not just *peculiar*, as they call it. It is cruel. It cannot be God's way. Why do Negros perpetuate it? Why do slaves want to own others? Lordy, Lordy. Lord help us all."

"… Because the conquered always emulate their captors, my dear Louisa," countered John. "It has been that way since the beginning of time. The Romans conquered England, now England conquers others. The enslaved become the next enslavers. We do not create new. We just copy the past. That's why we need a forgiving God."

"If that is true, there will always be more blood spilled," said Louisa with a sigh.

"Again, I think you right. And the white planters are afraid the blood will be theirs," replied John.

"I hope you are wrong. Hope is all we slaves have ever had. The past does not have to repeat itself, if we learn from it. Look at the two of us."

"Yes, we are good together," smiled John. "I also foresee more mixing of races. It is human nature for people who live together to love each other."

"Must I remind you that most planters don't love their slaves, John. They are most cruel, crueler than any animal I've seen. They just take women, force themselves on them, like mad dogs in heat!"

Silence.

John and Louisa were comfortable dropping the conversation. They had had this same conversation many times before and it went nowhere. John loved his wealth, his plantations and his Louisa. Was it in that order? He thought so, but he wasn't proud to admit it. Finally, John broke the silence.

"I think the most disheartening thing about getting older is burying all my friends. I want to at least have one friend left who will cry at my funeral."

"I will cry," Louisa said, as she leaned over and kissed him.

"I know you will, Louisa. And I know you think my preoccupation with death is premature, but I want to talk with you about my will – and your welfare. You are still young and by the looks of it, you are pregnant. I assume that is my child," said John touching her protruding stomach.

"And if the child is as dark-complected as me? Will you still claim it?" she teased.

"Do not even jest about that," said John. "Please sit by my side."

Louisa sat beside John and put her arms around him. They had many fond moments. Was she his equal? No, she wasn't. John was in charge of his household and his plantation. It had been the same with his wife and first mistress. But then, white, freed or slave, was any woman a man's equal?

"I have recently sent a lengthy missive to Thomas Hanscome in England that includes a copy of my will. But because he is not present, he cannot be an Executrix. I truly don't know if this flu will claim me or if I will live to see young Thomas' return. He promised to see James complete his medical degree, but I know he misses his plantations. Still, he will not abandon the only family he has left. He is committed to James. Thomas is of our land, our people - a hunter, a shooter, a sailor and a planter. His slaves say he has a black soul.

Fine manners and English superiorities do not suit him. I assured him that his plantations are well managed.

"I know I digress, my dear. The point is I want to manumit you now, Louisa, instead of at my death. If you are not free, our child will not be free. Thus, I have asked my attorney to prepare the necessary documents. I will also direct that a sum of money be set aside in my will for your welfare. I want our child to be educated. I want him accepted into Charleston society, not the white society, but the affluent mulatto society. For that he needs to have money and be educated.

"You can remain here on the plantation after I am gone, I will make provisions for that, but that choice will be yours after I pass. I also have left a home for you in Charleston. But even free, you will need a white planter to vouch for your good character. I have asked young Hanscome to be your guardian. I trust him. I don't ever want these white supremacists, and they are growing in number, to take advantage of you."

"Oh John, this sounds so serious, as if you are on your deathbed. I hate to hear you talk so. But yes, I do want our child to be born free. And keep in mind, she might be a girl."

"There's no need to get huffy, Louisa. I would actually prefer a girl, as I think my sons would feel less threatened."

"We will have what the good Lord chooses, dear," said Louisa as she set up the backgammon game. "Tonight it is my turn to win at backgammon, which is more important than any of our previous discussions."

Louisa had a way with her John. She never bruised his ego, but she wouldn't let him ever win their nightly game without a true battle.

And did John Randall die before his child was born? No, he died six years after her birth. The sight of his little girl, made him forget he ever wanted a boy. She was coddled by her father, much to her mother's dismay. How would the girl ever know humility? How would she ever learn her proper place in society? She knew no fear. She expected to be loved and adored. Why not? She had a loving mother and father. She had a legal surname. She was free.

What was her name? Her name was Nancy Randall.

CH. 11. Lucy Moor's Quagmire

1790

Charleston

On the same day as Nancy Randall's birth there was another celebration in Charleston.

"I am free!" shouted Lucy Moor, as she hugged and twirled her daughter Susanna. "Soon you will be free, too. Thank you, Emperor! Praise be to Allah!" Lucy was now a strong, determined, fair-complected thirty-one year old with dark eyes of steel that had just been lightened by great news.

The South Carolina Assembly had passed the "Moors Sundry Act" as per the 1786 American Friendship Treaty with the Sultan of Morocco. It had taken four long years to enact. With the flash of a pen in 1790, the eight petitioners, Moors or Turks, as they were sometimes called, became white! No longer were they subjected to the laws from the 1740 Negro Act. The petitioners were English prisoners of war who had been sold into slavery by a disreputable captain in Charleston. Eventually, through years of hard work, they saved enough to buy their freedom and hire an attorney. They were given the same rights and privileges as white people, including a jury trial. But were they really included in the white hierarchy? No, they were different and thus suspect. The Moors tended to socialize and intermarry with the elite class of wealthy mulattos.

"My child should be freed, Miss Sarah," begged Lucy. "I was never meant to be enslaved, thus she should be free, too."

"It is a law that all children born to slave mothers are slave and become the master's property. Talk to the freed mulattos in the market. They will tell you they had to purchase their children. I will manumit Susanna once you've paid me £500."

"That law you refer to is the Negro Act Law. It does not apply to Moroccans. We are white. All Moroccans, including my Susanna, are subjects of the Emperor and to be released. I have mistakenly been your slave for sixteen years!"

"You will have to hire a barrister. And while you may be considered white, Susanna is a mulatto. Her father is a Negro."

"Her father was freed at the time of Susanna's birth and he is also a mulatto."

"As you know, it is only the mother's status that counts, and you were a slave, my slave," said Miss Sarah with her clipped speech, superior attitude and pursed lips. "And Susanna is a bastard child, since you are not married. She is also strong and dark enough to be a field worker. I could sell her or have my husband put her to work in his rice fields. You would never see Susanna again, regardless of the Sultan."

Lucy just sighed – more threats. She knew the conversation was over. What good was her freedom? She was trapped. It seemed fair that her wages as a seamstress should go to providing a home for them, but then as a slave, fairness was an illusion. Now she would continue to work for Miss Sarah until she had acquired £500. Should she just steal her daughter after she saved enough for two passages back to Morocco? Freedom and passage to Morocco were both guaranteed under the new law.

But that was not to be. Miss Sarah kept track of Lucy's wages on a ledger, but not one actual coin did Lucy see. Now there was a further complication.

"Who is the father?" asked Lucy of Susanna, now sixteen. Initially Lucy worried that Susanna had the dreaded influenza, but that was not the case. She was pregnant.

What made Lucy ill was the fact they would never be freed. Lucy would now have to pay off yet another bond, her grandchild's. She would never abandon Susanna or her grandchildren to Miss Sarah.

"Please, say you know who the father is," implored Lucy.

Susanna left the room in tears. She left with no confession. Susanna and her mother were usually inseparable. Lucy protected her at all times - rarely let her out of her sight. Apparently, Lucy's vigilance had failed. Now she was worried that Miss Sarah might sell Susanna before the baby came, rather than lighten Susanna's work load. A buyer wouldn't know she was pregnant – for a month or two. Pregnant women didn't sell well. It was too chancy for a buyer, a most poor investment if both the mother and child died in childbirth.

However, Lucy's fears did not materialize. Miss Smith seemed satisfied as long as the work was completed. Lucy was now working for three. Finally, the baby was born.

"You have a baby girl," said Lucy to her daughter. "What will you name her?"

"I will name her Catherine Lucy, after you, Mother. I am so thankful she is alive and healthy."

"And most light-skinned. Please tell me who this white father is. I pray he will help us buy your freedom. Else we are doomed to this servant status."

"The father is Miss Sarah's son, Edward. He says he will help us, but right now he has no money. He has three years until he turns twenty-one."

"And then what are his intentions?" asked Lucy with a sigh. Edward could remain penniless, if his mother suspected he was the father.

"Edward says he will keep me. He would marry me, but the law will not allow it. He says he will be forever true to me and our children," stated a proud Susanna.

Did Lucy share her daughter's enthusiasm? No, she did not. Lucy cried and cried. She felt trapped in the South Carolina quagmire of slavery.

CH. 12. Where is Home?

1797

England

Ten years magically passed since the Hanscome brothers left Charleston, but isn't that the result of living life to its fullest? James had finished his medical education and the question of returning to Charleston loomed large. Where was their true home?

"I want to speak with you, Thomas," said James, as confidently as he could as he practiced his words in front of the mirror. "I am soon to complete my practical study at the Radcliffe Infirmary, then I will graduate from Oxford. This is difficult for me to say, but I do not intend to return to Charleston. England is my home."

Yes, James had practiced this speech, or variations of it, many times. He finally decided a short declaration of his future intentions was the best tack. James was no longer a lad and was as tall and handsome as his brother. His hair was dark brown, like his mother's, but his blue eyes definitely marked him as a Hanscome. He smiled less than Thomas felt he should, but then James found his older brother much too light-hearted. Together they were a good balance.

James had purposefully selected their annual October trek to the Newmarket races to discuss his decision. The horse races, win or lose, always placed Thomas in a superior state of mind. He went from breeder to breeder discussing the merits of his favorite thoroughbreds. And it was an outing Jenny didn't usually attend. James wanted this private conversation to go well.

Newmarket

"This is indeed a bit of a shock, James. Our plan has always been to return to Charleston after you completed your medical degree." Thomas frowned, but he wasn't angry. "I will need some time to digest this change."

"I am sorry to ruin your horse race euphoria, but England now feels like home and Charleston? Well, its customs seem distant, archaic and foreign, especially slavery."

"I thought the purpose of your degree was to find a cure for swamp fever, to save lives," reminded Thomas.

"I was young then. And there still is no cure. The best that can be done is the quinine treatment from the cinchona bark. I knew as much from Great Aunt Ann's journals, salvaged from the fire, as I've learned here about malaria, as it is called. My professors humored me when I postulated her theory that the mosquitoes caused it. Their scientific community attributes malaria to bad air. I have held my tongue since then, but Aunt Ann was correct. I have not abandoned my interest in saving lives, but there are lives to be saved here – right here in England, too."

"But they are not Carolinian lives."

"No, they are not. But a life is a life. I see little difference. I feel more English than Carolinian." James paused before changing the focus to Thomas. "And you? You and Jenny have been sharing her residence for years. Do you propose to take her to Charleston as your consort? I thought you might marry and remain in London, in the fresh, open air. The London commodity markets have been most profitable for you. Even the Charleston horse races will not be challenging." James strategies fell flat. Thomas became quite serious.

"I will return to John's Island. Creekside is my true love, James. It always was and will be. Vanessa and I shared those plantation roots. It was the glue of our affection. And Jenny? What a delight. We amuse each other. We want no children. Yes, we love each other but she understands my life with her has always been temporary. If I am correct, she loves her freedom too much to want to be any man's wife, even if I were to remain in London."

"And if you are wrong?"

"Then Jenny and I must talk, again." Thomas smiled. "You can choose your own home, James. I am disappointed, but I will come to grips with your decision to stay. You were still a lad when we came and I have witnessed how Oxford has formed you into a man, a fine man and, unfortunately for me, an Englishman. You have a few months to consider your options. Right now I want to place my bets and see who wins the cherished *Plate* trophy. Then I will buy some thoroughbred studs. Wait until you see these beauties. I may buy two, an Arabian and a Godolphin Barb. I wonder how they'll enjoy our strong marsh tacky mares! They are as good on the turf, flats and hurdles as any."

James was relieved. His conversation with Thomas had gone better than he thought. And how would Jenny respond to Thomas' desire to return to South Carolina? James bet on Jenny working her spell on Thomas, so he wouldn't have to choose between England and his only remaining family.

London

"You appear deep in thought," said Jenny as they left the concert. "Did you enjoy the baroque concertos?"

"Yes, indeed. The acoustics in the hall are even better than St. Cecelia's," teased Thomas.

"Must you compare every event to Charleston, even after all these years?" replied Jenny, somewhat annoyed. After all, could any place in the world surpass London's culture?

"I do know my habit irritates you, dear Jenny. I am preoccupied, I'm afraid. I have been planning our return to Charleston."

"When you say 'Our' are you referring to you and me – or you and James?" asked Jenny.

"Do you want to go back to Charleston with me?" asked Thomas.

"Do you want to stay in London with me?" asked Jenny. She was aware that she had answered his question with a question.

"Touché," replied Thomas. "I think our parting will be very difficult, unless we can reach agreement."

"You are, of course, right. I, too, have been preoccupied with our future." Jenny paused, like James she had practiced for this moment many times. "Thomas, I will not go back to the land of slavery, even as a freed woman. I shudder at the thought! As your consort I would live on the margin of Charleston life – and afraid that if something happened to you I could be re-enslaved, right in front of our gorgeous mansion. Here in London, I am part of it, not marginal, not dependent. I have no fear. I don't think you even know how a slave is conditioned to fear. But lose your love? That also is unthinkable."

"It is as I thought. Oh Jenny, what are we to do? Just say goodbye?" asked Thomas. Their initial irritations dissolved in the obviousness of their dilemma. No one was to blame.

"I love our present arrangement and I want it to go on forever. We do not control each other. And when we are together it is for our pleasure, not obligation," replied Jenny.

"I heartily agree. Our life together is perfect. I love you, Jenny."

Silence.

"Let me ask you a question. If I remained, would you marry me?"

"Are you asking me to marry you, Thomas?"

"Yes, I am."

"And what about your love for Creekside? I'm afraid I could never replace it. I believe over time you would grow to resent me. Then our love would fade. You know I am right, don't you? I must refuse your marriage offer, as much as I've longed to hear it."

Silence.

"Yes, you are right, once again, my Jenny. You say I don't understand your fear of returning to Charleston, but I do. It would be your ultimate sacrifice to honor our love, but also you would chafe at your restrictions and soon resent my freedom and grow to despise me. Do you also understand the hold my land has on my heart?"

"No, I really don't, Thomas. Why is the land more important than people? It killed your whole family, except for James!"

"Ah, that's a very good question. The land continues beyond our mortal lives, Jenny. It has never betrayed me by death. It has never judged me. My plantations and I are one in spirit."

"I suppose that is like my union with music. All I have to do is play my piano and I feel I have reached heaven." Then she laughed. "Except when I'm with you!"

"Thus, if you had to choose between your music, the arts, fine literature, theatre and my love, which would you choose?"

Silence.

Jenny had no answer for Thomas. They had finally discussed the unspoken - the limits of their great affection. Neither wanted to be vulnerable, again. Land and music - they were constant. They spoke to their spirits. They gave them peace. People had enslaved Jenny. People had broken Thomas' heart when they died. People were not permanent. Love was transitory.

That evening they clung to each other with their deepest passion. Gone was the normal playfulness and lightness of spirit when they touched each other. Their eyes, their bodies fiercely held each other in bruising desperation. This union had to last for an eternity. The memories of this night would be stamped in their hearts and their dreams, forever demanding to be recalled and never forgotten. "Remember me! I am real! I love you! We are!" Why couldn't the passion go on forever? Why wouldn't Thomas stay? Why wouldn't Jenny leave? Why wasn't love enough? Why did it always end?

Thomas spent the next few weeks settling his London accounts. He knew he must adjust to being alone, again. Finally, his departure day arrived. He was relieved. He respected that none of them wanted to change their decisions. Not James, not Jenny and not him.

Thomas settled his three stallions on the ship. He had decided to buy three, knowing that the difficult voyage could easily claim one or two. Thomas was serious about becoming a breeder. He was anxious to set sail and leave this coal smelling port. He was homesick for the warm, heavy, moist air. Yes, his soul hungered for warmth and sunshine. He was finished being sad. If he had remorse over leaving the two people he loved behind, he would deny it. He had said his goodbyes to Jenny and James. He was on to next. He was going home.

Suddenly, Thomas heard a welcomed voice.

"I can always move back to London if I don't readjust to Charleston, can't I?" James came aboard with a broad smile.

"Yes, you can, brother. Yes, you can! Now help me with these steeds, Dr. Hanscome."

Neither Hanscome looked back as the ship left the wharf. The painful deaths of everyone they loved had taught them to move forward, never back. Take the risks, leap in faith. The future was always the wisest choice. And just sometimes, it miraculously surpassed all expectations.

Neither Hanscome noticed Jenny watching their departure, tears sliding slowly down her cheeks. It seemed like an eternity for the ship to leave the harbor. She waited. She felt a painful tug at her heart. Would she jump in the water and swim after the vessel?

No, she didn't. As Jenny watched the ship disappear beyond the horizon, she stood tall and smiled. She knew she had made her best decision. She not only loved her freedom more than Thomas. London was her home.

Charleston

Once the Hanscomes reached the Charleston harbor, they also smiled. They were home.

"Ten years! We are finally home!" shouted Thomas to his brother as they led the stallions down the planks. All three champion sires had survived. "How does it feel to you, James?"

"I reserve final judgment, but my heart is racing with excitement. I feel like the horses, happy to be on solid ground again. And that dank, hot, and yes, deadly, infested air that we left years ago? It feels like soft, kind air and smells of warm sunlight and magnolias."

"What is the first thing you want to do, Dr. Hanscome?

"I want to go to 37 Meeting Street and unpack. If I remember correctly, it will make a fine medical office and town home for me. Do you want to come along?"

"No, no dear brother. I am going directly to Creekside with my steeds. But I will be back in Charleston in a few days to see to business - and find a trainer."

And did they go their separate ways? No. First they found a secluded spot, stripped and swam in the turquoise, warm sea. Ah! How they splashed and laughed. Now they had reclaimed their home.

Charleston Neck

Thomas noticed many freedmen with tatters for clothes and the absence of white faces on this side street. Squalor, he thought. Thomas knew Ietrow had quit his oversight job at Creekside years ago. Ietrow simply informed John Randall that he only knew about overseeing a mansion. The truth was Ietrow had no stomach for disciplining the field slaves. Was Thomas irritated? After all, he had freed Ietrow. No, he wasn't. Thomas was aware Ietrow was not strict enough with the slaves. He was too likeable and unable to instill fear. Ietrow had not a mean bone in his body.

"Greetings, Ietrow! It has been years since I last saw you. How are you doing?" asked Thomas. Ietrow, his constant companion and servant as a boy, looked good. The two men exchanged warm smiles and embraced, like lost brothers. "This Charleston Neck is an unpleasant place. Please tell me you don't live here. I had a difficult time finding you."

"This is my home, Master Thomas, but I love my life as a freedman and am most indebted to you. I am more fortunate than most. I have a position."

Thomas winced. Ietrow was free, true, but he still called Thomas "Master." Was that due to respect, fear or habit? After London, it seemed strange to Thomas. Yes, Thomas winced, but neither did he ask Ietrow to call him Thomas. In moments like these, Thomas knew he was home, indeed.

"How are you making a living, Ietrow?" asked Thomas.

"I am a butler at St. Cecilia's. My fine training as your valet makes me most agreeable as a servant. Many here in the Neck have difficulty finding work."

"It looks like their lives were better as slaves. Why aren't they working?"

"Unless they have a trade, they compete with the slaves whose masters hire them out. And they can't live very well on hired out wages."

Silence.

"It is good to see you, Ietrow," said Thomas, averting the freedmen's listless eyes that surrounded them, yes, avoiding the eyes that would not meet his.

"I imagine you are happy to be back at Creekside," offered Ietrow, wanting to change the subject.

"Yes, I am most happy to be home. My ten years absence was far too long."

"And Master James? He was but a boy when I last saw him. I hear he is Dr. Hanscome. I assume he has more patients than he can handle."

"Hopefully soon. But he has opened an infirmary for the poor, too. You must tell some of the freedmen here. James says it's essential to improve everyone's health, regardless of color. He says we all breathe the same air. His most exciting project is growing an orchard of cinchona trees. He is making a medicinal powder from its bark – for tea. He wants all of Carolina, rich and poor, free and slave to drink the tea daily from spring to fall. He says it will prevent the severity of the fevers."

"He is quite ambitious. To be free of the fevers would be a miracle. Please give him my best regards."

"I will," said Thomas with his wide grin. "Ietrow, I visit you for a specific reason. While I was in London, I saw Jenny. She wanted me to give you this envelope. It bears her seal. You may open it now."

Ietrow read her note, aloud. "… My benefactor and late husband, Thomas Downing, wanted me to share his inheritance with you, Ietrow. My husband thought we both could have been sired by the late Aaron Hanscome and wanted us to enjoy a freedman's life with some means at our disposal. I am teaching music and enjoying my life in England. I wish you happiness in yours. Thomas has assured me he will help you begin a business of your choosing…" Ietrow stared as his old master, flabbergasted.

"Let us take my carriage to the Exchange and I will open an account for you," offered Thomas.

"Right now?" asked Ietrow, still shocked.

"Why not?" answered Thomas. "Do you have any idea what you would like to do with this money?"

"Open a haberdashery, for gentlemen. Charlestonians always like to look their best."

"What a brilliant idea. As I recall you always dressed me like a prince - that is when you could get me to change my clothes. I can help you import goods from some of London's finest merchants - that is if you'd like my assistance."

"This is all too good to be true, Master. I would be honored to have your aid. I know some fine seamstresses who might work for me. I might also hire a milliner to create a line of fine women's hats. And perhaps also sell Dr. James' tea!" Ietrow's enthusiasm was infectious. He had never dreamed of such an opportunity.

"Jenny is a good artist. She might be able to copy some of the latest London designs and send them to you. She'd enjoy helping, if even from a distance. She likes to think of you as her brother."

"Do you think Jenny would ever return to Charleston?" Ietrow wistfully asked. "It would be good to see her."

"No. I asked her to consider it, but you see in London she lives like an English lady. Of course London society has its strata, but her darker complexion is not an issue with the merchant class. She is a talented musician and teacher, well-respected, and the widow of a prominent man - my cousin, Thomas Downing. In Charleston, as you know, there are distinct limits and levels of freedom and laws against miscegenation."

"Yes, I do know." Ietrow knew only too well how tenuous his freedom was. "Did you see much of Jenny?"

"Yes, we did. James and I were spoiled by her Carolina feasts. Oh, we will miss her laughter. Once again, she became part of our family."

Thomas decided to say nothing about his deep love for Jenny, but perhaps Ietrow had guessed the truth. Thomas missed her more than he thought possible and he knew it showed. But what Ietrow surmised was of little consequence. This was Charleston. The most obvious was easily denied. And no one questioned a prominent planter - ever.

Home had its rules and Thomas accepted them. He was now determined to be the best planter.

CH. 13. Compromises for Love

1801

Charleston

"Finally, we are all free!" cried Lucy. And just in time. Susanna was now expecting her third child. This one would be born free. Both little Catherine Lucy and wee Elizabeth were freed at the same time as Susanna. How, pray tell, did that happen?

"Mother, I want to talk to you about Susanna and her children. I insist you to free them. Today!" demanded Edward.

"Oh, and why would I do that? Lucy has not paid me for their manumissions," said an indignant Miss Sarah.

"They are Moors – all of them!" shouted Edward. "I went to see an attorney today, Mother. He advised me they do not need to pay you to release them from bondage. You have already enjoyed their services for ten years longer than was legal. Would you like me to advise Susanna that she could ask for her back wages? And what you pay for Lucy's continued service as a white person is robbery! It is a mere pittance of her true value. You intend to chain her to your dictates and I will not have it." Edward was finally standing up to his mother.

"Edward, where did you get the money for the attorney's fees?" asked his cunning mother.

"Father finally paid me my due. I told him that if he wants me to work for him, I need to be paid - and handsomely. I have no intention of being treated like a slave myself until I receive my inheritance."

"It sounds like you gave your father an ultimatum. That could be most dangerous for you."

"I did. But that is not all I said. I sired Susanna's children, Mother. I threatened to leak that news to your prestigious St. Cecelia's Society. There would be no advantageous marriage between planter families for me - ever."

Miss Sarah exploded at that news.

"How could you disgrace us so! How dare you blackmail us?" Miss Sarah was beside herself. How could she fix this bad situation?

"And what if I intend to keep Susanna and my children?"

"You must be in jest, Edward. That will ruin your future. You can never marry her," retorted his mother.

"Of course I can. She is a Moor and thus white. The miscegenation laws do not apply."

"But Susanna isn't white and although her two girls appear white, they are not. Susanna has a mulatto father!"

"Legally, I can marry her. As you know color is only one criteria of whiteness. There are several well-respected planters you know who are dark-complected, but have bought their white status. Now you need to sign these freedom papers and I will file them with my attorney. A manumission form is not necessary as they were never truly slaves," said Edward calmly. He intended to be very matter-of-fact and not return his mother's rage, but he was ready for battle.

"I refuse to do so. You will not blackmail me or you will lose everything!" stated his fuming mother.

"No, I am not blackmailing you. I am simply telling you what I intend to do. I will see you in court."

Did Edward take his mother to court? He wouldn't be the first son to do so, but he did not. Miss Sarah signed the freedom papers. Edward reached an agreement with his parents. He would agree not to marry Susanna if they would release a large sum of money and a residence in Charleston to the Moors. In return, Edward would marry a planter's daughter, one of their choosing, not Edward's. And would Edward give up Susanna or keep her as his consort? That matter he refused to discuss with his parents.

"My life with Susanna and my children is not your concern," he said. "On the day I marry, I want my rightful inheritance or there will be no wedding."

The Smith's reconciled themselves to Edward's proposition, but neither Edward nor his parents were happy. But someone else was. Lucy Moor was ecstatic. Her life was coming together.

"Susanna, Ietrow has hired us in his haberdashery as seamstresses!" said Lucy. Yes, Ietrow, Thomas Hanscome's manumitted personal slave had his very own haberdashery in Charleston. His business was thriving. Of course, all the planters trusted his expertise as Thomas Hanscome vouched for his character. "He also wants us to create fashionable hats from the London patterns he recently received from his London sister, Jenny. He has the finest fabrics – felts, silks, brocades and velvets and yes, plumes! We will be well paid. And thanks to Edward, we have a respectable home. We will not be forced to live in the filth of Charleston Neck. Edward has done well by you, Susanna. I wonder how he bargained with his parents for that home?"

"He promised to marry a planter's daughter of his parents' choice, instead of me," said Susanna as she broke into tears. She did not share her mother's happiness. To her love was more important than wealth and security.

"Don't you know that Edward traded his marriage to you for our best welfare, Susanna? You might have had Edward as a husband, but his parents would have disinherited him. Poverty can destroy love, particularly with someone as coddled as Edward. With the money he obtained, we will even be able to send our girls to school. Doors will open for them, if they are literate and polished ladies. Don't you agree?"

"Yes, mother, I see the advantages, but I wanted to marry him! We love each other. I wanted to be respectable, even if poor."

"If your affection is true, you can be his consort. It is a common practice in Charleston. Think of your children. They will know Edward is their father, and there is status in that, even if they are his bastards."

Susanna turned from her mother in disdain. Lucy spoke about practicalities, but Susanna felt like she had just been bartered for, like a slave.

"Susanna will come to her senses," thought Lucy. "Allah is merciful. Allah is great!" she chanted.

Lucy was grateful her family was together. She was grateful for her new home and her Muslim community. She felt she had finally stepped out of the quagmire of slavery.

Susanna closed her ears to her mother's prayers. She had prayed to God for a different outcome. She and her children had become Christian, as that was Miss Sarah Smith's command and Edward's desire, but Lucy still clung to her Muslim ways.

Susanna cried when the baby was born. She was healthy and free! Her name was Martha Sophia Moor. And she looked white, but with Susanna's mulatto father, all of Susanna's children were considered mulatto. Susanna's life was still steeped in the quagmire.

Was Edward ecstatic with the news of his third daughter's birth? No, he did not visit or even send a gift of acknowledgement. But how could he? He was on his European honeymoon with his bride, a plain woman no other planter could love. But her dowry was most generous and included a plantation his father had coveted.

CH. 14. The *Peculiar Institution*

1801

Charleston

Since their return to South Carolina, the Hanscome brothers focused on their true loves - Thomas his plantations and James his medical practice.

"Thomas, I have decided to make some changes in my life this new year and wanted your opinion. I might purchase Robert Deas' land on the Stono on John's Island. What do you think of our being neighbors?"

"Are you referring to Alexander Chisolm's old plantation?"

"Yes, about 550 acres, mainly highland and some pine."

"And marsh, too," chuckled Thomas. "Well, why not? You like new challenges, but aren't you spreading yourself a little thin - medical practice, assemblyman, planter? You'll need many slaves, very expensive, for it to be profitable. And maybe a doctor to treat your exhaustion."

"I'm going to sell 37 Meeting Street to pay for it, well part of it. My most rewarding medical work is with the mentally ill and my clinic for the poor. I've decided to close my practice. Deas is fine with my making several payments on my plantation. Yes, Meeting Street definitely has to be sold now that I have to be in Columbia while the Assembly is in session. I wish they hadn't moved the seat from Charleston."

What precisely were James' legislative interests?

Columbia

Dr. James Hanscome approached the dais.

"My fellow legislators: I have several items I wish to have this honorable assembly address.

"First, the restriction on slave importation needs to be lifted. The increased demand for cotton has increased our need for inexpensive labor. The slave trade was closed after the Stono rebellion more than sixty years ago. Why? It was assumed that our labor demands could be met by the natural increase of our more docile, native born slaves. It was further assumed that future slave rebellions would be fueled by new African slaves, many of whom were educated and freedom bound. For our safety, the Negro Act of 1740 was instituted, limiting the education and the freedom of movement of slaves. Since then, we have had no rebellions, save our own from England. Simply, our circumstances have changed. Our slaves are now more costly than the land we plant! We must have additional sources of labor. We have been unsuccessful at increasing the appeal of indenture bonds, and, as you know, light-skinned Europeans die in our sun and from our fevers. Or, at the first opportunity, they simply run away and disappear into whiteness. We need an influx of new slaves. We simply must change the law.

"I now speak to the concerns of the northern states. One of the objections to slavery from our northern states is the inhumane treatment slaves. Have we not learned from our errors? Punishment and capricious lashings never served our purpose. We want productive, healthy and happy servants. Thus, I suggest we include in the new slavery bill the following humane treatment guidelines:

1. Church attendance: No slaves will be forced to work on Sundays. We forbid slave only churches. Instead, we want slaves to attend the same church as their masters. This will increase proper slave attitudes, religious guidance, baptism, peace and harmony on the plantation. The church balconies will be open to all worshipping slaves and freedmen.
2. Task system: No slaves will be required to work from sunrise to sunset. Plantation tasks will be assigned to each servant. When the task is completed he or she may help family members complete their tasks or they may choose to work in their own vegetable gardens, care for their hearths or sew clothes. Land must be provided for slave gardens. Time must be available for personal welfare. In this way slaves can provide for their own food, shelter, and clothing, indeed a fine cost savings for planters. Proper rest, cleanliness and nutrition are necessary for prime health and prime production. Consequences for misbehavior must be understood. Expectations must be clear.
3. Family life: No slaves will be forced to breed. Natural affectionate partnerships will be encouraged for the promotion of child increase and nurturing child care.
4. Movement restrictions: All slaves must wear copper tags if owners hire out their labor. The current pass system must be enforced, with fines paid by negligent owners. Organization and management are essential to proper social order.
5. Awards and recognition: Humane planters will be recognized annually.

May I also suggest that the northern states adopt a similar humane model for workers in their textile mills.

"My second issue is the need for state funding of an insane asylum. Our current county philanthropies are unable to provide for their special needs. Families, try as many may, do not provide humane treatment for their strange ones, their idiots, those who mutter under their breath, rage, cry or wander away. Beatings and purges do not cure madness. Some have died from abandonment, lack of care or in chains. The rare few who are loved fare much better. We must follow a compassionate model of care. Insanity is a medical illness, not the punishment of an angry god. The Lord Proprietors in the 1690's set a precedent by placing the responsibility for the mentally ill in the public domain. An infirmary was established for the mentally ill in the 1760's, but we must progress further. A lunatic asylum, open to all, regardless of color, is the answer."

What happened to Dr. Hanscome's proposed legislation?

Bill # 1. Passed. The slave ships returned for five years. During that time more than 40,000 African slaves were sold in Charleston's slave markets. Proper treatment for slaves was outlined in the bill.

Bill #2. Not passed. Funding was denied for an insane asylum. This issue was considered a county responsibility. Twenty more years would pass before an insane asylum was approved.

Creekside

"Have a cigar, James," said Thomas as he patted his brother on the back. "I want to congratulate you on lifting the ban on slave importation. That's really a fine feather in your cap. I suppose you intend to benefit from your own legislation."

"Thank you. Of course, this was legislation was a boon to me. My new cotton fields will be much more profitable with additional slave hands. I must say, I am dismayed that the insane asylum wasn't funded, but it speaks to the lack of concern our public has for the unfortunate mentally ill. Humane treatment is necessary."

"Don't be discouraged, James, you did accomplish one major goal."

James did not run for the South Carolina Assembly again. He needed more time to devote to his plantation. Did the Hanscomes not see that slavery, that *peculiar institution*, in any form, was inhumane treatment? No, they did not. They had donned their blinders, just like Thomas Hanscome's thoroughbreds.

What, pray tell, happened to James's Oxford views that slavery was archaic, foreign and inhumane? He, like Thomas, fell back into the arms of the society that pampered them. They rationalized. They denied. They prospered. They were planters.

CH. 15. Spring Love Blossoms

1807

Creekside

"I do believe we have an agreement," said a pleased Thomas Hanscome to fellow John's Island planter, Charles Freer. Thomas had just expanded his plantation by 600 acres on the Keeabrook (Kiawah) River, excluding a ¼ acre family burial plot for Charles Freer and his heirs. "Let's have a brandy and smoke a cigar." Now that Thomas had sufficient slaves for his 1574 acres he could capitalize on that cotton market. But his land was not his only love.

1810

Charleston

Thomas' marsh tacky mares had accepted the Arabian stud's advances earlier than usual this year. "This will be the best foaling season," thought Thomas. The closer the births to January first, the more competitive his three year olds would be. His crossbreeds had been stealing the shows and the races. They were champions of speed and endurance.

"Are you not also a stallion in search of a mare?" teased Thomas' imported English horse trainer. "Rich planters are in as much demand as our stable's foals. You could have your pick of the belles."

"Maybe next spring, but I am encouraging James to rise to the occasion this season," Thomas jested in return. The truth be known, Thomas had little interest in the local ladies, for marriage anyway. It would be up to James to carry on the Hanscome lineage. Thomas, now fifty, felt relieved. He had loved two ladies in his life and lost both. He could devote his life to his plantations, horses and fine cadre of life-long planter friends. They were his family. Building wealth had been easy for him. Love had not.

The mating season was productive in Charleston, too. The season opened during the holiday balls. By March the ardent planters looking for mates were frenetic. And the unclaimed belles? Their dowries grew larger as the season progressed, until they became most beautiful and very desirable. Pairing of family fortunes was always a consideration.

"I don't have time!" was always James' lament when Thomas prodded him to learn to dance. He had just celebrated the last payment on his plantation, but his true love was his infirmary for the poor and the mentally ill.

"You are thirty-eight years old James. Our Hanscome line will disappear unless you find a wife," entreated Thomas. Guilt had never worked on James before, but why not keep trying?

"I am not sure I want that yoke, but you Thomas? You are not too old to marry. I trust you have not yet been gelded," said James, not taking Thomas' bait.

And so it went year after year, each Hanscome passing the wedding gauntlet to the other. This year romance would claim them both. It was in the air. Romance was contagious in Charleston. Not even Dr. Hanscome had a cure. Still, he refused to attend the balls.

"I admire your dedication to the paupers," said Dr. Hanscome to his assistant, Miss Grace Jones. "Why aren't you at the ball tonight?"

"I have grown tired of the annual parades and charades. At twenty-four I am relegated to the undesirable camp," she laughed. "To my parents' dismay, I have no interest in marrying. And why are you not at the ball, good doctor?" she retorted.

"I have patients to serve. My calling is to heal. It is my life's purpose. And I have a plantation to oversee. I have no time for balls or courting," smiled James.

Be wary of what you deny, he thought to himself. Grace Jones could be the one. She was a tall, pleasant-faced, curious woman with a keen interest in medicine. What a stroke of kismet that she showed up at the infirmary one day, seeking to volunteer. She was so kind and gentle with the most difficult of his mentally ill patients. Grace was most well-named, for his patients were miraculously healed by her calm presence and warm smile. James, however, was not calmed. Instead, he grew quite excited, indeed, and found it most difficult to stand too close.

They were engaged by the end of the season. Yes, James never attended one ball. Her parents, old planters, and Thomas could not have been more pleased. Did it free Thomas from his breeding responsibility? It did. A wedding date was set.

"Ietrow, I need a miracle in grooming. My outdated London formal wardrobe will not do for James' wedding."

"You are right, sir. I am the miracle man at your service. I have only London's newest attire for Charleston's best. Your pauper style will hardly do for the wedding of the season. What happened to that man of London fashion? Did he become an overseer or a stable boy? I do think you need a new valet."

"It is nice to see you, too," said Thomas, enjoying a good spar. "I have no valet. No one could ever replace your services, Ietrow. I am pleased your haberdashery has flourished."

"As your cotton business booms, my business also thrives. Upstairs from my shop, I am boarding my tailors and seamstresses, in separate rooms, of course. I have hired three new temporary slaves for the season at $3.00 a month, in addition to the four more slaves I own. I want to thank you. I couldn't have succeeded without your patronage. And to celebrate my good fortune, I have chosen a bride."

"And who is your heart's desire, Ietrow?" asked Thomas. Ietrow and Thomas shared a fine repartee. They were close, as close as a slave and a master could be. They grew up together, but of course, since Ietrow's emancipation, they did not socialize. Ietrow was proud of his status as part of the wealthy Charleston mulatto strata of society and also a slave owner.

"A white woman," laughed Ietrow, as he knew that would get Thomas' attention.

"Charleston never ceases to amaze me. Now how did you manage that?" asked Thomas as his eyebrows rose in disbelief.

"She's a Moor, legally white, but she actually is white, too. Her name is Lucy Moor, Moroccan, as her name suggests. I admire her struggle for freedom and her artistic talents. She has designed all my fine millinery. And she loves me with a passion, old as I am."

"Congratulations to you, Ietrow. This spring is the time for passion - brother James' passion, your passion, my horses' passions. I want to hear more about this Lucy."

"Our love has been a slow ember burning. She has worked for me for years. She is very feisty, like a cat. At first I was afraid to tangle with her. If you casually glance toward the ladies section, you will see her selling one of her latest millinery creations to that lovely, young mulatto."

"I see them both. Their beauty could put London to shame. The mulatto reminds me of Jenny. Her carriage and posture are a bit haughty. What is her name?"

"Nancy, Nancy Randall. She is more than haughty - she actually believes she's a princess."

"And what do you attribute that elitist attitude to?"

"She's the daughter of John Randall, your father's lifelong friend. He raised her to be a fine lady. She has been asked to join the women's auxiliary to the Brown Fellowship Society."

"What an interesting piece of news. John Randall helped oversee my business while I was in London. Unfortunately, he died before my return. I am actually Louisa's and Nancy's guardians. I have met with Louisa many times regarding financial issues, but the last time I saw Nancy she was just an awkward school girl. She is indeed a surprise, a most lovely one. John must have cared a great deal for them as he provided well for their future."

"Of course I don't really know, but some say Louisa, John Randall's mistress, was actually the granddaughter of his Mammy, Pearl."

"Gossip is sometimes quite true, Ietrow. I should come to Charleston more frequently for the social news. So tell me, now that you are a wealthy, slave owning merchant, have you been invited to join the Brown Fellowship Society?"

"I have and I am a proud member. But we are more than just a group of artisans and merchants securing cemetery plots for our loved ones. We also have social functions and philanthropies, such as helping your brother treat the new batches of African slaves - close to 40,000 imported in just a few years. His clinic can't treat them all, thus our society helps distribute health education to the slaves."

"I'm sure James appreciates your assistance. Yes, it was a boon to all planters that the slave trade was reopened. We had no labor, at any price, for our new cotton fields or your haberdashery. James also helped with the legislation that insisted on fair treatment of slaves, encouraged the task system and baptisms. Now he is insisting we drain our swamps that breed the mosquitoes."

"Dr. James is always working on a worthwhile health project. Miss Jones was fortunate to be his nurse, or they never would have met. And speaking of meeting, Miss Lucy and Miss Nancy are coming our way. Would you like to be introduced?" offered Ietrow.

Thomas nodded in the affirmative. He had been remiss in executing his proper guardianship duties. It was high time he met the beautiful Nancy Randall.

"Mr. Thomas, may I present to you my bride to be, Miss Lucy Moor and Miss Nancy Randall..."

"May I offer my carriage to take you to your door?" asked Thomas, after pleasantries had been exchanged.

"I thank you for your invitation, but as we have just been introduced, I think a carriage ride is a bit presumptuous," replied Nancy. Her words may have been a bit discouraging, but her smile was inviting. "That and my home is only a short distance from here. But if you'd like to escort me, we can walk."

Miss Nancy Randall paid no deference to the highly esteemed Thomas Hanscome. She definitely was not stepping into a total stranger's carriage. She had not remembered meeting him in the past. Had her mother neglected to tell Nancy that he was their guardian? It was an unpopular practice that freedmen still needed a guardian to vouch for their good character and take care of their assets. Many mulattos, like Ietrow, still had that slave mentality that positioned them one down, regardless of their education, wealth and character. Nancy refused to comply with such nonsense. Her father had instilled a high sense of worth in her.

"How refreshing and unique she is," thought Thomas with his mischievous grin. He liked that this Nancy was her own person and did not bow to his position of planter superiority. Her regal carriage, warm brown eyes, European features and bronzed skin reminded him of his London Jenny. Was it just that he missed his Jenny? He thought not, although his heart pinged every time he thought of Jenny. Should he tell this young Nancy he was her guardian? He thought not. Not today. Thomas Hanscome felt a stirring. He was intrigued.

Did Nancy Randall's curiosity outweigh her logic? Or did she foolishly believe that the rigid rules of color would not apply to her?

"Catharine Lucy, do you think I should allow myself to be courted by this Thomas Hanscome?" asked Nancy of her best friend, Catharine Lucy Moor. Catharine Lucy was the granddaughter of Lucy Moor and the daughter of Susanna Moor and the planter Edward Smith. Edward had his white family, but he found time to keep his promises to Susanna. Catharine Lucy loved her father, but she cringed when she heard the term, "bastard octoroon."

Nancy and Catharine Lucy had been schoolmates. They could read, write, figure numbers and speak French. They were the ladies of the brown smart set, schooled in the fine arts of dance, piano, harp, flute and vocal music. As much as possible, they emulated their whiter planter sisters' practiced refinement. Did they go to school with the planters' daughters? No. The schools were segregated.

"I can hardly advise you," replied Catharine Lucy, but of course, she did. "If you want a respectable marriage, do not begin this dalliance. You cannot marry a white man, but there are many prosperous Brown Fellowship Society members who would gladly offer their hand, men of good character. Your dance card at the last ball was full of marital prospects. Marry for the security. Please don't see this Thomas Hanscome as a light-hearted flirtation. Please nip it in its bud," begged Catharine Lucy. "He's a planter. He can do anything he wants, but your reputation will be forever lost."

"I have counseled myself with your very words, but..." Nancy was wavering.

"No hesitations, please Nancy. Be resolved. Do you want to be his consort, like my mother was to my father? Do you want to see him off to his social engagements while you dutifully stay behind? Do you want your children raised as my sisters and I were, by our mother? My mother is lonely. Do you want to hear the street gossips murmur 'bastard mulatto,' to your children, as they did when we were school girls? And what about his older age? He could inadvertently leave you with young children to tend, just like your father, who died when you were six. Not all white planters provide well for their bastards. You could end up in Charleston neck, a pauper, with hungry mouths to feed."

Catharine Lucy wanted to spare her dear friend Nancy pain. She didn't want to see her used and discarded, as happened so frequently with these liaisons. And even worse, she could be beaten and left by the side of the road for the buzzards.

"You are correct, dear friend. I will discourage his advances. I will consider a Brown Fellowship Society marriage proposal."

Nancy sighed. She had found no other man who set her heart aflutter like Thomas Hanscome. In just one meeting, she felt he was the one. Perhaps it was the fiery, red tint in his auburn hair that caught the sunlight, like a halo. Or perhaps it was his always ready grin. Or his quick mind. Or that he didn't touch her, but teased her and watched for her disappointment. He was a master of subtlety, as though he had a master plan of seduction. It was as though he was grooming a horse for a most exciting race. Of course, all of this closeness and no action made her a veritable lioness, ready to spring. How silly. How ridiculous.

To trust him could be her ruin. But then John Randall, her father, had openly loved her mother and her. And Catharine Lucy Moor's father had also been honorable. Still, most of these dalliances ended up not much different from the night-time prowls of the planters in the slave cabins. Their light-skinned children were never claimed and often sold before they were weaned. The planter's wives could not tolerate proof of their husband's true proclivities. Sold, mind you. Sold. Babes torn from their mothers' breasts and sold.

"Yes, I will stop Thomas Hanscome's advances, but I could be in trouble if I am not tactful and polite," she counseled herself. "He could even enslave me if he chose. Who would question his word? No one. I am determined. He is too dangerous a temptation. He certainly is not acting like my guardian angel. He is trifling with my affections."

What was a mulatto? Was it a fourth, an eighth or a half of white, black or Indian descent? All the fractions were confusing. One hundred and fifty years of mixing made this unique class. Some had recently been slaves; some had been freed generations ago. Some looked white, had blue eyes, fine hair and

African features. Others were dark-complected, dark-eyed, curly-haired and had European features. More often than not, their skin was golden – not palest white, not blackest black.

In Charleston the ratio of white to black was one to eight, but it was unclear how many were truly mulattos. Security was an illusion for these freedmen. All knew that their freedom and relative privilege could be wiped out by one slave rebellion. Many planters, while they profited from slavery, were also rightfully afraid for their lives. Many slaves lived in terror and were also rightfully afraid for their lives. The mulattos were the relative glue of safety in this powder keg of the *peculiar institution*.

What was this mulatto message of hope for the planters?

"We are one with you, white planters. We are your sons and your daughters. You have nothing to fear. We support you. We love you. We also prosper by the institution of slavery. We are the brown slave masters. Trust us."

What was the mulatto message of hope for field slaves?

"We are one with you, slaves. You, too, can be free and prosper. Do not give up hope. You can aspire to be us. You can hire out, buy your freedom and your family's freedom. We have done it and so can you. If you prosper, you can buy your own slaves."

There were also wealthy mulatto planters who paid many dollars for legal whiteness and eventually whitened out every African feature by careful intermarriage. And there were also very white slaves, like Lucy Moor. The age of indentured servant had passed. Since the latest importation of Africans, the term Negro became synonymous with slave and inferiority. In fact, the darker one's skin, the more inferior they were thought to be.

Visitors to Charleston often remarked about the handsome, well-dressed mulattos. These same visitors also found it peculiar they were also slave owners. How could they enslave when they had been slaves? Did they step down when a planter passed them on the street? No, they did not. But did they defer? Yes, they ingratiated themselves. Good relationships with the planters ensured their success.

Openly and brashly, Thomas and many other planters found mulatto women the most beautiful in the Carolinas. Did they care if they broke the fornication laws? No, they did whatever they pleased. No one would be lashing the planters' backs for flaunting the rules.

Nancy Randall knew all this to be true. As Catharine Lucy had predicted, Thomas Hanscome came courting. Did Nancy turn her head when his carriage followed at a distance behind her? No, she calmed her blush and stilled her heartbeat, held her gaze forward and wished him away. "Breathe, Nancy – just breathe and walk tall. He is the devil incarnate. He will soon be gone."

Finally, he offered her a ride and a picnic lunch on his sloop in the harbor. Did Nancy refuse? No, she did not. She simply smiled and took his arm as he opened the carriage door. Her heart raced and her golden skin turned a delicate pink. Her determination melted as his first grin flashed. He was exciting. This was meant to be.

And Thomas? He was lost in Nancy's gaze alone. Her gold-flecked, brown eyes were that entrancing. She had curly, black hair from her mother and her father's fine pointed English nose and features. Perhaps her high cheekbones and thin, tall frame hinted of her Indian legacy. The result was simply stunning. She was beautiful.

"Nancy, I do not want you to be afraid of me or think of me as some stranger. Apparently, your mother hasn't informed you. I am your legal guardian."

"No, I did not know that. She never told me I had a guardian," responded Nancy as she visibly relaxed. A dutiful guardian would certainly behave himself. Simply, she had misconstrued his intentions.

"Yes, your father appointed me to be your guardian. And when I return you safely to your door, I will talk with your mother. You will see that I am harmless and only have the best of intentions."

Was Thomas the devil incarnate or the haloed savior? Nancy thought the latter, when he took her in his arms and gently, oh so gently, kissed her. Then he gently guided her inside her home.

And was Louisa Randall displeased when Thomas explained his desire to see her daughter? No, she heartily agreed to their courtship, if it could be called such. Soon, Thomas picked up Nancy every time he was in Charleston for an outing. They strolled the promenade, attended horse races, sailed and picnicked on his schooner. Of course, he did not take her to his private clubs. Did the greater Charleston planter society take notice? Yes, they did.

"I hear, Thomas, you have taken a consort, one Nancy Randall," said James, after they finished discussing cotton futures.

"You heard right," said Thomas with a smile. "The social news of Charleston flies faster than a carrier pigeon. I do find Nancy to be the most captivating, young lady. She is John Randall's daughter. Actually, I am her guardian."

"Do you think that is wise? You may gain the disdain of our planter friends. I know your penchant for those of a darker hue. I worry about you, older brother. Is this Nancy just a substitute for that fine London Lady, Miss Jenny?"

"I find it interesting that you fondly call Jenny 'The London Lady.' Had you remained in London, as was your initial plan, you would have thought nothing about our marrying. You loved Jenny as an older sister. Now you have readopted the *peculiar* Charleston mores."

"Well, please say you aren't considering marriage," admonished James.

"No, I am not. As you know that is impossible. I leave that venerable institution to you." Thomas smiled. When had James become so self-righteous and parental toward him? Was he that old or was James simply being an arrogant doctor? Thomas changed the focus back to James.

"And speaking of that subject, are you ready for your wedding?"

"Yes, I am ready for my wedding and I am ready to return to work. My face cracks from too many smiles from these engagement parties. We will be leaving next week for a short honeymoon voyage up the American coast."

"Ah, as Vanessa and I did. Our marriage was a wonderful time in my life, but so long ago. My memories are as a dream."

"And Nancy Randall is real? You know she will not be welcomed at St. Cecelia's for my wedding."

"Yes, I know that. But I do want you and Grace to meet her."

"Of course, I will meet her. I will also ask Grace, but I leave that decision up to her. This is not London."

Did any of the other planters discuss Thomas' choice of companions with him? Of course not. To air the taboo subject would give his liaison permanence. Poor taste would then follow poor taste. Definitely, if they waited, Thomas would certainly tire of her and come to his senses.

And from the elite Brown Fellowship Society, did Nancy receive support? She only confided in her friend Catharine Lucy when she was in despair. Oh no, Nancy was tight-lipped about the nature of her love trysts with Thomas. She would not put into words their laughter and sensual compatibilities. She would not put into words Thomas' patience as he taught her the art of making love. She would not tell her best friend how it was she first thrust herself upon Thomas. Yes, Thomas had suggested a swim in the turquoise sea and Nancy simply jumped overboard, clothes and all.

"You will drown in all those garments," Thomas had grinned.

"Well then, you'd best hoist me aboard and help me find something more suitable," Nancy cleverly retorted.

Of course, Thomas was too gallant not to comply.

Today, however, Nancy did not feel so clever or much loved. She had discovered her proper place in Thomas' planter life. She was excluded. Her proper place was to be always waiting, alone. She was hurt and angry.

"You are right again, Catharine Lucy," wailed Nancy. "I have barely seen Thomas in weeks. He said he wished he could include me in his brother's wedding festivities, but he could not. He asked for my understanding."

"So now you understand the role of a consort - only welcomed in bed," quipped Catharine Lucy, looking intently at her friend, as though to ask her for the details of their private intimacies.

"My mother counsels me to be patient. She says love finds a way. But I am out of control - elated one moment, despondent the next. I am no longer in charge of me."

"You are just in love, which knows no sanity. However, your mother accepted your father's rules. Will you?"

"My mother was raised a slave, so her discreet life with my father was heaven by comparison. I am looking into passages to Philadelphia. They no longer have those nasty miscegenation laws, a sign that we are no longer in the subhuman category. I could walk down the street and not worry about being snatched. I want to be truly free. I want to be able to marry someone I love."

"If you want total freedom, no marriage will suit you – anywhere," laughed Catharine Lucy. "Men will always expect deference. They must rule the roost."

"That may be the case. I can accept that, but not being invisible. Slaves are invisible."

"Once your father's money is gone, how do you propose to support yourself in Philadelphia?"

"I can teach. I have heard glowing reports from some of our Brown Fellowship Society friends who have relatives there."

Yes, Nancy had run into the true limits of Thomas' affections. She was miserable. The spring blossoms of love had wilted in the heat of the Charleston summer. And what was Thomas' response to Nancy's planned move to Philadelphia?

"I love you. Please don't leave me, Nancy," begged Thomas. Yes, he begged. Nancy finally consented to see him, to say goodbye. "I will buy two adjacent homes in Charleston for us. Both will be yours to oversee, but we must be discreet, if we want our relationship tolerated. When we live at Creekside, we will have more latitude. And I promise I will provide for you and our children in my will. We can live as husband and wife."

"I will consider your offer, Thomas, but I want to marry the man I love and live as husband and wife in the open. Your friends will never welcome me in their homes, nor will they accept our invitations. We might grow to feel like prisoners in our own mansions. I know *discreet*. I was raised with *discreet.*

"I am angry Thomas, with myself as much as you. Tell me why you call me a mulatto? Am I truly like a mule? A hybrid, just like your horses? And what about our children? Will they be called quadroons? Bastard quadroons? I don't care if you withdraw your offer. I am a person, Thomas. Call me a person. If you truly want me, you must know who I am. And I will not be hidden away in a bedroom. I will not be *discreet*." And with that her rage dissolved into tears.

Did Thomas leave in a disgusted huff or embarrassed fluster? No, he did not. Instead, he held and comforted Nancy while she sobbed. When she quieted, he softly spoke.

"I am not responsible for the Carolina rules, dear Nancy."

"You may not think so, but you and all the other white planters are responsible for slavery, awful slavery. You grow rich from slave labor." Nancy wailed again. "And you do have the power to change the laws."

"I cannot defend slavery or the laws that protect it. Nor will I change them. Slavery is woven into the very fabric of our life. I accept it and prosper from it. Please turn your face to me, dear Nancy. Look at me. I want you to hear my words. I love you, I love my land and I love being rich. And you will grow wealthy, too. Nancy, you must accept our system of slavery, if you accept my offer. You will own slaves, too. They are my property and they will become your property when I die. I do not want to have uncomfortable conversations like this with you, again."

"Do you think I can live with you, without sharing my true feelings, because they run contrary to your own? Because they make you uncomfortable? I don't want to pretend."

"Nancy, you must simply deny the parts of the Carolina system you don't like, simply block them from your thoughts. If you can't, you would be miserable with me. Then your plan to move to Philadelphia is a better option. I won't like it, but it is an option."

"I will not lie to myself - deny my truths. Is that what you mean by denial?"

"I don't want you to be untrue to your soul, but you can change your perspectives about life. Focus on the beauty all around us. Focus on our good fortune. Our children, the light, the dark and the golden of them, will be equally loved. And won't it be fun to see who they resemble? You are too concerned about what they will be called. Now smile. They will be envied and called rich."

"You have that uncanny way of ruining all my intense emotions. I must laugh. I truly don't want to move to Philadelphia and live alone. All the same, I have spoken my truths. And you have heard them. They will always be there, but I need not dwell on them, at least not often. I love you, too. I will do my best to honor you. I will focus on the beautiful life we can make together. But please promise two things."

"And what are they?"

"First, please do not call our children by those derogatory terms, mulatto, octoroon or the like. It reminds me of descriptions used at the slave market to describe the merchandise."

"And what terms do you use for yourself? Our children will not be white or black."

"Call me a lady. You don't normally say, 'I'm a white man.' You just say, 'I am a man.' If you must designate my color for some legal document, use the term colored. I don't like the term brown, as in the Brown Fellowship Society. But I find that less objectionable than mulatto."

"I will call our children lucky and you my queen," laughed Thomas. "I like your golden brown color. Maybe I'll just call you and our children 'golden' and you can call me 'pale.' And I truly hope their ears don't stick out from their head, like mine. You need to be less sensitive to the labels. When it gets right down to it, Nancy, we are all mixtures in the Carolinas – English, French, Dutch, Scottish, Irish, Moroccan, Spanish, German, Angolan, Senegalese, Indians, East Indians, Muslims and Jews. Maybe we should call all of us mulattos! Or better yet, thoroughbreds, like my strong horses. I like that description, the thoroughbred Hanscome children. Strong. I can see by the look on your face, you don't like that term, either. And since you don't like the term mulatto, 'colored' it will be. And what is your other wish?"

"Do not die before our children reach their age of majority. I want them to know who you are. I have only a few memories of my old father. Most of all I remember him telling me how bright and beautiful I was. I cling to that memory."

"And you are bright and beautiful. I will tell you stories of your father and my father, if you you'd like. Uncle John was kind and he hated slavery, too. In spite of his feelings, he chose to stay. He chose the planter's life. He chose to profit from slave labor. You could call him a hypocrite – like we all are, in some way or another. But I cannot promise you how long I will live. I am fifty, old enough to be your grandfather. I will promise to cherish you for as long as I live. Now will you accept my offer?"

"Yes. Yes I will, Thomas. And I will cherish you, too. All I can do is to tell Dr. James that he needs to keep you alive." Nancy smiled.

"It is nice to hear your spirited laugh, again. I am relieved. We will do well together. I am wealthy. We will travel, laugh and play. Let's forget about Charleston for awhile. The world is at our disposal. The world does not operate by Carolina rules. You are the best and we will have the best. James' would like to meet you when he returns from his honeymoon. But let's not be here when he returns. Let us take a long voyage ourselves."

"You mean like a honeymoon without the marriage?"

"Think of ours as a marriage of love and affection, just not a legal one. Yes, a honeymoon."

If Nancy's friends were worried for her, they held their tongues. Ietrow and Lucy put together a fine trousseau for Nancy's honeymoon. Even Catharine Lucy became excited. She secretly thought, "What a privileged life Nancy will have."

Nancy's mother wept tears of joy when she read Nancy's letter:

Dear Mother,

I am having the best time in France. This trip is magical. We are welcomed everywhere. I am treated with great respect in the finest hotels and restaurants. There is no segregation! However, I do imagine this will never happen in Charleston in our life time, but it will happen. Oh, I wish you could experience, dear Mother, such joy, such freedom. The next time we travel abroad, I will insist Thomas take you with us. The shopkeepers so kindly take my money, but that is to be expected. Money speaks all languages and all colors. Tell Lucy I am collecting the in vogue hat patterns and fabrics for her.

Thomas asked a priest to marry us, but no papist certificate would be honored in Charleston, even if I were lily white! I am accepting my fate as a mistress, because I am Thomas' love. If only we could live here, in the open air. He commissioned our oil portraits to be painted, to hang in our parlor, side by side. I find them good likenesses, but Thomas wishes his ears protruded less. I am beginning to believe gentlemen are as vain as ladies.

Soon we will be leaving for Italy, then Constantinople. I had wanted to travel to London, but Thomas said it was too cold this time of year. He promises to take me another time. Thomas wants to return for the spring planting. I am gathering ideas for the wondrous gardens I will create. I see love in all that blooms.

Thomas is taking me to dinner to celebrate my twentieth birthday… and his fiftieth, facts that darken his countenance. I feel so proud to be on his arm. You were right, dear mother. I love him. I love my grand life.

I miss you dreadfully. I will write when I can.

Your loving daughter,

Nancy

CH. 16. For Better and For Worse

1811

Creekside

"It is so wonderful to finally meet you, James," said Nancy as she graciously welcomed him to his childhood home.

Nancy had practiced her greetings, probable rejections and proper responses in front of the mirror. She wanted all to go well. Why was she so afraid? She knew, truly she did know. This was her debut in the white society and she needed to tread lightly. Flawlessly, she hid her anxieties. "I must accept what is," she counseled herself. Stand tall. I will not be wounded. I am charming. Thomas will be most proud of my conduct."

"And will Grace be joining us for dinner?" she casually inquired.

"No, she is not feeling well. But she thanks you for your kind invitation," responded James.

"Please relay my sympathies to your wife. I do hope she recovers soon. Will you be spending the night then?"

"Yes, I accept your gracious hospitality. I would like to hear more about your European trip," said James as he escorted Nancy to dinner, lightly touching her elbow, a gesture she interpreted as acceptance. "Someday I would like to take Grace. Perhaps we might all travel together."

Thomas was relieved that James' manners were impeccable. James had done a fine job of masking whatever reservations he held, if indeed he had any.

Thomas pulled out Nancy's chair, the same chair his mother had used. Nancy rang the delicate silver bell. Dinner was promptly served and delicious. She had asked her domestics to make James' favorite dishes. They, too, were excited to see James. After dinner, they adjourned to the parlor where the slaves kept replacing the candles and refilling the brandy snifters. Laughter was heard late into the evening. The slaves were happy that their master was finally happy. Did they care that Nancy was his choice? Not one bit. Perhaps one of their daughters would be that lucky.

What created the festive air? Was it the brandy? Was it that James saw the light in his brother's eyes that had disappeared when they left London? Was it that James had disclosed that Grace was pregnant and quite ill? Was it that Nancy had told James she was pregnant, too? Was it that Thomas was pleased with James' acceptance of his Nancy?

It mattered not. They were becoming a family. There were going to be children. To celebrate his new family, Thomas announced he intended to renovate the mansion at 143 Tradd Street and purchase an adjacent house on Greenhill Street for Nancy. He wanted both homes ready before the July birth. What could be better?

Nancy was even more elated when Grace reciprocated with a dinner invitation for them.

"I am delighted to meet you, Nancy," said Grace as she squeezed Nancy's hand. Rarely did a white planter touch a person of color, not even in a hand shake. Nancy was relieved. She had dreaded this meeting.

"And congratulations to you on your pregnancy," replied Nancy.

"And to you, too. I hope you are feeling well," replied Grace.

"I am finally feeling wonderful. Thomas told me you are back at James' side, nursing his patients. It must be quite rewarding."

"I enjoy working with the paupers, perhaps because they appreciate our efforts the most. Would you like to help?"

"Yes, thank you for thinking of me. I would like to be of service, but after the baby is born. I would be afraid I might catch some dreadful disease and harm my baby right now. Aren't you concerned?"

"I only work with those patients who aren't infectious and only half a day so I can rest."

"I will ask Thomas what he thinks, perhaps that would be good for me." Why had Nancy acquiesced? Because she desperately wanted to be accepted by one white lady. She was hungry for a friend.

"Absolutely not," said Thomas later. "I understand it is important that Grace accept you, but I don't want you jeopardizing your health. Philanthropic volunteering, like nursing, could be good for you, but please consider it later, Nancy. Do you want me to talk to Grace?"

"No, I agree with you. This is not a good time to become ill. I must learn how to say *no, thank you* to a white person."

"Just smile and say *no, thank you*. You don't have any difficulty saying no to me," replied Thomas with his broad grin.

"Yes, yes. I will work on this, dear Thomas." Nancy vowed she would return to her mirror for practice. "It's just that my mother taught me to always say *yes* to a white person, as if my life could depend on it."

"How silly," Thomas said. "You're not a slave." And he embraced her.

Later Nancy thought, "How can I expect Thomas to understand? He tries, but he's white. Just breathe and pretend Grace is a school friend. Pretend she is Catharine Lucy. Practice." Then Nancy laughed at herself. "I think my best friend is my mirror." After a moment of silent reflection, she came to a new realization. It was not her image in the mirror or practicing pretense that made her courageous. In her heart she was becoming her own best friend, honoring her true self, bit by bit.

Nancy was amazed that when she simply said, *No, thank you* to Grace, she pleasantly accepted her decision. Why had Nancy even worried about this? She didn't even need to use Thomas' negative reaction as an excuse.

As the months passed, the two expectant mothers spent more time together. They marveled at their changing bodies, prepared their nurseries, shared their contentment and lightly touched on their hopes and fears of motherhood. Deep inside, each also knew she would never be the same again. But those feelings they didn't discuss. There were limits to their friendship Nancy knew, but she was nonetheless grateful for the common ground of their pregnancies and their men.

Was Nancy lonely? She had her school friends, her mother, but no other social interactions with the planter class. James and Grace were her only white associates. Thomas entertained his planter men friends, but Nancy never ate dinner with them after they kindly greeted her. Of course, Thomas always greeted Nancy's friends politely, before excusing himself. She tried not to feel hurt when a few of her school friends made excuses not to visit. Instead, she focused on the positive, denied any loneliness and gingerly straddled two worlds. She comforted herself with thoughts of: *Thomas spends as much time with me as he can.* Or, *Soon the baby will be here.* And most importantly, she reminded herself that *Life can't be better.*

1812

Charleston

"I love this bassinet," said Nancy as they shopped in Charleston. "What do you think, Grace?"

"I adore it. Buy it before I do. And look at this perambulator," exclaimed Grace.

Grace even offered to help Nancy with the décor of their Tradd Street mansion. In the place of honor over the fireplace mantel, Nancy boldly hung their oil portraits, side by side. Next she filled their home with priceless furnishings purchased on their European grand tour. Finally, Thomas insisted she buy a new grand piano so she could entertain him in the evenings. And, of course, their children would need music lessons, too.

Creekside

"Look at this steed. He is magnificent," said Thomas proudly to James, as he patted the neck of his prize Arabian.

"I'm looking forward to riding him after our breakfast," replied James. "It is thoughtful of you to let me take him through his paces. I want to see if he can jump."

"I want to see if he can win," laughed Thomas.

Grace and James had arrived the evening before this special occasion. Nancy had the servants prepare an outside breakfast feast similar to the English fox hunts that Thomas so much enjoyed. Neither Grace nor Nancy would ride, due to their condition. Nonetheless, all were festive. The ladies perched themselves atop a carriage to watch the brothers race. The oval race track by the stables was groomed. The hurdles had been placed by the trainer. Thomas would ride his last season's winner, but he wanted to see what his new purchase, the Arabian, could do. The groomsmen had the two horses saddled and ready.

The brothers always enjoyed a good competition. They smoothly moved their horses through their gaits before aligning them at the start. Four sets of hurdles had been placed around the oval track. And then, at the sound of the trainer's command, they were off! Nancy and Grace cheered. What a glorious, sunny spring morning for a family race.

Then the unspeakable happened.

"James! No! James! Thomas, do something!" screamed Grace.

The worst had happened. The Arabian stumbled. Yes, he went down, but not before James flew off and crashed headfirst into a hurdle. Thomas raced to James' side only to find him bleeding profusely from his head, limp and unresponsive. Thomas was dumbfounded. Grace and Nancy also ran to his side. Grace felt James' pulse and sobbed. There was no doubt James was gone. He was only thirty-eight years old.

Thomas sat between Grace and Nancy at the St. John's Presbyterian service attended by all the planters. He forcibly took Nancy's hand and marched her to the front as though to say, "Damn what others think! You belong right here at my side, not in the balcony."

The service was a blur. Thomas was more angry than sad. He felt responsible. After James' burial in the family plot at Creekside they returned home. Silently, Thomas helped Nancy into the house then swiftly left for the stable.

"No!" screamed Nancy as a gun shot rang out. Was it Thomas? No, Thomas was alive. He had shot his Arabian.

And Grace? How was she? She lost her baby and would receive no visitors, not even Nancy. One day Thomas sadly informed Nancy that Grace had followed her dear James to the grave. Grace, the epitome of health, simply stopped eating, took to her bed, shuttered the windows and waited for the inevitable.

"I don't know if I want to go on with our charade, Thomas!" sobbed Nancy after Grace lay next to James in the Hanscome cemetery. "I miss Grace so and now I have no friends. I believe I should go back to my mother's in Charleston. I am so lonely. And you? You need to marry and have legitimate Hanscome heirs."

"I don't care about the legitimacy of our children, Nancy. Just look at the color of Charleston. It is brown. We are not alone. Please don't abandon me. I love you! Our children have my name. They will also hold their heads high as the true Hanscome heirs."

July 24, 1812

"It's a boy!" shouted the Creekside slaves.

"Isn't he beautiful!" declared Nancy, as she handed him over to Thomas. "Beautiful, just beautiful!" she repeated over and over.

"Yes he is, but *Beautiful* is no name for a boy," laughed Thomas. "What do you want to name him?"

"I'd like to name him Joseph, that is, if you agree. I like that Biblical name, as Joseph overcame being enslaved and rose to great heights. And Joseph was beautiful on the inside, where it counts. That is, unless you want to follow the Hanscome tradition with another Thomas?" asked Nancy.

"That tradition can be most confusing," replied Thomas. "Traditions were meant to be changed. I actually prefer the name Joseph. And let's not tell him your first choice for his name was *Beautiful*. Do you feel lonely now?" he teased.

Nancy smiled. "I am most content, Thomas. A child is just what the doctor ordered. And you?"

"I'm just getting started. Joseph is simply the first of our line of Hanscomes."

"We will be the talk of the town, Thomas."

"Well then, let's give them more to talk about."

1815

"It's a girl!"

Both Nancy and Thomas were thrilled with another healthy baby. But poor little Joseph was miserable. At first he was bewildered, but when the baby wasn't taken away, he threw himself on the floor in a rage. Poor child! Finally, when Nancy passed the baby to Thomas he quickly scampered to her side. What did they call her? Louisa Rebecca, after Nancy's mother. What a special child to have two names. Thomas had preferred Rebecca, but deferred to Nancy's wish to remember her mother. Yes, many times Thomas deferred to Nancy's wishes, asked for her ideas, and this respect made her love him even deeper.

Nancy was busy. She had decided not to have mammies for her children. Thomas thought she would be exhausted and she was, in spite of her personal slave, Sally. When Nancy became pregnant with their third child she relented. They purchased a young girl who would remain with the children until they came of age. And Thomas was pleased to have Nancy's undivided attention at dinner, again.

1817

"It's a girl!"

She was named Elizabeth Sarah, for Thomas' mother. This time little Joseph held her and even gave her a kiss. And it was Louisa Rebecca's turn to look forlorn and abandoned. Soon the mammy took the babe away to the nursery and Thomas took the other two to the kitchen for a snack. Nancy closed her eyes in contented peace and thought, *Life is grand.*

1818

Charleston

"I am so excited," said Martha Sophia on her 15th birthday. She was Catharine Lucy's youngest sister. The room was full of well wishers, including Nancy Randall.

"What a festive party! Thank you for inviting me, Catharine Lucy. I have been cooped up with my children and in need of friends," said Nancy Randall.

"I thought you needed an outing. You rarely leave Creekside these days. Do you feel like you are being held captive in the country?" asked Catharine Lucy.

"Do you mean kept like a slave?" Nancy laughed. "I actually love my life. And while Thomas has taught me much about farming, he has agreed to move part-time to Tradd Street. For me, yes for me, he is actually selling 600 acres to Hugh Wilson. I do miss Charleston, you, Catharine Lucy, and my mother. None of you felt comfortable at the plantation. I could just sense it."

"How wonderful you are moving home. You are correct, Nancy, I always felt awkward at Creekside." Then Catharine Lucy's eyes narrowed as she digested the implications of this news. "Is he giving up planting? Selling all his land? Are you moving to Europe? I know you felt so equal there. Truly free."

"Mother says now that I am fifteen I can accept suitors," interrupted Martha Sophia with great excitement.

"You certainly have blossomed into a radiant beauty. You resemble your grandmother, Lucy Moor. Is there anyone who turns your head?" asked Nancy, not wanting to answer Catharine Lucy's probing questions, questions she needed to discuss with Thomas, first. Nancy trusted him completely and sometimes Catharine Lucy could be too nosy. *Deny the unknown future and enjoy today* was Nancy's new motto.

"Why thank you, Nancy, for the compliment. Actually, Ietrow says Thomas Inglis, one of his Brown Fellowship Society friends, is interested in courting me."

"I thought he was married," said Catharine Lucy, the protective older sister.

"He is, to an insane woman named Rachel, but he is looking for a place for her so he can be free to marry again. He has taken care of her for ten years," said Martha Sophia.

"It's too bad they haven't been able to fund a state lunatic asylum. Thomas' brother, Dr. James, tried, but to no avail," offered Nancy. "Tell me, why does this Thomas interest you?

"He is a wealthy barber and slave owner. His planter father helped set him up in business. Handsome, too, and very kind. I admire a   man who cares for an ill wife as he has," stated Martha Sophia.

"Well, you'd better look elsewhere. There will be no courting until he can free himself from his demented wife. I hear she has aberrations – talks and cries constantly about her visions," added Catharine Lucy.

"Martha Sophia, do you want me to help?" asked Nancy. "My Thomas knows Thomas Inglis' planter father who may put in a word for his son at the Infirmary for the Mentally Ill. Perhaps there is room for Rachel Inglis."

"Yes, that could solve our dilemma. Do they allow freedmen at the Infirmary?" asked Martha Sophia.

"There are a few, but they have to pay an extravagant sum," answered Nancy. "And, of course he'll have to give a generous donation to the church for his divorce."

Soon Rachel Inglis was placed in the Infirmary and Thomas Inglis began courting Martha Sophia. Why would such a wealthy man be interested in a woman with no dowry? Because she was born free with lovely, light skin and was young, twenty-two years younger than he. He wanted a family and heirs for his business and properties - land and slaves. He was ready to live.

1819

Creekside

"It's a girl!"

Nancy looked deeply into Thomas' eyes to see if he was disappointed that the babe was yet another girl. She was pleased that he happily held her.

"It will be interesting to see who she resembles," Thomas remarked. "So far we have Joseph, our blue-eyed, curly dark-haired, golden-skinned boy. I actually believe he resembles his Grandfather John's fine features. And little Louisa Rebecca actually has fair skin – I thought her tone would deepen as she grew. She's going to be quite stunning, like you, with her big brown eyes."

"I wonder if any of our children will look alike?" smiled Nancy.

"Time will tell, but so far, each of our children is quite unique. And very beautiful. Do you think we dare name this girl, *Beautiful?*"

"Be serious, Thomas. *Beautiful* is not a traditional name. What would you like to call her?"

"I like Mary or Ann, my two sisters' names. I wish you had met my sisters. It still saddens me that they both died so young and childless. It broke my mother's heart."

"We are indeed fortunate, dear Thomas," said Nancy as she gently touched his hand.

"Yes, we are."

After a moment of gazing into their new babe's eyes, Nancy ventured an idea. "Thomas, I'd like to change my name, but I want to know what you think."

"And why would you want to do that?"

"I know we can't be married, but is there any reason why I can't take the name Hanscome? I'd like to have the same name as my children."

"I have no objection to that. But legally it will still have to be Randall. Nancy Hanscome it is, unless you don't like your first name and would like to be called *Beautiful*," teased Thomas.

"You are so silly sometimes, Thomas. Nancy is fine. My parents gave it to me," replied Nancy. Nancy Hanscome has a nice ring, don't you agree? I'd better start practicing it in the mirror." Then she asked Thomas, "If you could have any name in the world, what name would you choose?"

"I'm happy with Thomas. If not Thomas, I'd choose Aaron, after my grandfather. No one is named after him." Then he pondered, "I find it an interesting phenomenon that few people ever change their names, even if they dislike them." Nancy laughed.

"What a strange observation. I don't find that to be true. White ladies change their names when they marry. And my one planter friend, Elizabeth Hanscome Grimball, has chosen to keep your deceased cousin's name in spite of remarrying. And slave owners change their slaves' names whenever it pleases them. And English royalty change their names when they inherit earldoms. The more names, the better, seems to be the rule."

"That's indeed enlightening. You are right again," chuckled Thomas.

"So back to our precious baby girl. Which sister's name do you prefer?"

"I pick both, Mary Ann. Just like English royalty she gets more than one name."

"Then how about four or five names?" challenged Nancy. "Mary Ann *Beautiful…*"

"You mean like the papists? Absolutely not!" protested Thomas with his wide grin. "Mary Ann, she will be."

"Are we having fun, Thomas?" grinned Nancy in return.

"Yes, we are. And here I was ready to foreswear children."

"You see, you are not too old to be a father, or have fun. Oh, I almost forgot. Our trainer told me he saw some strange slaves visit our groomsmen in the middle of the night."

"I wonder what that was about. Did he check their passes?" asked Thomas.

"No, they didn't stay long enough. When our trainer questioned our slaves they said they were church friends."

"Very strange behavior, indeed," frowned Thomas. "They should have presented a pass from their master. I will look into this matter tomorrow."

But tomorrow was a busy day. Thomas was meeting with his good friend James Legare. Why? To discuss the possible sale of his remaining Creekside acres. Thomas was feeling stretched. He had his plantation in Craven's County and secretly wanted to spend more time breeding horses. When he broached the subject with Nancy, she was ecstatic. She had never confessed her deep loneliness to Thomas or even herself.

1820

Charleston

"Do you Martha Sophia Moor take Thomas Kissick Inglis to be your wedded husband?"

"What a touching ceremony!" said her oldest sister, Catharine Lucy, dabbing her wet eyes with a fine, Belgium lace handkerchief.

"Do you think Catharine Lucy regrets never having married?" whispered a friend.

"She had no money for a dowry," gossiped another.

"Look at Nancy Randall. Why is she crying? She has everything a woman could want."

Yes, Nancy cried. She was not jealous of the beautiful wedding, the gowns, the orchestra, the dancing or even all the resplendent gifts. The truth be known, Nancy wanted to be married. And she also wanted her husband by her side at this wedding.

"Acceptance," Nancy counseled herself. "Thomas will never attend social functions with me. It just isn't done. I am loved by the best of the best, a white planter. I must deny my sadness. I must not expect the impossible. I promised." Nancy dried her eyes, put on a smile and approached her friend.

"My sister and I are equally blessed. Nancy, you won't believe this!" said Catharine Lucy, hardly able to contain her enthusiasm. "Now that Martha Sophia is married to Thomas Inglis, Elizabeth and I have been accepted into the Brown Fellowship Society Auxiliary. And you know what that means. In spite of our not having dowries, we will be considered the best of the best! Soon we, too, should be wed. Thank God for our beautiful, younger, fair-faced, born free sister. I am thirty and had almost given up on finding a husband!"

"I will dance at your weddings then," said Nancy as she shared her friend's joy with an embrace.

Nancy remembered her participation in the Auxiliary, but that seemed a lifetime ago. Her financial inheritances from her father, John Randall, and her European features made her quite desirable to other elite mulattos. Did they now mind that she was the mistress of Thomas Hanscome? Oh, no. They saw her liaison with him as one step further away from the dark slaves. Nancy found it interesting that Thomas had counseled Ietrow to accept membership in the elite mulatto society, but definitely discouraged Nancy from participating.

"Are not both Ietrow and I mulatto, Thomas?" asked Nancy one day. "Have I lost my color in your eyes?"

"Those are very interesting questions, dear. You are a Hanscome now and we are privileged, regardless of your lovely golden hue. Your station is above the Brown Fellowship Society. Now what do you think of that?"

"I find it all ridiculous, dear." For a moment she entertained the notion of having all their gilded mirrors removed. Could she then think herself white? After all, she was the mistress of the mansion.

February, 1821

Creekside

"It's a boy!" announced the mid-wife.

Thomas gave Nancy a gentle hug. He was almost speechless, a rarity for him, as he took his son in his arms.

"He looks like a Thomas, don't you agree?" suggested Nancy.

"Yes, his name can be Thomas." Thomas finally agreed to a namesake. Secretly, he was most thrilled. "As a present to you, I want you to know I finally signed the Creekside deed over to James Legare today. Now I can spend more time with you in Charleston. I have an inkling that will make you most happy," he said with a grin.

"I am delighted with the news, Thomas. I am delighted to be close to my mother and my friends, but you are giving up your childhood home. I'm sure you will miss all this. Are you pleased with the price?"

"Yes, indeed." Thomas' famous grin reached ear to ear. "James made me an offer I couldn't refuse: $19,400 for 650 acres. I am going to keep 324 acres on the Stono, at least for now. I have bought up a few more mortgages in Charleston and intend to invest the rest. Be ready to see much more of me."

"And your horse breeding?" she teased.

"You know me too well, dear."

A jubilant Thomas handed out cigars to all his house servants, before wandering through his slave quarters, distributing more cigars and shouting his news.

"What is his name?" asked his slaves.

"Thomas!" replied Thomas with pride. "Let me know if any of you have a young daughter who could serve as his nurse."

Thomas laughed as he sang and danced with his slaves. He hadn't done that for a long time. He felt they were also his family. All was well on his plantations. Life was as it should be.

Did he tell his slaves he was selling 650 acres to James Legare? No, he did not. What would be the fate of his slaves? Would Thomas sell them to Legare? Would he separate families, too? Of that, he was not sure. That decision, his decision, was for tomorrow.

CH. 17. Rebellion and Restriction

Spring, 1821

Creekside

"I want to be free, but I don't want to kill Master Thomas!" exclaimed one Creekside field slave, at a late night meeting in a blacked out slave cabin. "He works right beside us. He doesn't whip us."

"But you must. He owns you! He is evil! We must kill all the planters for us to have a new life in Haiti. We are the Israelites returning to the promised land!" said the rebellion organizer, Denmark Vesey.

"Our redemption is near. We will soon rise up. We are now five thousand strong! When we are ten thousand strong we will strike. We can do this with God's help. The slave rebellion in Haiti was successful, with fewer soldiers than we have. The French were routed and five thousand whites were killed. The Republic of Haiti was formed - almost twenty years ago. Think of it. If you had been born in Haiti, you would be free. Yes, free! God has ordained we shall be set free. He held the Hebrews' hands as they escaped Egyptian bondage. He will hold our hands, too. But, we have to answer God's call. We can no longer be sheep. Are you with us? Will you kill the Hanscomes? All of them?"

"Even the Misses and the children? She is a mulatto, like me!" cried one.

"Yes, she must be killed! Nancy Randall has never been a slave, has never known a lash. She is arrogant! She thinks she is white! She is the reason the rebellion has been so long in coming. She is one of those Brown Fellowship Society uppity freedmen who do the planters' bidding. Raise your heads higher than Nancy Randall! See beyond the fields! See beyond the Brown Fellowship Society! Want more than just pretending to be free. Do you see her grovel? Yes! Do you see her having white planter friends? No. She is a hypocrite and as evil as the planters. She is a traitor to her color. Do you want more than those traitorous mulattos? Say yes!"

"Yes!"

"Do you want land for yourself?"

"Yes!"

"Do you want to be educated?"

"Yes!"

"Do you want to give glory to the Lord in your own church with your own people?"

"Yes!"

"Do you want your families by your sides?"

"Yes!"

"The noose has tightened around our necks. No longer can we purchase freedom - not ours, not our wives, not our children! Soon we will be tethered to our beds at night, powerless. Do you want to claim your rightful destiny of freedom? Say yes!"

"Yes!"

"Death to all whites! Say yes!"

"Yes!"

"Swear to fight for freedom. Promise to kill all, even the house slaves, if they try to protect the Hanscomes. We have recruited no house slaves and only deserving freedmen. Most freedmen have mistaken beliefs and divided loyalties. Cry out for God's will to be done! Are you with us?"

"Yes!"

"Here is the plan. When the lantern signal shines bright, you will rise up, kill the Hanscomes and the horse trainer. This must be done first. Then you take all the guns, ammunition and horses and light the fires as you leave. Several must sail the large schooner to Charleston. The rest will liberate the slaves at the adjoining plantations as you ride for Charleston. At the same time, our Charleston soldiers will take the Arsenal and the ships in the harbor. By the time you arrive in Charleston both the city and the fields will be ours. Then we will sail to Haiti. We must be gone before the state troops arrive. Are you with us?"

"Yes!"

"Let us pray. Mighty Jesus, give us strength to overcome our captors. Hold our hands steady as we slay the white oppressors and any of our kinfolk who resist. Keep our vision of freedom strong!"

"Yes!"

"We pray for strength!"

"Strength!"

"We pray for justice!"

"Justice!"

"We pray for freedom!"

"Freedom!"

"Take our hands, Lord! Death to the Hanscomes!"

"Death to the Hanscomes!"

"Amen!"

"Amen!"

June 21, 1821

Charleston

"Congratulations my dear friend, James Legare. Creekside is yours!" Yes, the sale of Creekside was finally recorded.

Nancy and Thomas moved to Charleston. The next day, Thomas was off to the races.

June, 1822

Charleston

The rebellion had been carefully planned for five years. Were the field slaves ready? Yes they were, but the signal never came. Why? The rebellion was thwarted by one of their own. At the last hour Denmark Vesey and his cadre were betrayed by a loyal slave who informed his master of the plot. The instigators' bodies were hung and left dangling, rotting in the sun for all to witness. How dare the slaves rebel!

All hope was silenced for the slaves.

And the planters? Their fears and paranoia ran rampant. They could have been murdered in their sleep by their faithful domestics. The rebellion fanned the flames of white panic. No one was safe. The freedmen and yes, even the coveted Brown Fellowship Society elite were suspect. The fact that Vesey and his cohorts went to the gallows silently and proudly increased planter fear. Not one of the rebellion's organizers divulged the extent of the plot.

What solidarity. What purpose. The legislators tightened the restrictions, again. Control was essential.

All freedmen scurried to find white guardians to register them. These planter guardians had to sign and swear, again, to their good characters. A travel ban for freedmen stipulated that if they left the state they would not be able to return. If they did return, they could be jailed or even sold back into slavery. Yes, the freedmen were no longer welcome in South Carolina. There were too many of them and their presence gave hope to the slaves. All slaves had to display passes and wear copper tags. Slave patrols roamed the streets of Charleston. Planters were held accountable for controlling their slaves, who could be imprisoned and resold at a whim if they were at the wrong place at the wrong time. Manumissions were almost impossible to obtain. One notable exception was the slave who informed on Denmark Vesey. He was freed by the legislature and given a pension.

Brown Fellowship Society member Thomas Inglis asked his planter guardian, Henry Middleton, for help in freeing his slave, Alick, from conspiracy charges and sure death. Was Alick saved from hanging and public display? Yes, he was. And was Thomas Inglis awarded the return of his most valuable property? Yes, he was. Was Alick truly innocent? No one would ever really know. All slaves' lips were sealed shut with solidarity. And Alick thanked his Lord for his life.

The trials of the other slave conspirators were swift, as swift as it took to tie the noose.

Did Thomas Hanscome ever know his slaves planned to take his life? No, he had no inkling that his loyal slaves planned to slit his, Nancy's and their children's throats. Regardless of his ignorance about his slaves' intentions, Thomas was most relieved that he had sold Creekside. He needed liquid assets. Yes, assets for his family to leave South Carolina, quickly.

Tradd Street

"Push, Nancy, push. Your child is coming!"

"Thomas, we have another son!" beamed Nancy as she handed the babe to him. "What should we name him?"

"Let us name him James, after my brother."

"James, I like that. And for a middle name, what do you think of Randall, after my father?"

"Yes, a fine idea. In this nasty political climate two respected planters' names, Randall and Hanscome, might help him attain credibility and respectability."

Thomas smiled, then sat by Nancy at her bedside. "And I think wee James should be our last child. I believe we have reached our *plenty*." And he laughed. "Six is a cornucopia of blessings, my Nancy."

"*Plenty*? What a strange comment, but it seems it tickled your funny bone."

"It's an old family joke and I don't know who started it. It could have come from Kittery. Apparently, someone was going to name their last child *Plenty* and, of course, they kept having more children."

"I'm not sure I see the humor, but since you are well and quite vigorous, Thomas, let's keep having more!"

"Thank you for the compliment. I do feel like a stallion in his prime, but I'm actually serious. Wee James should be our last child."

"Why stop? I don't see the problem," replied Nancy, puzzled.

"Because I don't know that I can keep my promise to you to live long enough to see our children prosper. I am concerned about you having to raise our children alone, without my protection. As it is, I may not live to see any of our children reach the age of majority. Neither can I foresee the opportunities our children will have as freedmen. I will do what I can to appoint guardians who will see that my will is executed, but after the last slave rebellion even our whitest children may not have legal rights. I'm afraid paranoia reigns, Nancy."

"I see your point, Thomas. I must admit I do feel an unsettling change in the air, too. Your friends' eyes no longer meet my gaze. No one will converse with me."

"I am concerned about another rebellion. My most logical planter friends are applauding John Calhoun's pompous speeches about God's ordination of the white race to rule the inferior Negros."

"How preposterous, Thomas. My father told me that historically the colors of the enslaved and the masters changed with the civilization and had nothing to do with superiority or inferiority of races," said Nancy.

"That sounds like your father, but Nancy, you do remember he wanted his wealth more than to abolish slavery. He liked being in charge of his destiny and also his slaves."

"Like you?"

"Yes, like me. And like you, dear Nancy, my golden Queen. You enjoy your fineries, as we all do. I will not justify slavery, as we profit by it. The battle over slavery is being played out in Texas and Missouri. Our precious institution may be doomed and with it our children's welfare. If they are to make their way, our children may need to migrate to the northern states. There is talk of disenfranchising anyone with even one drop of Negro blood."

"Well, that will never happen," huffed Nancy. "Many of those white planters might be surprised by their true dark lineage."

"Yes, that is quite true, my dear feisty Nancy."

"You have not even begun to see my sparks fly," retorted Nancy.

"I promise not to warn my legislator friends of your ire," laughed Thomas. "We can talk more of this, later. But in the meantime, I am rewriting my will so that money, rather than land, will be available for our children. Property distributions can be challenged whereas bequests of money cannot be. There is talk of not allowing any people of color to own land."

"But this is their home," said Nancy in disbelief. "Joseph follows you everywhere and talks incessantly about becoming a planter. If any of our children were to leave South Carolina now, the new law states they may never return."

"We need to remain open to the option of leaving. Right now they can be educated in the Brown Fellowship Society School. As they grow older we may need to send them to England, permanently. I don't like that idea, but we must be ready for all possibilities. I do know I promised you a trip to England." Thomas was having difficulty being light-hearted about the possible of the loss of two things – his wealth and his children's freedom. Slavery was both the gift and the culprit.

"You have made your point, dear. James will be our last child. With this great uncertainty on the horizon, do you believe we should move to England?"

"I do not know. However, I will begin courting my old London business contacts. We must be ready."

1824

Charleston

How did the elite Brown Fellowship Society handle the restrictions?

Ietrow died, but not by the hand of any man. Lucy's screams should have roused him, but he was already gone. He quietly passed in his sleep. Thanks to the Brown Fellowship Society, which was formed to provide church cemetery plots for freedmen who, of course, were not allowed to be buried with the light skinned, Ietrow was laid to rest near St. Phillip's Church, where he and Lucy had been married.

Ietrow's burial was a solemn affair, attended by most of the freed artisans of Charleston. Also in attendance, was one white planter face, a notable exception. Thomas had accompanied his Nancy to the graveyard. Why not? Why shouldn't he be there? It just wasn't done, that's why. But Thomas was never much one for observing the proper protocol. He had grown up with Ietrow's daily presence. He was as constant as the sunrise until Thomas took James to London. And after his return, Thomas' patronage helped Ietrow's haberdashery prosper. Thomas decided to attend the funeral, but not his wake.

Only a year ago, Thomas had signed another guardian certificate for him in accordance with the new law. Thomas was happy to vouch for Ietrow's character, but did he see that behind Ietrow's smile was the deepest sadness.

Was this the cause of Ietrow's death then, the gradual loss of his freedom? How was having a guardian any different than having a master? This issue was the substance of talk at Ietrow's wake. Of course, Nancy paid her respects to his widow, Lucy Moor.

"Martha Sophia, have you and Thomas obtained your new guardian certificates?" whispered Nancy when Martha Sophia served her tea from her gleaming silver teapot. Ietrow's closest Brown Fellowship Society friends had gathered at the Inglis' home after the funeral service. All remarked at how lovely the music sounded on their newest grand piano and how the domestics kept every platter and glass refilled. This was refinement at its best.

"No, Thomas and I just haven't found the time," replied Martha Sophia. "His businesses and properties have been demanding. And you?"

"Yes, I have a certificate I must carry anytime I leave our home. I laughed when Thomas had to sign certificates for me and our children. I laughed when I asked him to sign 'husband' instead of 'guardian.' But inside, my soul wept. I became so ill I went to bed for a day. Just to think someone could steal us, sell me or our children if we didn't have those papers."

"I had best force the issue with my Thomas. He is so proud," sighed Martha Sophia. "I know your Thomas signed for my grandmother Lucy and Ietrow and my mother has my father's signatures for Elizabeth and Catharine Lucy. I also know that Henry Middleton will sign for us. But Thomas has to humble himself and ask."

"My Thomas thinks there will be an end to the institution of slavery, unless South Carolina leaves the Union. But when? Perhaps not in our lifetime. We must protect our children and our fortune," said Nancy.

"How can Thomas talk like that?"

"He is white. He sees no contradiction. He says we are one of the last holdouts in the world for the institution of slavery. He also says he will work his hardest to make as much money as he can – so our children have a legacy when it ends. He plans to sell the last of his plantation, 324 acres, to James Legare for $9,720."

"This is all indeed strange, isn't it?" mused Martha Sophia. "Thomas Hanscome will no longer be a planter. How do you feel about that?"

"I am relieved. I feel safe with him in Charleston. And I try to keep him as healthy as possible. And you? Your Thomas, like mine, is also growing older."

Martha Sophia simply smiled. Some fears were better not discussed. "Would you like more tea, Nancy?"

"Certainly. Thomas has left a carriage for my safe return. I will have him wait."

The next day, Henry Middleton signed Martha Sophia's and Thomas Inglis' certificates of freedom and good character. Was it humbling? Yes, it was.

CH. 18. Denial

1829

Charleston

Leave South Carolina? No. The Hanscomes did not run to England or scurry to the northern states. The truth was freedmen were not wanted anywhere. Thomas had waited too long to leave.

In the nation's capitol freedmen threatened the social order. Their relative prosperous existence reminded slaves everywhere, "You could be free, like me." And those dangerous freedom ideas could incite more rebellions. In Congress, colonization back to Africa was touted as the best national solution to the freedmen problem. In New York and Philadelphia freedmen were attacked by angry, white immigrant mobs who wanted their jobs. New laws passed in the northern states further addressed the dilemma. Freedmen could not assemble, meet in their own churches, travel or be gainfully employed. Discrimination ran rampant. Legal due process was withheld from anyone with dark skin. Abolitionist mail was seized by the US postal service.

At least in South Carolina, freedmen knew the rules and could prosper. The mulattos counted on the continued support of their white planter fathers. The Hanscomes decided to remain. Gratefully, the Denmark Vesey rebellion did not foment further mass uprisings. Thus, planter paranoia hid its head. And hadn't the freedmen always lived in a tinderbox? Charleston seemed easier with the passage of time. There were fewer slave patrols. Sometimes what you can't fix, you might as well ignore. Cotton was King. The planters were making money and the freedmen artisans, craftsmen and shopkeepers followed in their prosperous footsteps.

How did the Hanscome's cope? With denial, like everyone else.

"And they're off!" Thomas hoped his two-year old entry would show or place in his debut race. His lineage was impeccable. In his owner's box, his good friends were cheering. Of course, they all placed large bets. When did Thomas' horses ever lose?

"You have the touch," laughed John Legare as Thomas' horse came in first. "I wasn't certain he could win, but my show ticket is as good as gold."

"Drinks all around," said Thomas. "I must go to the winner's circle."

"That jockey is superb, a mulatto, isn't he?" asked Paul Grimball, now married to Elizabeth Jenkins Hanscome, Thomas' cousin's widow. Yes, Thomas had a cousin also named Thomas Hanscome, Moses' son, and one of the Grimballs five children was also named Thomas Hanscome Grimball. Why the namesake honor? Thomas had paid off the Grimball's mortgage at 97 Warren Street. He actually sold it to them for $5.00 along with five other lots on Warren and Vanderhorst Streets. Thomas had also generously purchased a home for the newly widowed Ann Legare Holmes on Tradd and Friend Streets. Why the extravagant gifts? Hugh Wilson had just made the final installment payment on his Creekside purchase. Why not share the wealth with his family of friends?

"Yes, my jockey is a freedman – and, if he saves his earnings, a prospering one at that," replied Thomas. "He is always my first jockey choice."

"Well, I wouldn't bet on a darkie to save a dime," laughed Solomon Legare.

"You just did, Solomon. You did just that, and he can ride better than any of us," retorted Thomas with a smile.

The racetrack stables

"Albert, I want to give you a bonus for your fine race," congratulated Thomas. "Would you like me to help you invest it?"

"I appreciate all your bonuses, Mr. Hanscome. I actually have a purchase in mind," said Albert as he dismounted after the ceremony and handed the reins to the trainer.

"An apartment in Charleston or a piece of property?" asked Thomas as they walked through the paddock to the stables.

"I have been saving to purchase two slaves. Can you help me with that?"

"Well, yes I could, but certainly you don't need any domestics."

"I want to buy my wife and child," said Albert.

"Ah, I see," said Thomas. "I didn't know you had a wife and child. I don't know if that's possible. These new manumission laws make it next to impossible to free anyone."

"Yes, I see you understand my dilemma. I need to buy them. I want my family with me, even if they are still slaves. But I need help with the purchase papers."

"Who owns them now?"

"John Legare," replied Albert. "I am afraid that if I don't purchase them soon my boy may be sold away from his mother. He is now ten and I don't want him working in the fields. I have saved over $1000, my purchase offer. My wife is an excellent chef. I think we can make our way."

"I will talk with Mr. Legare and arrange the necessary papers."

"What if he doesn't consent to the sale?"

"Oh, he will. I will ask him as a friend." And Thomas did.

"John, how much money did you win today?" asked Thomas.

"I made $1000. Thank you very much!"

"How would you like to double your money?" asked Thomas.

"Surely you jest. I am not a greedy man, Thomas. You needn't give me any of your winning tickets."

"Actually, I want to purchase two of your slaves for $1000."

"It depends on which two slaves. Field workers?"

"No domestics, a mother, your cook, and her son."

"Oh, my wife would dearly miss Bess," John lamented. "She is like one of our family and her sturdy son will bring a good price in a few years. I will make him a field worker next season. You have an excellent cook. Why do you want them, if I may ask?

"I want to reward Albert with them after his next win, a well-deserved bonus. They are his family."

"That is indeed a surprise. I didn't know Bess had a husband. You know most of them don't, unless you call jumping the broom a marriage. Why on earth would you give him such a large bonus? He's just your jockey."

"I attribute my stellar record to Albert's way with the horses. He has a natural talent. And he has saved half the money from his winnings."

"As a favor to you then, I will sell them to you. But I want no part in the transaction with Albert. I think we are paying freedmen too much, if they can afford to buy their families."

"Albert deserves to have his family with him, John. He was born free and has worked hard."

"Your lovely Mistress Nancy aside, a nigger is a nigger is a nigger. Wake up, Thomas!"

Thomas did not reply, but he was not in total denial. He knew hate and fear had frozen his friends' minds.

After Albert's next win, Thomas kept his promise.

"Albert, I have purchased your wife and child for you. You owe me $500. The rest of your savings you will need. Do you have lodgings for them?"

"I have a room and Bess can work as a chef. I expect we will be able to buy a small place of our own in a few years. You have made me a happy man, Mister Hanscome. I will forever be in your debt."

"Let me know if you want your son to work in the race track stables. I could arrange it. If he has your talents with the horses, I will pay him well."

1831

Charleston

Was Thomas' life truly golden? The answer was, yes but...

"Nancy, how do you feel about my going to Philadelphia with the trainer and our prize stud? I don't want to sell him, just sell his services during the mating season."

"I wish we could all go, Thomas. Do you still think it's too risky for us to leave the state?"

"Yes, it is too risky and I hate to leave you alone. That John C. Calhoun has changed his tune from being a Union man and wants South Carolina to secede. He wants the tariffs lifted and is taking a hard line on slavery. He's still preaching that slavery is good, not just a necessary evil. It's more of his banter that Negros need ruling by a superior class."

"And that superior class is the planters?" asked Nancy with a smirk, already knowing the answer.

"Yes, we are ordained by God!" Thomas laughed. "I share your sentiments, Nancy, but you know how susceptible my friends are to flattery. Calhoun's ideas have taken root. They have forgotten that our ancestors, like my grandfather Aaron, just needed labor. The planters, Indians, Negros, slave or indentured, all lived and worked together. They would have laughed at the idea of a master class ordained by God to rule others. But fearful men need to feel superior. In any event, I would never risk having you taken upon our return from Philadelphia. You could be jailed or worse, sold on the auction block. Have you seen those full slave pens, next to the jail?"

"Yes, I have seen the pens, full of the re-enslaved. I shudder thinking our children could be stolen. And I lament they cannot run, walk or play anywhere in Charleston, even though some are white enough and can pass."

"I wish it were different," sighed Thomas. "I have refrained from speaking frequently to you about these dangerous state codes, but we must safeguard our family. Rational people are acting like the Puritans in Salem hanging witches or in Kittery lashing my Great Aunt Ann for fornicating with a slave. Now the devils are anyone of color. Fear has defeated truth and logic. I have fortified our wrought iron fences so the children can play outside. I also have made four copies of your freedom certificates. Each child must carry one, we need two duplicates and one I will hold in my bank. I also want you to make sure a carriage takes the children to and from their Brown Fellowship Society School. I don't care how elitist it seems, they are vulnerable to the slave catchers. You are all too precious to me, Nancy. I love you and I must protect you."

Thomas held her while she cried. "Oh Thomas, you should have married a white woman. I fear I am a hindrance to you – and our children."

"Do you know, dear Nancy, that much of my success I owe to you? I have valued your wisdom in my business decisions as much as I value your dedication to truth, our children and our home. I marvel at your refinement, beauty and grace. There is an old story in our Hanscome family that the men need to be tamed. And for my *taming*, I thank you. Now dry your eyes."

"And is there any other reason you chose me?" Nancy smiled.

"Yes, you can really sit a horse and run a cotton crew."

"Now you are being silly!"

"No, only truthful. Your laughter is what keeps me alive. We must live above the codes, close our ears to the politics."

"And Philadelphia?"

"I've been there. I've decided not to go. I'll send my trainer. We will vacation at the seaside this summer, instead. The children will love it and we will be beyond prying eyes. But speaking of our children, let's eat dinner. I want to hear how each is doing."

"Thomas, Joseph is still angry with you for selling Creekside. Please talk with him about this. All he's ever wanted to be is a planter. And, please ask Louisa Rebecca about her debut ball, dear. It is every sixteen year old girl's dream," whispered Nancy.

Louisa Rebecca prated on and on about her dress, the engraved invitations, the banquet at the Brown Fellowship Society, the RSVP's arriving daily and most importantly, the eligible young men who might court her. Finally, she gathered the courage to ask her father a question.

"I have a serious question for you, Father. Will you be my escort?" she asked with bated breath.

Louisa Rebecca and the other children knew that their father was of a different social class. It was the reason he was noticeably absent from their school functions. Thomas put down his fork and considered his answer, but only for a moment.

"Yes, of course. I would be honored. But first someone better give me dance lessons."

Thomas was surprised by the elegance at the ball. If the faces had been whiter, the event was identical to a St. Cecelia's gala. He had debated feigning business as an excuse, but Nancy said his presence would enhance their daughter's marital prospects. The truth was Thomas could not disappoint his Louisa Rebecca. Was the ball a success? Yes, her dance card was full. One William P. DeCosta, a Jewish mulatto cotton gin maker, danced five times with her, one more time than was permitted. And Nancy was thrilled to have Thomas by her side.

Summer soon arrived and the Hanscome's moved to the seaside. Thomas and Nancy watched their children frolic in the warm, crystal clear water. They sat in the shade of the wide veranda of their beach home, drank fresh squeezed lemonade, read books and listened to the laughter of their children. They were content, but all was not well.

"You have been quiet since we arrived, Thomas," commented Nancy. "I notice you do not sleep soundly. Are you well?"

"I am fine," replied Thomas.

However, Thomas knew he was not well. He had hoped his family could have a memorable summer before he died. He had no fever, but as the summer progressed he turned noticeably gaunt and tired. The family returned to Charleston when he was unable to leave his bed. The doctor just shook his head in response to Nancy's questioning eyes. Thomas' father had died at sixty-three and wore that same bone-weary, wasted look. Thomas was seventy-one.

Thomas decided it was time to summon his executors, Paul Grimball and the Legares.

"Paul, Thomas, John, Solomon and Thomas, I would like to review my will with you. I'm afraid death will soon claim me," sighed a tired Thomas from his bed. Nancy sat by his side.

"Nonsense. We expect a full recovery soon," kindly said Paul Grimball, the chief executor of Thomas' will. Thomas considered Paul as family after he married his cousin's widow, Elizabeth Jenkins Hanscome.

"I see my father's withered face in the mirror, Paul. No amount of leeching will restore my vigor, but I thank you for your kind words. I want to go through the particulars of my will, since you all have consented to be its executors. Nancy is present, as I am designating half of my $330,000 to be distributed to her and the children."

The room was deadly silent as the executors hid their surprise – surprise at the extent of Thomas' wealth and surprise at its distribution.

"I know my relationship with Nancy Randall has vexed some of you. I want you to know that if it were possible, we would have married. We have been together for twenty-five years and have six children. I am asking that as my executors you treat her as my legal wife. I have also told Nancy that she may use my Hanscome name," Thomas smiled. "I see a few raised eyebrows among you, but legally she is entitled to use any name she chooses. Please speak now if you want to withdraw as my executor. I will not hold it against you. Do you have any questions?"

Silence.

"The other half of my estate I have dispersed among you and others. I have designated from five to ten thousand dollars to each of my Godsons and name sakes – Thomas Hanscome Grimball, Thomas Hanscome Walpole, Thomas Hanscome Legare, Thomas Hanscome Fripp, my cousin John Hanscome and my father's adopted orphan, John Jeffords. The particulars are precisely detailed in my will.

"The proceeds from my sold properties, over one hundred and sixty thousand dollars, are to be used for Nancy's and my children's welfare. Each child will receive a proper education, clothing, one slave and other necessities as Nancy deems important. At the age of majority, they will receive their inheritance. When my daughters marry, each husband must sign away any rights to her inheritance and recognize the amount is not a dowry. It is intended for each daughter's sole use. Nancy Randall will retain the house on Greenhill Street and the contents of 143 Tradd Street. If Joseph chooses to purchase the mansion from his inheritance, he may do so. Nancy will receive stocks, monies and slaves for her continued welfare.

"Yes, lest I forget, I have also bequeathed St. John's Island Presbyterian Church, the Orphan House of Charleston and Charleston College endowments for their continued good works.

"Please read my will now in its entirety."

Silence.

"Any questions?"

"Your will is very explicit, Thomas. And you have been most generous with us," said Thomas Legare.

"I am humbled that you have released my bond of indebtedness to you," replied Solomon Legare.

"We will do anything to help you rest in peace," added John Legare.

"My children are young. I expect you to take the time to fairly administer my estate, dear friends. Nancy will also need your continued support. I want you to protect my family when I am gone. In keeping with the current laws, please sign these letters of good character for my children and Nancy. I have nothing more precious than my family."

Silence.

As Nancy collected the signed documents she felt afraid and silently wondered, "Is this a bad dream? My life feels over." Nancy, forty-one, would soon be a widow with six children to rear. Could she really trust that Thomas' executors would have her best interests at heart?

"I thank you for your lifetime of friendship," said Thomas. "Had I to do my life over, I could not have chosen better friends, nor a better wife or children."

After more sad goodbyes, his friends somberly departed.

"You called me your wife, Thomas!" Nancy exclaimed, most deeply touched. "In front of your friends!"

"I am so grateful for you, dear Nancy. I broke my promise to you when you asked me not to die until our children were grown, but I seem to have no control over that. Yes, you have been my wife and I wanted to impress my executors that that is how you should be treated. I have left them more than enough money to ensure their loyalty when I am gone. Now, I think it is time for me to see our children, to say goodbye."

Nancy called the children to pay their last respects to their father. His strength was spent. Time was of the essence. Thomas wanted to die and he wanted to do it well. He knew a simple phrase or a few kind words had the power to erase bad childhood memories, change his children's' life views and set them on a course of success. He knew they would need more than he could imagine in this new age to come. Then he smiled, let them be, he thought. They are up to the task. They will figure it out. Thomas gathered his children to his bedside.

"Joseph, I know you are unhappy that I sold Creekside. In a few years you will be twenty-one and able to buy a plantation, if you so desire, but I want you to consider going north, all of you. I was selfish to remain in South Carolina when I know that we could have moved north or to England or Europe. Your lives would have been easier without the hardships of the codes and your illegitimate legal status. I want you to know, I am proud of all of you. I thank you, Nancy, for your guidance as their mother. You are all bright, kind and of sound moral character.

"Children, I want you to all listen carefully to me. I expect there to be a war, sometime in your lifetime. Maybe in ten years, but it will happen. Why?

Slavery will end - and with it our prosperity. Our land will be worthless. Please think about that, Joseph. I cannot predict an exact date, but you will need money to flee, perhaps in haste. I hope you all will have reached your age of majority by then. Please heed your mother's wisdom. South Carolina is like a clock wound too tight. The laws against slaves and freedmen will become more restrictive. There is even talk about rescinding the freedom of all of Negro blood. In that case, I want you to leave South Carolina, unencumbered by land and with money in hand.

"I have given you - Louisa Rebecca, Elizabeth Sarah and Mary Ann - money that will be yours, regardless of whom you marry. Your groom must sign a waiver of rights to any of your inheritance. It is for your sole use. Make the most of your education as you can take that anywhere. I have divided your inheritances into six equal amounts. But whatever you do and where ever you go, promise me you will always honor and care for your mother."

As the children filed by his bedside, Thomas held each one and whispered a special goodbye. He ended by saying, "I love you."

After the children left the room, not really understanding the significance of their father's death, Nancy held the vigil with her dear Thomas for two more days and nights. They spoke little. There was little to be said. When he was alert, they gazed in each other's eyes. Nancy did not weep. Finally, Thomas Hanscome took one last breath, released her hand and died. Then, Nancy wept and wept.

At the funeral service at St. John's Island Presbyterian Church, Nancy and her children sat in the Hanscome pew for the first time. Elizabeth Jenkins Hanscome Grimball had insisted and sat with them. Thomas' lifelong friends and executors were pallbearers. Thomas' body was laid to rest with all the other Hanscomes in the family cemetery on The Point, the only parcel of land the Hanscomes still owned on John's Island.

In the days following the service, no guests visited their home for refreshments, as was the usual custom. Nancy cried and cried when the prepared food went untouched. Her children were most bewildered by her behavior. Where had their strong mother gone? Nancy said nothing to them, went to her room and locked the door.

For the first time in her life, Nancy felt vulnerable. She looked in the mirror and her skin appeared much darker than she remembered. She wished her dear departed mother, Louisa, was here to give her counsel.

I am sorry I left us behind, Mother, the you and me, and all our darker skinned relatives and friends. I thank you for loving me so much. I felt your applause and pride as you shoved me from your nest, and set me, your best present to the world, free. But I never meant to abandon you. I know you wanted me to shine, to be loved, to be affluent and to be an example of gracious living. And I feel I was, but now, with Thomas' death, I feel so alone and afraid. Will I find the strength to carry on?

But her mother wasn't there. Nor was Thomas. Nancy faded in and out of sleep in rhythm with her silent tears.

Joseph took charge and the children distributed the uneaten food to their slaves. Yes, their slaves. Nancy and her children were now slave owners. Nancy stayed in bed for an eternity of days. In desperation, Joseph finally sent for Catharine Lucy Moor, Elizabeth Moor and Martha Sophia Inglis.

"Please get out of bed, Nancy. You have a life to live, in our world, not the planter world. You have us, your mulatto friends. You need to be the pillar of strength for your children. Their lovely eyes are hollow, all of them. You need to protect them. There are also suitors waiting in the wings, ready to marry you."

"I will rise and resume my responsibilities," said Nancy with a deep sigh. "But suitors? No, I will never love another man."

After the obligatory year of mourning, Nancy closed up the Tradd Street mansion and moved to her Greenhill Street home. The executors had been more patient and helpful than she expected. It had been time consuming to go through the mansion at 143 Tradd Street before it was sold. They had accumulated priceless paintings, family portraits, gilded mirrors, rugs, tapestries, furniture, linens, china, silver, pianos and a complete library. Carefully, Nancy divided the treasures into seven lots, one for her and each of their children and prepared them for storage. They would need fine things for their new lives.

Who purchased the mansion? Solomon Legare bought it for $6,500. Nancy tried not to question whether or not the price was fair. She reminded herself to be grateful each day for her abundance. Where would she be without Thomas' generosity? She was determined to see her children thrive.

CH. 19. Moving Forward

1833

Charleston

The August following Thomas' death brought the Nat Turner Rebellion in Virginia. Slaves were killing their masters, again! Why were the slave owners surprised? While fear and angry debate consumed the legislature, the Brown Fellowship Society held its breath.

"Colonization back to Africa? What a ludicrous idea," thought Nancy. "Thomas was right, we should have moved north. Now we are too late. Our existence is precarious, but I must see that my children flourish. I will not lower my head in dread. I must take this one day at a time and instill hope in my children. First, they need to marry and form important alliances. Alone we all will perish."

At least Nancy had Thomas' executors' support. They settled Thomas' estate, paid the annual free Negro taxes and raised no objection when she changed her name in the city directory. And what name did she choose? Why Ann Hanscome, of course! Nancy decided to take the first name of Thomas' great Aunt Ann, known as an independent, honorable and strong woman. Ann Downing had changed her disgraced name when she arrived in Charleston, unmarried with two illegitimate children and one, a mulatto, left in Kittery, Maine. She had always been a source of admiration for Thomas as a youth. She was his moral compass and the conscience of the family. Nancy had used the Hanscome name in private, but she publicly armed herself with it now. Ann Hanscome, what a powerful name. What a name of inspiration and protection. In this era of fear, Ann commanded herself to stay strong.

"What a surprise to see you, Nancy, or should I say Ann?" asked Thomas Grimke with a smile as Ann entered his Charleston law office, exuding her usual style and beauty. "I have seen your carriage about town, but it has been a long time since we have spoken. I hope you and the children are well."

"Yes, we are well, thank you for asking." Ann hesitated, then sat straighter and spoke clearly and calmly, as she had practiced in the mirror. "I am seeking your advice on a delicate matter, Mr. Grimke. Everything in Thomas' estate has been settled, except for one item. I am not sure I have any recourse in the matter, but you would know better." Was she confident, yet humble? Did she bend, ever so slightly to his superior white, male status yet appeal to his sense of fairness? She hoped so.

"I will try to be of assistance. What is this delicate item?"

"I inherited in Thomas' will by name, a young slave boy - Abraham, the son of Black Die. Thomas' executor, Paul Grimball took him and refuses to return him. When I asked for his release or a $1,000 payment, Mr. Grimball told me that Thomas had given him Abraham as a gift, along with his house on Warren Street. When I asked again, he said he had 'lost' the boy. I even asked Elizabeth for her assistance. She sadly told me Paul had no intention of honoring Thomas' will. What do you suggest I do?"

"I am sorry to hear that, Ann. I will speak with Paul about your property. If he remains stubborn on releasing the boy or paying his fair market value, I will file a suit in court. Court suits over slaves are fairly common and routine. It is my responsibility to see that Thomas' wishes are respected. I understand that you and Elizabeth are friendly. Hmm, this is indeed a delicate issue, for several reasons."

"I am not sure that this boy is worth losing Elizabeth's friendship over. I do understand my place, as a person of color. On the other hand, I do not want to set a precedent for being victimized, by anyone. I must learn to assert myself, for the benefit of Thomas' children."

Thomas Grimke smiled at her finesse. He was one of Thomas' planter friends who appreciated Thomas' choice of Nancy Randall. Rumor had it that he also had a second family with a mulatto mistress. Of course, Ann Hanscome knew this was true, thus had sought his advice, instead of one of the other executors.

"There are many states that have taken away freedmen's rights to due process, Ann. South Carolina has no such law, but the courts may not recognize your rights anyway. On the other hand, the will is clear. Let me talk with Paul. If he refuses to comply, do you wish to take him to court?"

"If you believe I can win, yes, I want to try," replied Ann in great earnest. Thomas Grimke smiled again.

"Thomas always appreciated your courage, in spite of your delicate situation as a colored woman. I want you to know, Ann, that I sympathize with the abolitionists, having my law degree from Yale, but I do not challenge my planter friends' views. They are also my best clients. Nonetheless, I promised to execute Thomas' will."

Paul Grimball insisted that the slave Abraham was a gift, thus Thomas Grimke filed a suit. Did the Court uphold Thomas Hanscome's will?

"The court finds that the slave boy Abraham is the rightful property of Mr. Paul Grimball. He has testified that Thomas Hanscome gave him the boy as a gift. Regardless of the will, a gentleman's word cannot be challenged by a freed woman. Mr. Grimke, I admonish you. You should have known the outcome of this case. You have insulted Mr. Grimball and this court. In addition, Nancy Randall, you are assessed the court fees of $32."

They lost! Ann Hanscome left the court dismayed. She had lost more than her property; she had lost her right to legally defend her property or even change her name. In spite of the court ruling, Mr. Grimke congratulated Ann for her tenacity.

"Oh Ann, I am so sorry about the court decision," sighed Elizabeth Hanscome Grimball. "I agree the boy belongs to you, but I have no influence over my husband. My deceased husband Thomas and your Thomas held women in higher esteem than most planters. Please do not be too despondent, Ann. I think the court would have honored any planter's word over a woman's, regardless of color."

"Thank you for your reassuring words, Elizabeth, but I'm not sure I agree. You have no idea of the precarious situation of women of color, slave or freed. Nonetheless, I must move forward. Perhaps you can help me with a more personal issue. I know you were heartbroken when your first husband died, but your life went on. I feel I need to start anew, but I must confess I am a bit uncertain. Why did you marry again?"

"I wanted children, so I married again. I didn't need the money or protection, but I coveted a family. I was alone. A single woman is not well accepted in planter society. And you are correct, Ann, I cannot fathom what it would be like to be in your position, a mulatto woman with property and children to protect."

"I have no legal rights it seems, but I will focus on what I do have – money, a home and my precious children. I may just buy a small plantation north of the city. Thomas taught me how to manage a plantation. I want to lead a private life, but I will keep the Greenhill Street home for the children as long as they are in school. Louisa Rebecca's betrothed has offered to help me. He makes cotton gins. Now that the seeds can be more easily extracted from the boll, the upland cotton business is booming. Maybe I will aspire to be a cotton picker!" laughed Ann. "And a wealthy one."

"I am amazed at your light-heartedness over such injustice. I do admire your courage. But more than that, I miss your laughter, Ann, and your friendship, now that Paul no longer allows me to visit you."

The two women hugged as they parted, knowing this might be their last conversation. They were used to acceptance.

Once alone, Ann thought, "I must move forward and deny the unpleasant things beyond my control. I must be resilient. My life may be much better than

Elizabeth's. She settled for a husband of poor character, a common thief. Now, I have Louisa Rebecca's wedding to plan."

CH. 20. Joy and Pain

Feb 12, 1833

Charleston

"To have and to hold, for better or worse, in sickness and health, until death do us part," vowed Louisa Rebecca Hanscome to William P. DeCosta.

"Your two souls have found each other, never to be separated again," declared the rabbi. Cheers resounded when William shattered the glass. What joy!

Theirs was wedding of the season. As William's family was Jewish, the ceremony was held at the magnificent Brown Fellowship Society Hall and not St. Phillip's Episcopal Church. Ann had spared no expense for the reception and even hired a full orchestra. William was mulatto, the grandson of a Jewish tailor and part of Charleston's prospering community of Sephardic Jews. His grandmother, a slave from Morocco, was also a Sephardi and a friend of Lucy Moor's. William gladly signed the prenuptial agreement protecting Louisa Rebecca's inheritance. He didn't need it; his cotton gin business was thriving. Louisa Rebecca's money was safe.

Did it bother Ann that theirs was a mixed religion marriage? Not in the slightest. She had adopted a more practical, social view towards Christianity, like Thomas and many of the planters. Ann was actually quite relieved. She felt the DeCosta's would provide both protection and a sense of family for Louisa Rebecca. It goes without saying that William, like Louisa Rebecca, was light-skinned.

And how was the wedding received?

"It is so nice to see more of Ann, not that I would have wished Thomas Hanscome's passing," commented one guest.

"But I can't believe her audacity. She took his name - a white planter's name!" gossiped another.

"Why not! Now she even has her own plantation and slaves," defended another.

"I do believe she has white airs that don't belong with her brown skin," smirked another.

"I admire her. Look at Louisa Rebecca's light skin and blue eyes. Our Ann did right to have a white man's children. They will have a future."

"That is, if any of us have a future."

"The DeCosta's are Jewish. I wonder if Louisa Rebecca converted."

"Mazeltov!" toasted several guests.

"I wonder who Joseph will marry," pondered another, ready to move on to the next entertaining Hanscome wedding. Yes, anticipation was half of the fun.

"He certainly was most handsome as he escorted his sister down the aisle. He has his mother's curly hair, is dark-complected and oh how those startling, blue eyes captivate. I predict he will be married next."

"This is a lovely wedding. Let's be merry tonight and forget the sad state of our political affairs."

The guests danced and celebrated in the best Charleston tradition. More importantly, Ann laughed and danced, too. Was she lonely? Absolutely not. Ann Hanscome was a social success, at least among the elite Brown Fellowship Society. She had almost forgotten what it felt like to be included in a social set. And when the gay festivities were over, Ann relived the whole magical wedding again in her bed with Thomas. No, Ann was truly never alone.

And Joseph Hanscome? He also found magic the night of his sister's wedding.

1834

"To love, honor and obey…" promised Mary to her groom, Joseph Hanscome.

What, pray tell, were the comments of the wedding guests?

"Who is this Mary? She has caught our wealthiest bachelor," lamented one guest.

"I hear he bought a 600 acre plantation in St. James and Goose Creek Parish, not far from his father's second plantation, just north of Charleston. And he's only twenty-two."

"He has named it Woodland, and rightfully so. This venture could be a folly. He will have to clear many pines before he can plant his cotton."

"Well, his brother-in-law, William DeCosta, had to help him trade his slaves last year. Joseph's domestics were terrible field hands. What was Joseph thinking?"

"I predict success. Armed with William DeCosta's time saving cotton gin and strong slave backs, Joseph should thrive. It seems Joseph has caught his father's plantation fever."

"I also hear his new mansion is quite similar to Creekside's with large north and south verandas, a kitchen house, barn, cotton shed with gins and sturdy, slave huts with brick chimneys. He must be intending on having a large family. It has ten rooms! Mary is indeed a fortunate girl."

"She is beautiful - has those lovely European features, but her skin is a shade too dark."

"I think she actually resembles Ann. Some boys are prone to marry duplicates of their mothers."

"Oh, don't be ridiculous!"

"You know Ann's children are quadroons. With the three generation rule, her grandchildren can apply for legal white status."

"It all depends on whom they marry. Joseph would have needed to marry a whiter girl for that to happen. And, of course, gone are the days when even dark-skinned mulattos could purchase legal whiteness."

And thus time passed. Ann tended to her own plantation and had more of a social life than she ever had with Thomas. She was content. All she wanted was marital bliss for her children. "So far, so good!" she told her Thomas in their nightly consultations.

1837

"My granddaughter, little Ann, and your daughter are delightful companions," said Ann to her old friend Martha Sophia Inglis.

"At two and a half they are still our little cherubs," replied Martha Sophia. She and her youngest children were visiting Ann for the day. Martha Sophia was redecorating her home and wanted Ann's expertise on gilded wallpapers.

"What a gift for Joseph and Mary to name her after you, another Ann Hanscome," replied Martha Sophia. She had lost her husband, Thomas Inglis, just two years earlier. Martha had been his executor, a privilege few women of any color were given. Now the two widows were free to spend time together. Their children had become great friends, like family, although Martha Sophia's were younger.

"Yes, it is. I used to believe naming people after grandparents was just a silly tradition, but now, on the receiving end, it gives me a sense of continuity. I like to believe a bit of my soul has passed along with my name to wee Ann."

"Little Ann does seem to have your determined spirit," replied Martha Sophia as they watched the children play with their rag baby dolls on the wide piazza of Ann's plantation home. "Let's just keep them away from these wallpaper samples."

"And what do you think of your wee Martha, your namesake? Does she have your easy going temperament?"

"She is a sweet one, but I'm not sure that has much to do with me. Her older sister, Mary Sophia, plays with her constantly. I just want to live to see little

Martha married. I have talked with my older sisters. We have a pact that if I die, they will care for the children."

"But you are much younger than I, just thirty-two. Please don't entertain thoughts of your demise so soon. Why don't you remarry and have more children?" asked Ann.

"I do miss Thomas' company, but I have no desire and no need to remarry. Sixteen years was sufficient. My Thomas, like your Thomas, was very generous. I am quite busy managing my slaves – ten of them are hired out right now. I want to make certain our children have a financial beginning. I had nothing, except my education and freedom when we married. And although Thomas's white plantation father left him no property in his will, he did help Thomas get started in his barbershop business."

Martha Sophia, like her dear friend Ann, had known she might be widowed young, since her husband was twenty years older. She had inherited his barbershop, his four houses, his slaves, his stocks and bonds and even the gallery pew at St. Phillip's Episcopal Church. And each of their five children had inherited two slaves each. Did she resent his bequest for Rachel's, his first wife's, expensive care in the insane asylum? No, she did not. She cherished his memory as an honorable man.

"I have no desire to tether myself to a man, either," laughed Ann. "Men can treat you like slaves - fetch and carry!" Ann laughed, in spite of her heart ache. She still secretly yearned for the smell of Thomas' bedclothes. "But it's all worth it for the children. I see Thomas in each of them - and little Ann, too. Elizabeth Sarah is already planning to have her as a flower girl in her wedding."

"I didn't know Elizabeth Sarah was engaged!" said Martha Sophia.

"She isn't, but at twenty she is seriously courting."

"And who is the lucky man?"

"John Garden. He's the youngest son of John Garden, the wealthy mestizo rice plantation owner from St. Paul's Parish."

"It's definitely an advantage to have Indian blood from his mother's side. He doesn't have to pay the Negro taxes, or abide by the nasty new Negro laws."

"It's a wonderful advantage. Unfortunately, the Negro laws will still apply to their children."

Of course, Ann wanted the best for her children. Joseph's plantation was thriving. She had successfully launched two of her children. Elizabeth Sarah would be next. She hoped her Thomas was smiling down from heaven. Life was good.

November 19, 1837

Woodland Plantation

"No! Oh no! Not little Ann!" cried Grandmother Ann.

Her granddaughter was gone! Her little Ann's precious light was snuffed out like a candle in a gust of wind. Joseph and Mary were beside themselves with grief. It was late in the season for the fever to hit but nonetheless, fever it was.

Joseph grew concerned about Mary's health. She was again pregnant. Rest, the doctor ordered. However, Mary would not stay in bed as she was flooded with the memories of her wee Ann's endearing habits, like placing her little ear on Mary's belly to hear the new heart beat, then joyfully clapping her hands and exclaiming, "My baby! My baby!" Each memory of little Ann dealt a blow to Mary's heart.

Surely that was enough despair for the family to bear. But another pain followed the first when Mary gave birth early and the baby failed to thrive.

"I promise you, Mary, we will have more children," assured Joseph. "Our lives must move forward."

August 4, 1838

Was it true that bad luck came in threes? That seemed true for Mary Hanscome. On the fourth day of August her Joseph was taken by swamp fever. Mary's grief would not cease. She was not eating or sleeping. Finally, Ann moved to Woodland Plantation to rescue her daughter-in-law from herself. In her own way, Mary was also courting death.

"Mary, Mary. You must get out of bed," implored Ann as she opened the curtains to expose a sunny, albeit warm, humid morning. "You must eat."

"This pain is more than I can bear! Why should I live?" screeched a ghostly, disheveled Mary. "Everyone I loved has been taken from me!"

"I loved my son and wee Ann as much as you, but we cannot let their deaths overtake our lives. You are a Hanscome. We are your family and we love you. You must rise and go on. You must find a new purpose to live. It is a lovely day and I want you to go for a walk with me. Please, dear Mary, we have much to discuss. Tomorrow we have an appointment with John Legare, who will help execute Joseph's will. Joseph's executors, William and Thomas, will also be there."

Mary silently rose, washed, dressed and went for a walk with her mother-in-law. A determined Ann was hard to refuse.

"It is a pleasure seeing you again, Ann," said John Legare.

All of Thomas' friends had disappeared from Ann's life, but she could almost detect a nostalgic note in John's voice.

"My condolences to you all," said John as he formally greeted each before they began the business of the will.

"I don't believe I've had the pleasure of meeting you, Mary. I almost mistake you for a daughter of Ann's, your resemblance is so striking. I am so sorry to hear about Joseph's passing. He was a fine young man, a true planter like his father."

"Thomas, you look even more like your father than when you were young. I must say, I miss your father's company."

"And William, you must be the lucky man who married Louisa Rebecca. I clearly remember Joseph and her as they grew up at Creekside. Why don't we all sit?" cordially offered John Legare with a gracious smile.

"This is a simple will. Young Thomas and William DeCosta are the executors. The time consuming part will be selling Woodland Plantation and the slaves. I assume you can help Mary with that, William?" asked John Legare.

"Yes, I will take charge of the sale. I've been told I am quite skilled at selling all types of properties," replied William.

"From the property profits you are to deduct your expenses, William, and pay Ann, legally Nancy Randall, $2000. The remainder of the proceeds are to be invested in stocks and added to Joseph's other bank assets. Joseph wills you, Mary, the dividends for your lifetime, but not the principle. For those dispersals you will need the executors' approval. You are, indeed, a very wealthy, young widow, however, I am certain you would rather have your husband by your side. Joseph also wanted to protect you from fortune hunters. The money is intended for your own use. Should you remarry, your husband will need to sign a pre-nuptial agreement, as stated in the terms of this will. Upon your death, Mary, Thomas will become the recipient of any remaining assets. You will become a full executor, Thomas, when you reach the age of majority. Do you have any questions?"

"We have no questions. Thank you, Mr. Legare," replied Ann. "May we consult you if we need help with the banks?"

"Yes, of course. I am always available."

Did young, widowed Mary Hanscome return in despair to her bed? No, instead she threw herself into helping with Elizabeth Sarah's wedding. She did not have her husband or child, but she had a family. Elizabeth Sarah needed to experience the joy of her wedding, thus Mary put on a happy face and denied her pain. Ann nodded her approval. Mary was learning to survive her pain through being of service to others.

1839

"I, Elizabeth Sarah Hanscome, take you, John George Garden, to be my wedded husband."

The vows were promised and the bells at St. Phillip's Episcopal Church rang out the happy pronouncement.

"What a handsome couple," sighed one adoring guest, as she tossed a handful of rice on the couple.

"What a wealthy couple," declared another. "Throw some of that rice on me. I need more prosperity."

"I wonder who young Thomas will marry. He looked like a man when he escorted Elizabeth Sarah down the aisle."

"He hasn't reached his age of his majority, but he must be careful with whom he dances tonight."

"Yes, his complexion is the lightest of all Ann's children. He is very tall and handsome with his straight, jet black hair. I hear that Mary Sophia Inglis has eyes for him."

"They are like brother and sister, thrown together often by their mothers' close friendship. I doubt they are the next match."

"I thought the ring bearer, little Joseph Hanscome DeCosta, stole the show. He is Ann's oldest grandchild at five and quite the little man."

"Oh, I disagree - not that the child isn't adorable. Mary Hanscome positively glowed as Matron of Honor. She is living in Ann's Greenhill Street home. I wonder if she is accepting suitors? It has been over a year since Joseph passed. She deserves some joy after all the pain she has had."

"We will find out at the reception at the Brown Fellowship Society."

"It definitely is advantageous that John Garden is classified as mestizo."

"His father sold 140,000 pounds of rice last year. Cotton may be the new king, but rice is still golden."

"I hear the newlyweds will have a home in Charleston, not far from his parents. The Garden's Hermitage Plantation has overseers, thus John may be spared from that deadly swamp fever."

"It appears another Hanscome may catch the wedding fever. Mary Ann just caught the wedding bouquet."

1840

"I, Mary Ann Hanscome, take you, John Lee, to be my wedded husband."

Again, the bells of St. Phillip's Episcopal Church pealed out in celebration. Was anyone tired of attending these Hanscome weddings? Absolutely not.

The reception was held in the fashionable boarding house owned by the groom's parents, John and Eliza Lee, and patronized by the wealthy planters. Eliza was known for her fine talents as a chef. More than one traveler lamented that the famed establishment was closed to the public for the wedding. The Lees, both mulattos, owned many slaves and apprenticed others. Some were taught the fine art of southern cuisine in the boarding house and others sewing and pattern-making in John's flourishing tailor shop.

"Look at that cake!" coveted one guest. Eliza's specialties were pastries.

"What a feast! I shan't be able to dance tonight!" protested another.

"Don't you find it interesting that all the Brown Fellowship Society eligible young men are marrying the Hanscome girls, but none of the young Hanscome men joined the Society? Why do you suppose that is?"

"I think Thomas Hanscome believed his sons to be a cut above the rest of us. He probably wanted all his children to marry as white as possible. His grandchildren would then be considered legally white."

"Yes, marry up, marry light, marry well. I think Ann Hanscome is doing a fine job. Her daughters won't be lonely, like she was. Soon, we'll see how her sons fare."

"Thomas and James are young, give them time. They will need the Brown Fellowship Society's support, like we all do. Thomas Hanscome cannot protect them from his grave."

"I wonder who will be next to marry?"

"Thomas has danced more than four times with Mary Sophia Inglis."

"That means they're almost engaged!"

1841

"I, Mary Sophia Inglis, take you, Thomas Hanscome, to be my wedded husband, for better or worse, for richer or poorer, in sickness and in health, until death us do part."

Again, the bells rang out at St. Phillip's Episcopal Church. And again, the guests could hardly wait to discuss the match.

"This wedding gossip is so much fun and harmless, don't you agree?" said one guest. "What do you think of this young match?"

"Ann and Martha Sophia are so pleased. But what could they expect? The two families were constantly together after Martha Sophia's husband died."

"I think they're terribly young to marry. Thomas won't reach his majority until next year and Mary Sophia is not yet 18."

"In a few months we will know if they played too much without a chaperone," laughed another guest.

"I think Ann simply wants all her children secure and married well."

"It is too bad Thomas Inglis wasn't able to escort his daughter down the aisle, but Mary Sophia's brother, William, is a good substitute."

"I noticed several young ladies blushing when he glanced at them. He is young, but quite eligible as he will inherit his father's barbershop."

"What interesting red hair Mary Sophia has. Where did that legacy come from?"

"Martha Sophia says her hair is a gift from Thomas Inglis' lineage - the red from his white planter father's Scottish background and the curl from his African slave mother."

"Do you find her beautiful?"

"I'm not certain beautiful accurately describes her. I'd say she is unusual and most definitely interesting. She has the most broad, welcoming smile. Together they are a handsome couple, both so pale in complexion. What do you think of Thomas' goatee?"

"It ages him, makes him look at least twenty-one, but I prefer a clean shaven man."

"What would we do without all these weddings to attend?"

"Life would be boring!"

"I always feel hopeful after a wedding, don't you? I wonder if James will be next?"

"Certainly Thomas' younger brother is too young to be married anytime soon."

Charleston November 10, 1841

I, James Randall Hanscome, take you, Serena Elizabeth Walker to be my lawfully wedded wife."

"Yes! I do!" shouted James and Serena, simultaneously. The guests positively chuckled and tittered with their enthusiasm.

 The church bells happily resounded and the guests celebrated in style. How could it not be?

"Ann is weeping! Look at her. It is not a good wedding omen when the mother of the groom cries."

"It looks like a fine match to me. The bride is lovely and a wealthy slave owner. Ann just doesn't want to lose her baby, her darling James."

"James has chosen a slave to marry!" exclaimed another guest. "That's why Ann's crying!"

"Serena is only a slave because her wealthy, white Scottish father, John Walker, was unable to manumit any of his eight children. He even petitioned the legislature, but to no avail. Everyone knows John Walker and his slave, Ann Jones Walker, live as husband and wife, openly in Charleston. Serena brings her own slaves to this marriage. James and Serena are deeply in love and financially a sound match."

"But their children will be slaves. I would cry like Ann."

"Ann could never control James. He likes the race track life, like his father."

"Just so he doesn't gamble way his inheritance."

"If he does, his wealthy father-in-law can pay his debts."

"He is only nineteen. Hopefully, he will grow more responsible with his husbandly duties."

"His duties may come earlier rather than later. Look at the bride's gown – see how it hides her growing belly. It is a gift that the Reverend agreed to marry them."

"Like brother, like brother. Do you see that Mary Sophia is also with child?"

"I will miss these lavish Hanscome weddings. Ann is so welcoming and gay."

And were the guests correct in their assumptions about James' and Thomas' wives? Yes, they were. Mary Sophia and Thomas had a baby girl, Alice, later that year. And James and Serena also had a baby girl, Sarah. How were they doing? The Thomas Hanscomes appeared to be in marital bliss, but it was rumored that James needed some *taming*. He was still spending time at the race track. The Hanscome girls seemed quite content in their wifely roles. All the new grandchildren were baptized at St. Phillips' Episcopal Church, except for the Jewish DeCostas.

Thomas Hanscome 1760 -1831

Unrestored oil portrait, circa 1810. Owned by current Thomas Hanscome. Identified, by Muriel Hanscome in 1950's letter to her California cousin as her great grandfather Thomas Hanscome from Scotland. No mention of Charleston.

Thomas Hanscome 1821-1894

Oil portrait, circa 1840's, restored in 1950's at the Smithsonian. Owned by current Thomas Hanscome. Identified by Muriel Hanscome in 1950's letter as her Toronto grandfather, Thomas Hanscome.

Mary Sophia Inglis Hanscome 1823-1899

Oil portrait, circa 1840's, restored in 1950's at the Smithsonian, owned by current Thomas Hanscome. Identified by Muriel Hanscome in 1950's letter as her grandmother from Buenos Aires. No mention of Charleston.

James Randall Hanscome 1822 - ? or his son James Hanscome II

Portrait restored at the Smithsonian in 1950's. Owned by current Thomas Hanscome. Identified in Muriel Hanscome's 1950's letter and diagram as James Hanscome II, son of James Hanscome of New York, Muriel's grandfather's brother. No mention of Charleston.

37 Meeting Street, Charleston, SC

Aaron Hanscome willed home to his son Dr. James Hanscome in 1760, who sold it in 1801 to Jervis Henry Stevens. However, the current Simons House has the same address and a different ownership history. Apparently, house numbers changed in the 1800's, thus the historical record of deeds need further research.

143 Tradd Street, Charleston, SC (front view)

143 Tradd Street (side view on Greenhill Street)

143 Tradd Street was willed by Aaron Hanscome in 1760 to Thomas Hanscome and was sold in 1831 to Solomon Legare.

143 Tradd Street front gate

CH. 21. Hard Choices and Promises

1843

Charleston

"Oh no!" wailed Ann Hanscome. "Martha Sophia has passed! I cannot believe it!" Ann embraced her grief stricken daughter-in-law. "I am so sorry, Mary Sophia. I have lost my best friend and you have lost your mother!"

Mary Sophia's eyes were glazed over. First, she had lost her father, then her sister Naomi and now her mother. She was in shock, speechless. Martha Sophia Inglis had been only thirty-eight years old.

Mary Sophia worried. What would happen to her eight year old sister, Martha, and her other siblings - Claudia Angelina, William and Helen? Orphaned! Mary Sophia's sister Naomi had died of influenza just last year. After her death, her mother was never the same. It was rumored that she died of a broken heart, but others said that was hardly the case as she had five other children to live for. Regardless of the cause, one day she simply clutched her bosom and keeled over, never to wake again.

Thomas Hanscome and the senior John Lee were named as her executors. William Inglis would inherit his father's barbershop when he came of age. Other properties, including slaves, were sold and the proceeds saved for the education and welfare of the five underage Inglis children. How long would the $37,000 last without the income from hiring out the children's slaves? Martha Sophia had counted on that income.

Mary Sophia was a married lady, thus not a beneficiary of her mother's will. However, since she and Thomas offered to care for her siblings, she indirectly would gain from her mother's estate. At age eighteen, Mary Sophia Inglis Hanscome became an adult. She and Thomas would have hard choices to make. What would they do?

1845

"The court of Charleston denies James Randall Hanscome's claim to Indian status, based on his great, great grandmother's Indian heritage. You claim an Indian woman, slave or indentured servant, was your mother's direct ancestor. Your claim goes back to the early 1700's and Robert Randall's plantation. You also claim from this woman on, each child was erroneously enslaved. It is true that the Lord Proprietor 1670's codes said Indians could not be enslaved, but in practice many were. This court recognizes an Indian name, but there is no documentation as to her status. In any event, your grandmother Louisa became a freed Negro and your mother Nancy Randall was a born free mulatto, as are you. Be content with your current freedman status. You could be a slave."

Yes, the unsympathetic Court had spoken. Hadn't these Hanscome mulattos learned they have no rights?

"I am sorry, Serena. I had thought if I could prove my Indian status and claim the same rights as a legal white person, our children might be manumitted due to their Indian blood. This hope is today lost. Our little Sarah is forever doomed to slave status, regardless of her color or lineage." James held Serena as she cried.

"We are powerless, James. I accepted that I would always be a slave, but not my precious Sarah and all our future children. Their futures are no brighter than the slaves I own!"

"I think your father needs to officially sell you and Sarah to me. He is getting older. Then in my will, you will be under the care and protection of my executors, my brother Thomas and my brothers-in-law, John Lee and John Garden. I will see that John Legare draws up the papers."

When the day came to meet with John Legare, Serena surprised them all.

"I have made up my mind to divorce you, James," said Serena. "I refuse to bear more children, which should be sufficient grounds. Many are surprised that the Reverend consented to marry us, given my slave status. I will raise our Sarah in my father's house. She will be educated, protected and know you are her father. I should never have given my consent to be married. We live in a caste system and you are a freedman. You deserve to live as such."

Did James agree to a divorce? He did. And despite his gay demeanor, gambling and drinking, James was truly heartbroken. Furthermore, he refused to consider the future plans the other Hanscomes were making plans for their own precarious futures.

"James, please go to Philadelphia with Thomas and Mary Sophia," begged Ann as she summoned all her children. "Serena is right, we live in a caste system and even the freedmen's rights are disappearing. You must leave. Please forgive me that I did not heed your father's wisdom. We appreciate your courage in petitioning the courts, James. Thomas and your sisters all routed for your success. However, hope is extinguished and our freedmen status remains. Opportunities in South Carolina have closed to us."

"I must remain in South Carolina, if I want to see my little Sarah. If I were to leave, I could never return. I will make a future here, dear Mother," answered James.

"And what are the rest of your plans?" Ann asked her other somber-faced children.

"William and I have decided to remain in Charleston, too. The Jewish Community and all of William's relatives support us. William's parents would cry if we were to take our little Joseph Hanscome away forever. We simply pray the laws do not grow more restrictive." Louisa Rebecca DeCosta put her head in her hands and sobbed. "Our Hanscome family will be split apart, forever!"

"John's tied up with his father's estate, as an executor," said Elizabeth Sarah Garden. "First, his family needs to sell The Hermitage Plantation and his other properties. It will be hard on his mother if we leave, but we are considering following Thomas and Mary Sophia. We had also hoped James' court petition would make our mother and thus us Indian, but our status remains mulatto. We don't want to raise our children in this fear. Even though John has Indian status, the children and I never will. What are you going to do, Mary Ann?"

"Perhaps John and I can travel with you, Elizabeth Sarah," suggested Mary Ann Lee. "My baby is due in April, so we cannot leave until after that. The Lees have encouraged us, like you, Mother, to begin anew in Philadelphia."

"And Mary? Will you come with us?" asked Thomas of Joseph's widow.

"Yes, thank you, I will. I am reminded daily of my lost Joseph and baby Ann. If I move, I hope to be freed from my sad Woodland memories. Nonetheless, I must follow my money and you, Thomas, my trusted executor." And with that they all laughed. What a relief from a very tense situation.

"And you, Mother? Will you please come with us? Our Alice and little Edwin will be heartbroken if you remain," begged Thomas.

"No, Thomas. I will remain here. I will not be alone as I have James and Louisa Rebecca and their children. Even Serena reaches out to me. When her father, John Walker, dies, she is in for a rude awakening. It may be I can buy both Serena and wee Sarah. I'll not have them auctioned at the market. And although John Lee, Sr. will oversee Mary Sophia's younger siblings, I can help with them. They are my family, too. I think you are right to have their Aunts care for them until you are settled in Pennsylvania. Here they have their school friends and familiar surroundings."

"Yes, you want to be needed, I can see that, Mother, but we are now orphaned," lamented Thomas.

"The truth is, son, at fifty-five I feel no desire to begin anew. Sometimes I sail down the Stono and reminisce about your father. I have so many memories that spark to life when I visit our special haunts. I feel his spirit, if not his body. When I plant my cotton I think of him. This is my home. And I know I can be demanding." Ann smiled as she added, "You may feel an additional freedom, yes, freedom from me, as you set sail."

Ann's children chuckled, in spite of their sadness. Ann Hanscome had become quite the matriarch. When she called, they ran to her side. When they had a question, she answered it. When they had a problem, she solved it. And now she wanted to orchestrate their trip. They smiled. Did her children want their emancipation from her? Not really. They adored their mother.

"I have written a letter of introduction to the mulatto Purvis family in Philadelphia. The wealthy white William Purvis sent his children to school in Philadelphia. They never could return. I wish Thomas and I had followed his lead, but that is history. As soon as I hear back from his son, Robert Purvis, you can book your passage."

"William and I will oversee your slaves and send you their hired out wages," offered Louisa Rebecca.

The family's hard choices were sadly accepted as the children quietly dispersed to their own homes. Laughter could no longer mask their inner despair. Once Ann had waved the last goodbye, smiled her last smile, she closed her door and copiously wept.

"Thomas, did I do right to push our children from their nest?" she asked her deceased, but ever present, Thomas.

No answer came, but Ann hugged her bed pillows as though Thomas were by her side. She cried through the night, dreamt of each child's birth, first bites of food, first walks, first swims in the sea, first horseback rides, first recitations, first balls and first loves. She woke knowing she would never see Elizabeth Sarah, Thomas, Mary Ann or their children again. She was heartsick. Was she right to firmly push them from her bosom? She took a deep breath, set her jaw and decided her decision was correct.

"We have done well, Thomas," Ann thought. "Our children will not only thrive; they will fly! They are the best of me and you - Hanscomes."

The plans for leaving South Carolina were soon finalized.

"Documentation papers, please." Thomas was perspiring, but not from the heat. He was reserving passage for Mary Sophia, Alice, little Edwin, sister-in-law Mary and all their household goods to Philadelphia.

"Five one-way reservations in a private stateroom, with two adjoining bedrooms, and storage for household goods," said Thomas handling the ticket master his papers.

"Yes sir!" said the ticket master. "This will be quite expensive, but the sea views are spectacular from our elegant balconies." Then he hesitated. "Oh, I'm afraid I cannot offer you those accommodations. I mistook you for a white gentleman. No freedmen are allowed in staterooms. And, of course you know, no return tickets can be purchased."

"I am a gentleman, just not white," laughed Thomas. "I want a stateroom, just the same, even if it costs an additional fee."

"I recognize the name, Thomas Hanscome," said the ticket master. "Your father was a good man. He gave my family a house in Charleston. You see my father was an orphan that your grandfather raised at Creekside. Your father was a true brother to him. He had no obligation, but he left us quite a legacy in his will."

"Now that he's gone I hear many nice stories about his kind acts," replied Thomas. "You must be a Jeffords."

"I am John Jeffords, named for my father. Let me see what I can arrange. If you and your family take your meals in your stateroom, no one will suspect you are not white. Your papers are all stamped 'M' for mulatto, but if you have a stateroom ticket, you may not be asked for them. I could lose my job, if you are discovered." He hesitated. "And if any of your family look Negroid, have them wear their largest, most fashionable hats. Perhaps you could feign illness and board early." He hesitated. "I am sorry to be offering this advice to the son of Thomas Hanscome. I do wish you well."

"Do not apologize, please. This new life will be more than a sea voyage to us. We may have to become champions at subterfuge. I am forever indebted to your kindness. It is traumatic for my family to be leaving, but there is no future for us here. We will remember most of our past as glorious."

"It is an honor to return your grandfather's and father's kindness."

Ann took charge of dividing family belongings and packing household goods. She encouraged cheerfulness and levity. Yes, Ann was in charge. There would be no agonizing or grieving for the renting apart of their family. None. Their love would exist and persist without their physical presence. As long as they had shared memories, they all lived.

"It is time to unlock the storage bins and divvy up the treasures I have been saving for you," said Ann cheerily to her children. "What you don't want we can donate to the Orphanage. I have no need for any of it. Those of you who are traveling north need to keep in mind the shipping fees. It may be cheaper for you just to buy all new furnishings. But please remember - don't imitate the drab, Spartan look and don the simple pearls of the Quakers. Honor your lessons in South Carolina charm and style. Grace is the key to fine living."

"I suggest we draw straws for the pieces, as I'd like us all to part on friendly terms," offered James.

"You are leaving a lot to chance, just like a gambling man," laughed Louisa Rebecca. "I suggest I take the larger pieces, since I will remain in Charleston, unless you have room for them James. Some of these old, ornate cabinets from Europe are still lovely."

"I think we better draw straws," said Mary Ann. "Just because you'll stay in Charleston and are the oldest doesn't mean you get first dibs on our memories."

And so the auction for the Hanscome treasures began. Thomas drew the longest straw so he chose first, very pleased with his stroke of luck.

"I'll take the three brass candelabra with the crystal prisms. I'm glad I didn't have to fight tooth and nail for them. I believe our grandfather bought them on his European tour. I hope their rainbows will mesmerize Alice and wee Edwin as much as they did me. I know they are not worth as much as other items, but I want them."

"And I'll take the gilded mirror that hung in the parlor," said Elizabeth Sarah.

"Yes, I remember you dreamily taking all the mirror time before we went anywhere," teased Thomas. "You can remember your youthful vanity with each glance."

"Touché, dear brother!" she retorted.

"And I'll take the dinner plates and silver," said James.

"Do you plan on getting married again?" teased Louisa Rebecca. "I can't believe you are becoming domestic and tamed."

"Yes, actually I just might marry again," said James. "However, don't put off your departure for that possibility. You might have to wait some time."

"My turn," said Louisa Rebecca. "I'll take the grand piano," and she grinned from ear to ear. "Applause, please." And she took a bow.

"Each of us needs to take our own family portraits," suggested Mary Ann.

"As your father's namesake, I want you to take your father's portrait, Thomas," said Ann. "His countenance is etched in my memory forever, and I'd like to think his spirit travels with you."

"Me, too?" timidly asked Alice, now age three and a half. "My turn?"

"What is it you want?" asked her mother, as her little hand reached for the delicate sliver dinner bell her grandmother used to summon the servants.

"Go ahead, take it. Perhaps it will be an omen of future wealth, but there will be no slaves to summon in Pennsylvania," said her Uncle James.

The auction of their past memories became a party. No one drew blood and most received a few treasures they cherished. Why didn't anyone cry? Crying was against the rules.

They were exhausted, but the bins were emptied and good will maintained. Their slaves packed the wagons.

"Very nicely done, children. Now you won't have to do this after I pass," laughed Ann. "I also have a copy of my will for each of you. As you can see, there won't be much left, so use your inheritance from your father wisely. James and Thomas, you will need to be gainfully employed, in some fashion."

"I don't want to leave you, Grandma!" wailed Alice. It had finally donned on her what 'moving' meant.

"I will miss you, too, my dear Alice. I always wanted to visit Philadelphia, now you can be my eyes and ears. Your mother can write down all your impressions and send them to me. Pictures are the best gifts."

"I promise to be good, but I am afraid. I don't want to go," said Alice with a trembling lip. "I'll have no friends."

"Sometimes the best things happen, out of the blue, like magic," said Ann hugging Alice. "Expect all good things and they will arrive, sometimes when you least expect them. Little Edwin will soon be a fun playmate and you will make lovely new friends when you go to school."

"Promise, Grandma?"

"I promise."

Thomas liquidated some of his and his sister-in-law's stock investments and other assets, including their domestic slaves. He needed capital for his land purchase in Pennsylvania, but left other slaves in the care of William DeCosta, Louisa Rebecca's husband, who promised to hire them out and send Thomas the proceeds. William would also manage Mary Hanscome's slaves.

"Done," said a resolute Thomas. "The past is over and I'm ready for next."

Finally, the day arrived to say goodbye. More promises to write were exchanged as they embraced and bid each other adieu. They had never been separated before. They had never been individuals before. They were part of the group, the Hanscome family. Those left standing on the wharf watched as more tears quietly streamed down their faces. Their eyes fiercely clung to that dot of a ship until it disappeared. They all had made promises for future meetings, in spite of the slight possibility that the current laws would change. Would Ann have the stamina to part with her daughters, Elizabeth Sarah and Mary Ann, and their families in a few months? Yes, she would.

Ann prayed to her husband as she wept in her bed that night. She felt she had made the hardest choices in her life and sought his blessing. She and Thomas had lived their lives together based on *what was*, not on *if onlys* or *maybes* and blocked out the future. Now Ann followed her gut that told her the future was dangerous. Charleston was no longer safe for anyone. A big storm was brewing.

CH. 22. Philadelphia, Land of the Free

1845

Voyage to Philadelphia

"I do believe we will have to buy more woolens in Philadelphia," said Mary Sophia with a shiver as she leaned over the balcony adjoining their stateroom. "This is more than a brisk sea breeze. It's bone-chilling cold."

"Are you complaining about this fine March day?" asked Thomas with a grin. "We might even catch a glimpse of snow when we land."

"I am not complaining, simply reporting the truth that my body is the coldest it's ever been. However, I am learning that I must expect my new life to be quite different, more than I could ever imagine. I'm sure Philadelphia has many hidden lessons for us, beside this winter weather. I am having the best time on this voyage, in spite of eating our meals in our stateroom. I was exhausted. To read, tend to little Edward, watch the sunsets and play games with Alice and Mary was exactly what I needed."

"And is that all you have enjoyed?" teased Thomas.

"It goes without saying that our very warm time together has been special, thanks to Mary's helpfulness with the children. And you? How do you feel about our new adventure?"

"I remember my mother telling me how her spirit soared in Europe, that to taste such freedom could not be imagined by any person of color in South Carolina. I hope Philadelphia will do the same for all of us. We may not have much space on this voyage, but I feel freer than I ever did in Charleston. The only limits are the endless sky and the sea!" said an expansive Thomas. More softly he added, "Thank you for trusting me. I was afraid you could not part with your sisters and brother."

"It would have been selfish for us to uproot them. With no slaves, how could I care for them and our children? My childless aunts leapt with joy to have their arms filled. I do know they will adjust. Once we are settled, we can send for them, but I am aware they may remain forever in Charleston," sighed Mary Sophia. "The sad looks on their precious faces are forever imprinted in my heart."

"I am truly sorry we had to leave them behind, but as my mother says, we cannot foresee the future. Let's just take care of each day the best we can and our future will be grand," replied Thomas with a gentle embrace.

"Do you always believe what your mother says?" teased Mary Sophia.

"Absolutely not, but you must indulge me. I want to have her resolute strength. When I repeat her words, she feels closer and I feel stronger. I also must confess I miss her. Don't you miss your parents?"

"More every day. They both died too young. I ask them for their wisdom and guidance, even now, but sometimes I think I'm just talking to the air. And none of us has any answers for what comes next. I think Ann is correct, slavery as the means to wealth in South Carolina will soon pass."

"Now you sound like my mother," laughed Thomas. "Let's just enjoy our voyage. The future will be upon us soon enough." They watched the sky and sea change luminescent rainbow shades in the sunset, silently comfortable in each other's arms.

"I had hoped to travel by land, but you were wise, Thomas. The travel restrictions on freedmen and the risks of being spotted by slave catchers were too great, even with my blazing, red hair. I must admit I was afraid of the sea. Now, I am enthralled with it."

"Perhaps I'll turn sea captain after this fine trip," mused Thomas. "It runs in my blood – pirates, mermaids and sirens."

"And leave me alone in the strange land of Pennsylvania while you cavort with the sea nymphs? No, thank you," laughed Mary Sophia.

"We haven't laughed like this in a long time, have we?" said Thomas giving her an affectionate squeeze. "Perhaps we should go inside, warm ourselves and take advantage of our private room. Who knows what awaits us in Philadelphia?"

"Hopefully, a helpful Robert Purvis awaits us. From his letter to Ann, he seemed quite keen on meeting us."

Philadelphia

"Welcome to the City of Brotherly Love," said a smiley and rotund Robert Purvis. "You must be exhausted. I have a carriage waiting and also arranged for your belongings to be stored."

"Thank you so much, Mr. Purvis," said Thomas, shaking his hand. "We are most fortunate that you agreed to help us settle. Actually, we feel quite enlivened by our trip. Let me introduce my family…"

Thomas felt relieved that Robert Purvis was so welcoming. He also noticed Robert tipping several Irish workingmen for loading their trunks and boxes into a wagon. Strange, thought Thomas, these servants aren't slaves.

"Philadelphia's busy harbor looks like Charleston's," observed Thomas. "There are the tall-masted vessels, smaller schooners and the noisy loading and unloading of cargo. I believe a busy wharf is a busy wharf, but I see workers, whites and Negros working side by side. That you would never see in Charleston. To not have slavery will be an adjustment for us."

"All is not as peaceful as it seems," said Robert. "The newer immigrants, the Irish, don't like the free Negros and vice versa. Don't let yourself be caught at night in this ward. It can be dangerous."

"But you have no slavery here. Why is this dangerous?"

"Competition for jobs. They fight like animals, all of them. The Irish stick together. The Negro freedmen have their own turf. I am working hard for the abolitionist cause, but even mulatto freedmen, like us, are not free. Luckily, money is respected, regardless of one's color."

"What do you mean, not free? That is why we moved here!" Thomas was astounded. Had he made a terrible mistake?

"There are no slaves here. We are free, true, but we have not gained citizen status. We cannot vote or hold office and the courts do not protect our rights. And traveling is ill-advised with the slave catchers ready to snare even a gentleman of a lighter color," said Robert. "Please do not go out at night unaccompanied."

"I appreciate your tutelage, but this sounds little different from being a freed quadroon, like me, in Charleston," sighed Thomas, disappointed. "I admit I was expecting more."

"Do not lose hope, dear Thomas. If one is clever and industrious, one can be successful. Do you see the buildings our carriage passes on the right? These sail lofts were owned by James Forten, my friend and father-in-law. He employed both freedmen and whites in his lofts and they respectfully got along. Some worked side by side for over thirty years. He died just three years ago. Although he was wealthy, born free, as was his father, he did not have citizen status – nor do I.

"James Forten's grandfather, who bought his freedom, was one of the first settlers as a slave in the late 1600's. James was proud to fight in the Revolutionary War and did not join the loyalist ranks as did so many men of color. He was even imprisoned for years on a British ship. He could have turned bitter at his misfortune following the war, but he persevered. His funeral was attended by both freedmen and white merchants. He was the most respected Philadelphia freedman. Some whites declared they were honored to shake his hand."

"That is indeed different from Charleston. You'd see no shaking of hands between the races. I would have liked to have met James Forten. He sounds most remarkable."

"He was. And you shall meet his son, Robert Forten, at dinner tonight. My wife, his sister, has invited him. Let me first drop you off at your boarding house. I believe you all will regain your land legs after a short rest."

And what a dinner it was. The Purvis' home was large and as opulent as the Brown Fellowship Society members' homes in Charleston. They were served by Negro servants, as well trained as any Charleston domestic. Harriet smiled as she beckoned Mary to sit next to her brother, Robert.

"I am surprised to see you have servants," whispered Mary.

"Oh, they really aren't servants. These are cousins who live with us, until they can make their own way. We help them and they help us," smiled Harriet. "We are active abolitionists."

"I'm not an abolitionist. I own slaves, even to this day," Mary blurted out. A deafening silence fell at the dinner table. Unapologetically she continued, "They are the source of my wealth. They are my property."

"You could be a slave, Mary. Have you no empathy?" commented Robert Forten with a bristle. "How can you separate your condition from theirs? Your money does not make you a more worthy human."

"I understand the Carolinas of my youth," interrupted Robert Purvis, trying to smooth over the friction between Mary and Robert. "My father was a wealthy planter and as such, I was untouchable, like you, Mary. We owned slaves, too. I try to not feel guilty that our family money came from the backs of slaves. We need not criticize each other for our past, a past we did not choose. You will need time to adjust. I toast to you, Hanscomes, in the spirit of both my white father and my mulatto mother. Eventually, may you view life through a different lens, one that values equality."

"Hear, hear!" resounded around the table, but Mary did not raise her glass. Thomas politely clinked his glass of cider with the Fortens and breathed a sigh of relief when the topic of conversation changed. He enjoyed his cigar in the library after dinner and tried not to miss his snifter of brandy. The Purvis' served no alcohol, but the camaraderie was familiar.

"Tell me, Thomas, what efforts have the abolitionists made in South Carolina?" asked Robert Forten.

"South Carolina is a powder keg, ready to explode. The mail is censored. If a freedman, like me, were caught with abolitionist pamphlets I could be jailed and sold as a slave."

"But surely the effort persists," replied Robert.

"There are freedom rumblings among a few slaves, but the freed mulattos do not promote abolitionist sentiments," said Thomas.

"That surprises me. Why do you think that is?" asked Robert.

"We freedmen have our own society and we all own slaves. I come from a planter family - that has been our way of life. When slavery ceases our economy and whole society will collapse. Everyone will lose. The white planters supported the freedmen and vice versa until recently. Today few whites trust anyone of color. Our freedmen status may be changed any day by our fearful legislators."

"And did you sell your slaves before your journey?" Robert asked Mary.

"No, I still own most of my slaves." And their eyes locked with a shocked understanding that they were from different worlds. Would they ever find common ground?

"Your Negro brothers and sisters need your help. They want and deserve that same freedom you enjoy. I am astounded by your viewpoints. Don't you find them hypocritical?"

"Yes, I do. I cannot defend slavery. I want my freedom, so why shouldn't I champion that same freedom for all? But I haven't. We South Carolinians have lived with our hypocrisy for hundreds of years. It is the ultimate paradox. The truth is we mulattos have championed the cause of our white fathers, not our slaves," replied Thomas.

"And your mothers? You abandoned your slave mothers - your very own mothers! I trust you will change your mind. Slavery is doomed."

"In spite of the fact that my educated, sophisticated mother was never a slave, we have finally found common ground, Robert. I agree with you, slavery is doomed. It is why I left."

What Thomas didn't say was that he would have stayed if the white planters still upheld the freedmen's rights. However, it served no purpose to alienate his newest friends, further.

"I hope that after you settle you will help us with our cause," said Robert Forten. "First, we need freedom for all and then we need full citizenship rights."

"I thank you for your viewpoints, gentlemen. In no parlors in Charleston would we have had such a conversation. I will reflect on your words," replied Thomas, as politely as he could.

The underlying question remained in both Robert's and Thomas' minds. Would the Hanscomes embrace the abolitionist cause? Nonetheless, Thomas had enjoyed the evening. Hope was in the spring air.

And Mary Sophia? What did she see at dinner? She saw a happy family, a lovely home and new friends.

And little Alice? Alice met a new friend, just her age, one of the Purvis' children. Her grandmother Ann was right. She would have friends.

And wee Edward? It made little difference to him where he was. He was fed and lulled to sleep in loving arms.

And Mary? She tried not to be excited by Robert Forten's charm and eloquence. His cause, abolitionism, puzzled, even frightened her. Is that why her heart raced? What would happen to the social order if all the slaves were freed? What would have happened to Joseph's plantation, Woodland? Chaos! Yes, chaos, and equal poverty for all would reign.

The Hanscomes rode in silence back to their boarding house, each absorbed in his or her private thoughts, but all centered on the similar questions of "Can we live here?" and "Did we make a mistake?" For the first time each felt pangs of homesickness. Thomas vowed to buy his own fine brandy and Mary decided to steer clear of the self-righteous Robert Forten. Mary Sophia was not feeling well. What did all this mean? Finally, Thomas spoke.

"Mary Sophia and Mary, we must accept that we are the strangers with the strange viewpoints. It behooves us to keep our beliefs among our family or we will have no friends."

In the morning they awoke to the unfamiliar sound of snow being shoveled from the path to the street. It was not just a Carolina dusting that would melt by noon. This was a heavy, wet snow, at least two feet deep. It clung to the newly budding leaves and the snow-laden branches bent in deep arcs toward the ground. The sun shining on the snow was almost blinding to the eye. Dazzling!

"Oh, how lovely!" cried little Alice, as she looked out the window. "This is a wonderland!"

And from the stairwell below they heard the friendly voices of Harriet and Robert Purvis. "We are distributing galoshes, hats, muffs, mittens and wool scarves to needy Carolinians today. Is anyone interesting in venturing outside?"

"Oh, you are lifesaving angels," said Mary Sophia. "We certainly are not prepared for snow."

"Would you like us to take you on a sleigh ride to see the countryside? We can travel northeast along the Delaware River in Bucks County and have a spring picnic. We have packed blankets and food. Robert Forten has brought his fine sleigh."

"It hardly seems like spring to us, but we'd love to see the country. As you said last night, I might want to buy farm land in Bucks County," responded Thomas.

"Do you want to see me free a tree?" asked jolly Robert Purvis of little Alice as he shook a tree branch. The clumps of snow fell on Alice's head and she laughed with glee. "Let me. Please, I want to free a tree!" And she did. Robert hoisted Alice on his shoulders and they shook the tree limbs, showering all with snow as the branches, released from their weighty burden of snow, sprang toward the sky.

"Me, too!" said Edwin as he stretched his little arms up to his father. Soon all were laughing and frolicking in the snow.

Robert Forten winked at Mary. "You see, the trees like their freedom, too," he said as he escorted her to his sleigh.

"Tomorrow the roads may be impassable from the mud, but today we can travel swiftly and smoothly. Listen to the bells jingling. I believe the horses are ready to run. Welcome to spring in Pennsylvania," laughed Robert Purvis.

As they passed through the gently rolling hills, Thomas wondered how he would adjust to farming this strange land. He was familiar with plantation style farming, but the lowlands were flat, not hilly. Well, he would just have to hire help to teach him what and how to plant. And they'd have to buy plows to do the work the slaves did. As a gentleman, he had no trade to ply. Farming he could do.

"You are quiet, my Thomas," said Mary Sophia.

"Yes. I am pondering where to live and what to farm. This snow will soon melt and it will be spring planting season. I think I must move fast or I shall lie fallow like the land until next spring."

"We can take our time, dear Thomas," she said as she patted his arm. "We will have another child this summer. Can we just rent a house in Philadelphia and take our time to adjust? Perhaps you might find a different calling in the city. You could be a cotton broker or a trader. Do you really want to be a farmer?"

"That is a fine question, my dear. I won't know until I try," laughed Thomas. "But I can wait until after the baby is born. Why didn't you tell me your news before? We certainly need a home soon for our growing family."

Early summer, 1845

"I think I must cry," said Mary Sophia as she toured one home for sale. "This house is little better than a slave hut! We cannot live here."

Finally, the Hanscomes found a spacious and gracious home, large enough to host the soon arriving Gardens and Lees. Mary Sophia and Mary were busy decorating, buying new featherbeds and hanging all their South Carolinian pictures and family portraits.

"Temporary, yes, but this house has a good feeling. I have cried for my own home," said Mary Sophia. "Thank you, Mary, for coming with us. I couldn't have managed the children or this new home without you." Mary Sophia caught the sadness in Mary's eyes. "I am insensitive, dear Mary. Perhaps one day you will have your own home and children again. In spite of Robert Forten's political views, he can be quite charming. I think he is definitely interested in you."

"Or perhaps he is just interested in my money - money stained by slaves' toil," Mary angrily retorted.

"Remember Mary, Thomas is your executor and your money will never belong to a future husband. But Robert Forten doesn't know that. I have heard rumors that he does not have the same good business sense as his father. He might even have to declare bankruptcy. On the other hand, his daughter Charlotte is so quick and lively – truly a joy. And you both have lost your spouses. Be open to all good things, as Ann would say."

"I am not interested in that dark-complected Robert Forten!" yelled Mary. "I miss my Joseph's blue eyes. I miss my little Ann," wailed Mary, now dissolved in tears. "I miss our plantation and, yes, I miss my slaves!"

"I will speak to Thomas about getting us some help. The new babe will arrive any day. We both have been laboring like scrubwomen today."

Later that night another kind of labor began.

"We have another little girl!" Mary Sophia proudly announced to her Thomas.

"How sweet she is," said Thomas taking his newest babe in his arms. "Let's show Alice and Edwin their baby sister." And what was their reaction? Alice proudly held her, but Edwin just wanted his mother's lap, all to himself.

"What should we name her?" asked Mary Sophia.

"Let's name her after your mother. May our baby girl be blessed with Martha Sophia's sweet South Carolina temperament," smiled Thomas.

And so it was wee Martha Sophia Inglis Hanscome was named. Four names, what an honor, indeed. Wee Martha Sophia's first outing was to the wharf to meet her Hanscome cousins.

"Look! Look! I see them," shouted Mary, pointing to the boat deck and waving frantically.

"I see them, too!" cried Alice holding her Aunt's hand and jumping up and down. "My cousins! I see all my cousins!"

Waving back from the ship's deck were Elizabeth Sarah and John Garden and their three children, Daniel, age five, Walter, age three, like Alice, and little Amanda, age one. Next to them were Mary Ann and John Lee. In Mary Ann's arms was their new baby boy, Drayton.

This time it was Thomas, Mary Sophia and Mary who did the welcoming. Oh yes, and Robert Forten, too.

"Welcome to Philadelphia, the land of the free," Thomas said.

Tears of joy were shed by all. Household goods were carted away to be stored and the Hanscomes were packed into the waiting carriages.

"Dear Lord, we are thankful for our family's safe arrival. Please send our love to dear Louisa Rebecca, James, their families, our dear mother Ann and Mary Sophia's family who remain in Charleston. May they forever be held in your safe keeping," prayed Thomas, seated at the head of the spacious dinner table. Yes, Thomas had replaced his mother as the head of the family.

"The candelabras!" exclaimed Elizabeth Sarah. "How I remember the lovely rainbows cast from those crystal prisms at our dinners. I will have to write a long letter to Mother, describing everything we ate. Oh how she loved her family dinners."

"How is Ann?" asked Mary Sophia.

"She did her stoic best not to cry when we left, but I think sending us off almost killed her," answered Mary Ann. "She looked very ill, indeed."

"What a terrible thing to say, Mary Ann," chastised her older sister Elizabeth Sarah, but inside she also knew her mother grieved. "Our mother will always be fine. Her cotton crop promises to be the best this year and she is busy helping Serena with little Sarah. Oh, Louisa Rebecca wants you to know she will have another baby this fall. On the surface nothing has changed in Charleston, but a few of our friends are moving north to New England. In Washington DC the freedmen now outnumber the slaves, so we are not welcome there."

"We are like the Israelites being sent to the desert," wryly commented Mary Ann.

"I see nothing has changed between you two," laughed their brother Thomas. "Mary Ann, you will always be dramatic and you, Elizabeth Sarah, the logical, big sister. Oh, how I have missed you both. But Mary Ann, Philadelphia is hardly a desert. How about this pleasant summer air? Admit it, Mary Ann. Is this not a pleasant change from the stifling heat in Charleston?"

"Yes, yes. This is glorious weather. And I so adored the sea breezes on our journey. But dear brother, is this Philadelphia truly the promised land, the land of the free?"

They all laughed. No one commented that all the food was placed on serving platters in the center of the table to be passed, as on a picnic. Why? There were no servants. And did anyone ask where the mammies were? No, they did not. And did Robert Forten join the men as they sipped their brandy on the back porch in the evening air? Yes, he did, but he did not imbibe. And did Mary find Robert's advances to her liking? Yes, she did.

CH. 23. Simple Farmers

October, 1845

Bucks County

The three families purchased small acreages adjacent to each other near Warminster. Each family had a home, barn and chicken shed. Still, they ate many dinners together, family style, as was the German custom. The Philadelphia demand for produce, hay and oats was booming. The city had an insatiable appetite for more – of everything, except laughter, music and dance. The Friends and the Germans took life very seriously.

The Lee's home

"What glorious autumn weather," exclaimed Mary Ann as she rocked wee Drayton on the porch swing. "I don't know which color is my favorite - every day brings a new hue of red, orange and yellow."

"You are our true weather bird, chirping with praises of autumn," teased Mary Sophia, watching her children at play. "If I were a betting lady, and I'm not, I'd bet you croak with the first snowfall."

"As long as we are warm, I won't care. I do know I am much happier here in the country than in Philadelphia. It has as many problems as Charleston. I wish our mother could see the colors of these leaves and meet some of these quaint Germans," said Mary Ann.

"The quaint Germans are called the Pennsylvania Dutch. I believe soon we will all be speaking like them," laughed Mary Sophia. "They have been very helpful, true, but their demeanor is so serious. I certainly hope our children don't imitate their dourness!"

"I don't think they're dour," said Mary Ann. "They actually are not as judgmental as we are, but their simple, plain clothes would have been given to the slaves. I did see Karl hide a smile as he tried to teach John how to use an ox and plow. And at least my John had the good sense not to retort, 'this is slaves' work' - a phrase he is using more and more frequently."

"None of us were prepared for the physical demands of this farm life," reflected Mary Sophia. "Other than Joseph, bless his soul, we were raised in Charleston and grew mainly flowers to grace our dining room tables."

"Thomas was right to buy this land with its planted fields, now we are reaping this bountiful harvest," laughed Mary Ann.

"I hope this isn't our last harvest. Joseph worked with his father and knew how to toil. Unfortunately, Thomas was a mere eleven when his father died and never learned to work with his hands. He admits that being a young Charleston race track dandy has not been advantageous." Mary Sophia sighed. "My own back is sore, but now that the first harvest is in, we will have the winter to prepare for next spring. We will know in a few years if we can prosper. I told Thomas that if we don't like it, we can move to a city, where he could be a trader in goods. At least in the country we are not afraid of our shadows as we were in the streets of Charleston or Philadelphia."

"I love watching our children run and play, freely. I think this is a good life for them," reflected Mary Ann. "And the schools for colored children in Philadelphia are better than Charleston's."

The serenity of the Hanscome pastoral existence soon faded with the first frosts of fall.

The Hanscome's home

"Oh No! No!" wailed Mary Sophia, during the middle of the night.

Edwin's fever had broken the day before, a good sign they all believed. But now he was cold, stone cold in his crib. Mary Sophia clutched her limp boy in her arms. Soon little Alice and wee Martha Sophia were also wailing with their mother. Thomas and Aunt Mary awoke with the commotion and ran to the nursery.

"My son! My son!" cried Thomas in disbelief.

And Mary? She was stabbed again with the pain of losing her own baby Ann, at about Edwin's same age. Angels! Their angels had been stolen away.

No one had planned a family cemetery. Life, not death, was center in their thoughts. Robert Forten offered a plot at St. Thomas' African Episcopal Church in Philadelphia, but the Hanscomes declined.

"We will bury him on the hill overlooking our land. It's an old Hanscome tradition," said Thomas.

He was speaking for Mary Sophia, who had not uttered a word all day. She just lay glassy-eyed in her bed.

"Mary Sophia, wee Martha Sophia will need to nurse soon. Please try," encouraged Mary Ann. But Mary Sophia just turned away. Mary Ann, still breast feeding wee Drayton, finally picked up her niece and offered her breast.

Thomas' sisters, Elizabeth Sarah and Mary Ann, finally took their nieces to their homes. Alice and even baby Martha Sophia were confused and upset by their mother's withdrawal.

No one was left unscathed by little Edwin's death. Many hidden wounds and fears were opened.

"I don't believe in God," cried an angry Aunt Mary, rocking herself as her grief from too many deaths bubbled to the surface. "How can a kind God take my wee Ann and little Edwin, innocent children? Why would a kind God take my young husband, Joseph? Why does a kind God let us suffer so? He is not kind at all! I refuse to acknowledge such a God."

Finally, Mary allowed herself to be comforted by Robert Forten.

Robert had no answers for her, but he had great empathy. He knew grief. He, too, had lost his young wife. His daughter Charlotte had lost her mother. He held Mary Hanscome in her unfinished grief, simply held her. And he wept, too - for Mary, Mary Sophia, his dear departed wife and the slaves who lost their lives running for freedom. Robert truly felt the pain of others.

The Garden's home

"This is the end of it, John," cried Elizabeth Sarah to her husband. "I will have no more children without help. Our Walter is Edwin's age and a handful. We just celebrated Daniel's fifth birthday, and it was all I could do to keep track of Walter who teased wee Amanda until she cried. We need to hire help or you can move to the guest bedroom. Poor Mary Sophia was exhausted, and look what happened - little Edwin is gone! Now she is catatonic. We need help."

And who did they hire? Karl Amundsen's thirteen year old daughter, Emma. If anyone thought it was strange for a white girl to work for mulattos, no one mentioned it.

Their losses brought the Hanscomes closer together. And to no one's surprise, Mary Hanscome opened her heart to Robert Forten.

The wedding

"Do you, Mary Hanscome, take Robert Forten to be your lawfully wedded husband?"

"I do," replied Mary.

Theirs was a simple country wedding, held at the nearby Neshaminy Presbyterian Church. The November leaves were at their most glorious. Yes, the Reverend had just been to the Hanscomes a month earlier for little Edwin's sad burial. But today he was welcomed by smiling faces, even Mary Sophia's.

"I am glad to officiate this happy occasion, Thomas. Pray tell, what made Robert and Mary decide to marry after such a short engagement?" inquired the minister.

"We were all tired of sadness," replied Thomas. "Why wait? We needed to celebrate. It is the Charleston way. After Mary's loss of my brother and her daughter, she is finally ready to live again. Young Charlotte needs a mother, which delights Mary. More than anything, we want Mary's happiness."

"Well, love is the only thing that can heal broken hearts," said the pastor. "Look at Robert's daughter, Charlotte. She is bubbling with joy. All she needed was a mother's care. This marriage is a blessing for all."

"Please join us for our wedding banquet, Reverend. We have made a feast that rivals the most elegant in Charleston."

Even the minister drank more than his fair share of the finest champagne in the finest of crystal. Everyone but the bridal couple imbibed. Robert, as all the Fortens before him, was a staunch supporter of temperance. Apparently, it was one belief of Robert's that Mary had accepted.

The servants served and removed china plate after china plate that had been filled with the most delectable food. Servants, you say? Yes, the Hanscomes had hired the best caterers in Philadelphia. Laughter and toasts rang loud. What gaiety. What an enamored bride and groom.

What Thomas didn't tell the minister was that the wedding date was pushed forward by the availability of forty acres adjacent to theirs. The price was good, $4000, and included a small house, barn, chicken shed, plows, lathes, saws and even livestock. In addition, Robert Forten agreed to sign the prenuptial agreement. In truth, the farm was Mary Hanscome's. As was thought, Robert was in debt and Thomas did not want Mary responsible for them, now or in the future. In addition to the prenuptial agreement, Mary signed a will leaving her fortune to her children and not her husband.

Yes, they had talked into the late night hours of their common bond, their hunger for more children. What Mary and Robert didn't share were their political views. Mary thought politics of little consequence and Robert surely thought his compassionate wife would embrace his abolitionist cause. And did she?

The Forten's home

"Mary, please accept my sister's invitation to join the Philadelphia Female Anti-Slavery Society. You already know Harriet, Sarah and Margaretta and you'll enjoy their company. Perhaps you'd like to ask Mary Sophia, Elizabeth Sarah and Mary Ann to join you?"

"I will ask them, but I don't know what they would do with their children."

"Emma and our Charlotte could take care of the children at the Purvis' Philadelphia home," suggested Robert. "Or I'm sure Harriet or Sara Douglas could arrange help."

"I will ask, Robert, but I am not optimistic," replied Mary. The next day Mary invited the women for tea and to show off her new home.

"Thomas says no to the trip to Philadelphia," said Mary Sophia, curtly, without even consulting him.

"John says no to my joining the Philadelphia Female Anti-Slavery Society, even if it met here in Warminster," firmly added Mary Ann.

"And my John says I could go if I wanted to, but I know Emma's parents would feel it too dangerous for her to travel to Philadelphia with us," added Elizabeth Sarah. "Let me ask you a question, Mary Hanscome Forten. Don't you feel it's a bit sanctimonious, as a past plantation and slave owner, to join an organization that boycotts food and cotton grown by slaves?"

"I suppose I am a hypocrite – and I told Robert that. He just laughed. He said I was duped, that we mulattos were all duped into supporting the white institution of slavery. Now that I'm no longer a part of it, I can change my mind and support freedom for all," replied Mary, self-assuredly.

"But Robert lives on the wealth, your wealth created by Joseph's sweat and slave labor," added Mary Sophia. "I believe your Robert to be the worst hypocrite."

"What better use for my money than to help Robert with his cause? Don't you think it is wrong for a person to own another? Isn't that why we left South Carolina, so we wouldn't be enslaved?" asked Mary, trying not to be defensive. It had taken her time to change her perspective, with Robert's patient tutelage. Why had she not seen the atrocities of slavery before? Why did she think they were the privileged few, the special mulattos who deserved freedom? Her views gradually changed like a shade slowly lifted to let the sun shine in the darkest places in her brain. Robert was afraid he would lose Mary if he challenged her beliefs too quickly. She, in turn, was patient with her Hanscome sisters, not by blood, but sisters of her heart.

"Yes, you are right - slavery is an evil, Mary, but inequities in circumstances are nothing new. Strata in social class have existed since time began. We are in Pennsylvania living on our fat profits, yes, profits from slave labor. Also in Pennsylvania men live off the profits from others' sweat - just not the sweat of slaves. Look at the toiling coal miners who are freedmen, poor Irish and Germans. And the coal mine, canal and train owners are as wealthy as our Grandfather Hanscome. It's just another system of exploitation. So my John says we can choose whether we want to be the wealthy exploiters or the labor class," said Elizabeth Sarah.

"At least the freedmen have a chance. James Forten, my deceased father-in-law, had a chance," said Mary. "And he became wealthy and respected. He was not an exploiter."

"Well, this conversation is useless," sighed Mary Ann. "I support you supporting your husband's calling, which is abolitionism. But it is not our battle, Mary. I wouldn't feel good about missing my slaves, as I do, and sending money to free them."

"What if you freed them, then paid them wages?" asked Mary Forten.

"They'd still be poor," joked Mary Sophia. "And they'd still do my bidding. Yes, Miss Mary Sophia! Yes, Miss Mary! Anything else, Miss Mary Ann?" Mary Sophia bowed and kowtowed as she imitated the proper servant subservience. All laughed except Mary, who had become most passionate about her abolitionist views.

"Poverty is unnecessary, sisters. It's the Anti-Slavery Society's point. It's what Robert's speeches are all about. We need to raise money to give to the freedmen so they can be educated, learn a trade, make their own money. We need to help them. We need to be proud of their persistence to live, in spite of the hardships we forced them to endure. Yes sisters, we need to make amends. They need our money to begin anew."

"We like Robert, even if he gets a bit long-winded at times, but we won't be joining the Society. Just tell him we won't be hypocrites, or are too afraid of having our farms burned in retaliation, or can't leave our children or are cowards - whatever story you choose. Your beloved husband tried to reinstitute the right for freedmen to vote, right here in Bucks County. That was ten years ago, and still we are barred," said Elizabeth Sarah.

"Who are the 'we' you speak of, Elizabeth Sarah?" asked Mary Ann. "White women are disenfranchised, too, subject to every whim of their husbands, like servants. The penners of the constitution only sought freedom for themselves - the white, male, property owners."

"Remember, it is those very same white males that made us wealthy. Without our inheritances we would have nothing," added Mary Sophia. "Thomas honors his father as my father honored his white father. Just make sure Robert doesn't leave you penniless."

"What should I tell my Robert?" asked Mary Forten. "I don't want to tell him you miss your slaves!"

"Well, that would be the truth," offered Elizabeth Sarah. "Tell him what you think he wants to hear, you're his wife now. You chose him. We admire Robert, but his cause is not our cause – and you be careful when you go to Philadelphia, please, dear Mary.

"Tell him we are not heartless," added Mary Sophia. "Even in Charleston we gave to the poor. What I will do is prepare holiday clothes and food packages for the freedmen at Guinea Run, not far from here. Thomas says they are little better off than slaves. They don't make much as coal miners and this winter will prove to be cold. Nonetheless, they are very grateful to Thomas for getting them jobs at the mines. He says it is just a beginning for them and next year their harvests should be better. If that happens, they hope to quit the mines."

1846

The Hanscome's home

Clang! Clang! Clang! The bell rang from the Hanscome's porch.

All the relatives came running. What would this summons be? Good or bad news?

"It's a girl!" shouted Thomas as he rang the bell, again.

"What is her name?" asked John Lee.

"Anna Louisa," Thomas replied, handing out cigars to his brothers-in-law. "She is named for those left in Charleston - Anna for our dear mother and Louisa for our dear sister. They will be overjoyed when I write them the news of their namesakes."

"And how is Mary Sophia?" asked Mary Forten, now proudly pregnant herself.

"She is well, tired, but well. Mary Ann is with her now."

"Anna Louisa will be a great playmate for our wee Ellen," said Elizabeth Sarah, cuddling her newborn.

"If only our animals would be so prolific," laughed John Garden placing his arm around his wife and new babe. John laughed, but the reality was that Pennsylvanian farming was not profitable, not like the Carolina low country. Why? The planting season was shorter, their acreage was smaller and their hired hands cost them dearly, but the biggest reason? Cotton was absent. They had no cash crop like cotton.

"I'm thinking we need more boy babies to make our land more profitable," ventured John Lee in return.

"Don't let Mary Ann hear you say that you intend to turn her into a broodmare or your son into a field hand," teased Thomas. "She has plans for an education for little Drayton. And don't let my Mary Sophia hear you talking about the need for more sons, since we have only girls. Next year our new orchards should produce a bumper crop and little girls hands are as gifted at picking apples and cherries as boys."

The truth was all their children were still too little to help in any significant way. What would they do, these gentlemen farmers from Charleston? They had invested more money than their farms returned. They had planted orchards, harvested timber, increased their flocks and herds. Every year production increased, but would they prosper? Thomas felt certain his new purchase of fifty acres would be money well spent. They had owned six hundred acre plantations in South Carolina. In Pennsylvania, the Hanscome clan had a mere two hundred and fifty acres. They had become simple farmers.

In spite of their changed circumstances, the Hanscomes, Lees and Gardens kept their Charleston celebrations and festivities alive.

The Fourth of July

"Happy Fourth of July!" shouted Charlotte Forten to her Hanscome cousins as she, her step-mother Mary and father climbed into the buggy for the drive to Philadelphia. She was excited to see the fireworks and the grand parade. She also promised to bring back American flags for all her cousins. Mary was most excited to hear her husband speak at the Anti-Slavery Society rally. He had been practicing his speech for a week. Alice had begged to go, but Mary Sophia said she would miss out on her favorite game of egg toss with her father.

The Gardens, Lees and Hanscomes were hosting their own party. They had invited the Amundsen's for a picnic and games. Was their celebration also a tactful way of escaping Robert Forten's lengthy oratory?

"But your children are too young for foot races," said their nanny, Emma Amundsen.

"But we aren't," laughed Mary Sophia. "Do you think we can get your father, Karl, to race with us?"

"You can ask, but he will think such games too childish," smiled Emma. "However, he might consider racing his new mare."

"On your mark, get set, go!" shouted Karl Amundsen. Yes, he had refused to play the games, but he didn't mind declaring the winner. And Karl's new mare won a simple horse race, much to Thomas' chagrin. Thomas apologized to his horse-racing father in heaven for that loss. And Emma hid a smile of her own when she detected a certain pride in her father's stance. Pride was considered a sin.

The Hanscomes, Lees and Gardens played as hard as they farmed. They had contests of who could stand on their hands the longest - John Garden won. They played horse shoes, which Karl Amundsen won. Who won the traditional Hanscome egg toss? Mary and John Lee were victorious while Thomas and

Elizabeth Sarah were called "the good eggs." Even Thomas laughed as the broken egg splattered the whole front of his shirt.

After the picnic, decks of cards were brought out for games of whist, which they taught to the Amundsens. They wouldn't gamble, but Karl saw no harm in the game, much to Emma's delight. As the sun set, they shot off rockets and ended with a volley of thirteen rounds from their rifles. Why thirteen? One round represented each original colony. Their happiness may not have mirrored their grandfather Hanscome's feelings when independence was gained from the British, but holidays were meant to be celebrated. Did they give any thought to independence for the slaves they left behind in South Carolina? No, they did not.

The next day the Fortens returned from Philadelphia. Was their Independence Day more meaningful? Charlotte was excited to recall every bit of the parade - from the horses and soldiers to the drums and the bugles, and especially the ear breaking cannon booms. However, her father's speech was her highlight. Robert warmed many hearts to his call of "Freedom for All!" Mary was very proud of her husband and Charlotte decided right then and there to also dedicate her life to the cause of freedom for the slaves. The Anti-Slavery Society was also most pleased that Robert had inspired many to empty their pockets.

1847

The Garden's home

"Thank you, Elizabeth Sarah, for my new field hand," smiled John Garden as he held his newborn, Joel. "What a fine looking son."

"Yes, our Joel is a handsome one, and I can tell way too smart to be tricked by his father into becoming a common laborer." retorted his mother. "Now please go ring our porch bell."

The Forten's home

"I am more in love with you every day, my dear Mary," said Robert Forten as he held his son, Wendell Phillips, named after his abolitionist friend. "I never thought I would have another child. I must write a poem about his miraculous birth. And we must have him baptized as soon as possible. I'll ask the Purvis' and the Phillips to be his God parents, if that pleases you, too."

"Yes, they are the best Godparent choices. I owe my life to my Hanscome clan, but your Philadelphia friends will see best to wee Wendell's religious instruction." Mary smiled at her gifted, and sometimes zealous, husband. He was gifted with words, enthusiasm and a kind heart. Unfortunately, he was not gifted as a farmer. "However, we need my Hanscome family to teach our son to prosper."

"May I hold him?" asked Charlotte, now ten and a seasoned nanny for her Garden, Lee and Hanscome cousins.

"Of course, dearest Charlotte," answered Mary. "And please ring our porch bell."

After two short years, Mary could not imagine life without Charlotte. She was so talented with words, as was her father. Robert and Mary had discussed Charlotte's future education at great length. While they appreciated the tutelage of their Philadelphia Forten Aunts, Charlotte had an insatiable appetite for knowledge and untapped abilities. A boarding school in the North would be the best, costly, but best. Mary was very grateful for her Robert, but was secretly also thankful that Thomas was managing her estate. She would gladly pay for Charlotte's education but her financial contributions to his cause needed to be curbed.

1849

Were they prospering? If wealth were counted by children, they were most wealthy. No, their means were quite modest.

The Forten's home

"It's another boy!" shouted Robert Forten as he rang his porch bell.

"Thank you, dear Mary. Indeed, we are most 'fortunate' to have such fine sons," he jested.

"Now all we need is the fortune to go with the Forten name," she laughed.

"Don't worry, Mary, God will provide."

And what did they name their second born? Edmund Quincy Forten. He was named for Robert's Massachusetts friend and cohort in the American Anti-Slavery Society. It was said that Robert's orations and Edmund's writings inspired wealthy abolitionists to support the cause, from Boston to Pennsylvania. Why not the South? It was still impenetrable due to the US postal service censorship of all such inflammatory literature.

Elizabeth Sarah joined the celebration with her new baby, Joanna, in her arms. "You might have a Congressman with a name as impressive as Quincy."

"First, freedom for all, then the vote, then the Congress. Why not? The Quincy's will support us," touted Robert.

"The Quincys might support a Forten for Congress, but they are not going to support all these babies we are having," reminded Mary.

The Hanscome's home

"Twins! Twin girls!" yelled Thomas as he rang his porch bell. In his excitement he doubled his cigar gifts for all the men.

And their names? Virginia Emeline and Eugenia Angeline.

"And my surprise for you is a nanny, dear Mary Sophia. Emma's younger sister has agreed to help. When we're old and gray, I trust our girls will return our good care."

"Or more probably hire a nurse," retorted Mary Sophia.

"And my other surprise is that our dear mother Ann has agreed to move to Pennsylvania. First, she plans to sell her plantation and slaves. She writes she has spent four years without us and can no longer live without our company," reported Thomas holding her letter in his hand.

"What about James and Louisa Rebecca and their families?" asked Mary Ann. "She won't be able to return to South Carolina, once she leaves."

"Mother Ann says they are both prospering and will not leave. James is marrying this year - this time a freed mulatto girl with impeccable Brown Fellowship Society background and wealth. Her other great news is that Sarah will accompany her, as much as Serena hates the thought of losing her daughter, she wants her free in Philadelphia."

"How can Mother take Sarah? She is designated 'slave' as is her mother, Serena."

"Mother will find a way to get documents forged, but because of the mail censorship, did not elucidate on how that would happen."

"I wish we really knew what was going on in South Carolina," added Mary Hanscome Forten. "We have to read between the lines."

"With all these levels of 'free' and 'slave', how can your relatives breathe?" commented Robert Forten.

"They are used to it. And really, Robert, we do not have citizen rights right here, in the most liberal Pennsylvania."

"But here slavery is banished," defended Robert. "That is a huge difference. Sarah will be free as soon as her feet touch our soil."

"Yes, that is a true gift for Sarah. I do long to see her and mother. But I, for one, also miss the grandeur of our Carolina life," sighed Mary Ann. "I miss the balls, the dancing, the music, and the fresh oysters. Oh, and the lovely warm sea in the summer. You cannot appreciate how we lived, dear Robert. But we cannot return. I so hope mother is not shocked by our lack of refinement, our simple farm life."

1850

The Hanscome's home

"A warm house! I am so thankful for this coal and our new furnace," said Mary Sophia, kissing her Thomas on the cheek as he took the hod carrier to the basement to stoke the furnace. "What a thoughtful husband. What a wonderful present. I know I laughed at you last summer when you had it installed. I no longer think it is a folly. The hot air keeps our children toasty warm until the morning. We could live without coal in South Carolina, but these Pennsylvania winters are beyond cold, bone-chilling frigid better describes them. Today I smile. I even find this snowfall lovely."

"Does that mean you will shovel the path to the barn this morning," he teased.

"Yes, I will," laughed Mary Sophia. "I think it's even warm enough for the girls to help with the chores. And later we can make snowmen."

"It's a good thing Emma taught you to knit wool hats and mittens," laughed Thomas. "We certainly are getting use out of them this winter."

"Even fancy Charleston ladies need to keep their hands busy. Do you like that we each have a separate color?"

"They are a blessing," smiled Thomas. "I certainly don't hear anymore fighting over the mittens."

"The Three Little Kittens, they lost their mittens," sang Alice, now five, as she donned her pink mittens and matching hat.

"And they began to cry!" added two year old Martha Sophia, mimicking her older sister. Her mittens and hat were blue.

"Put your mittens on, Father. We are getting hot," bossed Alice. The children shrieked as he put on Mary Sophia's red mittens and hat. "No, those are Mother's mittens!"

"But I have these drab mittens," he complained, holding up his big, dark brown mittens. "Boo Hoo, Boo Hoo!" Thomas imitated the three little kittens crying and rubbing their eyes and his girls laughed with glee.

"They are stunning, not drab at all," defended his wife as she changed the subject. "Listen girls. I hear the animals calling you! Moo Moo…"

"Moo Moo!" added the girls as their mother whisked all that silliness out the door.

"I'll race you to the barn," challenged their father. Accepting his challenge, they waddled as fast in the deep snow as their galoshes and fat coats allowed.

"I get to feed the cat, please Father," begged Alice.

"Me, too," said Martha Sophia, clapping her hands.

"First, we need to milk the cows, slop the pigs and feed the horses and oxen. You can help me. And that cat is supposed to be eating the mice. He is not doing his job," said their father with feigned disgust.

In spite of hearing yesterday that Mary Sophia's brother and sisters were not leaving Charleston and in spite of Thomas' holding her as she cried all night, he smiled at their morning antics. They were happy in spite of their losses. They had made a good life for themselves. Thomas was content. He looked up to see his wife shoveling the path to the house, wee Anna Louisa strapped to her back. She had finally gotten over the loss of their son, Edwin. However, he thought, it is unfortunate we are not making much money. He decided to talk with Mary Sophia, later.

"I have been offered $1000 more than I paid for our new fifty acres, Mary Sophia. I think I will take the offer."

"If you sell the acreage, what is your next plan?" asked Mary Sophia, concerned. She was aware that their funds were dwindling.

"We will keep the farm, the hired hand, but I am going to become a coal merchant. I have been meeting with The Delaware and Hudson Canal Company and the mine owners on my Philadelphia trips. I have also corresponded with brother James and William DeCosta in Charleston. I think they could make money as coal brokers for us. I predict coal will replace timber as the best heating source, even in the warmer climes. And transportation by the new railroads might defray the shipping costs. Much of the timberlands close to Charleston have already been cleared."

"That means you will spend more time away from us, Thomas," lamented Mary Sophia. "But I would not part with our coal furnace, so I imagine others will gladly make the change from wood stoves, if the coal is reasonably priced."

"Yes, that is what I hope. Coal could make us wealthy. And you will also be able to travel to Philadelphia with me. I know you miss the Purvis and Forten sisters, the shopping and the concerts."

"I don't want to move back to Philadelphia. Do you, Thomas?"

"I love our family farms. I think I can travel from here to do my business. I am also going to sell furnaces, like ours."

"What I don't like is you traveling by yourself. The slave catchers could claim you."

"Come, look in this parlor mirror with me, Mary Sophia." And he led her to stand before the mirror.

"What do you see?"

"Don't be ridiculous, Thomas. I see us in the mirror."

"And what color is our skin?"

"Light, now that winter is here, our skin is quite pale."

"And what color is your hair?"

"Red."

"And haven't you always envied my straight, black hair?" he teased.

"Indeed, I have," she laughed.

"I think it is time we consider changing our racial designation to white. It's a matter of perception. I know a man in Philadelphia who will change our traveling papers, for a small fee. It's simple to change an 'M' to a 'W', at least on our traveling papers. It's time we live beyond fear."

"And what about our girls' African curls?"

"That's what bonnets are for," smiled Thomas.

Had Thomas forgotten that the 1850 census had recently listed the Hanscomes as "M" for mulatto?

CH. 24. The Noose Tightens

1850

Philadelphia

"No! This cannot be!" said Robert Forten to Robert Purvis as they read the latest news, the passage of the Fugitive Slave Act.

"What will this mean for us, Robert?" asked Robert Purvis, equally upset.

"It means fear will now be a part of our lives again," replied Robert Forten. "But it also means our anti-slavery work has succeeded," he thoughtfully added.

"How can you say that? Now any slave discovered in a free state can be returned to their masters in a slave state. The slave catchers will be fruitful and multiply. And what's more, we can be fined and imprisoned for helping runaway slaves. We have slid backwards since 1838 when you published your *Appeal of Forty Thousand Citizens, Threatened with Disfranchisement to the People of Pennsylvania,* beseeching thinking men to award us the right to vote."

"It is like the French Revolution, only fifty years ago, my dear friend. Our abolitionist cause is more than a thorn. We are the instrument for social change. Things may get worse before they can improve – look at history. The southern states are hanging onto their institution of slavery for dear life. It may be as my friend Edmund Quincy predicts. The South will secede and our Union will dissolve. Then we will be finished placating them, with ridiculous laws, like this Fugitive Slave Act. We must continue our work. We will prevail."

"But the blood! More blood will be shed," lamented Robert Purvis.

"We must increase our efforts to help the courageous runaways on the underground railway, before the noose swings right here in Pennsylvania," said a determined Robert Forten.

Bucks County

And how did the farmers receive the new Fugitive Slave Law?

"Clang, clang, clang!" tolled the Garden's porch bell. "I have just received bad news from our mother," said Elizabeth Sarah to her extended family. "She bemoans that she will not be able to leave Charleston. Her papers are in order, but Serena will not release Sarah. Serena's white father, John Walker, has died and Serena needs her Sarah to remain."

"Read between the lines. What does she truly mean?" pondered Mary Ann.

"I think it is a code that Serena fears for her daughter, if she is caught leaving the state. These fugitive slave laws have created a panic. Sarah, really all of them, could be imprisoned, then sold at the auction block. Even our mother, if she assists, could lose her freedom. It could also mean that Serena and her mother now need our mother to protect them. We don't know who their white guardian is in her father's will. Perhaps our mother will have to buy them. But certainly Serena and her mother will inherit a good amount," offered Elizabeth Sarah.

"This is all mere conjecture," said John Lee. "My parents' letters also mask the truth. All I know is that their hotel and restaurant are still in favor by the cream of the white gentry. They are prospering, but they bow and kowtow. They also say we made a good decision to leave, in their subtle ways. One day I expect them to show up at our doorstep."

"My brother says all the rice plantations are suffering their share of runaways," stated John Garden. "And the tariffs, good for the north, are killing our agricultural prices and profits. The newspapers he includes have long postings of rewards for runaways and list many plantations for sale. Of course, he does not explain further. We must surmise that the golden age of plantations has passed. It was a good thing we sold our plantation and slaves when my father died."

"Yes, I have directed our brother-in-law, William DeCosta, to sell the remaining slaves owned by Mary and me," added Thomas.

"I have difficulty listening to your evil words, dear relatives, although it is an education for me," said furious Robert Forten. "You discuss the sale of humans and land in the same breath. And you hold yourself above it all. Your sense of entitlement must have been a gift from your white fathers. And when the gild was off the lily, you left. You abandoned the ship of slaves, when you, the models for successful living, left. You simply betrayed them, your darker brothers and sisters."

Silence.

"You speak of them, the darkest and most uneducated of field slaves, and us in the same breath, Robert," interjected John Garden. "What we have been trying to tell you is that for over a hundred years, we have been a breed apart. We come from good families. We are now homeless and belong nowhere. I was proud that my father, a mestizo freedman, had the most successful 600 acre rice plantation – and slaves. I myself disciplined them. For those deeds I am most sorry, but that was our normal life, our culture. We see your cause, Robert, but we're not there - yet. We have many layers of fine clothes to shed first. Perhaps one day we will see our past quest for acquisition as a sin, like the Quakers. But doesn't the law of acquisition - of aspiring to be the best, own the most land, make the most profits - guide most human actions?"

"Not at the expense of your brothers and sisters," shouted Robert Forten.

Silence.

The Forten's home

As a new dawn approached, Mary was stoking the cellar furnace with coal. Upstairs the wood stove was burning hot. She was cooking a slab of bacon, eggs and grits for breakfast. It had been a cold winter's night. Soon her family's nostrils would guide them from their comforters to the kitchen. She smiled. Bacon worked every time to rouse her family.

"Knock, knock, knock." Three short, distinct knocks was the signal for the travelers. Mary opened the door wide and saw no one. Then Mary softly sang, "Swing low, sweet chariot, coming for to carry me home..." and figures appeared from behind a stand of pines. Mary motioned a welcome sign and the five weary adults ran to the porch.

"Is this a station?" cautiously asked the woman carrying a young child.

"You need no ticket at this depot," answered Mary. "Come in, warm yourself, breakfast is on the griddle."

Mary called for Robert. "We have passengers this morning."

"If you go down the basement, which is toasty warm, you can bathe in private. I'll have my husband fill the bath tub with hot water and bring clean towels and clothes. You must have had quite a night."

"We have been traveling for two days with little sleep. I think we are off course, but we have been following the drinking gourd and the star on its tail."

"You are safe here. We will help you get your bearings, draw a map, and discuss your route after you are rested and fed."

Mary added pan cakes and another slab of bacon to the griddle. Charlotte added five more places at the dining room table and placed apple butter, cherry preserves, cheese and milk on the table. The eggs sizzled and the guests hungrily sat down to the feast.

"Dear Lord," prayed Robert Forten. "Thank you for allowing us to be instruments of your hand and help these passengers reach the promised land. Thank you for this fine food and bless us all. Amen."

"Amen," the travelers chorused.

Where were these runaway slaves from? Near Raleigh, North Carolina. They hugged the mountains traveling north at night and stayed in "conductors" homes during the day. They kissed the ground when they reached the free state of Pennsylvania. But that is where they ran into the slave catchers.

"We killed a man, preacher Robert. He was going to take us back to our master, but we outnumbered him. Somehow the Lord helped us slay the devil, but we do not feel right inside," said one of the men to Robert.

"As Daniel slew Goliath, you were led by God. You have left the den of iniquity and God will reward, not punish you. Take comfort in God's grace, dear people. You are meant to be free!"

The travelers slept close to the furnace on cots in clean linens and warm quilts. The babies were placed in the Forten boys' cribs and slept contentedly. When they awoke, Mary and Charlotte welcomed them with a southern fried chicken dinner. In addition to the crispy chicken, they were served green beans, sweet and Irish potatoes, gravy and apple pie with the freshest cream for dessert.

"Let's discuss the rest of your journey to Canada," said Robert.

"Will Canada be any different?" hesitantly asked one weary guest.

"That is a good question. Like the rest of England's colonies, slavery was only outlawed twenty years ago. None of us know what the future brings, but anywhere in the world is better than the United States for runaways."

"Are there folks like us, families?" asked the mother of the small child.

"You will find many slaves, like you," assured Robert. "Many fought for the British during the Revolutionary War, were freed and relocated to the Canadian east coast provinces. But there are pockets of freed Negros - farmers and artisans in many areas. We have been told that London, Ontario, has a good community of escaped slaves. That is where we suggest you live. The Anti-Slavery Society of Canada has helped many, like you, start afresh."

"And the slave catchers can't bring us back to our masters? We are so afraid of them our hearts pound with fear."

"You are not safe from the slave catchers until you cross the big lake of Ontario. But there are many safe depots and many who deplore slavery, who will hide you, help you and feed you. Friends like us. You must follow the Delaware River, a bit east of here, north to New York, then follow the Hudson River until you come to a big canal. Follow the Erie Canal west to the big lakes. I have marked the rivers and depots on the railroad on this map with X's. Travel close to the rivers and cross them frequently, so the slave catchers' dogs will lose your scent. Study this map, all of you, in case you lose it. Many station masters are white folks, but do not be afraid of them. You will be free, like we are."

Elizabeth Sarah was at the door, but did not knock when she heard the singing and praying. Instead, she turned and walked back to her home. She knew the Fortens were an underground railroad station and she feared for them. Would she help, if runaways came to her door? Yes, she would turn no one away, but John would not like her risking her family's safety. She left her pie, beef jerky and jars of vegetables on the window sill, along with a box of outgrown coats, wool scarves and mittens. Mary Sophia and Mary Ann also helped by supplying the Fortens with old clothes and precious canned food. Outgrown children's clothes and boots were especially needed.

"Thank you for our comforts, dear Lord," the Hanscomes prayed at their family gatherings. "Help us share our bounty with the needy." Yes, Robert Forten had slowly and patiently made an impact on his elitist southern relatives.

1852

When Thomas traveled his coal circuit northwest, he made an effort to stop at Guinea Run, the town of poor freedmen miners.

"Where have they gone?" asked Thomas of his German neighbor, Karl Amundsen, as he returned from Guinea Run. His wagon was full of clothes and food for the barely thriving town. "What happened to them?"

"The slave catchers took them, took the whole lot of them that weren't working in the mines. They drove carts and chained them all together, mainly women and children. I have never seen the likes of it!"

"Where were the men? They all have guns to protect their families. I know. We collected weapons for them!"

"They were working in the mines. The brazen slave catchers simply came in broad daylight and snatched their families. And when the colored men returned from their mine shift, they chased after the catchers, with guns. It sickens me. How could this happen? Right here in Bucks County!" Karl shook his head in amazement. "Now the town is deserted. It's a frightful thing, to have your freedom taken in such a way. None of them from Guinea Run were runaways. None of them had been slaves, at least none of the young ones. They just wanted better lives, away from Philadelphia. This has got to stop, but what can we do? The law is still the law." Karl paused, "And how are your people?"

"We are safe, thank you, but we keep a watchful eye on our families. We don't let our children play outside alone anymore. I don't know what we would do without your daughters' help. We are grateful for your trust."

"You are good neighbors. Emma and Karen are most happy in their work. They come home laughing and singing. And their English and reading have improved. If you have any trouble, send a rider for us. We will help you."

"Thank you. Let's hope that never happens."

1853

"Robert, don't let them take our passengers - do something!" pleaded Mary from the safety of their house.

"What can I do?" shouted an angry Robert storming in from outside. "I did what I could do. I showed them our papers, but they took them along with the runaways and threatened to be back for the rest of us! They said the sheriff will arrest us for aiding and abetting the runaways. Now we have no papers, Mary!"

"I'll ring the bell. Get both Johns and Thomas to ride after them!" she screamed as she sounded the alarm signal. "We need to help those runaways! We need to get our papers back!"

All came running. And Mary beseeched them to chase the slave catchers. But did they? No, they did not. They made other plans.

"Mary, you and Robert, your family, all of us are in jeopardy. We cannot go after the runaways. Do you want us to kill the slave catchers? And then what? Think, Mary! Think!" implored Thomas.

"We must also leave here and soon," said John Garden. "The Guinea Run freedmen all had certificates of freedom, like us. And these slave catchers are getting braver and braver."

"We can go to Philadelphia," suggested Mary Ann. "Or the Purvis' will take us in at their country estate."

"I think not. Nowhere in Pennsylvania is safe. The Purvis' children can't even go to the public school he pays huge taxes for. And he is the richest man in the county," said Thomas. "I think it is time for us to seek safety in Canada. I've had it with the Pennsylvania politics. This feels more and more like Charleston freedom. We are in danger."

"But we need time to put our affairs in order," cautioned John Garden.

"We need to move fast," countered John Lee.

"Slow down, John," cautioned Thomas. "We must sell our land first. We have made profits on our investment. Our farms are finally prospering. But in the meantime, we must guard our families, day and night. We must be armed and ready." Thomas' affable ways were cut cold. His eyes turned hard and determined. "We will take time to plan, but I intend to leave before spring. Let's hope the slave catchers lie dormant this winter."

"I cannot abandon my mission, Thomas. Mary and I will stay. Pennsylvania is our home. But if you do indeed leave, we will move back to Philadelphia, near my family. We can get new papers there. As much as the Purvis' enjoy their country estate in Byberry, they are finding increased sentiment against them."

Robert consoled his Mary as the others drew up a night watch schedule.

April, 1853

The Hanscomes, Lees and Gardens were ready to leave by the spring.

"It has been a pleasure doing business with you," said Thomas to John Henderson, the attorney who finalized the sale of the Hanscome fifty-one acres to Robert and Elizabeth Bicknell. "I may need your assistance at some later date as I will be keeping my other investments. I will be in touch with you from Toronto."

The farewell to the Fortens and the Purvis' at the Philadelphia wharf was most difficult.

"And my best to you, Robert," said Thomas. "I remember you and the Purvis' welcoming us from this very same pier just eight years ago. We had thought this would be our permanent home. And Mary, remember you always have a home where we are, should you and Robert change your mind. We should be in Toronto within the month."

"I never thought I would live anywhere except Pennsylvania, but we, too, will be moving north, to Boston," said Robert Forten. "I will be able to continue my anti-slavery work there, but also keep my family safe."

"Robert and his sister, Harriet Purvis, are taking Charlotte to grammar school in Salem this fall and will look in Boston for a new home for us. Edmund Quincy has most kindly provided introductions," added Mary. "The boys and I will remain in Philadelphia until Robert and Harriet return."

"Are you excited?" Mary Sophia asked Charlotte, a fine young lady at sixteen.

"Oh, yes. I hear the prejudice against us is much less in New England. I will be attending a school with 200 white pupils, the Higginson Grammar School in Salem. After I matriculate, I will enroll in the Normal School," said Charlotte proudly. "When I've finished, I promised Margaretta to consider a teaching position at her Philadelphia school."

"We will miss you. You have already been the best teacher for our children. Please write to us and continue your poetry. Your writing is as moving as your dear father's prose," added Elizabeth Sarah.

"All aboard!" The ship's whistle blew as the conductor opened the ramp gate.

As they embarked, their sadness could not be contained and their tears could not be stanched. Again, they were homeless. Did the young children realize their Forten cousins would not be going with them? Did they realize they would never be returning to their warm kitchens or their baby pigs and chicks? The Fortens watched the Hanscome, Garden and Lee families wave from the upper deck, until the speck of the ship was swallowed by the ocean.

"Tell us again, Father, where are we going?" asked Alice, seeking reassurance, as she viewed the sunrise from the ship's bow and snuggled into her father's warm shoulder.

"On a spring time adventure," said Thomas. "We are like a babe taking its first steps, a bit uncertain of the result, mind you dear Alice, but enthusiastically open to the future. Toronto will be our new home."

"I mean how will we get there? I know New York City comes first," asked an impatient Alice. Sometimes her father could prattle on and on.

"Oh, I see, you want a geography review. New York is an island with a bustling harbor, like Philadelphia. There we will disembark and transfer to a smaller vessel that will sail up the Hudson River. At Albany, we will disembark again and travel the Erie Canal."

"Why can't we just stay on this ship?" asked Alice. "I like our stateroom."

"Because the Hudson River is like the Delaware and the channels are too small for such a big ship. In a few years they will have a railroad with a steam engine that will go from Pennsylvania to New York. Look at this map. Travel by land is too slow and cumbersome, especially since we have many trunks and household goods to move with us. What happens at Albany, Alice?" quizzed her father.

"A barge. We will take a barge on the Erie Canal, like the barges on the Pennsylvania canals. And from Lake Ontario a ship to Toronto." Alice had been through this recitation before, but talking about the journey made it seem less like a dream.

"And I will celebrate my eleventh birthday in our new home, right Father?"

"Yes, we will have a party."

"Will we have another farm, Father?"

"No, I will be a coal and wood merchant, thus we will live in town, in a nice big house, where you and your cousins will finally go to a good school. Your education is important."

"I have a question about my papers, Father. Why does it say 'W' white for race? I've always been 'M' for mulatto."

"Because you are more white than Negro and in Canada no one uses the word, mulatto. We won't use it either or the word colored. Now you will be white. We all are white."

"The Gardens and the Lees, too?"

"Yes, all of us. All our papers say white. Please remember that."

"I like it. Now we won't be different. We will be the same."

Thomas smiled. He hoped in Canada his children would find a home and school free from prejudice.

The Gardens, the Lees and the Hanscomes changed their racial designation on their South Carolinian baptismal, confirmation and marriage certificates in Philadelphia. Only the 1850 Pennsylvania Census still listed them as 'M' for mulatto. Apparently, money could still buy most anything. Buying white status was nothing new. It had been done by wealthy mulattos in Charleston, but that was before Thomas was born and before the new laws, those awful laws that made manumission impossible and restricted freedmen. Before they left the farm, they lit a bonfire with their damning certificates of freedom from South Carolina. No whites were ever asked to carry such certificates.

"If the Negro race is so inferior," reflected Thomas, "why is it necessary to pass the laws to contain them? Fear. Regardless of racial status, we all have the same potential and talents. Robert Forten is right, about so many things, but he is just not practical or realistic. None of us mulattos will ever see true equality in our lifetime. As white, my family will thrive."

CH. 25. The Fresh Canadian Air

1854

Toronto

How were the fair Hanscomes faring one year after their immigration?

They were busy, most practical by day, but at night indulged their memories as they longed for the warm, soft, low country air. Yes, Charleston and the Sea Islands still captured Thomas' and Mary Sophia's dreams. They would lie in bed, laugh and replay grandiose tales of their lavish weddings and grand parties, horse races, sailing regattas and the subtle courting games of the refined, mulatto elite. They were convinced they would never see so much opulence again. Oh, make no mistake, the Hanscome coal and timber business was thriving, but these northerners did not believe in ostentatious displays of wealth.

"Canadians are frugal to a fault," sighed Mary Sophia. "What good is wealth, Thomas, if you can't enjoy it? I'd love to sing and dance again in fine silk dresses. I'd love to be served my meals and be waited on hand and foot." There seemed no harm in reminiscing, but some nights Mary Sophia dissolved in tears. "Oh, Thomas, I shouldn't have left my brother and sisters behind. Why did we do that, Thomas? Do you think they despise me? Will we ever see them again? Or do you think they have simply forgotten us? Why haven't they written to me?"

"Stop blaming yourself, dear. I excuse us because we were both too young, barely adults, to envision the consequences of our actions. We are not clairvoyant. We could not foresee the passage of the Fugitive Slave Act or even the reluctance of your Aunts to part with your brother and sisters. Do not forget that in Pennsylvania we tried to have them and my mother join us. I don't know how my mother found the strength to shoo us from her nest, but in retrospect, her actions were the wisest. She let go and now we must let go of your family. They have not returned your letters since we moved to Canada. We can only hope our prayers will make a difference. Let's assume it is a problem with the mail rather than jump to the conclusion that they are soon to be sold into slavery."

"My family has no claim to Indian blood to save them from the Negro Law restrictions," said Mary Sophia, distraught. "It made no difference that Lucy Moor was a Moroccan, thus white, to my family's status as freedmen. Slavery is supposed to follow the mother's lineage. I'd like to hear that my aunts petitioned the court, then my brother and sisters could leave South Carolina, but I think they still are registered as "M" for mulatto. Their silence is deafening to me. I think the absence of news is as cruel as the worst reality. Nothing!"

"I think that the courts granting James' second petition, awarding us Indian status and exemption from the Negro laws, is a blessing, if we are to believe my mother's cheery missives. I believe she writes optimistic, rather than truthful news. I'd feel better if we heard confirmation from James or Louisa Rebecca. They, too, have been silent since we moved to Toronto. Nor do we know that any of this legal status makes any difference to the slave catchers."

Silence.

"Our only recourse is to follow Ann's joyful lead, accentuate the positive, lest we become mired in grief," resolved Mary Sophia, shaking off her despondency.

Thomas smiled, as he shared his mother's favorite expression with his wife. "If you don't like something, just deny it, my dear!"

Hadn't this always been the case in the course of history? People moved to improve their lots in life. Families became divided. Plans to reunite became lost good intentions. Whole families emigrated and lost their roots. Survival became more important than love. But the memories of love were never forgotten. The Hanscomes were no different. When logic failed, they prayed with their hearts. "Please, Dear Lord, keep our family safe." Most of the time, they simply denied their pain. Click, over, next and smile.

And how were the children faring? They quickly adjusted to Toronto life, but nostalgia about their family farms, not South Carolina, claimed their hearts.

"I miss our pigs," whined Martha Sophia, "especially Bessie."

"As I recall, you despised slopping those muddy, slippery pigs," laughed wise twelve year old Alice.

"I miss winning the egg toss game," chirped Anna Louisa.

"You might have won a few games, but you seem to have forgotten that your sweet little thieving hands were bloody, black and blue, from the pecking of those vicious hens trying to protect their precious eggs," reminded Alice. Indeed, she was thrilled to be free from farm chores and herding her sisters. More than anything, Alice loved school.

The Hanscomes bought a large two story home with four bedrooms upstairs. The first thing Thomas did was install a brand new coal furnace in the basement.

"We have a monster in our basement, so you'd better be good," teased Thomas. Its fiery red mouth and threatening octopus arms made Martha

Sophia, Anna Louisa and the twins, Virginia and Eugenia, shriek with both fear and joy. When Thomas had their full attention he would add fuel to their fear, just like stoking the furnace. "And sometimes the monster likes to eat little girls!"Alice simply laughed, but all the same, she didn't like to go down to that dark, eerie basement, either.

Their house had both a front and a back stairs, perfect for playing tag, hide and seek and sliding down the wooden banisters, intentionally waxed bright and slippery. The more they polished, the faster they slid. Downstairs the dining room held a round mahogany table with lion paws for feet, large enough to seat twenty when the leaves were added. Of course, the Charleston candelabra with the crystal prisms glinted in the sunlight at the table's center. Meals with the Lees and Gardens were always served on the best china and silver platters. These Charleston traditions were cherished. As Thomas said, "Children might be conceived in the marriage bed, but they are taught gracious living, laughter and manners, the very foundation of civilization, at the dining room table."

Upstairs, the largest bedroom overlooking St. James Cathedral was made into a cheery dormer for the five girls. The adjoining small bedroom was given to Windsong, their servant, a Mississauga native girl. She eagerly went to school during the day and as eagerly helped Mary Sophia with the cooking, washing and cleaning. From her room, Windsong could keep an eye on the girls' shenanigans and study. She learned to treasure her first taste of privacy. Windsong was preparing to be a teacher for her village on the harbor islands.

Was their Toronto life good? Of course! Sadness was whisked under the table. Laughter had made every Hanscome home a most happy one. And tonight with the Fortens' arrival, the best celebration was about to begin. Their family would be reunited.

"Do you see them? Alice, do you see your Aunt Mary, Uncle Robert and the boys?" asked Mary Sophia as they watched the ship move closer to the wharf.

"No, I don't see them anywhere. Maybe they didn't come," despaired Alice.

"Impossible, we just don't see them," said Mary Sophia, frantically scanning the upper deck.

"Look down, at the lower deck. The ship is segregated, Mary Sophia," Thomas whispered.

"Oh, I forgot, since we had upper deck tickets. Thomas, how is this visit going to work for all of us? The railways, the schools are all segregated," worried Mary Sophia.

"We will make it work. They are family."

Everyone furiously waved as they spotted their cousins. All the Lees and the Gardens turned out to welcome Mary, Robert, Wendell and Edmund Forten. A sea of arms embraced as everyone fiercely greeted each other. Their faces beamed as tears raced down their cheeks. What a noisy and heart-warming reunion. Soon all were stuffed into the waiting horse-drawn carriages.

"What a lovely town! I am enthralled," exclaimed Mary Forten to her lost sisters. "The Toronto Islands and the harbor are magnificent. They remind me of the South Carolina Sea Islands. I didn't expect white sand beaches so far from the ocean."

"We have many surprises for you. This is called the St. James Ward," extolled self-appointed and proud tour guide Thomas. "We have a new hospital and you can see the lovely Cathedral, just rebuilt, in the distance. There was a devastating fire just a few years ago, 1849, I believe, but these hearty people will not be discouraged. It's the tallest building in Canada. This city is growing fast, Robert, and has many opportunities. They are forward thinking and have plans for a magnificent train station that overlooks the harbor. Soon a railway between Montreal and Toronto will be completed. Over here is the Mechanics Institute that John Garden attended before he opened his machine business. Tomorrow, we will walk the magnificent Scarborough Bluffs and eat in the Lee's Restaurant and Boarding House."

"And has segregation been implemented above the 49th parallel?" asked Robert.

"Yes, unfortunately, yes it has. Canada has no segregation laws, but people are expected to know their proper place. What a disgusting phrase that is, *to know your proper place*. English law supports freedom for all, legal freedom, but in spite of the many Canadian abolitionist voices, the neighborhoods, the schools, even the railways are all segregated."

"Well, at least you have no extradition laws," commented Robert, trying to sound positive.

"There are no slave catchers here. Thousands of slaves are free and safely settled in Ontario. This is the end of the Underground Railway, but you already know that, Robert. I thought you might enjoy meeting the editor of *The Daily Globe*, perhaps even write some articles for the paper. It supports the Anti-Slavery movement."

"And your neighborhood?" he asked. "Is it segregated?"

"We will have a look around tomorrow and you can judge it for yourself. But I do believe it is dinner time and trust you are hungry. We have missed you, Robert. I have missed you."

Thomas knew he was being evasive, but he wanted this evening to be a welcoming one. He had missed Mary and Robert, even his lengthy oratories. And the children? They were ecstatic to see their cousins. The candelabra were lit and the crystal and silver gleamed on the finest white linen tablecloths. Name cards, inked in Alice's best calligraphy, graced each of the thirty place settings. It had taken Mary Sophia, Mary Ann and Elizabeth Sarah days of preparation. Of course, much of it had been prepared in the Lee's large restaurant kitchen.

When Mary Sophia rang her silver hostess bell, Windsong served the first course. As Mary Sophia raised her soup spoon to her lips, the signal for the meal to commence was given. The conversation was as fine as the manners and the food. The soup course was followed by silver platters laden with vegetables and meats, followed by fruits and cheeses. Even Alice was poured wine, but the Fortens, true to their temperance practices, did not imbibe.

"And how is dear Charlotte?" asked Elizabeth Sarah. "The children miss her – we all do."

"She is finding her Salem school an adjustment," sighed Robert. "As the only person of color, she is lonely. The other girls are polite to her, but she has no real friends. Poetry is her favorite companion. She hopes that next year when she attends the Normal School things will be different. Her host family, the abolitionists Sarah and Charles Remond, have been most welcoming and introduced her to many free thinking writers. Charlotte particularly delights in her correspondence with John Greenleaf Whittier. Then, of course, there are my friends, Wendell Phillips and William Lloyd Garrison, who take an interest in her writings.

"Sister Harriet and I went to Boston to look for suitable homes and were dismayed, to say the least, by the enforcement of the Fugitive Slave Law. In spite of our work with the Massachusetts Anti-Slavery Society, the Court decided to extradite Anthony Burns to his slave master in Virginia. Given that sad state of the law, why relocate? Instead, we decided to visit you."

"Well, Boston's loss is our gain," said Thomas raising his glass high. "Let's toast to the Fortens and our family."

Where did they all sleep? The girls vacated their large room for the Fortens and their two boys. Did the girls mind? Heavens, no. The twins, Martha Sophia and Anna Louisa bunked in the third bedroom that also served as their study and guest bedroom. And Alice was happy to leave her young sisters and their silly antics to sleep with Windsong, her idol.

Alice had been invited many times to Windsong's village on the Islands. There they rode ponies as fast as the wind through the surf and sand by day and gathered for camp fire stories at night. The legend of the Gibraltor Lighthouse and its haunting by the murdered light-keeper, sent chills up her spine. Alice felt accepted by the Village. Yes, she went to the white school, but she was considered *different*. Alice's best friend was her neighbor whose family had an East Indian mother and an English merchant father. She was also *different* – Caucasian, but a shade too dark. "If only I had your straight hair," Alice laughed. "And if only I had your lighter skin," resounded her East Indian friend.

And how did the Fortens find Toronto?

"I find it interesting that *The Daily Globe* published my articles, but when I asked for full time employment, the editor awkwardly refused my application," sighed Robert.

"Actually Thomas, the term *interesting* is an incorrect phrase - disheartening or even heart-breaking are more fitting descriptions of our feelings," added a discouraged Mary.

"Oh, we are so sorry," responded Mary Ann. "John and I could always use your expertise at the restaurant. John's parents arrived from Charleston and are helping us improve our business. The fine southern cuisine is as sumptuous as the view of the bluffs. We say we offer food for the body and soul."

"Or you could join my machinery business," offered John Garden. "We can hardly keep up with the growing demand for coal furnaces, thanks to Thomas' fuel business."

"And my coal accounts have doubled since last year," added Thomas, proudly.

"Or, if none of our businesses interest you," said John Garden, "there are other courses of study at The Mechanics Institute. It was a blessing for me. Like you, Robert, I had no idea how I would support my family when we arrived. Our son Daniel will join me in business, after he matriculates," said John beaming at his son. "But I'd be happy to have the placard read, Garden, Forten and Sons."

"I appreciate your kind offers, but I must be able to practice my calling. I must be of help to our people," said Robert.

"But you also need to find a paying position, dear Robert," spoke Mary softly, looking down at her plate.

Silence.

"Children, how did your day at school go?" brightly asked Elizabeth Sarah, tactfully changing the subject.

"We had fun at recess," replied Joel Garden, now seven. "The teacher put Wendell in the back of the classroom, all by himself. I offered to share my desk with him, but the teacher said I could sit with him in the back, if I wanted to – so I did. Then she gave me a note to take home to you."

"What did the note say?" asked Mary.

"We can talk later about that," said Elizabeth Sarah. "Right now we have two birthdays to celebrate. Virginia and Eugenia are five years old today! Let's sing happy birthday as Windsong brings in the cakes." And with that, Mary Sophia rang her little silver bell. All broke out in the Happy Birthday Song at the grand entrance of two identical snow white coconut cakes, flaming with candles.

After dessert, they retired to the parlor to listen to the concert the Hanscome, Lee and Garden children had excitedly prepared. All the children sang as Alice artfully played the grand piano. Too soon the party was over.

"Elizabeth Sarah, what did the teacher's note say?" asked Robert as the Gardens were preparing to leave.

"The note said that it was fine that Wendell visited, but that if he planned to enroll he would be better served attending the school for people of his color," said Elizabeth Sarah.

"I had thought that might be the case. Things are not much different across the 49th parallel are they?" His question was rhetorical. "You have enrolled your children in the white school, haven't you?"

"Yes we did - as you enrolled Charlotte in the fine Salem school."

"I am having second thoughts about my wisdom with Charlotte. And how are your children doing?"

"They are excelling in their studies and have made a few friends," answered Thomas. "We all miss the country life, but we ride our horses to the Toronto Islands regularly in the summer. We will go tomorrow if you like, take a picnic lunch. It is indeed lovely."

"But how are you adjusting to the segregation?" pointedly asked Robert.

"We haven't needed to adjust. As you see our neighborhood is mainly English and we attend St. James Cathedral. Next door lives an English merchant with his East Indian wife and children. The French live near the Catholic Church and keep their language, as much as possible. Just a few years ago there was a French rebellion for freedom from the English. The rebellion was quelled, but tensions still exist between the French and the English. And people of color live in another ward."

"Why then are you not in the colored district?" asked Robert.

"We have registered ourselves as white, Robert. Once we crossed that 49[th]parallel, we declared ourselves white."

"But you're not!"

"We are, Robert. Look at us - really look at us. We are light-complected."

"You are passing for white! You are traitors to your dear mother's heritage." Robert was livid and glared at Thomas.

"We are not *passing for white.* I detest that term!" seethed Thomas. "Do you *pass for Negro*, Robert, you with your white blood? We are white! We have claimed our English heritage as we are more white than Negro. It is logical. We are three generations removed from our African slave blood and many generations away from African soil. Should we call ourselves Negro, African, Mulatto? What racial designation suits us best? I suppose we could coin a new term and say we are bi-racial, but how ridiculous is that?

"Mulattos are held in as much contempt as those *half-breeds,* those of mixed Indian and French or English blood. It is a strange new prejudice for us, as in Charleston all the Mulattos wanted Indian blood – like the Gardens, to assure their freed status guaranteed by the Lords Proprietors in the late 1600's. Why would we want to be Negro? Negro, black and colored are synonymous with poverty and illiteracy, with inferiority. It conjures up the image of *the slave,* which we never were. We jumped to the white side of the fence, Robert, while you arrogantly maintain that racial fence with your rhetoric. Color is a blend, not an absolute! I have yet to see a truly white man or a black man.

"And we have voting rights here, unlike Pennsylvania. Yes, we are registered to vote, well the two Johns and I are registered to vote, not the women, but that is yet another battle to be fought. Our children are registered as white in school. And you insult me! Our mother would applaud our choice. As a mulatto she was raised as an English child, pampered by her white father, but always honored her freed Negro mother. She wanted us to thrive, have opportunity, regardless of racial designation. What is a race anyway, but external characteristics? Ridiculous! I tell my children to be the best they can be, a lesson I learned from my mother. How dare you say I don't honor her? I wish we could forget the words black and white, Robert. We are all people!"

Silence.

"Here we are, again, at the same place, Thomas," said Robert trying to control his rage. "Your Carolina lineage is an elitist one. Mary and I came to see how we would like Toronto, but we will not stay. You selfishly care only for your prosperity and turn your back on those enslaved. You deny your heritage. You are not our family anymore!"

"You will always be our family, Robert," sighed Thomas. "Take that fence down, at least between us."

"I am African and I want my children to honor my black heritage. We will be leaving in the morning."

Robert huffed up the stairs to pack their bags while Mary broke down in tears. She had never heard Thomas and Robert so angry.

"Mary, dear Mary, do you want to remain with us?" offered Thomas.

"I can't. I just can't leave him! Robert is my husband. I must remain true to him. And Thomas, we are not as light-skinned as you. I know he is hurt that you do not embrace your slave heritage, but I will always embrace my Hanscome ties. I will always embrace the mulattos in their quest to be the best and have the best, just like the planters. I will always honor my dearest Joseph and your dear mother Ann. I understand why you have made your choice, but Robert never will.

"Robert doesn't understand the beauty of Charleston, the spirit of the Sea Islands or the extravagances of the Brown Fellowship Society. Robert never lived music and dance. He never touched a soft cotton bowl or planted rice in the heel and toe cadence of a slave or lived side by side with a slave. We lived with our slaves! He knows about the institution of slavery, but he knows not a slave. Above all, he never lived laughter, as we did. His honorable but humorless father taught him the abolitionist cause and the cause claims my Robert. The cause is Robert. It is my Robert's soul.

"Unfortunately, James Forten never taught his son how to make a living or even how to hang onto the wealth he inherited. He raised a fine educated orator, a gentleman. In many ways my Robert is more of an elitist than he claims you to be. Am I sorry I married Robert? Absolutely not. I admire his tenacity and his principles. I love him."

"Principles? He didn't mind using all your money from the sale of your slaves. I know you love him, but how will you live, Mary, if he does not find gainful employment?"

"We will travel to London - London, Ontario - not too far from here, to assist the runaway slaves in their adjustment. Hopefully, he can work in some capacity. And I do have money left from the sale of my farm. Nonetheless, Charlotte's school tuition is expensive."

"And if he can't find work? There is great poverty in London but the Anglican Church has been helping. Our St. James Cathedral sends money to support a resettlement mission. Perhaps they will employ him."

"Robert would never become an Anglican," replied a despondent Mary.

"I do not feel good about your future in London, Ontario. What then, Mary? If you cannot support yourself in London, what will happen to you? Will you proudly join your darker skinned brothers and sisters, and yes, live in poverty? Poverty is the root of the problem – not skin color. Robert knows this to be true. He just fails to apply this principle to himself. What are you going to do if he doesn't find work?"

"He says he intends to find employment. Robert has a fine reputation, everywhere we go. Certainly one of his influential white friends will vouch for his character and recommend him for a suitable position. Wendell Phillips has lamented our leaving for Canada and has offered his assistance. We have also discussed traveling to London, London in England, where the Anti-Slavery movement is strong. Or we could always return to Pennsylvania, the Purvis' and Robert's family. We have lived under the fear of the slave catchers before. I support Robert's calling, but I am tired of feeling homeless and poor. And, oh how I have missed you, my family!"

Silence. Thomas held Mary as she sobbed and sobbed.

"Mary, please know you are always welcome in our home. I will send money for your passage, from anywhere. All you need to do is ask."

In the morning the Fortens left for London, Ontario. Robert did not notice Mary, Edmund and Wendell wistfully looking back at their sad-faced cousins.

1856

"It's a boy! Girls, you have a baby brother! Thomas, you have another son!" cried jubilant Mary Sophia.

"What do you mean another son?" said Virginia, one of the six year old twins.

"We had another brother, Edwin," answered fourteen year old Alice. "I remember his chubby little legs as he toddled around – and his laughter, in spite of his drooling. He died in Pennsylvania when he was a mere two years old. That was a sad day. We buried him on a hill."

"Oh," said Virginia. "I didn't know that. That makes me sad."

"Dear Virginia," said her mother, patting her hand. "We must take the bad things with the good in life. Many families suffer from losing babies, but see how fortunate we are to have all of you. Little Edwin is an angel waiting in heaven for us all. We are thankful for the short time he was with us. Do you think he is smiling today?"

"I hope so," said Thomas, giving his wife a kiss. "So what would you like to call our new son?"

"William, after my brother William," said Mary Sophia. "I miss him so. We have been gone eleven years. He is a grown man now. Still, I never give up hope that we will see each other again."

"You know, I had a relative named William. As the story goes, he was the mulatto son of my great, great Aunt Ann, from Kittery, Maine. As you know her given name was Alice and why we named our first born in memory of her. She could not bring Little Will to Charleston when she left Maine in disgrace. That very same William Black became a respected man. He owned an entire Island off the coast of Maine. Yes, I like the name William. May our child be doubly blessed with such an auspicious lineage, a namesake from each family. What is your desire for a second name?"

"Kissick. Kissick - after my father's Scottish lineage," declared Mary Sophia. "Since he is our first declared white son, he should have a white name, too. Do you agree or would you like to have his middle name be Thomas, after you."

"Oh, I think we have had too many Thomas Hanscomes. Let's use your Inglis name. Kissick, yes I like that. It is a distinguished sounding name. Does that mean he'll have your delightful red, nappy hair?" teased Thomas.

"His hair looks dark brown now, and blessedly straight, like yours, but who knows? All of our children surprise us as they grow – a real garden variety of beauties," laughed Mary Sophia.

"Girls, welcome your wee brother, William Kissick Hanscome, with a kiss." And each sister planted a kiss on the top of his sweet little head. Did they mind giving up their study for the nursery? They did not. They would rather play with him than tend to their lessons.

"Can we call him Little Will, like your Kittery ancestor, Father?" asked eleven year old Martha Sophia.

"Why not," answered her father, quite pleased.

Thomas reflected on his son's future as he watched his five daughters dote on him. Would we William be spoiled by too much affection? Probably. Would William join him in his business? Possibly, but that was too much to hope for. Whatever he becomes, William will choose. Thomas was keenly aware this was their first child born white in a truly free society. This bodes well, he thought. I have done right by my family.

1861

"It's a boy, Thomas. We are blessed with yet another son," smiled a weary Mary Sophia. She had thought Little Will, now six, would be her last, but alas, she would be nursing and washing diapers again. But then, that was a woman's life, quite good, if one could afford help. Thank goodness coal was in such great demand. They were making steam and lighting lamps with it. John Garden was giving them one of his new steam driven wringer washing machines and a mangle. Imagine that! Swift Doe was thrilled not to have to haul water, scrub and rinse clothes by hand. Windsong had matriculated with her teaching certificate, but her family sent her younger sister, Swift Doe, to serve the Hanscomes and be educated.

"Let's name this one Thomas," said Mary Sophia. "I'm thirty-eight and he should be our last child. Please, Thomas. You deserve one namesake and my body is tired."

"That's fine," replied Thomas, secretly pleased, "but let's give him his own middle name, one we will call him to lessen the confusion. Girls, would you like to choose a middle name?"

"I choose Henry," said Martha Sophia. "I have a boy in my class named Henry. He is very smart."

"But that's not why you like him," teased the twins in unison.

"We could name him Henry, for a middle name, but give him the nickname of Harry. I like that," said Alice.

"It has a nice ring to it – Thomas Henry Hanscome," said their mother.

"I really like Harry. It's a modern name," said Alice.

Did Alice have a special beau interest with the name Harry? Yes, she did. But Harry's real name wasn't Henry. His name was Howling Wolf. He was Windsong's and Swift Doe's cousin. He took Alice's breath away. She had never seen anyone sit a horse like Harry, simply one with the wind. And could he howl! Well, Harry's howls made the whole tribe question if he, indeed, was part wolf.

"I will write the happy news to my mother, Louisa Rebecca and James," said Thomas. "And you can write to your family, Mary Sophia. It seems so futile, but we must try. Perhaps someone will receive a letter. It has been a year since South Carolina seceded from the United States and our mail has gone unanswered, even from my mother. I am concerned about their welfare."

"How will the South survive without commerce from the northern states?" reflected Mary Sophia.

"It will survive. Eventually the trade will resume, just as our trade resumed with England after the Revolutionary War. We all must adapt to change. We have no choice."

"And if the South looses and returns to the Union?"

"Then it will be as Robert Forten predicted - slavery will be no more. But the news is that the Confederate forces have taken our dear Fort Sumter in Charleston. North Carolina, Arkansas and Tennessee have joined the southern battle to maintain their precious institution. Those eleven confederate states almost equal the Union's population of twenty million. Of course, the lives of four million slaves are counted in the South's census. And they are fleeing to the Union troops to fight for their freedom. Who can blame them? Nothing will remain of our old South Carolina."

"Do you have any desire to enlist, Thomas?" questioned Mary Sophia. "And, if so, for which side?"

"No, I don't want to enlist, not for either side. I consider myself a Canadian. I am not like Robert Forten, who abandoned his family in England so he could do his duty to the United States," fumed Thomas. "He just quit his stationery salesman position in London, quit it without a thought of Mary's and Edmund's welfare. First Wendell was taken by typhus. He was only thirteen, Mary Sophia. Then Robert sailed away, leaving Mary and Edmund with no means of support. His duty? He used our Mary up. He took her plantation and slave money until it ran out."

This was not the first time Mary Sophia had heard Thomas' rants about Robert Forten's lack of responsibility.

"Don't be so hard on Robert, dear Thomas. Mary said in her letter she insisted he return home, to do his patriotic duty. She will soon follow him."

"Even if the North wins the war, the die is cast for continuing prejudice and hypocrisy. Patriotic duty? He is in the colored corps. Why would I want to fight to claim such a future of segregation for us? I prefer this fresh Canadian air!"

And did Mary Forten return to the United States? Not for years and not before she was reduced to abject poverty.

1864

"It's a girl!" Swift Doe announced to Thomas and the other waiting Hanscomes. She passed the swaddled baby first to the proud father who in turn passed her to the girls for inspection and adoration.

And who named her? Mary Sophia did. She wanted namesakes for her two younger Inglis sisters left behind in Charleston, Naomi and Helena.

And who would share a room with wee Naomi Helena? The Hanscomes had settled just in the nick of time in their new six bedroom home, complete with inside water closets and bath rooms. Yes, Thomas' business was exceeding expectations. The new street lights used coal gas. Even the lighthouse on the Toronto Islands had switched from sperm whale oil to coal. Progress.

Mary Sophia thought certainly they would have no more children, but then she had thought that when William was born. Then Harry was a complete surprise. Who knew how many more Hanscomes would be born?

"Girls, it is time for you to get married," announced Thomas to Alice, Anna Louisa and Martha Sophia. "You have all graduated from high school and we may need your room for our children yet to be born."

"No, Father," they chimed in unison. "You and Mother need to discuss your dilemma of too many children and too few rooms, but we'll never relinquish our turret with the splendid view of the harbor and the new train station."

"There is no other space, the twins and your brothers are not ready to leave the nest and we still need Swift Doe for wee Naomi Helena."

"Who knows how long Swift Doe will stay," said Alice, gathering courage. "The Mississauga might be moving from the Toronto Islands. You know how the British are, they selfishly take any Indian land they want, call it purchasing a deed. But I might be able to help you out with more space. Howling Wolf has asked me to marry him and I accepted." There she had said it. Finally!

"I won't allow it, Alice. You cannot and will not marry Harry Howling Wolf under any name or circumstance!" Thomas was so irate he was shaking.

"I see what a bigot you are," screamed Alice in return. "Our Charleston family has declared themselves Indian, but I cannot marry one!"

"Poverty, Alice. Poverty is the reason. He cannot even provide for your basic needs or security. The Indians are the bottom of the barrel here. And you are correct, his tribe won't receive what they deserve for that Island land. They will have nothing and so will you. Nothing!"

"Money is not the issue, Father. Love is! I will marry him." Alice's eyes met her Father's straight on with equal fire. Her sisters looked on wide-eyed in amazement, but said nothing. Where did their father's rage come from? Where did Alice's courage come from? What had happened to the jovial repartee they just shared with their father and sister about vacating their room? Their laughter was gone, as fast as smoke up a chimney.

Did Alice marry Howling Wolf? No, she did not. She obeyed. But it was apparent to all that no other suitors were seeking Alice's hand. Thus, instead, her father placated her by allowing her to work. Work? No young ladies from fine families were allowed to work. It just wasn't done. It just wasn't proper. Thomas had just opened another kettle of worms. At twenty-two Alice took a position as a sales girl at Eaton's, heralded as the finest department store in

Canada. Alice felt so proud and independent, even with her meager salary. Soon her sisters followed suit. Martha Sophia took a position at the library, a great choice as her head was always stuck in a book. And the more sociable Anna Louisa decided to learn the restaurant business from the Lees. That she enjoyed food was evident by her rounder shape, but she truly had the talent of a chef.

Where were the coming out parties, the fancy balls, the suitors for these Hanscome girls? Painfully, nonexistent. Alice, Martha Sophia and Anna Louisa had no love interests or marriage prospects. Why? Although they were white, they were considered *different*. They had nappy curly hair and broader noses, although of fair enough complexion. With the passage of time surely Thomas and Mary Sophia guessed that even a hefty dowry might not bring their daughters suitable prospects: white, young men. Thus, employment was agreeable to everyone.

When Martha Sophia brought home an apprentice from Uncle John's machine shop, all were surprised. She was elated, accepted his proposal as did her parents, but was crushed when his parents would not bless their engagement. The same thing happened to Anna Louisa. She fell in love with the Lee boarding house clerk, but his parents would not approve of their marriage. Heart-breaking! How could parents be so cruel? Well then, what about their own father's prejudice? Of course, Thomas knew that's the way life was.

Now, the Hanscomes had three heart-broken girls.

Then came the sad news from Margaretta Forten in Philadelphia. Her nephew, Robert, had succumbed to typhus while serving in the Colored Troops 43rd Regiment. And Mary? She and young Edmund Quincy were left penniless, still stranded in London, England. However, Margaretta assured Thomas that she had sent them funds to hold them until Robert's military pension could be obtained. They were expected to book passage to Philadelphia, soon.

"Good," thought Thomas. But it wasn't good.

CH. 26. South Across the 49th Parallel

1865

Toronto

"Who wants to cross that ominous 49th parallel with me and visit South Carolina?" inquired Thomas at dinner. "Now that the Union has won the War and we are free to travel, I must return to our old home."

"I have no desire to see the devastation in the Carolinas caused by the War," stated John Garden. "My family news is that prosperity has fled the city and the low country plantations have been taken over by the new freedmen. My brother says everyone has equality now - equality in poverty. I have sent them money to relocate here. Our old cherished way of life is over. It is obsolete. You must let it go, Thomas," counseled John.

"I am not interested in a permanent move, but I want to visit our Charleston families. James, Louisa Rebecca and Mary Sophia's brother and sisters remain. My dear mother and Mary Sophia's aunts, all in their seventies, may still be living. We have written, and continue to do so, but our only recent news has been from your family, John. We have had no word from the Hanscomes or Inglis' in over five years! It is not safe for Mary Sophia to go with me as she is pregnant again. We have heard of great lawlessness and hardship in the Carolinas."

"I cannot give up hope," added Mary Sophia. "I may never see any of my family again, but I want Thomas to find them. They may be destitute, as we would have been, had we stayed. Don't you shudder at the thought of having absolutely nothing? I can only hope that my Inglis family will once again thrive, as we do now. Perhaps Thomas can entice them to move to Toronto. This has truly been a land of opportunity for us. True wealth is better than the old Charleston dazzle. And that is gone. And yes, it is high time slavery ended."

Had Mary Sophia turned the corner on her previous life perceptions? Yes, she had. The inevitable passage of time had most kindly freed her. Charleston no longer captivated her heart. Toronto was home.

"I want to go with you, Father," begged Alice. "I want to visit Charlotte Forten in Philadelphia. I miss her. I also want to see where I was born. I want to see the places of your Carolina stories. I want to see my Grandmother, Aunt Louisa Rebecca, Uncle James and all my Inglis cousins. I want to know where I came from. Please, Father, take me with you. Please."

"I actually like that idea, Alice, but you must understand this trip is for business as well as pleasure. Would you, Martha Sophia and Anna Louisa, like to join us?" Thomas had secretly hoped he could interest his daughters in traveling with him. He had toyed with the idea of finding suitable mates for them through the old Brown Fellowship Society. Certainly he had enough money to entice many a young gentleman to Toronto. And if suitors were not found, a trip would uplift their spirits after their recent broken hearts.

"Do you think that is wise, Thomas?" asked his wife. "We have no idea of the true destruction of Charleston. It could be demoralizing."

"I think it's an educational opportunity for the girls and a business opportunity for me. The first stop will be the breath-taking Niagara Falls. Then we will follow the coal route from the Erie Canal to the New York trains that connect the Pennsylvanian canals to the coal mines. I need to renew my coal business acquaintances and contracts and promote John's improved iron furnaces. It is safe to travel by land and there is so much to see. I want to explore buying coal barges from the Delaware and Hudson Canal Company." Thomas stopped with a smile.

"Have I enticed all of you to travel with me? We could also visit our old German neighbors in Bucks County and the Purvis and Fortens in Philadelphia. Charlotte is recovering from her smallpox and can educate us as to the state of the Sea Islands and Charleston. She admirably did her duty teaching the freedmen for three years during the war. And from Philadelphia we would take a ship to Charleston. My only regret is that you are indisposed, Mary Sophia, and cannot travel. I could delay my trip until after the baby is born."

"Nonsense," said his wife. "It would take several years for me to free myself from our young children. Now is the best time. You have my blessing to take the girls."

"We want to go, too," begged Eugenia and Virginia in unison. "Please, Father!"

"You must attend to your studies and help your mother with the little ones now that Swift Doe has left our service," tactfully explained their father.

"How long do you plan to be gone?" asked Elizabeth Sarah. "Perhaps I can travel with you. Joanna is finishing her last year in school and the family can manage without me."

"The girls and I will leave in March and follow the spring south. I have no intention of spending a disease ridden summer in South Carolina, so we will return by June, just in time to greet another Hanscome babe. Three months at the most. I would welcome your company, sister."

"John," said Thomas to his brother-in-law, "would you mind writing to your brother about our return to Charleston? Perhaps he can find the DeCostas or my brother James. I need to believe they are still alive."

March, 1866

They left Toronto just after the melt of a major March blizzard, dressed in their warmest clothes, wool mittens, hats and scarves for the passage across Lake Ontario.

"Behold the power of God!" cried Anna Louisa as they witnessed Niagara Falls from a ferry boat. Pictures usually depicted the Falls in summer, but this mixture of winter ice and spring thaw made the rising steam surreal.

"This is a place that inspires men," added Thomas.

"And women," scolded Alice.

"I remember the romantic story of an Indian Princess who killed herself when she canoed over the Falls rather than marry a man she didn't love," added Anna Louisa.

"Another romantic Romeo and Juliet legend," sighed Martha Sophia, clutching her heart and feigning a swoon. "You read too many romantic novels."

Alice winced as her heart remembered her love for Howling Wolf. Had she been in error to heed her parents' wishes? Should she have galloped to his side or thrown herself on a bonfire? No, Alice knew she was not a blind romantic. Her affection for him would not have survived a fierce winter in his Village. She smiled, knowing she never would have killed herself for Harry or thrown herself into these ferocious Niagara Falls. One question remained in Alice's mind. Would any man marry her? Or was marriage even important to her? She loved her position at Easton's Department Store.

"This is the place of many battles, as well as weddings," taught Thomas. "The War of 1812 and the Upper Canadian Rebellion for freedom from the Crown in 1837 were both fought here. It has been bought and sold, desired by the British, the French and the United States. Timber and flour mills have flourished on its shores, but its true power has yet to be harnessed. I predict more battles unless the Canadians and Americans can share its wealth."

"Can we travel across the suspension bridge?" begged Martha Sophia, uninterested in her father's history lesson. "Please, Father. It looks so frightening, but the views must be majestic."

Thomas smiled, "Of course, we can." He always had difficulty refusing his daughters' requests.

The girls yelled and yelled in a loud contest of shrieks and delighted as the Falls drowned out their feeble attempts to equal its roar. Never had they heard such a deafening sound. "Can we stay longer, Father?"

"Girls, we must be on our way, but the Falls will greet us again on our return. This is only the first secret of many to be revealed," promised Thomas with a teasing wink.

Winter and gray skies followed them until they navigated the Erie Canal and were headed south on the Hudson River. What a damp, cold spring. Did the girls complain? No, they did not. Their curious natures were enthralled. They felt free, after being cooped up all winter in Toronto. And the anticipation of the glorious unknown held them tightly in its vise.

Finally, sunshine and the blue skies of spring appeared. They didn't want to miss one day of new scenery, new people or new modes of transportation, especially the trains. They were equally impressed with their father's business acumen as he purchased barges and negotiated contracts with the transportation and mining tycoons. But it saddened them to see the lot of the Pennsylvanian miners with their blackened faces, deadened expressions and filthy clothes. They had hungry stares.

"Keep your eyes lowered, girls," ordered Thomas. "It isn't becoming to stare at other's misfortune."

"The miners do not seem to be as healthy as the slaves we once owned," observed Elizabeth Sarah.

"They aren't. They are caught in the traps of the mine owners as they acquire more debts with no means to repay them. Most of the miners are uneducated immigrants, who will take any kind of work."

"Do you think it wise for the girls to witness their plight, Thomas?" asked Elizabeth Louisa.

"It is part of their education. Men have always enslaved others. A few, like Robert Forten tried to right these wrongs, but he sacrificed his family for his cause. It is unfortunate Robert did not live to see the end of the war, to see the fruits of his labor. And I want the girls to kiss the Canadian soil when we return to our relative abundance."

Bucks County

The smells of budding leaves, grasses and the brisk spring breezes enlivened the Hanscomes as they rode to their old homesteads. The winter in Warminster had been more severe than Toronto's. Temperatures had plunged to minus 18 degrees and even the Delaware River had frozen. Now they skirted the creeks overflowing with the winter snow melt. In spite of the chill, the girls were thrilled to see their old family compound, the rope swing, the remnants of their tree house and the chicken coop, home of those wicked beaked birds that drew blood from their tiny hands.

"Just think we actually slopped those pigs," squealed Martha Sophia with delight.

"I do think city life suits me better. The town of Warminster is smaller that I remember," added Anna Louisa. "And our old homes look so, well shabby and small, too."

"I think this is the best day of our trip – and the warmest," said Alice. "I am only disappointed not to be able to see Emma Amundsen. At least I know she married and has a family of her own. She was like a big sister to me. As for the condition of our homestead - I only hear the laughter we lived. I love this place. I am so glad we came."

"Let's stop at Edwin's grave and plant a few spring flowers," suggested Thomas as they approached a familiar hill. "I am glad we can still find it."

"Swing low, sweet chariot, comin' for to carry me home," sang Alice. When the prayers were over, she tried to sing Edwin's favorite lullaby, "Rock-a-bye Baby, from the treetop…" but she broke down in tears. Her sisters joined in to finish the song.

As they rode away, Elizabeth Sarah whispered to Thomas, "visiting Edwin's grave was worth the trip. I believe I needed to cry, not just for Edwin, but for our younger selves. We were so brave."

Thomas just nodded, speechless, as he feared the lump in his throat might bubble up into unstoppable tears.

That night after the girls had retired to their boarding house room, Thomas and Elizabeth Sarah sat by a toasty fire.

"Oh, Thomas, I have enjoyed our travels through New York, the rivers, the canals and even the mines. But the best part has been just you and me talking, getting acquainted again without our spouses. We have never done that. Today was so special to share with you. I feel I picked up scattered pieces of my heart with each familiar farm sight. We worked so hard here. I feel kinder to my younger self, a self I have been too hard on. How courageous all of us were in leaving South Carolina, starting out only with faith that our lives would be better. And then we were torn again from our homes to escape the slave catchers. I thank God daily for his guidance and for you, Thomas, our champion."

"Yes, we had fine memories farming this land and they surfaced today - along with my sadness that will forever remain on Edwin's hilltop grave. And I thank you for your kind words, dear sister, but I believe it was the fear of remaining that moved me rather than divine inspiration. Fear, like any emotion, has many faces - good and bad, cowardice and courage. The difficult part is that only in retrospect can we assess the correctness of our actions. Did we do the right thing to leave Charleston? Our worst fear, the loss of our freedom did not occur."

"We will soon find out. I do know that we did save our wealth," responded Elizabeth Sarah.

"Ah yes. Money," reflected Thomas. "The coal business has been good to me, better than my farm."

"My memories are bittersweet," added Elizabeth Sarah. "Our old farms are in disarray. And the Amundsens have moved. In retrospect, they were our only true friends among our neighbors. But we were too busy having babies and helping each other to notice we were set apart."

"Truly? Set apart? And now? Do you feel set apart from others in Toronto?" Thomas asked.

"I feel welcomed by the Anglican Church ladies, but like our children, we are not really included in proper society. We are not sought out, as we were used to – not special." She hesitated. "I worry Thomas. What are we going to do if our children find no mates? Should we encourage them to marry into the Toronto colored society, illiterate as they are? Or should we allow our Hanscome lineage to become extinct, like the mules we mulattos were named after?"

Thomas detected a note of bitterness in his sister's voice.

"I don't have the answers, but please don't be disheartened or embittered. I think time and events will pass as they should. Sometimes I think we set ourselves apart, not vice versa. When I return I am going to do more entertaining, perhaps join a social club, a sailing club or a card club. We just need to stop having babies. Mary Sophia and I need to see what we can do to bridge the social gulf. New immigrants and new opportunities arrive daily in Toronto. We have grown complacent."

Thomas and Elizabeth Sarah gazed at the fire in the old stone hearth, each privately recalling old memories. Their silence was comfortable. It wasn't important that they answered each other's questions or defended their positions as they shared their mental meanderings. It was sufficient they were together sharing their past and anticipating the future.

"Shabby or not, I missed our farms today. We would soon be planting the crops," said Elizabeth Sarah wistfully.

"We made a good life here," agreed Thomas. "Satisfying. Farming was satisfying, particularly after Karl Amundsen gave us a few tips. Oh, how he laughed at our initial planting efforts. We were babes in the woods, still in our twenties with more ambition than knowledge. Do you remember Robert's first attempt harnessing the plow to the oxen? We laughed until our sides ached. Even Robert and perhaps the oxen laughed. Nonetheless, Mother Nature was kind to us. And we were fortunate to have each other. Building my coal business gives me the same satisfaction, like growing children or tending crops. And happily, much more profitable."

"Did you mean to say tending children and growing crops?" she laughed.

"Aren't they the same?" Thomas mused."

"No, not exactly," laughed Elizabeth Sarah. "And I do appreciate that your coal business and our furnace business are much more profitable."

"I wonder how we'll feel about Charleston and our old plantations?" pondered Elizabeth Sarah. "What do you want to do, after we find our family?"

"I want to spend some time on a small schooner on the Stono fishing. I want to ride a fast marsh tacky through the dank lowlands. I can smell the rotting vegetation and the black humus. It is intoxicating, even as I imagine it."

"Moldy odors are not my cup of tea, dear brother, but I want to swim in the warm, salt water. Oh, how I have missed the beach – and the concerts. I will buy some fine fabrics for Mary Ann and Mary Sophia. Something other than boring gray, dull brown or widow black. And now I bid you good night, Thomas. Sweet dreams of our youth to you."

"Good night. I will write a letter to Mary Sophia about our old homestead, the flowers we planted on Edwin's grave and how Alice sang his favorite lullabies. I am truly sorry we couldn't see him grow."

"You tended little Edwin well. His death was not your fault, Thomas."

Philadelphia

On that very same evening, Charlotte Forten was also reminiscing. She had returned to her Aunt Margaretta's to recover from the small pox that ran rampant in South Carolina during that awful Civil War. She had mixed feelings about seeing her Hanscome relatives. At times Charlotte wished she'd never known them. She suffered nightmares, imagining the freedmen she helped on John's Island being whipped by her Uncle Thomas. She found no way to excuse his past and felt ashamed that she loved him still. Oh, she prayed to God to enlighten them, all her Hanscome aunts and uncles. She wanted them to confess their sins of slave-owning, as her mother Mary had. She prayed to God for guidance.

Thomas had been Charlotte's favorite Uncle, before she realized how different his viewpoints were from her father's - and from hers. Charlotte wondered how they could have shared that Warminster farm. How could her abolitionist father have married Mary Hanscome, part of that slave owning Brown Fellowship Society elite? Charlotte despised those new Hanscomes she met in Charleston. Oh, how she worked to reconcile her love for the Hanscomes of her Bucks County days, who had owned slaves, with her love for the new freedmen.

She loved Mary Hanscome, her step-mother, as her true mother. It was slave money that sent the Purvis' and the Ellison's children to Philadelphia for an education at Margaretta's school. Rich. Very rich from cotton and slave labor. How did her Aunt Margaretta reconcile taking that money? She could not reconcile how William Ellison went from slave to a black slave master in just a few short years. Charlotte knew that her education funds came from Mary's plantation profits, a fact that gnawed at her soul. She fervently prayed to atone for the sins of her slave owning kin and to assuage her own guilt. Were there degrees of hypocrisy? If so, how guilty was she? She only knew she had seen such strength in those new Sea Island freedmen. She had seen their eyes light-up with happiness as they learned to read, as they tilled their own land. She wanted to help them thrive, not just survive. How could she also love those who enslaved them? Charlotte sighed a deep sigh as she heard their arrival.

"Charlotte," cried Alice. "I have missed you so."

The two young women embraced as the Hanscome clan was welcomed into Margaretta Forten's parlor. Anna Louisa and Martha Sophia barely remembered Charlotte and shyly waited their turn to greet their old tutor, nanny and accomplished cousin. Soon all were talking at once, catching up on their lives since the Warminster farm.

"Yes, the thirteen years have flown, to where I do not know! I can't believe you have all matriculated and have taken positions," said Charlotte. To her Uncle she stated, "You are quite progressive, Uncle Thomas, to take your girls on such an adventurous trip and allow them to work."

"They admire you so," said Thomas. "It is nice to see you have recovered from your small pox. And yes, Charlotte, I am a supporter of women's rights, including the right to work. I certainly hope women's citizenship and voting rights will be included with the freedmen's rights in the new amendment. But then, because we are Canadian, we also need to push the Crown for such action."

"I know you viewed emancipation of slaves as a problem for the South. May I surmise that you have changed your mind and welcome the freedmen?"

"Yes, of course I do, but you have grounds for your distrust. My conflicting beliefs over the years have confused even me, dear Charlotte. I hope you are forgiving of my hypocrisy. I have protected the glorious past of Charleston and our precious plantations. My personal foundation was built on the denial of the most obvious poison, slavery. We accepted people were property. Even my precious mother denied the obvious, the evil of slavery. She ignored it her whole life. It was all any of us knew. And we loved our slaves at the same time - my father particularly did," joked Thomas as he smiled at his intense young niece.

"Please don't joke about this, Uncle Thomas!" replied an irritated Charlotte. "Your father may have loved your mother, but most plantation owners just took women, used and abused them, our people!"

"Yes, I see your serious view, but it's colored by your privileged Philadelphia life, just as mine is colored differently," replied Thomas. "Please laugh, dear Charlotte. You take offense at my jest, niece. Please don't. Your zeal without humor will ruin your life. We were the privileged, but we lived with our slaves. I want you to challenge your beliefs. Part of you knows not of what you speak. Did you ever know a slave, prior to your reconstruction teaching? No, you didn't. Did you ever live on a plantation? No, you didn't. Did you ever love a slave? No, you didn't or perhaps you are hiding that under your austere demeanor," he teased again.

"Sometimes I don't know whether to despise you or love you, Uncle. Today, I will let it be."

"Would you have held different views, Charlotte, if you were raised as we were? I can change my opinions and I have, but I had to get away from the South to see a new perspective. Slavery is horrifying but I didn't always believe so. It's like debate or logic. Once you accept the first presupposition - slavery is good - the rest naturally follows. That was my era. This is yours."

"And what do you think of my era, of me?" she warily asked.

"I admire your teaching. We all do. I had a great, great Aunt Ann who also championed education for all, including slaves and women. She hated slavery. Some say she was killed in Charleston for her beliefs, more than a hundred years ago. You would have liked her. Now, will you please settle down? I suppose you won't - and perhaps you shouldn't. Your zeal reminds me of your dear father, sometimes so self-righteous. You know we sparred, but we also deeply respected each other. And I still applaud him and you. I need to understand that you are a Forten and you need to understand that we are Hanscomes."

Yes, Charlotte did love her Hanscome cousins and her infuriating Uncle. He taught her how to fish, how to race horses, make snowmen, pick watercress and yes, laugh. He was so delightfully real and so bigoted. She also knew that without Hanscome money, her father could not have provided for her. With his head eternally in the clouds, her father was oblivious to his family's material needs. She wished her father could have done both, made money and inspire, like her Grandfather James Forten. He was her true hero, but he didn't live long enough for her to know him.

"Touché. Today I will enjoy my *white* cousins. Really, Uncle Thomas, how could you do that, claim to be white? But that's for tomorrow's conversation." Charlotte even smiled.

"And I thank you for giving me the doubt of being a decent human being. We find being white most advantageous, thank you." He smiled. "You have been a source of inspiration to my girls. I also want to hear about your teaching in the Sea Islands and your view of the future of my old home. I am afraid an evil institution has been replaced by chaos – and now I am serious."

"Not chaos, but poverty reigns. The whites are angry and poor, as are your old cohorts, the Brown Fellowship Society. The new freedmen are progressing, but they have much to learn - they were kept down, broken, ignorant and poor for too long.

"I went to John's Island in 1862 after the Sea Islands were evacuated by the planter families and many of their slaves. The Confederacy couldn't defend the Islands – they simply abandoned them to the Union troops. I witnessed the burning of the seaside summer village, Legareville, and many plantations by their owners before they fled. All the fields were devastated. Did they even think of the welfare of the slaves, what they would eat? No. Their only concern was that the Union soldiers wouldn't benefit. The freedmen had to forage for sweet potatoes, hunt wild cattle, swine and fish. They almost starved!"

"You do not paint a rosy picture. Do you know if Creekside is intact? Do the Legares still own it? My father sold it to them."

"No, I do not know Creekside's fate, but all the cotton and rice fields were gone to scrub and the animals eaten or turned wild. I imagine the Legare's joined the Confederacy."

"This is difficult for me to hear, Charlotte," said Thomas sadly.

"I wish I could travel with you, dear Uncle, but my body demands more rest before I return to Charleston. I am lucky to have survived this pox." Charlotte looked intently at her uncle before continuing.

"I only now understand the beauty of the low country. I am sorry it has been laid to waste. I am also sorry that my father wasn't able to see the South. It's lovely and I know it was your life. He never understood your views or how South Carolina slavery hypnotized you, but he never lived there, as you said. I have seen South Carolina, Uncle. I detest slavery. I hold you accountable for it. I hate you for it. I also love you."

Silence.

"Will I recognize Charleston?" ventured Thomas.

"Yes, you will, but you won't like what you see. And your relatives? I'm not sure you will like them, either. I must admit, I did not."

"You met the Hanscomes? The Decostas? The Inglis'? And I'm afraid to ask, is my mother living?" Thomas hungered for any family news.

"Your mother was alive and living with James on my last trip to Charleston after the war. But, Uncle Thomas, she lives in the old world and it is gone. She is frail and confused, but I glimpsed remnants of her old beauty and spark. She kept asking for her slave. Do you know how hard that is for me to hear? Sally, her old slave, still tends to her needs, in exchange for room, board and a small pittance. I do sense real affection between them, but the roles of mistress and slave permeate their interchanges. It nauseates me. Your brother James says they are both too old to change. He says they will die together, like family. It makes my heart sick.

"As for your other relatives, they are angry. I must say I did not find them very hospitable, but then a northern abolitionist like me is hated by most of the Brown Fellowship Society ilk. The Ellison children attended Margaretta's school, but their cotton gin and plantation fortunes are now gone. The brown elite resent having to start over from poverty, but they are educated and the hope of rebuilding Charleston lies with them. They can bridge the gap between the light and the dark of us. I hope they pick up the gauntlet. There is a vacuum of sane leadership. And Thomas, I suggest you consider returning. With your foot in two cultures you could help. I can never pretend to know the whole glue of South Carolina."

"I am a Canadian now, Charlotte, but who knows how I might be moved after my visit. If you would be so kind, would you please give me the new addresses of any of my relatives? We have heard nothing from them in five years."

"Luncheon is served and it is time for the two of you to put on your best manners while you sit at my table. No politics!" chastised Margaretta Forten, Robert's older sister and directress of Philadelphia's best school for the colored.

"How do you find Philadelphia after such a long absence?" Margaretta asked.

"We saw a steam engine fire truck putting out a fire!" exclaimed young Martha Sophia.

"We have had too many fires," lamented Margaretta. "Blocks of our city have been destroyed. Our hope is that these steam engine fire trucks will help. It's only been a year since the end of the war and so much has changed. Everything is steam powered. And we are building new bridges across the Delaware River."

"The streetcars are new, too, but we were surprised to discover they are segregated. We didn't expect that in Philadelphia," added Elizabeth Sarah.

"Yes, the general assembly is planning to reverse that awful practice. However, before there were segregated train cars, no one of our color was allowed to ride at all. Robert's colored troops had to walk, rent or borrow horses in order to return home from their patriotic duty. Slaves may be freed, but prejudice remains," stated Margaretta with a sigh.

No one asked if the Hanscomes had traveled in the white street car, which they had. They hadn't given it a second thought.

"And here I am talking politics, breaking my own dinner table rules. We are now over 22,000 of African descent in Philadelphia, but the Catholics, particularly the Irish are trying to keep us in our place. Competition for the new railway jobs has led to blows."

"So much for the City of Brotherly Love, Margaretta," replied Thomas before changing the subject. "We were so sorry to hear of Robert's death. It was just a year ago. How are you doing?"

"We are still grieving - for him and for Mary's entrapment in London. It is sad she was unable to be by Robert's side, but he was gone in three weeks. First, young Wendell succumbed in London, then poor Robert. I think we lost more troops to typhus and cholera than we did by guns. And Mary missed the tribute paid him at his funeral, attended by all the leading abolitionists, white and Negro. Like our father, Robert's life made a difference. His service to his country made a difference. That gives me solace."

"Margaretta, I don't understand why Mary hasn't returned," said Thomas aghast. "Your last letter indicated you had sent Mary and young Edmund fare for their passages? We had expected to greet them here. What happened?"

"As you know, the plan was for them to follow Robert shortly after he sailed for Philadelphia. But they had acquired debts and after Mary paid them, she had no money left. She kept waiting for Robert's pension for his military service, though a pittance that is. Finally, I had to write to Washington to find out the problem. She had not listed his Regiment as the Colored 43rd Regiment, just the 43rd Regiment and they had no record of his service. Now, she has reserved passages. In the meantime, they are making do with the funds I send," said Margaretta.

"We want to help! If only we had known!" said Thomas.

"Please do not concern yourself, Thomas. She is no longer a Hanscome, but a Forten and I will take care of them."

"Nonsense, Margaretta. You can ill afford such expenses. I'm certain your school enrollment is down since the War. Mary will always be a Hanscome, too. I will send them additional money. I want to do this. My brother Joseph would roll over in his grave with this news. I need to do this. I am horrified that she has no income. Mary was never meant to live in poverty, alone and in a foreign country."

Thomas wanted to scream – "And how could your dear brother have left them there? How could he have taken all of Mary's money for his cause and left her destitute! How could he have quit his London position with no concern for his debts or his family? How could he be so selfish?"

But Thomas didn't confront Margaretta Forten. Robert was gone and it was not proper to speak ill of the dead or upset his gracious hostess. He was learning perceptions were different on this side of the 49th parallel. He wondered how Charleston would also challenge his Canadian views.

CH. 27. Return to Charleston

The voyage

April, 1866

After they sadly waved goodbye to the Forten's and the Purvis' at the wharf, Thomas' and Elizabeth's anticipation mounted, like a groom waiting at the altar and a bride on her wedding night. Excited and frightened, both at the same time. Home! They were going home. Nothing could be more glorious. Soon they would glimpse their sweet Carolina shore.

"I feel like an exiled Israelite returning to the promised land," said a giddy Elizabeth Sarah.

"I don't know whether to feel ecstatic or embittered," reflected Thomas. "We were little more than fodder for the hungry *peculiar institution*. The assemblymen were discussing re-enslavement, isn't that why we left? Successful mulatto planters threatened the order. South Carolina wanted more slaves, not successful freedmen. How ironic! Now they have no slaves, only freedmen. In their greed, the planters lost everything."

"Doesn't it seem strange to use the term mulatto?" asked Elizabeth Sarah. "I shed my skin of color when we crossed the 49th parallel. Mulatto doesn't fit anymore."

"Soon we shall see, dear sister, what fits us and what is truly shed. Perhaps the words chameleons and molting snakes describe us better than the label mulattos."

And the girls? They lamented they could not stay longer with Charlotte. She regaled them with stories of her life in Salem, teaching in her all-white school, and her mission with the freedmen in the Sea Islands of South Carolina. Her life seemed so purposeful, even poetically romantic, as Charlotte might say. The girls were a bit envious of the new society she was creating. Aunt Margaretta had suggested the Hanscome girls receive Normal School Certificates and join her teaching staff in Philadelphia. Imagine. Philadelphia had unveiled new possibilities for them as young ladies.

And how did Thomas react? He had been polite, but thought, "Absolutely not. I'd rather have Alice married to Harry Howling Wolf, than to see her ensconced in Margaretta's and Charlotte's pious world." Why? Thomas knew his mulatto world had collapsed, but he didn't want his daughters to live on the dark side of the fence, like the Fortens. Still, they were family.

"Girls," called Elizabeth Sarah, thinking a distraction would calm their unbecoming weeping as the boat pulled away from the wharf. "Do you see the young men, rowing those flimsy sculls? They have raced down the Schuylkill River and will soon cross the finish line. I remember such tournaments in Charleston. They would start from the Cooper River and race to the harbor, in the best London Thames tradition."

"Look at the long boats, with eight men!" exclaimed Martha Sophia. "They resemble centipedes on a march."

"Yes, the synchronization of the long oars glinting in the sunlight is breathtaking," marveled Alice. "But centipedes are land creatures. I think the flashing oars resemble flocks of seabirds, exposing their white shimmering bellies to the sun as they swoop and soar to some hidden rhythm of sunset."

"I am not looking at the oars, silly. Watch those handsome, strong arms move in unison!" teased Anna Louisa.

"Handsome or not, they better watch out for the coal barges. This is indeed a busy harbor," added Martha Sophia.

"Wouldn't it be wonderful to catch a sailing regatta or a crew contest on the River in Charleston," said Thomas to Elizabeth Sarah. "We could have a picnic, like we used to, on the river bank."

"Yes, Thomas, but I remember you being in the races, not picnicking with the rest of us. You were such a dandy."

"That was twenty-one years ago. I think I might like to watch. There is so much I want to see and do. And did I forget to mention the horse races? I must spend some time at the track."

"Temper your expectations, dear brother. I think we better prepare for the destruction of our dearest memories," whispered Elizabeth Sarah. "It was only a year ago that Charleston capitulated and the war ended."

And what was Elizabeth Sarah's desire? She longed to dance in a filmy, pink silk dress to an orchestra in the balmy, spring air. She also doubted they would be welcomed by regattas, dances, concerts or races of any sort. What a folly. Why had she agreed to take this trip? As her husband John Garden had warned, "Close the door to Charleston. Slam it if you must. You can't go back. Think Toronto. This trip could ruin your cherished memories and break your heart, my dear wife."

"I know, sister. We must steal our hearts, hide our grandiose expectations from the girls," responded Thomas. "They will be pleased enough to see Charlotte's world of new futures for the illiterate. It will be interesting to see if they identify with the affluent or the poor, the white or the black."

"How ridiculous those dichotomies are. I have never seen a totally white or black person. Have you? We are golden, dear brother, kissed by the sun. I think we wax too mercurial today. Will we ever know who we truly are?"

"Does it matter? Right now I want to remember this voyage. I have so missed the salt air, the sea birds, and these majestic sails," said Thomas.

Charleston

"I see James! I see Louisa Rebecca! I see William Inglis!" shouted Elizabeth Sarah as she pointed them out to the girls and frantically waved. What jubilation! John Garden's brother had found her family. Even stoic Thomas wiped his eyes. This is why they'd come home.

No one noticed the absence of the harbor guards. There was no need to declare your race, be detained if you were a slave or denied a return entrance if you were a freedman. A placard simply said, "Welcome to Charleston." The harbor was alive with hawkers selling their produce and wares. Familiar odors of shrimp boils, spicy hot sauces and sizzling fried chicken awakened Thomas' and Elizabeth's long forgotten memories.

Before they were whisked off to the DeCostas, introductions were made. Oh, how Mary Sophia's sisters had grown. All the nieces and nephews were adults. It had been far too long.

Had they changed? Yes and no. The unique smiles were the same. They had joked that they were all adopted as youths, so dissimilar in features. Now their eyes and structure of their faces, minus the baby fat, announced, "You are my brother, my sister, my cousin." But the Charleston families were much leaner. Thomas thought, "If only you could be here to witness this miracle, Mary Sophia."

"And Mother? Will we see her at dinner?" asked Elizabeth Sarah.

"No," answered Louisa Rebecca sadly. "She is at James' and we will visit her tomorrow. Mother does not tolerate commotion well. We want tonight to be festive. We haven't had enough laughter in the last few years and are counting on you to fix that." Behind her joviality, Louisa Rebecca prayed her mother would recognize her other children. But that was tomorrow. They had learned not to anticipate during the war and its aftermath, but simply take each day as it came. Tonight was for celebrating.

What wonderful, strange cuisine, thought the girls as dinner was served. While the Toronto Lee restaurant boasted fine southern cuisine, much seafood, okra, peppers and spices were just not available. Plates and bowls were filled with turtle and crab soups, oysters, shrimp, okra gumbos, red rice, sweet potato pie, corn pone, butter beans, black-eyed peas, sugar snap peas, tomato gravy, pork sausages and grits. Gullah foods to some. New to the girls. Home to Thomas and Elizabeth Sarah. Delectable to all.

The DeCosta's house held fifty people to welcome the Hanscomes. The girls were amazed at the warmth, laughter and affection from all their new-found cousins. Southern hospitality was real. They wondered why Charlotte had found them to be hostile.

"Do you remember when we were surrounded by alligators on the Stono?" asked James.

"Do you remember the dance lessons and how our silly feet refused to comply?" asked Louisa Rebecca.

"Do you remember how that old bull chased us?" remembered another.

"Do you remember the horse races that you always seemed to win, Thomas?"

"Do you remember the baby pigs, Joseph's pride? Oh, how we miss him still."

"Do you remember the balls and dance cards? We were so beautiful, so young then."

"Do you remember the sailing regattas and capsizing in the harbor?"

"Do you remember summers at the seaside, the picnics, father out-swimming all of us to the Point?"

"Do you remember our parents dancing in the moonlight? What a distinctive laugh she had. How enamored he was."

"How is your business doing, William?" asked Thomas of his brother-in-law, William DeCosta.

"We almost lost everything, including our house, but, of course, there was no one to buy it. Our Confederate money became so inflated. It is, of course, worthless today. All six of our children moved home and together we survived. We planted a vegetable garden, fished and hunted, foraged like the Indians of old, wary of both Rebel and Union troops. There was no demand for my cotton gins and farm equipment. No cash crops have been grown for five years and the livestock were slaughtered or became wild. I laughed when both armies recruited our sons. We decided to sit this war out; we were losers either way. After you left, Thomas, the restrictions on our movement made us feel like slaves. Our planter guardians became less solicitous of us. All our merchants suffered. When the planters abandoned their fields, they didn't even bother to board up their mansions.

"Last year cotton was again planted, by both the returning planters and the new freedmen. It remains to be seen who will end up with the land titles and the crop profits. After the war, Sherman distributed old plantation land to all the new freedmen refugees - 4500 new Negros came to Edisto alone. The Yankees just gave the land to them and kept the old planters from returning. Then came the turnabout. The planters gained back their land rights, that is, if they hadn't sold them. Now, the freedmen are share cropping for them. William Seabrook's grandchildren sold his estate for worthless Confederate money. We were barely able to feed ourselves. The Freedmen's Bureau and the Union army are distributing rations, still. We had to bury our pride and take the handouts."

"How awful for you, William," empathized Elizabeth Sarah. On a hopeful note she added, "We did see firewood, chickens, okra, sweet potatoes and other produce for sale on the wharf."

"It is not business as usual, but better. One decent harvest has helped. Vanderhorst even made profits on his first crop of Sea Island cotton, planted with hired help. He had to fight to get his plantation back after it had been given to refugee freedmen. And the College of Charleston's doors are wide open, but I'm not sure any students have entered the gates. We had to evacuate Charleston, sit back and watch the Union troops destroy our homes, our beloved city." William recanted his unbelievable tales to an entranced Thomas and Elizabeth Sarah.

"Please speak on, William. We need to hear this," said Thomas. Soon all in the room had quieted to listen.

"Too many died from the smallpox epidemic. The Jewish Community helped us out. The Brown Fellowship Society is extinct. These northern preachers insult our ears. And the newly elected Negro Assembly wants to fund public education for all. Prey, where do they think the money will come from? We are bankrupt as a state. If we have no income, we can't be taxed. Fools all! A northerner, Daniel Chamberlain, is running for Governor. The old planter class has been decimated, and we along with it." William's eyes welled up in tears. "What do they mean by equality? We are now all equal - equal in poverty!"

"I am so sorry to hear this, William. John Garden in Toronto, used your exact words, *equality in poverty*, when he was dissuading me from returning. I want you to know I will help you. Reconstruction may sound like a nightmare, but there is money to be made. Buildings and bridges need to be rebuilt. You may need to change your focus from cotton gins to construction and refugee housing. I have a fuel and transportation business, timber and coal mainly, but I predict hydropower will be the next wave. Rapid rivers equal opportunity, not dread. Your western rivers are ripe to be harnessed. Let's toast to the return of prosperity, your prosperity." Thomas uncorked the champagne he had contributed to the feast and toasted to William.

"Hear, hear!" responded the crowd.

"I'm afraid I have ruined our dinner festivities with my woeful talk. Let us truly welcome you, dear Thomas," said William as he refilled Thomas' glass. "Let's laugh, sing, dance and toast to your dear Mary Sophia, the Gardens and Lees."

And they did. They drank and danced and celebrated as if there had been no war, as if their spirits had not been broken, as if family had never left. Good. This was the Charleston Thomas and Elizabeth Sarah remembered. Thomas' daughters, wide-eyed in amazement, had never seen such an unleashed spectacle. Uncle James daughter, Sarah, with her soft-voiced, southern charm enchanted her northern cousins. Her surprising hearty laugh, said to be an exact duplicate of her Grandma Ann's, only enhanced her mystery and charm.

"You are the only one ecstatic about the outcome of this war. I don't understand. Why?" asked Alice of Sarah, about her same age.

"I am free! You are looking, dear cousins, at a bona fide slave, in case you've never met one," drawled Sarah. "My mother and I are finally free. We have lost our wealth but we no longer have to be afraid. I can walk outside and even take a stroll to the harbor. I can be normal."

The Hanscome girls stared at their lovely, golden skinned cousin in disbelief. Sarah had been a slave, too, albeit not a poor one. She had also owned slaves, contrary to any lessons learned about slavery in school. There had been educated, wealthy, slave owning slaves and freedmen. Their parents rarely mentioned their pasts. And here was a room full of their very own relatives. Suddenly, their parent's elitist attitudes and family history became clearer. Their relatives might now be poor, but oh they were proud, elegant and fun. Yes, fun. Alice, Anna Louisa and Martha Sophia mimicked Sarah's sugar-coated southern accent, flutter of eyelids, and glide, as if she had no feet. She simply nodded, smiled and charmed. How could their cousin Charlotte ever have disliked her? They practiced speaking slowly, *Whatever pleases you, darlin', tickles me plum to death.* Sarah had them practice in front of a mirror. Then Sarah taught them to dance and float, making nary a clomp or a stomp. They howled with laughter but at the end of their lessons, the Hanscome girls felt beautiful, graceful. This was not Toronto. They belonged here.

In the morning, Thomas hired a carriage to take them to brother James' house.

"This is all too sad," observed Elizabeth Sarah as they drove through old familiar streets. The Hanscome Tradd Street mansion was occupied by soldiers and shabby. The tenements of Cabbage Row were overflowing with gaunt looking, hollow-eyed freedmen. Elizabeth Sarah covered her mouth, to hold down her sickness at the rotten smells, crumbling old elegant foundations and the hopelessness of human spirit. Devastation reigned.

"I cannot look in their eyes. I feel guilty in our finery, Father," said Alice as they passed street beggars. Philadelphia had its share of poor, but the girls were not ready for these hungry looks. They thought of all the food consumed last night and looked away in shame.

"How can you be so bright and happy viewing this squalor?" asked Martha Sophia of her father. "You and Aunt Elizabeth Sarah seemed so different last night - not your true selves," she added.

"You glimpsed a part of our true selves last night, a good part. The variety of a person's spirit is limitless, Martha Sophia," smiled her father. "We learned to deny the ugly years ago. Soon you will meet your Grandmother, the champion of denial and the indomitable spirit," answered Thomas.

"I do believe James' circumstances are better than I thought," observed Thomas as the driver stopped at a lovely old brick mansion, enclosed by a tall, wrought iron fence. A solid burnished wood door with an impressive knocker greeted them, but it did not have James' name engraved on it. "Ah, I see the truth now, Elizabeth Sarah. The old kitchen and carriage house is his - good taste, if one has to be poor. James always had exquisite taste."

Thomas and his younger brother had been quite similar as youths. Joseph, the oldest son, was the responsible one, who emulated and adored their planter father. Thomas reflected that he had now assumed the more serious spirit of Joseph. When had that change snuck up on him? After they moved to Pennsylvania? After they had so many children? Responsibility wasn't first nature to him, but it was necessary. Last night was a tribute to Thomas' old self. He felt rejuvenated and promised himself to honor his lightheartedness more.

"Welcome," said Hetty, James' second wife. She was originally from Savannah. Some said she married James for his wealth, but others said James married Hetty for her money. The origin of it was of little import, James had gambled it all away. Hetty was a widow and six years older than James. James' dandy and drinking days were over, or so he told Thomas. He was now a Charleston police officer and thankful for the work. They had an eight year old son, Peter, who shyly greeted them. Unfortunately, Sarah, James' daughter, was not here today. James and Hetty's home was small, but the back veranda opened to a spacious, lovely garden in its full spring glory.

"Mother," cried Elizabeth Sarah as she saw an older woman sitting under a pink cherry tree, sipping tea.

"Oh my! Oh my!" exclaimed Ann Hanscome, clapping her hands. "Unless my eyes fail me, it is my Elizabeth Sarah and my Thomas! Come here! Come here!" she beckoned, opening her arms. "I could not die without seeing you again. You are here! I have outlived this damn war and those inhumane restrictions. You have come home!"

They all cried, even Sally, Ann's former personal slave. Louisa Rebecca breathed a huge sigh of relief as she watched the touching reunion. Her mother was having a good day and recognized her children.

"Oh Sally, bring my children refreshments," ordered Ann.

"Yes, Miss Ann," answered Sally as she scurried with a slight limp to meet her old mistress' demands. When she returned, Thomas took Sally by surprise as he warmly greeted her with a hug.

"It is nice to see you again, Sally. I want to thank you for staying with our mother when you could have left."

"Well, Master Thomas, where would I go? No, I'm not going anywhere. It is my God-given duty to take care of her, as I always have. We have been together for fifty years, ever since Master Thomas gave me to her. That was my lucky day. I figure we will die together."

"Thomas," interrupted his mother. "Who are these lovely, well dressed girls? Are they yours or Elizabeth Sarah's?"

"Let me introduce my daughters – Anna Louisa, Martha Sophia and Alice," proudly announced Thomas.

"Martha Sophia? Is she named after my dear friend Martha Sophia?"

"Yes, Mother, the very same. Mary Sophia and I are soon to have our tenth child. She was disappointed not to be able to travel with us, but sends her love."

"You married little Mary Sophia? I don't remember that, but then I am told I don't remember many things!" Ann laughed. "No matter. Girls, come to your Grandmother so I can get a good look at you. Alice - I do remember a young child named Alice. You can't be the very same!"

"Yes, I am the same Alice, but I was so young I don't remember Charleston. I do remember your wonderful deep laugh - the same laugh our cousin Sarah has."

The light morning conversations passed quickly. Too soon Louisa Rebecca announced it was time to leave. They were to meet the Inglis' for lunch.

After they left, Ann turned to Sally and asked, "Now who were those nice people? Was one my dear friend, Martha Sophia Inglis? I do hope they visit again."

And Thomas' and Elizabeth's reactions, once they were back in the carriage?

"It makes me ill to see her like that," cried Elizabeth Sarah to her older sister, Louisa Rebecca. "How long has she been so confused and frail?"

"Her forgetfulness has been growing for years, but something snapped when the war began and she moved in with James and Hetty. Once she had no plantation to run, she just gave up and sat in a chair. The truth is the War snapped many minds. We should have kept her and Sally on the farm, but we all ran out of money. Today was a good day for mother. I am happy that she recognized you. However, don't be surprised if she treats you as strangers on your next visit."

"And Sally? She looks hardly capable of caring for herself, let alone our mother," added Thomas.

"Sally may be lame, but her mind is sharp as a tack. James and Hetty help with mother's physical care, but some days Sally is the only person who can calm her agitation. I think Mother gets frightened when she doesn't recognize her surroundings or even James. Just pray that Sally doesn't die first. I don't know what we would do," answered Louisa Rebecca. "On a positive note, we have arrived and lunch awaits. There is no need to focus on the negative, is there? William Inglis is waving to us."

They had a delightful lunch at a sidewalk café, an old Brown Fellowship Society haunt, right around the corner from William's barbershop on 4 Queen Street. William had inherited the building, business and slaves from his father, Thomas Inglis, along with the clientele, old friends of his white planter grandfather. The café owner, also the waiter and chef, remembered Thomas with an embrace. He hovered and fussed over them, as the twenty-five Inglis' were his only patrons.

William Inglis introduced his younger sisters, Claudia Angelina, Helen and "baby" Martha, now thirty-two, their husbands and a few of their children. They were touched to hear they had namesakes. And Thomas was pleased that Mary Sophia's orphaned siblings had not forgotten them. Thomas and Mary Sophia, newlyweds, had done their best to care for them until they left Charleston. Then their Aunts, Catherine Lucy and Elizabeth Moor, both now deceased, took over their welfare. They were thrilled to see their Uncle Thomas and also thrilled he was paying the bill.

"I never knew we had so many cousins!" said an overwhelmed Alice. "How could you have left your family behind, Father? All mother's sisters and brother?"

"Not easily, dear Alice. Not easily. The noose was tightening on affluent freedmen, like us. We chose freedom over our family ties. We were but your age when we left. And your Grandmother Ann almost pushed us out the door."

"I am recording every name of my new relatives. I know mother wants to hear about all of them," said Anna Louisa.

"They say we all look like our mother, but how could we? We don't have her red hair," whispered Martha Sophia to her aunt, who simply smiled.

"William, has your barbershop survived the War?" asked Thomas.

"Of course, I lost all my slave apprentices, but I hardly have enough work to keep me busy, anyway. At least a few of my old planter clientele keep their regular appointments."

"I see how hard life is in Charleston, William. Is there a chance I could interest you in moving to Toronto?"

Thomas had been asking all of his relatives the same question, but it seems none could be shaken from their precious Charleston.

"Well, yes, I might consider it. I think the others are correct in assuming our economy will return, but when, is the question. Let me talk with my wife. Our children are grown and have moved to find work. And you, Thomas? Do you feel like you have returned home?"

"No, William, today I realized Toronto is my home. The golden age has passed. Charleston will never be the same. But I did discover a gentle part of my heart that I left behind. I needed to reclaim that. I am glad I returned. I have missed you all, my family."

CH. 28. The Sparkle of the Sea Islands

John's Island

May, 1866

The pleasant, warm April turned stifling hot with the approach of May and reminded the Hanscomes they must soon depart. Relatives had visited, and they revisited them. True to his word, Thomas financed a joint building supply venture for William DeCosta and his brother James. It was exactly what the reconstruction of Charleston needed. What a happy day when their bids for government contracts were accepted.

It was time to play. And what could be more relaxing than a trip to the beaches and his father's beloved Creekside, which he had sold the year Thomas was born, 1821. Thomas wanted to pay his respects to father, buried in the Hanscome cemetery on the Point. Thomas rented a sloop and sailed his girls and Elizabeth Sarah to the Stono, as promised. They left at the crack of dawn, packed with food, tents, fishing poles, swimming suits and supplies for a week.

As soon as the Charleston Harbor was out of sight Elizabeth Sarah stood, albeit precariously and shouted, "At last! This is what I needed. Freedom from that depressing, poverty-stricken city. At least the miserable war could not destroy this lovely water. I would toss my hat in the air, but I don't want to go back to Toronto with skin too kissed by this glorious sun. See the dolphins dancing just for us, girls? What a beautiful May Day!" Elizabeth Sarah's display of happy relief was contagious as the girls sent their hats sailing. What free abandonment.

"Sit down everyone and put on your hats!" yelled Thomas, after he fished the hats out of the water, but he was smiling. He, too, had absorbed the sadness of his beloved city. It hung like a cloud of oppression that magically disappeared on the water. They had arrived at the Creekside dock in time for lunch. The old Hanscome home was gone, burnt to the ground. Fine, thought Thomas, we won't have to greet the Legares. But he spoke too soon. A rider on a marsh tacky swiftly appeared, gun in hand. "Legare?" asked Thomas. "You must be a Legare."

"And who might you be, trespassing on my property?" asked a handsome, young man.

"Hanscome, Thomas Hanscome. This was my father's plantation and I wondered if we could have a picnic lunch on your property."

"Well, I'll be! Another Thomas Hanscome! I am Thomas Hanscome Walpole, named after my father, Thomas Hanscome Walpole, who was named for your most generous father." He quickly dismounted and shook Thomas' hand. "I'm the great grandson of James Legare, who bought this land from your father. My father I barely knew as he died in 1850 from the fever and I was quite young. My grandfather, Captain Horace Walpole, died just days before the War began - bless his soul, I remember him well. He would have hated to see Creekside in its present state. I hope its demise is not too hard for you to witness. My two uncles and I own Creekside. I thought you were one of those northern land poachers. You are welcome to stay for the day or several days – I see you have some tents in that sloop."

"Thank you. Our plan is to fish, go to the beaches, swim in the surf, and shed the pathos of Charleston. Why don't you join us for lunch and tell us the twenty years of Creekside history that I missed."

And young Walpole did just that. "The Confederacy abandoned the Sea Islands. The lowland planters either defended themselves against the North or fled, leaving burned fields as gifts for the hungry Union troops. But we did not set our Creekside afire. That was someone else's pleasure. We planters begin, again, but with no capital and no slaves. We hope to make a profit on this year's crops and next year grow cotton again. Did you know the Grimballs?"

"Yes, Elizabeth Grimball was previously married to my father's nephew, another Thomas Hanscome. She was not really our aunt, more like a second mother to us as she was our mother's best planter friend. When my cousin died, she married Paul Grimball. Then there was a falling out over the custody of a slave left to my mother in my father's will and he forbade Aunt Elizabeth to see us. The court allowed Grimball to keep the slave."

"I don't remember the slave incident, but I do know of the famed Nancy Randall. Yes, of course, she was your mother. What a spicy legacy your parents left for Creekside. What a love story. Did you know my father, Thomas Hanscome Walpole?"

"Yes, I did. He was a few years younger than I, but, as you might have guessed, we didn't socialize with my father's planter friends. I am sorry you didn't have a chance to know your father better. And the Grimballs? What do you know of them?"

"They are in exile, but their grandchildren, friends of mine, recently claimed Longwood, the land that is. Their mansion was also burned to the ground. I helped them push a few old slave cabins together. It is a beginning." He smiled, excited about rebuilding, finding new opportunities in the old ashes.

As he spoke, the girls were rapt, not with his tale but with him - handsome Thomas Hanscome Walpole. Thomas had never witnessed them so entranced, but Elizabeth Sarah signaled him with a frown to keep his observations to himself. Thomas had mixed feelings towards this young man. He tried not to resent him for his charming ways with his daughters.

"I am going fishing in my canoe, is anyone is interested?" young Walpole asked.

"Yes," replied all three girls at once.

"Why don't we empty the sloop and all go fishing," suggested their father. "I think three girls would tip your canoe over and I have no intention of feeding them to the alligators."

Soon they were ready. They spied alligators sunning themselves on the bank and watched them silently slip into the water as they approached.

"Look for the alligator eyes in the water as we come around this next bend. Listen carefully and you can hear them slink into the water," young Thomas whispered to Alice. "Count how many pairs of eyes you can find."

As they rounded the bend Alice delightfully counted three pair of eyes staring at her. At the same time, the catfish started biting.

"Steady girls, don't rock the boat! I have a fish on my line and so does Elizabeth Sarah," cautioned their father.

They caught ample cat fish and speckled trout for dinner. After they returned, young Thomas taught the girls how to catch shrimp while their father made camp.

Elizabeth Sarah decided to forage for firewood and search for the Hanscome family cemetery. At fourteen years of age, she still vividly remembered her father's sad funeral. "I want to walk our old land, see if my feet remember it, as my eyes do not remember any of this undergrowth," she laughed. "I must remember to be wary of the snakes!" When she returned, disappointed that her foray into the overgrown brush yielded no family cemetery, she was free from snake bites, savagely bitten by mosquitoes and famished. "Charleston is not looking so unappealing to me at this moment," she laughed. "I need to slather some mud on these bites, fast."

"Don't be disheartened, we'll look together," said Thomas. "Perhaps young Walpole knows its location. And stay away from the swamps and out of the brush. Remember that swamp fever took our brother Joseph.

"Ouch!" yelled Anna Louisa, holding her finger for all to see. "These shrimp bite with the nips on their heads!"

The shrimp were added to the gumbo of fresh tomatoes, peppers, onions, and okra. The fried catfish and trout were also most tasty. What a feast. They drank young Walpole's cinchona bark tea, as a precaution against fever, around the camp fire as Elizabeth Sarah told long forgotten stories about Creekside.

The next morning they sailed the sloop to the beaches. Did young Thomas accompany them? Yes, he did.

"Oh, Father," cried Anna Louisa, "This water is warmer than a bath. I was expecting to shiver. How could I have found that frigid Lake Ontario so enjoyable."

At the end of the day, Thomas said to Elizabeth Sarah, "I think young Thomas needs to go back to Creekside. I don't like how he looks at Alice."

"Oh, Thomas, you're just acting like a protective father. I haven't seen Alice this happy in so long - too long. He is harmless."

"No young man is harmless, Elizabeth Sarah. I like the sparkle of the sea, but not the sparkle in Alice's eyes."

What fun they had. Young Thomas taught the girls how to hold the tips of their fishing poles up and give the fish some line before they set the hook. The senior Thomas rolled his eyes as his girls were mesmerized by their tour guide's vast knowledge of fishing and the sea. In turn, Elizabeth Sarah smiled at her brother as he always wanted to be in charge. Indeed, young Walpole had stolen the show and Thomas was dethroned.

"Be patient for the nibblers and ready for the attackers," said Walpole. "Watch the water at all times, notice the swells, currents and birds, looking for their dinner, too. Look beyond the surface. It teems with life. When the tide changes, the fish will bite. The big fish follow the jumping bait fish. The smaller, milder white fish like the sand fleas we dug up on the shore." On and on young Thomas went, like his elder namesake. But no one seemed bored with his lessons.

Thomas taught them how to spot star fish, pick up sand dollars with their toes, collect clams and find the smooth olive shells after the tide went out. He even picked a few spines from a purple sea urchin out of Alice's foot. Did he massage her foot and gaze into her eyes just a bit too long? The senior Thomas was watching him like a hawk.

All the girls whined and moaned when their father announced their beach holiday was over. As Elizabeth Sarah turned the sloop back toward Charleston, Thomas asked, "What will be your favorite memories from our Creekside trip?"

"The sea," they all yelled in unison.

"Swimming and captaining this boat," laughed Elizabeth Sarah. "Not the mosquitoes."

"Racing the marsh tackies that Thomas lent us," said Martha Sophia. "And watching you and Thomas kill the alligator."

"And eating alligator meat," said Anna Louisa. "And watching Alice fall in love!"

"The whole thing. Everything was perfect, Father." Alice ignored her younger sister's insinuation as she fondled the shells young Thomas helped her collect.

Thomas reflected on visiting his father's unkempt gravesite, almost hidden by dense scrub, and crying, for his lost father, his confusing youth and for the end of an era. Young Walpole had helped them locate the cemetery and promised to maintain it.

Charleston

At the DeCostas, they returned to sad the eyes of Louisa Rebecca and a house full of company. Something dreadful had happened.

"Mother has died," said Louisa Rebecca. "Blessedly, she quietly passed in her sleep two nights ago. Tomorrow is her funeral. I know I will miss her more every day, but today I am glad you are here to send her off in fine Charleston fashion. Today we will celebrate her life."

"We never should have left for Creekside," lamented Thomas.

"Oh yes, you should have," replied Louisa Rebecca. "You visited her daily for a month. You knew her condition. I hadn't seen her eyes so bright in years. She died a happy mother. It truly is fitting that we all bury her, together. Don't look so sad girls – it was a blessing for her to see you. It's a good thing to die and see hope in the next generation. That is the gift you gave her - hope."

James greeted them next and held his nose. "Go bathe, change your clothes and join us. You smell like the swamp, brother, and that our mother wouldn't abide. I must also say you look so healthy and colorful!"

"Aunt Elizabeth Sarah," the girls shrieked in horror as they looked in the mirror. "Come here! Please! Look at us!"

"Well, now you know how the Brown Fellowship Society received its name." Elizabeth Sarah actually liked what she saw in the mirror, perhaps a glimpse of her beautiful mother. For her it was a gift to be free of her hat. She felt beautiful. "Don't worry girls, we will fade and yet again be decent white ladies upon our return to Toronto."

Where was their sadness? This was a wake and the chatter seemed too lively, like a ball. Would Elizabeth Sarah open the floodgate and weep? Would she cry for her mother, for her Charleston family, for her Toronto children who had grown up northern, for her maturing self? No, she would not. What did she feel? If she could take their Toronto money and move back to Charleston, she would. She'd love to be brown again, in every sense of the word. Oh, how she missed the sun and the water. How she missed these people – her family, the smells, the food, the light-heartedness, the music. They had soul. But poverty and devastation is not kind and grows old, anywhere, she reminded herself.

Elizabeth Sarah dried her eyes, took a deep breath, held herself erect and practiced her flawless southern smile in the mirror, just as her mother had taught her. Tonight she was determined to honor her mother's words: "Tomorrow is tomorrow. Smile today, my dear." She unclenched her jaw as she slowly, gracefully, floated down the spiral staircase, followed by her nieces. Her smile magically warmed the room. What a graceful sight the northern Hanscome ladies were. And what a sight they beheld below.

A Nancy Randall, Ann Hanscome, tribute was in progress. There was a line of people waiting to view their mother. Black as coal old Hanscome slaves, old Brown Fellowship Society gentry and even a few old white planters paid their respects. Sally was seated in a chair of honor, a spray of orchids pinned to her best dress. Of what did these mourners speak? They recalled how Ann Randall and her Thomas Hanscome had challenged the rules. They gossiped about their audacity and even admitted to jealousy of their great love. Ann Hanscome's death symbolized the grand finale of Charleston's golden days. Champagne was opened, the memories flew and the music soothed. They were not mourning just Ann Hanscome. Regardless of their station in life, they were burying an old order.

"She was beautiful," commented one mourner.

"She cared for my mentally ill mother at the insane asylum," said another.

"She could plant cotton with the best of us," recalled a newly freed slave.

"Thomas was so proud of her," mentioned another.

Then Elizabeth Grimball appeared at the door. Aunt Elizabeth! She spent a long time staring at her old friend, Ann, before greeting her children.

"I had been in exile with Paul, but he recently died and I have returned to my dear Charleston."

"Oh, I am so sorry to hear that news," said Louisa Rebecca taking Elizabeth's frail hand. Thomas, James and Elizabeth Sarah drew close to welcome their Aunt, not by blood, but by her friendship with their mother.

"Please don't be sorry. I have come to terms with death and find it a kind thing. I am quite happy for Paul and your dear mother. To suffer and lose your dignity is unkind. I visited Ann last week when I returned and her mind was addled. Her younger self, oh so proud, would have hated to see herself so.

Please don't remember her like this. Remember her hearty laugh. Remember how much your parents loved you, and each other. I focus on the happy times I shared with her and you children. Your mother's life was not easy, to be shunned as she was by Thomas' friends and even treated so shabbily by my dear Paul. The Lord has been merciful to take them both. And when I die, be happy for me and have a lovely party, like this one.

"This is a new era. Make something of it. I am off to visit my grandchildren at my old plantation, Longwood, and give them the same speech."

Elizabeth embraced them all, then with no more ado, slowly and erectly floated out the front door. What a presence. What grace.

The biggest surprise was the appearance of Thomas Hanscome Walpole. He looked most handsome in his stylish Charleston attire.

"I rode to Charleston last night and heard the news of your grandmother. I am sorry for your loss," he said to Alice, who was unsuccessful in hiding her excitement. Unfortunately, her father noticed and was not excited.

"Young Thomas, may I have a word with you?" said Thomas, sternly, leading him to a private room.

"I do not welcome your interest in Alice. We are soon to depart for Toronto and it would be unkind of you to toy with her affections." Thomas' eyes had turned as hard as steel.

"Please be assured my intentions are honorable."

"And what might they be?"

"I missed her and wanted to see her again, to get better acquainted," replied young Thomas, hopefully.

"Well, that's not good enough young man. She wants to be married and you cannot provide that for her, at least not in South Carolina. If you are interested in marriage, you would have to come to Toronto with us, forsake your dear Creekside."

"Well, that I cannot do," sighed young Thomas. "I am fond of Alice but marriage is out of the question, anywhere. It is against the miscegenation laws for a white to marry a mulatto. You must be aware of that."

"Oh, I am painfully aware of those laws, young man. It is why my parents could not marry. Why would I want Alice to have the same lonely fate as my mother? Incredulous! But what you don't know is that in Toronto we are white. And even if we weren't legally white, they have no miscegenation laws. I challenge you. The only honorable intention I will consider is marriage. In that case I would also set you up in a most profitable business of your choosing. I am a wealthy man. If marriage is not your intention, I forbid you to see her. And, I want you to leave, now."

"I see. I know that I am poor, but I could never leave Creekside. My soul is in this land. If Alice is white in Toronto, she and I could marry and return here. No one would challenge such a marriage."

"Have you no enemies? Legally, you could risk being jailed and fined. The unfortunate truth is that her Hanscome racial heritage would precede her entrance into every room. She would never be totally accepted by your friends. Of that I am certain."

Silence. Finally, young Thomas spoke.

"Yes, you are right. I don't like it, but you are right. I will honor your wishes and not visit Alice again."

"Thank you. I need to protect my Alice's heart. I also understand your love for Creekside. It gets in your blood. I predict you will make it profitable again."

And they shook hands.

"Father! What did you say to Thomas?" asked a distraught Alice when she saw young Thomas leave the house. He had not even said goodbye to her.

"I told him to stay away. You do not need another broken heart, dear Alice. He cannot marry you, even if he wanted to. It's against the law. Did you want to be Thomas' courtesan? You need to marry an honorable man, a man from Toronto."

"How could you? This is the second suitor you have turned away, first Harry, now Thomas. You have ruined my life! I could love Thomas under any circumstance, courtesan or not. He would be true to me. I know!"

Alice ran from the room and up the stairs, consumed in rage and tears. She hated her father. She wanted to run after Thomas, never to return to Toronto. Did she?

Yes, she did. She packed a few belongings and took money from Elizabeth Sarah's satchel. Then she stealthily opened a window and climbed down a tree. She had defied her father, finally. She was free. She felt exhilarated, fueled by anger and anticipation. She rented a horse from a stable, purchased food and headed for John's Island. She prayed Thomas would go back to Creekside and that she could get there without incident, before sunset. Alice rode with abandon, until the horse was near exhaustion. Finally, she stopped at a grove of old oaks. On a normal day she would have marveled at the ancient trees with their massive trunks, arching branches and gray green Spanish moss flowing from their limbs. But she barely noticed their beauty. Instead, she rushed her mare to graze and drink before continuing on her journey.

"Please be there, Thomas. Be at Creekside!" she fervently prayed.

She arrived as the sun was setting, but found Thomas nowhere. Finally, she went to the pier, the place they had met, and waited. She was alone. Her anger was spent and she was tired. She wept. Was she a fool? She didn't care. She settled herself and finally slept.

In the morning, Alice awoke to the aroma of bacon.

"Good morning, Alice," greeted Thomas with his captivating, wide grin.

"Hello, Thomas," she smiled back. "I am famished. Is that food for me?"

"Yes, it is. Consider me at your service, Miss Hanscome," he said as he handed her a plate of grits, fried green tomatoes, eggs and bacon.

They talked and laughed. Alice helped him feed his chickens, do his chores and they fished. Lunch was speedily caught, cooked and served.

"Alice, you need to return to Charleston," Thomas said seriously. "I have nothing to offer you. Could I love you? Yes, I could, but your father is right. I cannot marry you and you deserve that."

"I want to stay with you," was all she said. Then Alice leaned over and kissed him.

"He will come for you. Your father will look for you here. I will not hide you," cautioned Thomas, as he held Alice at arm's length.

"Yes, I know, you are an honorable man. But until he comes, I want to be with you."

"Are you certain?" he asked.

"Do you love me?"

"Oh yes, I do. I love you, Alice. I would marry you this instant if I could."

"We could pretend," she shyly offered. "We at least share the Hanscome name."

"Yes, we do, indeed, Miss Hanscome." Thomas smiled and took her gently into his arms.

"Let's run away, if only for a day," Alice said. "My father will soon be here, if we stay at Creekside."

"This is not a good idea, but I will do it."

They packed Thomas' canoe with supplies and paddled until they found a secluded beach. There they made camp, swam and naturally found each other's arms. What a glorious picture of young love they made.

"Ouch," said Thomas as he stepped on something sharp. He held up his foot to see if it was bleeding, but it wasn't. "I do believe I have just found our dinner," said Thomas as he pulled up a large conch shell hidden in the sand. "Let's see if this one has a few friends." They dove under water, found two more large whelks and surfaced triumphant. "Are you ready to work, Miss Alice?" Yes, she was.

Together they banged metal stakes into the tops of the shells until the muscles released their suctioned feet that fiercely gripped the shells. First, they washed the muscles in the sea, cut off any black poisonous tissue, chopped them into small pieces and flattened them paper thin with a rock. Next they boiled the muscles for several hours to tenderize them, drained the foul smelling water, then added clean water, onions, garlic, tomatoes, okra, corn, potatoes, lots of peppers, including the seeds, and fried bacon chunks.

"This is not a quick meal," said Thomas, "but a must for all Canadian visitors to taste, at least once. Now it has to simmer for hours."

"That was a lot of work," said Alice. "I must admit I am relieved that it smells better now than that nasty foul water we drained off. I wasn't certain I could eat these sea snails."

"I like that you are a good sport, Alice, game to try anything new."

"And I like that we make a good team."

"Happy?" asked Thomas after they'd eaten.

"Happy," replied a contented Alice. "Very happy, very full and very satisfied in every way. This is a true paradise. I have white powder sand to rest on, crystal clear, warm water to swim in, gentle, undulating waves to float upon, and conch chowder cooked to perfect tenderness by my own personal chef."

"And what else makes you happy?" Thomas asked?

"Having your arms around me," whispered Alice in his ear.

"Are you embarrassed to say you love me out loud, afraid the birds and the dolphins will shout your feelings to the highest heavens? Here, Alice, watch me announce our love to the sun in the sky." Thomas raised his arms to the heavens and shouted, "Good day honorable sun. I want to announce that I love Alice Hanscome!"

"Will you also announce our great news to the moon tonight?" she asked, coyly, trying to keep from laughing.

"Of course, and maybe a star will shoot across the sky in our honor," he added as he leaned over to kiss her. "Now on a more serious note, bring that lovely, pink conch shell to me and hold it up to your ear. Listen."

Alice did as he asked, listened for a sound and gave him a questioning look. "I hear a slushing noise, is that what you hear?"

"Listen more carefully. And now what do you hear?"

"I hear the sound of the sea," Alice exclaimed. "Is that right?"

"You are correct. Many people hear the ocean's roar and the waves upon the shore. Please give it to me and I'll listen. Each shell has a unique message, a secret message." Thomas looked quite serious, intently listened and said, "Yes, this conch shell is special, very special. It is softly whispering, 'I love you, Alice.' Do you hear it? Try listening again."

"I do love that you make me laugh so, Thomas."Alice took the shell and pressed it again to her ear. "I hear no such words, but I believe you are a magician and have special powers, especially over me. I do love you, too. Catch me if you can," challenged Alice as she dove head first into the sea.

It was noon the next day when Alice's father found them. Was he angry? Simply, he looked old, haggard and disappointed.

"Alice, come with me," was all he said.

"Alice wants to stay with me," challenged Thomas.

"For what? For what should she stay? For another night or two? For years of back-breaking work in your fields? For a balcony view of you in Church? For shunning? For what, I ask you?" Thomas seethed. His full fury came unleashed. "I thought we had reached an understanding, but you are no man of honor!"

"It was not Thomas' idea. It was mine. I want to stay, forever, with Thomas," replied Alice, moving in front of him, as though to ward off her father's wrath.

"This is a new era. We can make this work, Alice and I. Wouldn't you like to see your grandchildren at Creekside? A place your family loved?" asked young Thomas.

"As bastards? No. Not as I was raised. Absolutely not!"

Alice was not moved by her father's anger or moving from her Thomas' side.

Silence.

"We are leaving in four days from Charleston, Alice. I want you to come with us, home to Toronto. I will not shoot your young man, but I implore you not to live in shame with him. You will regret it. We will wait for you at the wharf. Ask Thomas to return with us, where you can be married. I will purchase a ticket for him."

Thomas did not look back. His rage erupted as he sailed away. His inability to control Alice, save her from an ill-fated tryst that would ruin her life, gave way to the unfamiliar sound of a massive scream that came from the depths of his soul. "I am powerless, Lord! I cannot save you from foolish yourself. Oh, Alice!" Thomas lost control, the control that he carefully, diligently orchestrated his whole adult life. Yes, he was practiced at skirting danger and protecting his beloved family at every turn with every ounce of strength he possessed. He was the father, the protector. As his rage dissolved into sobs, years of contained grief surfaced. He let go, finally let go. He sobbed for his father, his mother, his lost Carolina youth and his lost mulatto society. Most of all he cried for his Alice. Would she return to Toronto with them or would she choose the sparkle of love, the Sea Islands and a prejudice she had never experienced?

Spent, he sailed into Charleston. He had done his best, but he was not in charge of Alice. He wondered if he'd really ever been in control of anything. He knew. He knew he could not spare his Alice another broken heart. He also knew young Thomas would choose Creekside over his Alice, but he bought a ticket to Toronto for him anyway.

And Alice and Thomas?

"I feel like an adult, Thomas. I finally stood up to my father. I looked him straight in the eye and said, No! And you did, too. I love you, Thomas!"

"You are stronger than you think. I am so proud of you. We can do this, Alice, together. I just know it. Trust me. I will take care of you."

"Are you asking me to marry you?"

"Yes, you can be Mrs. Thomas Hanscome Walpole, if it pleases you."

"It pleases me. Yes, I am so much more than pleased." Alice laughed. "And will you return to Toronto with me so we can be legally married?"

"Yes, I will," Thomas solemnly, solidly stated.

"And after we're married, then what?"

"I want you to return here with me. I'm a greedy man, I want both my land and you."

"Now ask me properly," she scolded, "in front of all the seabirds in this blue sky and the sparkle of the sea. "I want a memory of this moment that will last me a lifetime. Make it good."

And with that Thomas got down on bended knee and gazed into her eyes.

"I promise you my devotion for a lifetime, Alice."

"And?"

"I promise you the joy of our children's laughter as they frolic in this very sea."

"And?"

"I promise you we will rebuild our plantation and continue the legacy of our families, Hanscome and Walpole."

"And?"

"I command this sea to swallow me whole if I ever break my promise to love you eternally."

"And?"

"Will you marry me, Alice?"

"Yes, I will. I will! Now will you please kiss me?"

"I will do more than that, my love."

And with that they celebrated their betrothal in paradise and merged body and soul in timeless passion. Yes, together they created a memory never to be forgotten.

Charleston harbor

"I'm afraid Alice isn't coming with us," said Elizabeth Sarah, pacing the wharf. The whistle had blown and the passengers were boarding. "She has made her choice and I will not judge her for it. This South Carolina charm can be so seductive. Let's be happy for her, Thomas. We cannot predict the future."

Thomas said nothing. They boarded.

"Wait! Wait, I am coming!" shouted Alice as she ran down the wharf, hat askew. She was alone, but in the distance they saw young Walpole turning his horse around.

No questions were asked as the Hanscomes embraced their Alice. Thomas couldn't have been happier, as he wiped the tears from his eyes.

Who else was happy? Why William Inglis and his wife. They had left their Charleston property, now worthless, in the hands of a solicitor and decided to move to Toronto.

"Put your hats on girls!" ordered Thomas. All complied, of course, but Alice. She held her magic conch shell to her ear, listened in vain for some tune of love and, hearing none, heaved it far into the sea. Then she simply turned her face to the wind and allowed it to dry her unstoppable tears.

Thomas released the extra passage ticket to the wind.

They were going home.

Hanscom(b)e Genealogy

First Generation:

Children of Thomas Hanscombe and Katherine Alcock Bedfordshire, England:

1. Joan Hanscombe b.1597? England d.1670? Salem, Massachusetts Bay Colony m. 7/29/1627 Richard Claydon b.1594 England d.1640's Salem, Massachusetts Bay Colony.
2. Thomas Hanscombe b.1618 England d.1696? Kittery ME m. 5/16/1664 Ann (Downing?) b.1646 Kittery ME d.1719? Maine.

Second Generation:

Child of Joan Hanscombe and Richard Claydon:

1. Katherine b.1627? England d.1629 on ship Talbot crossing to Salem.

Children of Thomas Hanscome and Ann (Downing):

1. Thomas Hanscome b.10/17/1666 Kittery ME d. 2/1713 Kittery ME m. Alice Rogers. Five children. After her death m. Tamsen Gowell Sheares. Six children.
2. John Hanscome b. 9/15/1668 Kittery ME d.? No known marriages or children. He was a mariner.
3. Alice Hanscome b. 3/12/1671 Kittery ME d.? m. 1690 John Mederille who abandoned Alice after the birth of her first child by Black Will, a slave. Both were flogged for fornication. Black Will was the first slave to buy his freedom and settle in Maine. Alice had two more children, no identified fathers. Her first child, William Black Jr. b. 1690 Kittery ME d.? m. Elizabeth Turbot b.? Kittery ME d.? Settled Bailey's Island. Several children.
4. Samuel Hanscome b. 4/10/1675 Kittery ME d. young adult?
5. Job Hanscome b. 1679 Kittery ME d. 9/3/1779 Saco ME m. Mary Gowell b.? Kittery ME d.? Ten children.
6. Moses Hanscome b. 1680 Kittery ME d. Cape Elizabeth ME between the dates of 1748 and 1760 m. Hannah Rackliff b.? Kittery ME d.? Seven children.
7. Aaron Hanscom(b)e b. 1685 Kittery ME d. 1760 John's Island SC m. name unknown Two sons.

For further generations of New England Hanscoms consult Robert Hanscom's extensive genealogy on Face book: Family Hanscom Reunites.

Third Generation: South Carolina Branch

Children of Aaron Hanscom(b)e and unnamed wife:

1. Thomas Hanscome b.1723 John's Island SC d. 1787 John's Island SC
   m. Elizabeth, unknown surname b.? d. before husband Thomas. SC
   Assemblyman 1785-1786.
2. Moses Hanscome b.1730 John's Island SC d. 11/1771 South Edisto
   plantation at Ferguson's Ferry, St. Bartholomew's Parish SC m.
   6/2/1761Mary Brown b? d. after husband Moses.

Fourth Generation:

Children of Thomas Hanscome and Elizabeth, unknown surname:

1. Ann Hanscome b. 1757 John's Island SC d. between 1777 and 1786
   John's Island SC m. 4/24/1777 Col. Robert Rivers b. 1725? d. between
   1777 and 1786. John's Island planter. No children.
2. Thomas Hanscome, Jr. b. 1760 John's Island SC d. 12/29/1831
   Charleston SC. Never married. He challenged SC society by having
   six children with Nancy Randall, his colored mistress of twenty-five
   years. b. 1792 SC d. between 1850 -1865 Charleston SC?
3. Mary Hanscome b. 1763 John's Island SC d. 2/1783 m. 1782? John
   Geyer, John's Island planter. No children.
4. James Hanscome b. 1774 John's Island SC d. 1812 Charleston SC. No
   will, marriage or children recorded. He was a South Carolina
   Assemblyman 1800-1801, physician and planter.

Children of Moses Hanscome and Mary Brown:

1. Thomas Hanscome b.1760's Ferguson's Ferry, South Edisto SC d.? m.
   Elizabeth Jenkins b. 1786 John's Island SC d. 1850? No children.
   Widow Elizabeth Jenkins Hanscome m. Paul Chaplin Grimball b.
   1788 John's Island Longwood Plantation d. 1864. Several children.
2. Moses Hanscome b. 1760's Ferguson's Ferry, South Edisto SC d. after
   1787 m.? Children unknown.
3. John Hanscome b. after father Moses' death in 1771, Ferguson's
   Ferry, South Edisto SC d. after his Uncle Thomas in 1787. Children
   unknown. His Uncle Thomas Hanscome's will provided for John's
   care until age 21. Moses' two older sons were not named in their
   Uncle Thomas Hanscome's will, but were included in their father's
   will.

Fifth Generation:

Children of Thomas Hanscome and Nancy Randall:

1. Joseph Hanscome b. 7/24/1812 Charleston SC d. 8/4/1838 Charleston SC m. 1834 Mary, unknown surname. d. 1876? Philadelphia PA. Joseph died of fever as did their toddler daughter, Ann.
   In 1845 widow Mary Hanscome traveled with Thomas and Mary Sophia Hanscome to Bucks County PA where she married well-known abolitionist Robert Forten, son of James Forten, wealthy Philadelphia freedman sail maker and businessman. Robert d.1864 Philadelphia PA.
2. Louisa Rebecca Hanscome b. 1815 Charleston SC d.? Charleston SC m. 2/12/1833 William P. DeCosta b. 1808 Charleston SC d. 1873 Charleston SC. William was cotton gin maker and member of Brown Fellowship Society and part of Jewish Community.
3. Elizabeth Sarah Hanscome b. 1817 Charleston SC d. 1877 Toronto Canada m. 1839 John George Garden b. 1812 Charleston SC d. 1880 Toronto Canada. John was the son of the wealthy mulatto Hermitage Plantation owner and Brown Fellowship Society member, John Garden. The Gardens bought a farm in Bucks County, Warminster PA near brother Thomas, sister-in-law Mary Hanscome (Joseph's widow) and sister Mary Ann Lee and their families in 1845.
4. Mary Ann Hanscome b. Charleston SC 1819 d. Toronto Canada? She purchased the family St. James' Cemetery burial lots in 1877, but not buried there. m. 1840 John Lee b. 1821 Charleston SC d.? Canada. John was son of Eliza, restaurateur, and John Lee, tailor, also Charleston Brown Fellowship Society members.
5. Thomas Hanscome b. 1821 Charleston SC d. 1894 Toronto Canada m. 1841 Mary Sophia Inglis b. Charleston SC 1823 d. 1899 Toronto Canada. Mary Sophia was daughter of Martha Sophia and Thomas Inglis, wealthy Charleston barbershop owner, Brown Fellowship Society member and son of white plantation owner Thomas Inglis.
6. James Randall Hanscome b. 1822 Charleston SC d. after 1898, possibly Charleston, Toronto or New York m. 1841 Serena Elizabeth Walker, wealthy mulatto slave and slave owner, daughter of wealthy white planter John Walker and his slave mistress Ann Jones Walker, another famed Charleston love liaison similar to Thomas Hanscome and Nancy Randall. John Walker was unable to manumit his mistress or any of their eight children. Serena divorced James before 1844. James m. 1856? widow Harriet (Hetty) E. Geary b. 1816 Savannah GA. James divorced Hetty. James m. 1865? Charleston SC Emma, unknown surname. In 1872 James was Charleston police officer.

No further information for Moses Hanscome and Mary Brown lineage.

Sixth Generation:

Child of Joseph Hanscome and Mary, unknown surname:

1. Ann Hanscome b. 1835? Woodland Plantation SC d. 1837 or 1838 Woodland Plantation SC.

Children of Mary Hanscome (Joseph's widow) and Robert Forten:

1. Wendell Phillips Forten b. 1847 Bucks County PA d. 1860 London, England.
2. Edmund Quincy Forten b. 1849 Bucks County PA d. after 1875 England?

Children of Louisa Rebecca Hanscome and William P. DeCosta:

1. Joseph Hanscome DeCosta b. before 1841 Charleston SC d.?
2. Five other unnamed children.

Children of Elizabeth Sarah Hanscome and John George Garden: (St. James' Cathedral Cemetery source: nine children.)

1. Daniel Garden b. 1840 Charleston SC d.?
2. Walter Garden b. 1842 Charleston SC d.?
3. Amanda Garden b. 1844 Charleston SC d. 1911 Toronto Canada.
4. Ellen Garden b. 1846 Warminster, Bucks County PA d.? Toronto Canada.
5. Joel D. Garden 1847 or 1850 Warminster, Bucks County PA d. 1894 Toronto Canada.
6. Johanna Garden b.1848 Warminster, Bucks County PA d.? Toronto Canada.
7. Thomas Garden b.1850? Warminster, Bucks County PA d.? m.? Toronto wife unknown, but he is listed as father of two infant daughters buried in Hanscome St. James' Cemetery plot.
   1) Sadie Garden b. 1883 Toronto Canada d. 1885 Toronto Canada.
   2) Helena Frances Garden b. 1885 Toronto Canada d. 1886 Toronto Canada.
8. Iona Butler Garden b. 1852 Warminster PA d. 1876 Toronto Canada.
9. Helena Garden b. 1853 Warminster PA d. 1918 Toronto Canada m.? Gallagher.

Children of Mary Ann Hanscome and John Lee:

1. John Drayton Lee b. 1844 Charleston SC d.?
2. No other Lee children recorded. Mary Ann Hanscome purchased St. James' Cemetery plots in 1877, but her last name of Lee was not used in those records.

Children of Thomas Hanscome and Mary Sophia Inglis:

1. Alice Constantia Hanscome b. 1842 Charleston SC d.1929 Toronto Canada. Unmarried.
2. Edwin Hanscome b. 1843 Charleston SC d. 1845 Warminster PA.
3. Martha Sophia Hanscome b. 1845 Philadelphia PA d. 1906 Toronto Canada. Unmarried.
4. Anna Louisa Hanscome b. 1846 Warminster PA d. 1943 Toronto m. 1888 William Philip Marston b. 1821 d. 1901. William had child(ren) by first marriage. Anna Louisa no children.
5. Virginia Emeline Hanscome b. 1849 (twin) Warminster PA d. 1929 Toronto Canada. Unmarried.
6. Eugenia Angeline Hanscome b. 1849 (twin) Warminster PA d. 1942 Toronto Canada. Unmarried.
7. William Kissick Hanscome b. 1856 Toronto Canada d. 1945 Minneapolis MN m.1880 Toronto Rhoda Baldwin Cooper b. 1844 England d. 1919 Minneapolis MN. Rhoda Cooper was a widowed school teacher who moved to Toronto with her Baldwin family from England.
8. Thomas Henry Hanscome b. 1861 Toronto Canada d. 1891 Toronto Canada. Artist. Unmarried.
9. Naomi Helena Hanscome b. 1864 Toronto Canada d. 1960 Toronto Canada. Unmarried.
10. Arthur Randall Hanscome b.1866 Toronto Canada d.? Vancouver Canada? m. unnamed English woman in Vancouver Canada. No known children.

Child of James Randall Hanscome and Serena Walker:

1. Sarah Hanscome b. 1841 Charleston SC m.? d.?

Child of James Randall Hanscome and Harriet Geary:

1. Peter Hanscome b. 1858 Savannah GA d. 1916 Charleston SC m. Phoebe DeLyons b.? d.? Charleston SC.

Children of James Randall Hanscome and Emma, unknown surname:

1. Perhaps three or four unnamed children.

Seventh Generation:

No further lineage information for seventh generation Hanscomes, other than William Kissick Hanscome, below.

Children of William Kissick Hanscome and Rhoda Baldwin Cooper:

1. William Thomas Hanscome b. 1880 Toronto Canada d. 11/20/1964 Minneapolis MN m. 1912 Ethel Dixon b. 11/4/1881 MN d. 10/23/1969 Minneapolis MN.
2. Muriel Hanscome b. 1/1884 Minneapolis MN d. 12/10/1961 Minneapolis MN Never married. No children.
3. Rhoda Hanscome b. 10/30/1886 Minneapolis MN d. 9/30/1982 Minneapolis MN m. 5/22/1911 James Arthur Campbell b. 1884 Minneapolis (Camden) MN d. 7/5/1954 Minneapolis MN.
4. Robert Hanscome b.? Minneapolis MN d. as young child. Minneapolis MN.

Eighth Generation:

Children of William Thomas Hanscome and Ethel Dixon:

1. Thomas Dixon Hanscome b. 7/2/1914 Austin MN d. 11/01/1988 Irvine CA m. 11/8/1940 JoAnn Elizabeth Chandler b. 5/27/1920 Glidden IA d. 2/27/2012 CA.
2. Barbara Jane Hanscome b. 11/25/1916 Austin MN d. 2/13/2005 Richfield MN m. Detroit MI 7/13/1942 Edward Allen (Jack) Munger b. 8/27/1907 Anaconda MT d. 9/20/1983 MN.
3. William Dixon Hanscome b. 5/29/1925 Minneapolis MN d. 12/09/2011 Anoka MN m. 7/7/51 Donna Mae Sundberg b. 5/26/1930 Robbinsdale MN d. 5/11/2012 MN.
4. John Baldwin Hanscome b. 1928 Minneapolis MN d. 1994 Santa Maria CA m. 9/9/1948 Marjorie Ann Timm b. 1927 Omaha NE d. 2012 San Francisco CA.

Children of Rhoda Hanscome and James Arthur Campbell:

1. James Gordon Campbell b. 6/1912 Minneapolis MN d. 7/01/1994
   Scottsdale AZ m. 1/1940 Minneapolis MN Margaret Fuge b.
   11/23/1918 Minneapolis MN d. 1/12/2013 Scottsdale AZ.
2. Rhoda Jane Campbell b. 4/17/1915 Minneapolis MN d. 2/29/1994
   Minneapolis MN m. 6/23/1939 Minneapolis MN Wesley Adsit
   Dickinson b. 12/6/1913 Hastings MN d. 9/22/1991 Walker MN.
3. Jean Hope Campbell b. 8/27/1917 Minneapolis MN d. 2/17/1992
   Richfield MN m.1939 Minneapolis MN William Gage Donald b. 1915
   Pittsburgh PA d. 1960's, div. 1945 m. 1950 Edina MN Clifford
   Gardner Johnson b. 1/2/1918 Valley City ND d. 1978 VA div. 1962.
4. Miriam Patricia Campbell b. 4/9/1919 Minneapolis MN d. 8/20/2007
   St. Paul MN m. 8/25/1942 Minneapolis MN John Alvin Herrmann b.
   6/29/1916 St. Paul MN d. 6/20/2001 Minneapolis MN.

Ninth Generation:

Children of Thomas Dixon Hanscome and JoAnn Elizabeth Chandler:

1. Thomas Chandler Hanscome b. 07/02/1943 Washington DC m.
   11/18/1966 Sherry Lee Maxwell b. 11/17/1945 Visalia CA div.
   8/1/1971 m. 8/25/1973 Margaret Lee McDonald b. 3/11/1948
   Fayetteville NC.
2. Cheryl Dixon Hanscome b. 2/5/1948 Washington DC d. 7/27/1966
   Santa Ana CA. No marriage or children.

Child of Barbara Jane Hanscome and Edward Allen (Jack) Munger:

1. Edward Allen Munger, Jr. (Ned) b. 4/3/1948 Minneapolis MN m.
   7/15/1972 Hopkins MN Jeanne Ruth Stevenson b. 1/18/1949 Grand
   Island NE.

Children of William Dixon Hanscome and Donna Mae Sundberg:

1. Craig William Hanscome b. 5/20/1953 Minneapolis MN m. 8/31/1974
   Marilyn Ruth Phillips b. 9/ 5/1953 Toledo OH.
2. Geniene Marie Hanscome b. 2/14/1957 Robbinsdale MN m. 7/30/1983
   Chetek WI Peter Allen Haack b. 2/17/1957.
3. Ronald Edward Hanscome b. 7/4/1960 Robbinsdale MN m. 1982 Elk
   River MN Crystal Schlosser b. 2/17/1957 div. 1987 m. 7/23/1988
   Christine Eve Meinhardt b. 12/24/1964.

Children of John Baldwin Hanscome and Marjorie Ann Timm:

1. Jann Melanie Hanscome b. 1955 Minneapolis MN Unmarried. No children. Physician in Petaluma CA.
2. Barbara Christine Hanscome b. 1964 in Long Beach CA m. Matthew Todd Mumper b. 1963 Hayward CA.

Children of James Gordon Campbell (Gordon) and Margaret Fuge:

1. Heather Campbell b. 10/19/1940 Minneapolis MN m. Eden Prairie MN 1962 Christopher Angus Wurtele b. 9/24/1934 Minneapolis MN d. 8/30/2017 div. 1976.
2. James Gordon (Jim) Campbell b. 10/17/1942 Minneapolis MN m. 6/18/1964 San Diego CA Carol Lynn McCann b. 7/3/1942 div. 1987 m. 5/23/1991 Duluth MN Debra Lee Oftedahl Smoter b. 12/29/1954.3.
3. Scott Arthur Campbell b. 6/26/1946 Minneapolis MN m. 1978 Durango CO Barbara Lynn Hart b. 6/17/1952 Wildwood NJ.

Children of Rhoda Jane Campbell and Wesley Adsit Dickinson:

1. Rhoda Susan Dickinson b. 7/03/1941 Willmar MN m. 3/18/1967 Bloomington MN James Eigel Pedersen b. 6/1943 Tyler MN.
2. Nancy Jean Dickinson b. 8/23/1943 Willmar MN m. 6/18/1966 Bloomington MN Richard Raymond Dowell b. 6/6/1944 Bemidji MN.
3. Joan Adsit Dickinson b. 5/17/1945 Willmar MN m. Bloomington MN 4/21/1973 Richard Allen Laughlin b. 11/18/1938 Bakersfield CA div. 12/29/1979.
4. Robert Campbell Dickinson b. 2/8/1950 Willmar MN m. 9/27/1975 Blooming Prairie MN Mary Margaret Whitlock b. 9/28/1951 Mankato MN div. 9/2000.
5. Mary Jane Dickinson b. 4/03/1953 Willmar MN m. 8/12/1972 Bloomington MN Jerry Dexter b. 9/22/1951 Ft. Collins CO.

Child of Jean Hope Campbell and William Gage Donald:

1. Patricia Donald b. 9/8/1942 Minneapolis MN m. 2/27/1965 Minneapolis MN Robert Ruble b. 10/4/1944Minneapolis MN.

Child of Jean Hope Campbell and Clifford Gardner Johnson:

1. James Richards (Jay) Johnson b. 9/23/1953. Unmarried. No Children.

Children of Miriam Patricia Campbell and John Alvin Herrmann:

1. John Heck (Jack) Herrmann b. 3/5/1944 Minneapolis MN d. 12/2016 St. Paul MN m. 3/1968 St. Paul MN Rachelle (Shelly) Mitchell b. 8/9/1044 div. 1989.
2. Judd Campbell Herrmann b. 6/11/1946 Minneapolis MN m. 1971 Sue Ellingson b. 2/1952 div. 1981 m. 1992 Linda S. Lee div. 1994 m. 2006 Marcia Gage b. 1/26/1955.
3. Penny Lou Herrmann b. 5/16/1954 St. Paul MN m. 1982 St. Paul MN David Eden b. 5/2/1952 div. 2009.

Tenth and Eleventh Generations: (Eleventh Generation Incomplete)

Child of Thomas Chandler Hanscome and Sherry Lee Maxwell:

1. Heather Chandler Hanscome b. 06/06/1970 Newport Beach CA m. 9/30/2000 William Matthew Artukovich b. 11/2/1969 Sierra Madre CA.
   1) Barrett Matthew b. 3/26/2011 Newport Beach CA.

Children of Thomas Chandler Hanscome and Margaret Lee McDonald:

1. Jennifer Chandler Hanscome b. 8/6/1974 Cincinnati OH m. 5/10/2015 Robert James Bermudez III b. 10/28/1967 Orange CA.
   1) Addison Rose Bermudez b. 5/22/2007 Laguna Hills CA
   2) Ashlyn Rachelle Bermudez b. 1/27/2011 Laguna Hills CA.
   3) Robert Brandon Bermudez IV b. 1/27/2011 Laguna Hills CA.
2. Kimberly McDonald Hanscome b. 3/30/1978 Newport Beach CA m. 9/28/2003 Keith Frank James Wojciechowski b. 1/6/1971 Patchogue NY.
   1) Taylor James Wojciechowski b. 3/6/2001 Newport Beach CA.
   2) Tanner Chandler Wojciechowshki b. 11/24/2008 Newport Beach CA.
3. Lindsey Anne Hanscome b. 6/19/1980 Newport Beach CA m. 8/10/2012 Aaron Wesley Lee b. 3/8/1983 Modesto CA.
   1) Camryn Mackenzie Lee b. 3/4/2011 Laguna Hills CA.
   2) Danielle Anne Lee b. 7/21/2014 Laguna Hills CA.

Children of Edward Allen (Ned) Munger Jr. and Jeanne Ruth Stevenson:

1. Sheila Ann Munger b. 12/5/1967 Kenosha WI m. Melvin Loveday 04/12/1990 Div. 9/01/1998 m. 10/13/2001 RobRoy McGregor b. 05/16/1965.

    1)   Adam Wade Rassmussen b. 2/8/1988 St. Paul MN.

    2)   Emily May Loveday b. 7/1/1990 Fort Francis, Ontario Canada m. Cameron Block 6/21/2014 Niagara on the Lake, Ontario Canada.

    3)   Jered David Loveday b. 4/21/1994 Fort Francis, Ontario Canada.

    4)   Matthew Gerald Loveday b.11/23/1995 Fort Francis, Ontario Canada.

2.   David Ned Munger b. 11/3/1968 Kenosha WI m. 12/20/1995 Angela Lynn Visage b. 5/2/1971.

    1)   Madelyn Grace Munger b. 1/25/1999 Dallas TX.

    2)   Emma Isabella Munger b. 12/18/2001 Dallas TX.

3.   Derek John Munger b. 06/22/1980 St. Paul MN.

4.   Stephanie Jeanne Munger b. 9/30/1988 St. Paul MN.

Children of Craig William Hanscome and Marilyn Ruth Phillips:

1.   Joanna Ruth Hanscome b. 4/24/1978 Hicksville OH.

2.   Rachel Marie Hanscome b. 4/5/81 Ferkessedougou, Ivory Coast, West Africa m. 6/3/2006 Willis Gray III Toccoa GA b. 11/21/1979.

    1)   Joshua Evan Gray b. 3/10/2013.

3.   Daniel Paul Hanscome b. 3/17/1983 Ferkessedougou, Ivory Coast, West Africa m. 8/6/2005 Amy Chrissy Fincher Toccoa GA b. 6/27/1983.

    1)   David William Hanscome b. 7/12/2012 Birmingham AL.

    2)   Abigail Jean Hanscome b. 9/25/2014 Birmingham AL.

Children of Geniene Marie Hanscome and Peter Allen Haack:

1.   Kelsey Lynn Haack b. 6/4/1987 Anoka MN m. 11/24/2012 Christopher Frank Millette b. 5/4/1983.

2.   Collin Matthew Haack b. 6/30/1990 Anoka MN m. 8/13/2015 Katelyn Elizabeth James b. 5/13/1990 Minneapolis MN.

3.   Karina Noelle Haack b. 2/17/1993 Anoka MN.

Children of Ronald Edward Hanscome and Christine Eve Meinhardt:

1.   Nicolas Blake Hanscome b.7/20/1995 Minneapolis.

2.   Ryan William Hanscome b. 9/26/1998 Anoka MN.

Children of Barbara Christine Hanscome and Matthew Todd Mumper:

1.   Jackson John Mumper b. 2004 San Francisco CA (twin).

2.   William Jeremiah Mumper b. 2004 San Francisco CA (twin).

Children of Heather Campbell and Christopher Angus Wurtele:

1. Christopher Campbell Wurtele b. 1/30/1964 Minneapolis MN.
2. Andrew Lindley Wurtele b. 5/7/1965 Minneapolis MN.
3. Heidi Wurtele b. 12/17/1967 Minneapolis MN m. 2000 Napa CA
   Caley Castelein div. 2015 m. 5/21/2016 Alex Fisher San Francisco
   CA.

Children of James Gordon Campbell and Lynn McCann Campbell:

1. James Charles Campbell (Jamie) b. 3/18/1969 Minneapolis MN.
2. Kevin Bryant Campbell (Casey) b. 11/18/1970 Minneapolis MN m.
   7/24/2004 Boulder CO Anne Armstrong.
3. Robert Scott Campbell (Bobby) b. 3/18/1976 Edina MN.

Child of Scott Arthur Campbell and Barbara Lynn Hart:

1. Elijah (Eli)Fuge Campbell b. ? Steamboat CO m. 2010 Erin Elizabeth
   Di Santi b. 3/14/1984

Children of Rhoda Susan Dickinson and James Eigel Pedersen:

1. Ryan Wesley Pedersen b. 3/17/1972 Minneapolis MN m.1992
   Chanhassen MN Jordon Greer Dolentz div. 2005.
2. Erik Eigel Pedersen b. 10/17/1975 Minneapolis MN m.11/11/2016
   Phoenix AZ Katie Peters.

Children of Nancy Jean Dickinson and Richard Raymond Dowell:

1. Richard Raymond Dowell, Jr. b. 12/30/1970 Minneapolis MN m.
   Phoenix AZ 8/20/1992 Nichole Anderson b. 2/11/1972.
2. Kelly Rhoda Dowell b. 3/23/1972 Madison WI m. Kansas City KS
   6/7/1997 Chad Ingram b. 2/16/1971 Topeka KS.

Child of Joan Adsit Dickinson:

1. Sarah Adsit Dickinson b. 11/03/1975 Greeley CO m. 7/11/2008 Boston
   MA Brian Harry Berejik b. 11/04/1978 Boston MA.

Children of Robert Campbell Dickinson and Mary Margaret Whitlock:

1. Justin Friend Johns Dickinson b. 6/22/1971 Mankato MN m. 1990?
   Stephanie Daunche b. 1974 MN div. 1992?

2. John Wesley Dickinson b. 1/8/1977 Austin MN.
3. James Robert Dickinson b. 12/16/1977 Mankato MN. m. 2004 Mankato MN Catrina (Trina) Kote b. 1980 Mankato MN.
4. Robert Whitlock Dickinson (Jake) b. 8/17/1990 Mankato MN.

Children of Mary Jane Dickinson and Jerry Dexter:

1. Adam Wesley Dexter b. 8/26/1980 Apple Valley MN.
2. Michelle Marie Dexter b. 7/8/1983 Apple Valley MN m. 2/11/2007 Spokane WA Kevin Gawenite b. 4/3/1975 div. 2015, m. Joshua Sutton Spokane WA 8/19/2017.
3. Scott Campbell Dexter b. 5/31/1987 Anchorage AK m. 2/23/2014 Spokane WA Valentina (Tina) Romanchuk b. 12/15/1987 Ukraine.

Children of Patricia Donald and Robert Ruble:

1. Steven Ruble b. 7/9/1966 Minneapolis m. 6/27/1993 Spooner WI Susan Meyer b. 6/18/1967.
2. Elizabeth (Beth) Ruble b. 11/12/1968 Sioux Falls SD m. 10/28/1999 Ronald Blanchar b. 9/16/1965 Madison WI.

Child of John (Jack) Heck Herrmann and Rachelle (Shelly) Mitchell:

1. Danielle Herrmann b. 10/2/1970 Lake Tahoe NV m. Jamaica, Trevor Busby b. 1971 TN.

Children of Judd Campbell Herrmann and Sue Ellingson:

1. Trevis Herrmann b. 7/20/1973 Stillwater MN.
2. Jaymik Herrmann b. 8/26/76 St. Paul MN 2004 m. Nicole Cervantes.

Child of Penny Lou Herrmann and David Eden:

1. Max Campbell Eden b. 11/5/1988 Cleveland OH.

About the Author...

Joan Dickinson has worn many hats - history teacher, psychologist, professor, behavioral health director and international consultant, wellness columnist, public speaker, yoga and meditation instructor. She hails from Minnesota and kayaks with the dolphins near Anna Maria Island, Florida.

Also by the Author...

The UnPuritans is available on Amazon.com.

66374462R00177

Made in the USA
Middletown, DE
07 September 2019